THE
CHANGING
MAN

THE CHANGING MAN

TOMI OYEMAKINDE

FEIWEL AND FRIENDS
New York

A Feiwel and Friends Book
An imprint of Macmillan Publishing Group, LLC
120 Broadway, New York, NY 10271 • fiercereads.com

Our books may be purchased in bulk for promotional, educational, or
business use. Please contact your local bookseller or the Macmillan Corporate
and Premium Sales Department at (800) 221-7945 ext. 5442 or by email
at MacmillanSpecialMarkets@macmillan.com.

Library of Congress Cataloging-in-Publication Data is available.

First edition, 2023
Book design by Michelle Gengaro-Kokmen
All emojis designed by OpenMoji—the open-source emoji
and icon project. License: CC BY-SA 4.0
Feiwel and Friends logo designed by Filomena Tuosto
Printed in the United States of America

ISBN 978-1-250-86813-8 (hardcover)
1 3 5 7 9 10 8 6 4 2

The Changing Man is grudgingly dedicated to my dearest nemesis.

Without you, my writing journey would have been a much slower—gentler—burn, and this story would not exist here and now. Which has consequently meant less sleep, countless rejections, and limitless frustration.

Despite the obvious inconveniences to my peace, I am grateful. It's because of you I do not take the journey we are on for granted. You're somewhat encouraging, mildly funny, and healthily optimistic. But most of all, you help me hold on to *why* I write.

So, grudgingly, this book is dedicated to you, Rachel.

PS: Our bones never lied.

PROLOGUE

Even though the trees shivered and the ground was frosted, Leon Small was a furnace. Vodka snaked down his throat, searing his chest, and when the burning faded he realized the bottle was empty. He wiped his mouth with the back of his hand and flung the bottle at the weathered baby statue in front of him. He watched it fall short.

"Do you reckon Ros noticed my new look?" Henners asked, drawing up alongside Leon and offering him a Ferrero Rocher.

Leon passed on the chocolate. Henners should have known by now he loathed nuts. Even ones smothered in chocolate. "No clue, mate. But she *definitely* noticed the drool face you made at her all night."

"That obvious?"

Leon *hmm*ed, an unlit cigarette between his lips.

As they headed down the hill, back to Nithercott's grounds, one of Leon's pockets vibrated with a text from Benny asking where he was.

Out, Leon responded mentally.

When Leon's pocket buzzed again, he swore. He loved

his little brother, but Benny needed to stop leaning on him, else he'd never think for himself.

But looking at the screen, his right eyebrow quirked. It wasn't from Benny after all, and looking at the display picture, he bit down on a smile.

Judging by the image it was from the new girl, Leila.

WYD?

How does she have my number? She's barely ever said a word to me. Could she be . . . interested?

"Leon, bro, you alright?" Henners asked.

If Leon answered truthfully, he knew how it would all play out. Henners would tell him not to reply. He'd say she was the type to chew him up and spit him out. *High maintenance.* What he wouldn't say is that while she wasn't good for Leon, she was good for *him.* That he could "handle" her, as if she were some piece of volatile Bitcoin or whatever buzzwords made them feel relevant.

So he swallowed the truth. The hope that maybe—just maybe—she might be interested in him. "All good."

Henners raised an eyebrow and parted his lips. Leon held his breath, waiting for his friend to stop bloody staring. Finally Henners turned away. Sometimes Leon found it hard to breathe around him. They were good friends—Leon didn't want anyone misunderstanding—but they were from different worlds.

As he stared at those three letters, his heartbeat pulsed at the end of his fingertips. *She messaged ME, first. And it's LEILA.* What the hell was he supposed to say? The only option was to play it cool.

Nm, just heading back.

You didn't say goodbye 😦

Leon frowned, trying to find the meaning behind Leila's words. They hadn't spoken all night—and he'd been trying. She'd barely looked at him.

"What's up?" Henners asked. "Who hurt you?"

Leon angled his phone away. "It's . . . none of your business, Henry," he said in a jokey, please-leave-me-alone way. "Nah, it's just Benny. You know what he's like."

A shrug of Henners's shoulders meant Leon could type in peace the riskiest message he'd ever sent. Each tap of the screen sent the flutter of his heart up toward his throat.

You want me to kiss you good night?

But the moment he pressed send—instant regret. Several times Leila started typing and then stopped. *Oh God. She's definitely thinking about how to turn me down. Or she's going to air me.*

Leon needed to deflect, deflect, deflect. He was about to send a passably funny GIF and caption it with a joke, but then his phone vibrated.

Read my mind 😊 Meet by the abandoned cottage?

Leon's toes scrunched in his trainers as butterflies

3

swarmed in his stomach. It took everything in him not to fist pump. Energy zagged through his bones, and fantasies of him and Leila together swam through his head. He'd show everyone she wasn't "too much" for him.

Clearing his throat, Leon turned to Henners and said, "Uh . . . Benny needs me, so I'm just going to go see he's alright."

Even though Leon was sure Henners didn't believe his excuse, his friend didn't say anything. He never did.

He can be so . . . apathetic. Like everyone at this stupid school.

See you soon x

Within minutes Leon was striding toward the abandoned cottage. He paused and played with the rings on his fingers. Lately, Henry had started messing with him. Following him and then claiming he was making stuff up. Every other step he looked behind him, just in case his friend trailed him and messed everything up.

Henry was probably only here because his parents were former students and regular donors. In fact, the last three Nithercott Day events had been funded by his parents. Why not send their child here if that's what they wanted?

Meanwhile, Leon was all about what he needed, because a lot of the time what he *wanted* was out of his reach. Two different—

A branch snapped behind him.

Leon stopped to gaze into the velvet darkness. *Nothing.* His heart pulsed like it was drowning in his chest and trying to break free for air.

Squinting, he could make out the shape of the cottage up ahead. A crooked silhouette that leaned to the right. He forced himself to breathe.

Then he heard it again. A gentle rustle that turned his blood to slush. Someone was definitely following him. He reached into his pockets and grabbed at the bottle opener to use as a weapon. When he stopped moving, the rustling stopped also. When he moved, the rustling picked up again.

"The hell?" Leon muttered, whipping out his phone and texting Leila.

Walk toward me.

At that moment a siren blared from the country road a stone's throw away. His hands and shoulders jerked, sending his phone flying through the air to sink into a bed of autumn leaves. He got on all fours and wrinkled his nose at the strong smell of earth in his nostrils. *Where is it?*

Leaves crunched in a one-two rhythm. Footsteps, moving closer.

Leon stopped searching and turned. "Hey, Lei—"

No one to see. Instead there was a hazy orange mist that made the air shimmer. The stench of earth got stronger. He blinked several times, but the rippling mist didn't disappear.

What?

Then he felt the bone-curdling sensation of breath against his face. Leon's heart caught in his throat. His flesh was riddled in goose bumps. He was sure he would scream, or shout, but sound evaporated long before it could make it out his mouth. Leon swallowed as he stared into the orange mist. The breaths grew heavier. Tiredness and panic suddenly wrapped around him as something emerged from the darkness.

Two glowing eyes, too big to be human.

No, no, no—

Slowly, slowly, the world darkened.

Ben's world was dark. His eyes were squeezed shut as he washed some painkillers down with water. He leaned back in his gaming chair, the building migraine showing no signs of slowing down. And somehow, it wasn't the most annoying thing in his life right now.

It was Leon.

"Pick up, you mug," he grumbled, glancing down at his phone. *I don't ask for much.*

Okay, that wasn't fair, Ben mused, spinning around in his chair. Leon was usually good at getting back to him. It's just tonight he *really* needed his help with this English assignment—due tomorrow and not a single word written.

Ben was about to try calling his big brother again when his phone *pinged.* He couldn't unlock it fast enough.

> Hey, Ben, so sorry I missed your calls. Out on the hill, L

> Nws. When will you be back?

> I'll be out late. Don't wait up, L

But I need you for my English assignment.

You know what. Gimme your laptop password. I'll just get the one I need

Let's talk tomorrow, L

Bro ...

It can't wait till tomorrow.

Leon Small is typing . . .
Leon Small is typing . . .
Leon Small is typing . . .

And then nothing. Ben blinked. He took several deep breaths before letting out a torrent of profanity his mum would not approve of. Leon was royally screwing him over. The *one* time Ben actually needed his help, and suddenly Leon was following through on his threat to let him learn the "consequences of his actions."

Ben should have known something was up when Leon called him Ben instead of Benny—too formal.

Now he was left with two options. Pull an all-nighter and find a way to complete his assignment. Or hop on his Play-Station and drown his frustration in the sounds of *Call of Duty* gunfire.

There were several moments of silence before Ben

scooched his chair right up to his PlayStation and pow-
ered it on. He'd deal with the consequences tomorrow. And
when he saw Leon, he'd make sure to tell him *exactly* how
he felt.

One Month Later

CHAPTER 1

THE PHYSICS OF BAD LUCK

The roof crackles like hot oil as rain lashes against it. Insides tight and toes curled uncomfortably, I'm daydreaming in the middle of physics and wishing I could be somewhere else. I try staring past my reflection, sulking at me with tired eyes, to the A-road. If I concentrate, I can hear the cars zooming by—hurtling away.

I'd do anything to be in one of them.

Colored pieces of paper swirl in the wind. They zigzag through the air above the front lawn, evading the hands of the groundskeeper—a stooping man with pleasantly wrinkled features. The scraps of paper are what's left of a now-forgotten sign Leon's friends put up a few weeks ago to show support for him. I see them still going on lunchtime walks looking for possible clues. Anyone—student or staff—is welcome.

Leon went missing right before I joined. Some people think he ran away. Others whisper and blame the Changing Man—a stupid urban myth that's apparently been around forever.

"Go on, mate, do it," the boys behind me whisper, drawing my attention away from the window. The teacher's back is to the class.

Next to me, Ben—Leon's younger brother—makes a loud fart noise with his armpit, and his friends, scattered around the class, erupt into giggles. Mr. Morley hushes them with a dull, dark glare.

I go to side-eye Ben, expecting him to be smirking. Instead there's a tightness in his ocean-blue eyes. I'm trying to work out what it is when Ben turns toward me. I jerk my head back to the window and fix my eyes outside.

A few moments later a sleek car coasts down the driveway, coming to a stop on the side of the front lawn nearest to the school. A burly man steps out holding a coffee cup. The warden of the Nithercott Foundation. He gave a talk a few weeks back about how he, along with the headmaster, is making sure the values of Nithercott are upheld.

The warden hobbles on a jeweled cane that winks with each step. I roll my eyes, thinking about how he called Nithercott a *fundamental* and *accessible* institution of education, equipping tomorrow's leaders for public impact.

A mouthful of nonsense.

Mum and Dad are paying through the nose for me to be here, despite the reduced fees that come with being on the *Urban Achievers Program*. If I do well academically during my first year, the school's more likely to match me with a sponsor who'd essentially pay the rest of my school fees, and uni too.

My parents like to pretend there's no pressure or expectations, but I know that's not true. When they say they're proud of me, it's heavy with pressure. All my life they've tried to give me better. So when they asked me to take the entrance exam, I obviously couldn't say no. And when they asked me to give Nithercott a chance, I did.

A fizz of guilt bubbles in my stomach at my ungratefulness. But a month in, I'm running out of steam and motivation. The demands are higher even than the expectations of my very Nigerian parents, which says a lot. To top it off, even though I got in the program because of my art, they don't seem all that interested in it now that I'm here.

The art they've got me doing is so bland. But apparently it's the type of art that's more "esteemed."

If my bestie, Zanna, were here with me, then everything would be fine. I could be the person I was back at Archbishop's. Every single day wouldn't feel like the moment before the roller coaster drops.

Hoping to ease the storm in my stomach, I slouch in my seat, but it makes things worse so I sit up straight again. Through the sliding rain, I spy the centerpiece of Nithercott School—Porthaven House. It's wearing vines with cerulean flowers, and it's made of dimpled bricks the color of autumn leaves. I feel nauseous. Everything's so different here.

As my thoughts stew, I get distracted by the excited way my phone's vibrating against my chest. Fishing it out, I check the lock screen.

The group chat from my old school is blowing up, giving me a hollow feeling in my chest. I need those girls like I need my eyebrows. Without them backing me up from a distance, I'd feel so weird and out of place. Well, even *more* out of place.

Joining midway through the first term of year eleven means I've missed out on a lot of the schoolwork already. Plus, almost everyone's been at Nithercott since year seven.

I don't know where I fit.

I take a deep breath because as stifling as Nithercott is, I have a reason to survive—Malika. She's the only other Black girl in my year and the closest thing I have to a friend here. We bonded over our mutual dislike of nearly everybody else. The rest is history.

Tomorrow, Malika's helping me meet Zanna halfway between Nithercott and my old home of Orlingdon. A fluttery feeling drifts through my chest.

"Any of you able to describe to me the interaction responsible for keeping protons and neutrons together in a stable nucleus?" Mr. Morley is asking. With his shirtsleeves rolled up and faded tattoos peeking out from his collar, he's not the typical Nithercott teacher.

Hands punch upward until they're high in the air. Mine stays down. I *think* I know the answer, but this isn't the kind of school you survive at if you aren't sure.

My phone vibrates again. I look down and stifle a laugh. Zanna's sent me a GIF of Taraji P. Henson in the bougiest coat with the caption Ife's new look.

I mean . . . Taraji's killing it, but that'll never be me. I key a quick response in our made-up language.

> Ihnastic. Ownastic chaalsastic, imosastic ldaastic omastic.

> LOL really had to check our language rules! *New* elitist school, same old you, you mean. Anyway, can't wait to hear all about THAT life. Also feel free

to bring any friends along.
Would love to meet them!
Avolastic aeyastic x

My fingers hover over the keyboard, trying to think of the perfect comeback. After a moment I try a few GIF searches but can't find anything. Moving schools has zapped my GIF-picking superpower.

Stoking the flames of determination in my stomach, I scroll, search, and scan until I find it. Nah, this is it. Holding back a laugh before pressing send is usually a good sign. *I win.*

As soon as I press send, a message from Nithercott Quick-Talk comes in. It's from Malika.

So ... got an update on
tomorrow

Go on ... 👀

Cuz can't give us a lift, but my
step-nephew can. Just have to
meet him in the next town over
by 9:30.

Lights out at 10. Ms. P always
makes sure we're in bed ... Can
it be later???

He says he's got a gig that he
can't be late to.

There's a pinch in my chest. I swallow it down, my hands trembling.

> ☹️ Is there anyone else you can ask?

Malika is typing . . .

A chill burrows through my bones. Malika's step-nephew *has* to come through. I *have* to see Zanna tomorrow. She and I started plotting our reunion the moment my parents dropped me off here and flew out to Norway. I've been falling ever since, like a bloated blob of paint that's slipped off the edge of a canvas.

I didn't ask for any of this.

Malika replies.

> I think so . . . but can't promise anything.

My heart bangs against my chest. *Please God*, I pray. I have to see Zan—

"Ife!"

My shoulders tighten and my head jerks up.

"Y-yes, sir?" I reply, trying my best not to show fear. I swear it fuels him.

I focus on my breathing, not batting an eyelid as I let my phone slip from my hands and free-fall into my unzipped backpack.

Mr. Morley runs a hand through his spiked hair and shakes his head. "All I ask is for you to pay attention in my class, Jesus Christ. Goes for the rest of you. Starting now, anyone caught not paying attention—automatic detention." Mr. Morley sighs like he'd rather be somewhere else, and I get it. We're on the same side. He points at me. "If a nucleus decays by alpha decay, where two particles are emitted, how is the baryon number conserved?"

I clear my head and flip through the pages in my mind. This was in my prereading before I joined. I stammer my way through the answer in a way a Nithercott student would never. The way "before" me would never.

"Umm . . . a-according to the laws of conservation, the number of baryons must be the same before and after the reaction. That means in . . . alpha decay, the number of nucleons, protons, and neutrons doesn't change?"

Mr. Morley chews on his gum like it's really pissed him off. Pausing for a sigh, he says, "Wrong. In alpha decay a neutron changes into a what?"

It takes me a few seconds. "A proton?" I swear—

"A proton," he repeats. "Did you not go over the reading material we sent you?"

His words hammer down with disappointment. Like I should've known better. But I was so sure. I go over the question again and I see the mistake in his question and thinking.

Except fearless Ife isn't around anymore. Not when everything is so different here. When there's no Zanna to back me up.

My throat is closing and I just want to disappear.

A gentle voice punctures the silence. "Sir, actually, Ife's right. You're talking about beta decay."

A few groans sweep through the class. Ben chuckles next to me. Across the room, Bijal—little miss know-it-all—smiles in my direction. Her braces glint as scattered sunlight spills in through the windows. Ever since she found out Archbishop's was the sister school of her old school, she's tried to earn my approval.

She turns to Mr. Morley. "You got confused between alpha and beta decay. In alpha decay it's actually one particle emitted, not two. So actually . . . Ife's right."

Mr. Morley flips through his workbook. When he lands on the page he wants, he spends a good minute reading while chewing his gum harder and harder. He looks ready to explode.

I'm scared Mr. Morley *will* explode when Ben pipes up.

"Sir? Cat caught your tongue? It's basic physics. Oi look, he's all red. They say those that can't do, teach. What do they say about those that can't teach then?"

What the hell is he doing? I open my mouth to warn him, but nothing comes out. Even though Ben's wearing a smirk, I see how tightly he's curled his hands into fists in my periphery.

"This is a new low, even for you, *John*. Actually, nothing will top your wife leaving you for a sixth-form student."

Deafening silence. I scramble to understand. *Did he really just go there?* Not even Ben's friends are laughing.

"Ben." Mr. Morley's voice is calm, scraping at the silence. Not a raised decibel in sight. "Pack your things and get out. Now."

"No offense, but I only listen to teachers who actually know what they're talking about." Ben shrugs and leans back on his chair with his hands on his head. It's like he's trying to get himself in as much trouble as possible.

Mr. Morley flicks another stick of gum into his mouth

and leans back against the whiteboard. "I'm not going to get into a pissing match with you. Christ, I get paid regardless. If you want to waste your potential, then be my guest. Now get out."

I glance at Ben to see what he's about to do, but his smirk is gone and he's quietly packing his stuff away. His chair grates against the floor as he stands up.

I never noticed how tall he is. *And cute.* I swallow the sudden laughter trying to rise to the surface. Now's not the time. Still . . .

Maybe it's the hair? The back and sides are shaved and what's left is all over the place. He's scruffy, but it works with his shirt half untucked, top button undone, and sleeves rolled up.

Mr. Morley shakes his head as he watches Ben leave without a word. "Right. Now that—"

Everyone starts laughing and he frowns. Then he catches on and turns to the window behind him where Ben moons the whole class.

I'm laughing too, even though it's gross. Ben is *not* cute, I almost decide.

The lesson continues and no one tries anything because Mr. Morley is a roaming shark. For the last half hour he gives us a surprise difficulty-adjusted test. The radical type of education an elitist school like Nithercott would create. Apparently it's their way to make sure students are striving to reach their potential.

"Raise your hand if your current Dynamic Difficulty Score is between forty and forty-nine?"

My hand is the only one to creep up. I cringe at the soft

sniggers. Moments later a test paper and equation sheet plop onto my desk.

"Do not begin until I say so," Mr. Morley orders. When he's finished passing out everyone's papers, he sits at his desk ready to invigilate. "You may now begin."

I look through the pages and realize I can barely answer any of these. Which is soul-crushing, since my low DDS should mean I get easier questions.

"Sir, this isn't fair," a girl moans. "How come State School gets an equation sheet?"

Murmurs ripple through the room. A flash of heat rushes through me and my scalp prickles, all too aware of how I don't fit in.

As if it isn't bad enough that Urban Achiever (UA) students also have to wear a slightly different uniform too, as a show of "distinction" and "pride."

They might as well stamp *Urban Achiever Kid* on my forehead.

Mr. Morley ignores the complaints, pointing his pen at the scribbly message on the whiteboard:

Exam conditions.

This whole situation is Ben's fault. We're only supposed to get these tests once a week, not twice. This should be *his* punishment, not ours!

As I'm working through a question that looks relatively easy, my phone vibrates multiple times in my bag. Piercing through the exam-conditions silence. I cough and tap my pen against the table. *Crap.*

Mr. Morley jumps up and breathes out a laugh. "You . . . kids. Give me a break." He definitely wants to say a lot more than that. He's clenching his fists so tightly his knuckles are white. "Own up. If you do, I'll only give you a week's worth of detention. I'm feeling generous."

No one does for a full minute and a half. Which makes sense, because I should be the one owning up. For once, Mr. Morley seems too tired to do anything. Dealing with Ben was enough.

He sinks back into his seat.

I'm about to reach in and turn my phone off completely, but the preview messages on my lock screen are from Malika.

Malika: You in a free? Need to vent about this place. Also school's told me my grades have been good enough to get a sponsorship. 😎   *3m ago*

Life's good for some. Meanwhile, my parents are going to ask me the next time we talk if I've got a sponsor yet.

Malika: Sponsor wants to meet me #robtherich   *3m ago*

Malika: ???   *3m ago*

Malika: nvm, I checked ur timetable for week B. You've got a free.   *3m ago*

My eyebrows squish together. It's week A.

Malika: I'll call you in 2 mins. You
better pick up.   *2m ago*

Unease crackles through my gut. I scramble to power my
phone down and instead accidentally switch silent mode off.
It blossoms into song.

> *Cut my life into pieces, this is my last resort*
> *Suffocation, no breathing*
> *Don't give a—*

Mr. Morley slams his left hand on the table as he stands
up, his signet ring clacking against the wood. My shoulders
tighten, and hands loosen, as my phone tumbles to the
wood-paneled floor. I scramble for it at the same time a voice
squeaks, "It's State School's phone, sir."

I flinch. *Thank you, Stacey.* Even though she's an Urban
Achiever student like me, and *also* came from a state school,
she tries extra hard to act like she isn't any of those things.
It's embarrassing.

He points at me. "Up. Now!"

Like the prisoner I am, I obey. If the floor could swallow
me up, that would be great.

When Mr. Morley strides over to my desk my phone is
still singing, and the floor is clearly not hungry today.

"Jesus! Turn it off then!"

I crouch down, decline Malika's call, and power my
phone off.

Mr. Morley scowls at me like I'm the worst person in the room.

"State School's *actually* crying," someone announces.

Yes. I *actually* am, because it's so dumb. The whole situation is! Now here I am, my tears messing up my physics test.

"I—I didn't think . . ." My voice is shaky and quiet. I hate how tiny I feel. "I—"

My throat dries up. Before I can recover, Mr. Morley cuts in.

"*Of course* you didn't think," he spits. "You've wasted my time, and the class's time. We're here to learn, not to play guess who." He doesn't say anything else, and I realize he's waiting for me to play my part. To apologize. Except my mouth isn't working. "Well? You're not going to say anything?"

All I can do is gape at him, speechless. Confident Ife is in hiding. He frowns at me and I know what's coming next.

"For the love of God! Right, well since you clearly don't care," he starts. *I do.* "A day of detention for each person's time you've wasted here today."

I look around at the rows and columns of heads. I get halfway through counting the second column when Mr. Morley says something that spins me and I face him.

"Huh?" I want to make sure I heard him right.

He sighs. "For God's sake, girl, *listen*. I said give me your phone."

"But—You can't—I—"

"Oh? Now you can talk. Christ, I'm not asking you, Ife." His voice blasts over me like too-cold aircon. "You'll get it back after you finish your detentions."

My heart deflates like a balloon. *Zanna*.

I take a deep breath, hold back the tears, and hand my phone over to an unimpressed Mr. Morley. He huffs and steps back up to the front to go on one long rant about how he doesn't get the respect he deserves. But it's just noise to me. I bury my head in my arms, the tears dampening the sleeves of my school jumper.

CHAPTER 2

DRUGS, DETENTION, AND MADNESS

When the last bell rings, day students run to their parents' super-fancy cars or to the luxury school buses. The boarders rush to change into their own clothes and spend obscene money on snacks at the village shop.

Usually I'd head to the art block to unwind for a bit. Instead I'm dragging my feet to detention all the way on the other side of the school. Back at Archbishop's, walking from one side to the other took five minutes tops. Here it's closer to fifteen. I walk past Porthaven House, haloed in a pool of sunlight that flows through gray clouds. The wet vines shine as sunlight hits them just right.

It's a reminder of just how far I am from home.

I kick out at a loose pine cone and watch it bobble across the ground.

"They're saying Leon ran away because he had an argument with his parents," a lanky sixth-form boy gossips ahead of me. A shimmering brooch on his lapel marks him as one of the school's prefects. His green plaid tie matches my green plaid skirt, highlighting him as an Urban Achiever student like me. His arm wraps around the waist of a girl who I'm pretty sure is in the year below me.

I slow down and keep in step so I can listen.

"Really?" the girl questions in a southern American accent. "How boringly cliché."

The prefect leans in and does his best creep-face impression, which isn't hard. "*I* heard the Changing Man got to him before he ran off. You know who that is, babe?"

She shakes her head.

"They say he lives in hidden rooms at Nithercott, and from shadows of the night, his steps come soundless, his eyes glow bright. He leaves strange plants as he creeps away. Seeking those to"—the lanky sixth-form boy pulls her in tight—"*change.*"

I roll my eyes. Every school has an urban myth. At Archbishop's they used to say that in the abandoned public toilets behind our school, there was a man raised by ghosts. When night comes, he supposedly sneaks out to haunt the teachers staying late (which is silly; ghosts, aka the spirits of dead people stuck in the living world, aren't real).

The girl squirms and her shoulders swallow her neck like a turtle. "Stop, that's not funny."

"Oh, come on, I'm just repeating what everyone's been reading on CottsLore." The girl gives him a look. "Okay, I'll stop looking at that 'sensationalist bullshit,' I get it. Kiss?"

They slow down and lean into one another.

"Rupert and Marybelle, you know the rules," a voice barks before their lips meet. "Not too close for comfort."

Mr. Ingham, the headmaster, emerges from Porthaven's

front entrance in an elegant dirt-brown suit. He's quite tall and could be taller if he didn't have a slight hunch.

"Sorry, sir!" they both say in unison, pulling apart and hurrying off.

"Ife," he calls out. Pockmarks start at his temples and frame his high cheekbones. A hairless cat scratches at his trousers, meowing. Mr. Ingham tries to delicately shoo the cat away with the leg that isn't being used as a scratch post. It hisses and scratches at his ankle. "Ouch!" Taking out a ball of tinfoil from his pocket, he bends down and waves it in front of Hairless, who stops clawing. And goes racing after the ball when Mr. Ingham flings it away. As he rises, he gives me a knowing smile. "Art used to be an Olympic event; Jackson Pollock's nickname was the Grim Dripper; the *Mona Lisa* has her own mailbox. Which one's the lie?"

"That's easy," I say with a confident smile. "Middle one. Jackson Pollock was called Jack the Dripper, not the Grim Dripper."

Mr. Ingham *hmm*s. "Not bad. I was so sure I'd stump you with that one. What's that now? Three correct answers and—"

"No wrong ones." Art trivia is light work for me.

In my frustration, I consider telling him about Mr. Morley and my phone. Maybe he'd take my side. But something behind me catches his attention. His easy smile mashes into a frown, gaze locked onto Rupert and Marybelle, who have stopped by a tree and are *way* too close for comfort. Mr. Ingham sighs, clears his throat, and rearranges his face back into a smile. "I'll deal with them later. How are you settling in, Ife? You've been here a month, right?"

"Yeah. It's been . . . okay. Thanks, sir."

"Good to hear. Well, just know if you have any questions, or need support, don't hesitate to email the well-being email address or speak to Ms. Piddleton. She's seen it all."

"Thanks, sir." I smile and keep it moving. The weight of Nithercott sinks into my bones as tiredness grips me. I'm going to have to do this walk twenty-three times. All because Ben decided to put Mr. Morley in a bad mood. Yep, it's Ben's fault. I would have only gotten maybe a week of detention at most, if it hadn't been for Ben.

He's an idiot.

By the time my mind has called Ben all sorts of names, my legs have carried me to Room 19—Detention. The door is wide open. The teacher on duty is at her desk, joined by a steaming polka-dot mug. Looks like I'm the first one here. *Well, duh, you're early.* There's actually fifteen minutes to go before detention starts, but if I'd gone back to Beeton, Ms. Piddleton would have probably chewed me out and then forced me to volunteer for Nithercott Day as extra penance. That's my idea of hell: a day where the school opens its doors to parents, future students, and the community through various attractions that dutiful current students organize.

Talk about exploitation of labor.

"Ah, ah, ah," the teacher sings as I pull out a chair in the back. Her glasses sit on the end of her nose, matching her lilac cardigan. "Fill out from the front, please."

I'd argue, but I have no energy, and also, getting on another teacher's bad side doesn't seem smart. She smiles back before her head disappears below her desk, leaving behind a nest of frizzy blond hair. Moments later she pops back up and asks if I would like a Rocky Bar.

"Yes, please!" I'm not even ashamed how desperate I sound.

Chatter gets louder and louder and soon the room bursts with homework evaders, rulebreakers, and one classroom felon, aka Ben. He takes the spot next to me. Thank God the desks are separated by at least an arm's length.

When detention starts, I reach inside my blazer pocket to pull out my headphones—and then remember I have no phone. My eyes squeeze shut as I suck in a deep breath. I exhale and pull out my thick physics textbook and workbook instead.

We've got an essay on atomic structure due and I seriously can't be bothered. Plus, a short presentation on it tomorrow. My first thought is to find a way to skip it, but I'll just be prolonging the inevitable. Opening up the textbook, I flip to the relevant section. Tell me how I end up reading the same sentence *three* times.

This isn't working. *Focus.*

"You look a bit lost. If you want, I can get you a copy of the essay my brother did a couple years ago," Ben says. He's leaning toward me, invading my space with a crooked smile. "It's all yours, if you'd like?"

I ignore him and try to make some notes.

"He got a Goldilocks mark for it. Not too bad, not too great, but just right."

Ignore him. My eyes scan paragraphs about a whole bunch of diagrams that make no sense. How can anything be this boring?

"I bet the school doesn't even have it on file. You could

probably copy and paste, and these precious teachers would never notice. They never notice anything. Except if you fail to live up to the standards of Nithercott."

My head snaps to him. He's staring at me with brilliant blue eyes and a stony, expressionless face.

"I don't want your brother's essay. Leave me alone," I whisper harshly. For the first time I notice a faded scar that zags through his eyebrow.

Ben holds up his hands. "I was just trying to help. You looked like you could use it. Guess you don't." He points at my cheek and smiles softly. "Birthmark, right? It looks like a small puddle of spilled water. Leon had one on his—"

Heat rushes to my face. I'm not doing this. Not today. "Just leave me alone, please."

I look away, wondering what his deal is. The girl to my left is on her phone, scrolling through CottsLore. She grins when a text comes through. I feel a sudden strike of jealousy. Without my phone, it's like a piece of me is gone.

Twenty-three detentions. Two-three. That's excluding weekends. I do the rough maths in my head and the answer makes me sick. *That's like a* month.

I hope the group chat and Zanna know I'm not ghosting them on purpose. My foot taps against the carpeted floor. I hope they know I would never!

Okay. I get back to my prep—Nithercott's fancy way of saying homework—but can't focus. Too distracted thinking about how I'm going to speak to my friends. I'll just DM Zanna on Twitter and explain everything.

Still, I have no idea how I'm going to survive a month without my phone. I'll go insane!

A phone rings, and when I look up, Lilac Cardigan is scrambling for her purse. She brings her phone to her ear. "Hello? Oh—okay. Really? I thought you didn't—Oh, someone canceled? But I was told that—You need a scanned copy of my what? Well, erm, okay." She stands suddenly and faces the room. "I'll be back in time for the end of detention. If my classroom is in one piece, I'll give you all a Rocky, and one extra if you keep the fact I needed to slip out quiet."

"Bribery, Miss? Didn't think you were the kind," someone behind me says.

Lilac Cardigan chuckles. "I'm not! Just this once. Okay?" She doesn't wait for an answer before leaving.

Soon after, a sixth former with slicked-back hair walks in with a big fat grin. Another sixth-form boy with two gold-dagger earrings in one ear approaches and pats Slicked-Back Hair on his back. "You legend, it actually worked. How'd you know she'd nibble?"

"It's not what you know, but who," Slicked-Back Hair answers. He adds smugly, "She was my last lesson and let slip we shared the same medical fixer—Perry?"

Medical fixer? I make a note to google it.

Gold-Dagger Earrings nods. "I know him. We switched from him to Erman. Much better subscription offerings."

I twirl my finger in one of my afro puffs as they debate medical fixers. My stomach turns in disgust when I overhear Slicked-Back Hair faked a call as Perry saying Ms. Pearson (Lilac Cardigan) got a slot for the cosmetic procedure she'd been waiting for. All that just to get her out the classroom. *Nithercott kids are different.*

The sixth formers start playing a game that involves

throwing and catching a scrunched-up piece of paper. I have no phone, no tablet, nothing. Meanwhile, Ben's busy hunched over and scribbling away.

I lean in to try and peek over his shoulder. He stops writing and stares at me with a smirk and one eyebrow lifted up. "Can I help you?"

"No."

"Oh, really?" His smile is picture-perfect. "Because *I* saw you looking over my shoulder," he accuses, leaning in. I smell something Zara-y. "Don't deny it."

My mouth opens but words don't come out, stuffed back down by Ben's audacity. I take too long to finally find my voice. "Get over yourself."

"Yeah, whatever." He gets back to whatever it is he's working on.

I rock on the back legs of my chair and scan the room for some sort of way to reach out to Zanna. I could ask one of Nithercott's finest offenders. But they all look so much older and scarier. I think of Ben next to me and decide to summon my courage. When I turn toward him and open my mouth, all of a sudden, his name feels off-limits and my voice withers. Deep breath.

There's a *BANG* to my right.

"Sorry, mate!"

"Piss off," Ben spits.

He's on his knees frantically scooping up loose bits of paper. One of the pieces lands on my foot. He hasn't noticed it and his back is to me. I listen to a little voice in my head and pick up the piece of paper.

I start reading:

TRANSCRIPT-PAGE 3

Key:

A = Angela Anne Small
DW = Detective Wilson William

A: You already asked me that. Why am I still here? You should be finding out who took my son.

DW: We're doing our best, Ms. Small. I hope you can appreciate that. Are you sure he wasn't displaying any signs of unhappiness?

A: Are you saying I didn't know my own son?

DW: His friend, Henry, reported that before Leon ran off, he was acting odd. That he was easily startled whenever someone mentioned the Changing Man. He even accused Henry of following him as a way to mess with him. People were starting to tease Leon. Is it possible the teasing got too—

A: I told you already. He didn't run. We're done here.

That's where it ends. I should hand it back, but if Ben even suspects I read this, I don't wanna know how he'll react.

I panic, fold it up, and stuff it in my inner blazer pocket. My heart slams against my chest for the rest of detention.

I sketch a mini self-portrait to calm down, but it turns out all wrong. It's giving me long-lost-twin vibes, so I scribble it out.

Lilac Cardigan makes it back just in time for the piercing shrill of the two-minute warning bell. Her cheeks are super red when some of the sixth formers ask if she was at couples' corner. She's too flustered to notice a couple of students have left early.

Then the bells ring to signal boarders' prep time and we're dismissed. On my way out, a boy with the curliest mop of hair bumps into me. It takes me a second to recognize it's Louis. I've seen him around. He's friends with Malika, and a UA kid like us.

"Oh sh—I'm sorry," he says. His eyes light up when he recognizes me. "You alright?"

I purse my lips and nod.

"Not much of a talker, are you?" Louis laughs. "What are you in here for?"

"Phone."

"Ah, that's right, your phone rang out. Set Mr. Morley right off. Once a dick, always a dick." When he sees my face scrunched into a frown, his paper-thin lips curl into a smile. "You've been here long enough now. You familiar with CottsLore?"

I nod. A sensationalist gossip site. "Yeah. What about it?"

He leans in way too close and I jerk my head back. "Well, you're looking at the brains behind the operation. Nothing around here happens without me knowing."

Or fact-checking probably. But something tells me he doesn't care about any of that. "Oh."

"Got anything you want to get off your chest? One thing you should know about me, I protect my sources. I saw you and Ben talking. Did he say—Hey, I was—"

I've started walking away.

"I can pay you," Louis rasps, grabbing my wrist.

What the hell is wrong with everyone in this place? Spinning round, I snatch my hand away and come *this* close to snapping at him, but my stomach churns and I swallow down the boldness I was prepared to unleash.

I'm yawning when I walk into the classroom where boarders from my house have to do their prep before dinner. I find a cozy corner right at the back. Away from everyone and everything.

Soon after, other boarders strut in. I'm watching a fashion show. Fran, my new roomie, enters in a pink tie-dye crop top and high-waisted jeans. She's got a pink scrunchie on her wrist, pink nails, and a pink bubble-gum slushy.

"Girls," she beckons.

Three walking clichés assemble like minions—Stacey, Melanie, and Jessica. Each of them has striking platinum hair in a side bun, coupled with a pink scrunchie.

The international girls are next to arrive, unbothered and seriously fashionable. Unlike Fran and her backup dancers, they actually have personalities and *range*.

One girl's wearing white trainers with a long, faded-turquoise skirt and white jumper, with a turquoise designer beret to match her skirt.

Homesickness wraps around my heart and squeezes. Zanna has the same beret. She saved up for nearly half a year to buy it and only wears it to big parties to let everyone know she means business. Not as an everyday, after-school look. I can't believe this is my new normal.

I shouldn't be here.

I'm about to dive into this atomic structure essay when the door bursts open and Bijal stumbles in. Her hair is in a long plait that snakes all the way down her back, and she's dressed in a honey-gold jumpsuit that pops against her tawny brown skin.

"S-sorry I'm late, Miss! Had to get a few books from the library."

As she scans the room looking for a seat, I'm praying that she doesn't sit next to me. The chances are fifty-fifty. There's the seat to my left and another one by Franny. Immediately, I'm not liking my odds.

Bijal gives me a beaming smile and heads straight for the free seat next to me. "Hey, school sister," she chirps, sitting down and leaning into a bond that doesn't exist.

The nonstop references to the schools we came from, the clinginess in the lessons we share, and the subtle mimicking of everything I do . . . it's all really starting to annoy me. Just last night when she saw me mix apple and orange juice in a cup, she did the same.

It's not that I don't *like* her—it's quite flattering—it's more like I don't actually *know* her. "Hi." I shrug.

She just smiles at me for the longest time. Not saying a word.

Okay then. This isn't awkward at all.

"Tough break with Mr. Morley," she eventually says. "He's such a clown, right? I mean the way he—okay, okay, not interested. I'm sorry." She takes a breath. "I'm not good at this. Talking to people. Though I *should* be good at it; I'm part of the school magazine." Another breath. "Anyway, guess what?"

"I'm not really in a guessing mood."

"Oh, come on. Please, try and guess. I bet you'll never get it."

I frown at her. "So, what's the point in guessing?"

Her face scrunches at my question. *One point for me.* It's not every day the school know-it-all looks stumped.

"Ifeeee," she begs.

She's even pouting and lifting her thick eyebrows up like caterpillars on their front legs.

"You're saying it wrong," I whisper.

Everyone says it wrong.

"Huh?"

"My name. It's not *eye-fee*. It's Ife," I stress. "Pronounced *ee-feh*." I make sure the last syllable pops like a finger snap.

"Oh! Okay, thanks for correcting me. Mine's pronounced *Bee-jull*," she counters. "But you can call me Bee. So, are you going to guess?"

She's not going to give up, is she? Fine. I come up with the most random thing I can think of. The sort of thing I wish was true so they can shut Nithercott down and send me home. "The school is a front for a cartel selling drugs and all the teachers are in on it?"

"Who have you been talking to?" she asks in one breath.

"Are you—" She laughs and I roll my eyes. "You're an idiot, Bee."

As soon as the nickname slips out, I want to take it back. *Don't get comfortable*, I tell myself. The people at Nithercott aren't anything like my friends at home. My mind wanders to my phone that's locked away without parole.

I'd ask Bijal to use her phone, but I don't want to encourage her. After she's done laughing, she goes into a new mode of seriousness.

"So yeah, not even close. Does the Changing Man ring a bell?"

"Yeah, I've heard a little about that. Saying he's why Leon ran away." *An understatement.* "Some sort of urban myth, right?" I look around for somewhere else to move to, but all the seats are taken now.

"Well, *legend*, but yeah, I've been reading through some of the school archives for fun recently—"

Of course that's what she's been doing for fun.

"—and I think I've found the first mention of the Changing Man. It's a short article from 1992. I think I'm going to do a special feature on this in the next issue of the school mag . . ."

I look around the classroom at all the girls who seem so . . . comfortable. Especially the non–Urban Achiever students. They throw around the Changing Man like a missing student is just another interesting thing to happen at Nithercott. Another term. Another scandal. It's not hard to tell they've been living in this bubble their whole lives.

I feel uneasy. Will I be more like them by the time I leave? Carefree and wrapped up in my privilege?

". . . Ife!" Bijal says, snapping me out of my daze.

"Yeah?"

"I was saying that you can't bring up the Changing Man without talking about what happened in 1983."

"Oh?" *Still no free seats for me to move to.*

"Yeah. That's where it all began. Several students claimed they were being followed by someone strange. The police got involved. Soon after though, the students all withdrew their stories. But then a few days later, one by one those students started acting odd. One lost it in the middle of class, another during cross-country, and another on the way home. They either shouted random nonsense, or screamed, or simply went quiet and froze. That's probably when the Changing Man rumors started. Ever since then, whenever someone suddenly acts differently in some way, students blame it on the Changing Man. That's what they're saying about Leon running away. *I* think it's dumb and reductive."

Hearing about all the ways this school is messed up is not what I need right now.

"Yeah, reductive. Hey, why do you know so much about this myth?"

"Because I don't think it's a myth, but a legend."

"What's the difference?"

"Myths are usually supernatural in some way. Legends aren't. They're *real*. Anyway, I have my own theory. Namely, the Changing Man isn't some being with soundless steps or a thing who can make strange plants grow. Rather he was really a creepy, rich resident playing some sort of twisted game back then. Like in the *Most Dangerous Game*. Either way, I'm going to make sure the truth sees the light of day."

"A game would certainly liven the mood here." The words slip out before I can stop them. Bijal gives me an off look. "It's not—I mean I just—Miss!" I say with my arm lifted high.

A student has left one of the single desks and she's packed away her stuff. Granted it's by the window that doesn't shut, but it's an escape. "Can I move to the empty desk, please?"

"And what's wrong with your current desk, Ife?"

The way she butchers my name is rude, but I force my anger down because I want that desk. I smile sweetly and stand up. "It's a bit too warm for me here, Miss, and I'm feeling a little bit nauseous. I could use the fresh air."

"Very well."

"Thanks!" I look down at Bijal, who isn't even looking at me but at her phone. Her chin trembles. "Hey, thanks for sticking up for me with Mr. Morley," I whisper casually.

She beams at me. "No worries. We are school sisters after all. Besides, he was being an idiot and I've never liked him. How he got a teaching job here is beyond me." Her phone buzzes and she picks it up. I can't help but take a quick look.

> Ur on CottsLore AGAIN 😝 I didn't
> know u were such a beg. You actually
> paid for an online friendship course? 🤣

There's a flicker of a frown on Bijal's face, but she laughs softly instead when she catches me looking.

"You alright?" I ask, packing my stuff away.

Bijal nods. "Yeah, just . . . school banter. You know how it is. Us Nithercott lot are always winding each other up. I—It doesn't matter. I'm alright."

It's a bold-faced lie, but I don't push her. The part of me that desperately wants to reach out is trapped in a sludge of anxiety. "Well, see ya." Still, I can't shake the message I saw on her phone from an unknown number.

Messages like that remind me that there is no *us* when it comes to Nithercott. I wish Bijal saw it too. Sympathy clouds my mind, but I blow it away. With a shiver I settle into the single desk and get started on my prep.

CHAPTER 3

DESPERATION

Soon as the bell rings for the end of prep, I rush to Beeton House like the Olympic athlete I know I'm not. Internet filters are off, which means I can finally log on to Twitter. I'll apologize to Zanna and update her on everything that's happened.

I take the shortest route possible. Through Susanna's Yard, full of weathered statues to honor the old, old Nithercott alumni; past Webber's Tower, a bell tower built in Nithercott's early days; and down the cobbled path that cuts through the King of Beelsalam Garden opposite Beeton.

I key in the house PIN and rush through the doors. Kicking off my shoes, I bound up the short steps, down the hallway, and into the first room on the left. There's one free computer left. *Thank you, Lord.* Within minutes I'm typing Twitter into the address bar. I press enter, and when the screen loads, my stomach drops and twists. There's a big red STOP sign:

THIS WEB PAGE IS
UNAVAILABLE WITH

THE EDUCATION FILTER ENABLED. TO VIEW THIS WEB PAGE, THE NETWORK ADMINISTRATOR WILL NEED TO ADD IT TO THE WHITE LIST.

What?

The students around me are having the same issues with the filter. Each time I refresh the page, I get the same message. Anger crawls up my spine and I'm in Mr. Morley's class again, reliving the moment he made me feel so small.

I don't even bother logging out. I just hold the power button until the computer goes blank, leaving my vague reflection and that of a girl with a tightly coiled, teeny-weeny afro.

"That's going to take forever to set up now," Malika says. I turn in my chair. She's wearing an apologetic smile, her signature gold-chain choker, and a constellation of piercings in both ears. "I've been looking for you. I wanted to say sorry for calling. Got the weeks mixed up."

"It's alright," I reply, standing up. I notice her patchwork jeans and I feel a little jealous. I love them, but I could never pull them off. "Any luck?"

We walk toward my room. "Yes, actually. A friend of my cousin—family friend. He can pick us up on one of Silkhead's backroads at ten thirty and have us in Backemere by eleven. Let's meet behind the Silkhead bus stop around ten twenty and we can walk over together. You in?"

I nod. "Obviously."

"Good, good." We stop in front of my door and Malika

wrinkles her nose. "This is where I bid you adieu. Mum's going to be here any moment to drop off a care package. Besides, the stench of privilege is blocking my sinuses."

"Come on, Fran's not *that* bad." I giggle. "She's just . . . basic. Besides, the fact we're here means we technically share some of that privilege too."

Malika scoffs. "Yeah, yeah. That's one way to put it. Laters. Just don't let those fumes change ya."

I snigger. But when I push my way into my room, I freeze. *Should have asked to use Malika's phone before she headed off.*

This has been the longest day ever. Kissing my teeth, I kick off my shoes so they go flying into the corner. Next to come off is my hideous purple blazer. I chuck it at my laundry basket. It's halfway through the air and off course when my roommate walks in, her eyes glued to her phone. My blazer lands on her face. She peels it off with one hand and looks up at me with squished eyebrows before she looks back at her phone.

"I'm *so* sorry," I say, scrambling to take my blazer back.

This is our first proper interaction since she moved to my room a few days ago. My last roommate transferred to a different boarding house with more liberal house parents. I haven't even had time to say hello properly, and we're off to a great start. With my face burning, I attempt to be friendly, invoking her pet name. "H-hey, Franny. How are—"

She doesn't look up from her phone. "Fran."

"Pardon?" I wring my hands.

She looks up and bites at her lip. "Close friends call me Franny, but everyone else, it's Fran." Playing with her low ponytail, she looks around before stepping to her desk under-neath her bunk bed. She holds out a workbook in front of me. "What does that say?"

Fran Holding
English Language
Ms. Keating

"Fran Holding," I read aloud.

She nods. "Fran," she says softly. "And you're Ife. I hear you're good at art. So good you're an Urban Achiever student."

I smile weakly at that. "Yeah."

The sternness in her eyes falls away suddenly, and she smiles at me. "Daddy collects art actually. Who do you like? He might have one of their pieces."

"Uh . . . too many, but off the top of my head I like Harris Wynne a lot at the mo'."

Fran thinks for a moment, then *hmms*. "Yeah, Dad called him too chaotic. Doesn't uphold the art traditions, whatever that means. Also about the blazer, it's no biggie, by the way. Just don't make it a habit of hitting me with it, 'kay?"

"O-of course." I feel relieved at how nice she's being. Maybe she can help me. "I know we aren't cool like that, but . . . can you help me out?" She tilts her head. *Great*. I keep going. "I need to message my friend. Can I use your phone, please?"

She shakes her head at me. "Nope, using it."

"Oh, okay."

I stuff down my disappointment and turn away. I

shouldn't be surprised, to be honest. The students who aren't Urban Achievers tend to be pleasant in a don't-ask-for-anything-though type of way. My anger flares. Apparently lending a roommate a phone for five minutes max is a step too far. If you're not one of them, then don't bother. Sometimes I get the impression they think we're disturbing their peace, like someone constantly smacking their lips while eating.

As I said before, there is no *us* at Nithercott. Like calls to like.

I pull on my standard after-school clothes—a hoodie and black leggings—and pop a gummy bear in my mouth. If Mum were here, she'd say I'll ruin my dinner. But she's not. I smile and throw another gummy bear down the hatch.

Sliding into my chair, I switch on my desk lamp and get ready to do some more physics work before dinner. The glittery snow globe by my pile of books casts a long, stretching shadow that catches my attention. I'm reaching for it when movement stops my hand short. Emerging from behind the snow globe are two identical-looking spiders in the middle of a fight. Their stabbing legs tangle endlessly.

I'm startled out of my daydream by the *thud* of the door as Fran leaves. I grab my snow globe and turn it over. Zanna's handwriting begins to thaw the parts of me Nithercott has frostbitten.

If Nithercrap gets mega hard,
think about all the good reasons
that make it worth it
EvUL I 4vuru Fae xx

Determination hardens in my gut. Energy crackles in my fingertips, and I'm in the mood to sketch something. How can I be here on an art scholarship and have barely drawn anything? I should ask about why there seems to be no real arts program here.

The desire to pour out all my frustration into as many pencil strokes and scribbles as possible shudders through me. I've been meaning to draw the main characters from Tosin Ajayi's new dimension-traveling detectives book. She's my favorite author, and I know exactly which of her characters I'd draw first, but I'm forced to shake the thought from my head. What I need to focus on is my physics work, and the presentation I have to give tomorrow.

As I stand in the queue for dinner, my mouth waters at the smell of egg fried rice and salt-and-pepper ribs. Did I say I hated this school before? I grab a rectangular leather tray with metal handles and join the slow-moving traffic. While I wait, I look around the grand dining hall. It's been a month, but I can't help but always marvel at the sleek wooden tables, extensive windows, and the way a large, hollow square of LED lighting has been embedded into the ceiling.

"What's it gonna be?" the head chef asks with a warm smile, pulling me out of my awe. His hair is hidden behind a black headscarf with a gold-chain pattern.

"Don't tell me—fried rice and ribs?" Mr. Ingham says, coming up alongside me.

I lift an eyebrow and smile. "It's the only thing on the menu."

"I admire your sense of adventure, you know. Honestly."

Mr. Ingham's dry humor makes me laugh. "Thanks," I answer, handing over my plate.

"I heard . . . about your phone." He draws a breath. "Unfortunately, rules are rules, but I can assure you I've had a word with Mr. Morley about his tone." My lips part, but words don't follow. "A teacher passing by your class informed me of what happened. Mr. Morley has assured me it won't happen again."

Silence stretches like an elastic band before I snap to my senses. "Th-thanks, sir. You didn't have—"

"I want you to know," Mr. Ingham starts, "that at Nithercott, no one gets to tell you who you are. Not me, or any of our staff. Understand that, and you won't end up lonely." He says that last bit so quietly I almost miss it. Then he turns to the chef with a bright smile. "After all, as the kids say, we're not here for a long time, but a good one. Go ahead and give her my portion, Al. Watching my salt intake these days. That reminds me, we need to talk catering for Nithercott Day at some point."

"Certainly," Al replies.

As the extra ribs make their way onto my plate, I need a moment to swallow my expanding heart. "Thanks, sir."

"Anytime, Ife," he says, drifting off to find a table. He heads to the teachers' table after a few of them beckon him over with smiles. That would never have happened at Archbishop's, where the headmistress was a bit of a loner. I don't think a single teacher smiled at her when she roamed the hallways.

After I grab my banoffee pie from the dessert station, my head is on a swivel hunting for a good seat where I won't be disturbed. The dining hall is like the food court at the Eastgate Oxhall shopping center back home on a busy day. A seemingly mad rush for seats.

But when I look closer, I see the calculated decisions students make. Students alike in their privilege congregate like a flock of pigeons; sixth-form boys slide into seats next to younger girls they have no business talking to, flashing perfect smiles and blinding watches; and woven into everything are the students who don't quite fit, waiting to be thrown a bone, ready to be welcomed into the fold.

All of it sends a shiver down my spine. I look for Malika and see her sitting with Louis, whose curly mop of hair jiggles as he gesticulates. I find a seat tucked away in the corner instead. Franny smiles at me as I walk by her table. Stacey scowls, and my eyes roll. She's probably pissed I get to room with her lord and savior.

I tuck into my food, oblivious to everything. My bubble of peace is disturbed when two bodies plop down next to me. A boy with a purple streak in his side-swept undercut and Bijal. She gives me a quick hello, and I get ready for her to talk my ear off, except all her focus is on this boy and his on her.

"Okay, tell me," the boy demands in a gruff German accent.

"Well, while the architecture of this school is stunning,

it's antiquated. That means a lot of the security is lacking. I wouldn't be surprised if half the alarms didn't work either."

The boy gestures with his hand for her to hurry up. "Nein, tell me how?"

"It's easy. Most of the cameras aren't operational. You'd know that if you'd read the reference books about Nithercott in the library. There *are* working alarms though, but there are ways around those. I bet the legit Changing Man figured it out. That's my hypothesis anyway."

"Ja. I don't care. How do I get the answer to tomorrow's test?"

Bijal sighs. "Behind the east wing of the quad, there are large enough air vents. Find the one attached to her classroom. They're old, so just tug at it and it should come out easy enough. Crawl through and you're in. She usually keeps the tests in the bottom drawer."

The boy lifts his chin and stares at Bijal with probing eyes, before he gives her a crisp nod and produces a wad of cash, dropping it in front of her.

Bijal frowns. "You said you'd get Louis to remove the post from CottsLore."

The boy is already on his feet, carrying his tray of half-eaten food over to his friends. There it is again. That look on Bijal's face. Eyebrows bunched and head drooped.

I clear my throat. "A-are you okay?"

"Yeah, yeah, everything's fine." She stuffs the ten-pound notes into her pocket and plasters on the fakest smile I've seen. "Moritz probably just forgot about what we agreed.

He's harmless though. Acts like he's about that life, but he's not."

"Cool." I wince inside. If Zanna were here, she'd tell me off for not calling Moritz a jerk and standing up for Bijal. But it's hard. The air here is stuffy. I keep my mouth shut and we finish our food in silence.

"Hey," I say when it looks like Bijal is ready to leave.

"Yeah?"

"I, um, can I quickly use your phone, please?"

A slow smile builds on Bijal's face. "Of course, here. It's the first six digits of pi."

I stare at Bijal blank as an egg. "What about me makes you think I know the first six digits of pi?"

"Yeah of course." She bubbles into laughter. "The passcode is 314159. What do you need it for?"

"Just to message a friend," I say while unlocking her phone and heading to the web browser.

"Okay then. A friend from Archbishop's?"

I nod, logging in to Twitter.

> Hey Zanna.
>
> SorrySorrySorry >.<
>
> Phone got confiscated and web filters are messed up
>
> We're still on for tomorrow, right?

Of course!

Already know what I'm wearing.
Hope u know too.

See u soon. Can't wait! x

Me either x

I blink a few times, processing the fact it's really happening. I get to see Zanna tomorrow and I can't wait, I can't wait, I can't—

Bijal is staring at me.

"What?"

"Nothing, I've just never seen you smile so much before. It's . . . radiant. I like it."

Amusement pushes my mouth apart and I laugh. "Serious?"

"Deadly. Anyway, I'm planning to have a quiet one in my room, do some research. Do you want to hang?"

"I—ermm. I think I—I was going to draw tonight and I find it easier to do that alone."

Bijal drops her shoulders and lifts them back up again, flashing a false smile. "Actually, you know what? I think this might be an earphone in, world out type of evening."

She walks off and I hang back. My chest is tight as I replay my interaction with Bijal. I'm acting like Fran. Pleasant, but distant. A part of me wants to be warmer, but I just . . . can't. The way Bijal is trying hard to befriend me is the same energy I'm putting into not making friends.

Personality in, people out while I'm at Nithercott.

I look around the dining hall. Sound jumbles and fades. My shoulders sag and jaw unclenches. I imagine what it would be like to try and be myself here. But I can't picture it. Noise returns as the voice in the back of my head says, *You don't belong here.*

I get up from my seat, certain the voice is right.

CHAPTER 4

DARTH PIDDLETON

Tomorrow comes and Bijal is by my bed bright and early, already ready for the day. She nearly short-circuits all of my nerves and I groan into my pillow. How is she so comfortable just invading my space like that?

"Want to have breakfast together?" she asks. The longer I stay quiet, holding my breath, the more her eagerness starts to crumble. A nameless pang presses into my chest. "I can get them to make us cinnamon french toast," she adds.

"I've never had that before." But it sounds good.

"Is that a *yes*?"

I exhale and force the word "Sure" out of my lips.

Bijal looks at my desk. "Mummy showed me her drawings once, before she got pregnant with me, and her and Papa moved over here from India. They weren't as good as this." Bijal laughs. "You're talented. But what's up with the ominous clouds over Porthaven House?"

"Thanks, and it's—" A sudden yawn swallows my words. "It's too early to explain. Maybe another time."

I rush my way through brushing my teeth, showering, and

getting dressed, and we head to breakfast by cutting through Susanna's Yard. In the morning light, and slick with dew, the statues look more ethereal than weathered. There's an oak tree in the middle that has large twisted branches that reach more outward than upward. The lower ones are low enough to perch on.

When I did the new students' tour, it was one of the locations I earmarked as a peaceful place to do some sketching. But I found out pretty quickly it was a popular haunt of sixth formers who gave me evils when I tried to set up at the base of one of the statue pedestals.

"I need fuel before I use my brain in the mornings," Bijal muses as she stumbles over a pine cone, breaking our painful silence.

My nostrils flare as I prepare to spark a conversation. Her blazer buzzes at the same time I think of something to say. Fishing out her phone, Bijal takes a quick glance at the screen, winces, and puts it back in her pocket. Her strides lengthen.

Must have been something CottsLore related, I guess. The message she got in prep yesterday flashes in my head.

I speed up too, before taking a moment. "You know Mr. Ingham said there's this well-being email you can—"

"Ready for your physics presentation?" she asks, brushing off my words as we enter the dining hall.

Okay then. "Yes." The real answer is no. I'm terrified. I never used to be though.

"Same."

Bijal eyes the pastries, sausages, and pieces of bacon that

are on display. I can barely look at them. Anxiety swirls in my stomach. Why did she have to bring up the presentation?

"Only cereal?" she asks.

"Yeah. Not feeling that hungry."

"Could it be residual radiation?" she mutters to herself as she takes a seat at the table. "Huh. My horoscope did say I'd have a new idea for a project. Maybe I should explore this," Bee huffs to herself. "And this is why I prefer my horoscopes to Mummy's jyotisha."

I put another big spoonful of soggy Crunchy Nut and milk in my mouth. I chew. And chew. And chew. The lumpy clump of food in my mouth tastes like cardboard. Under the table my knee bobs like it's trying to drill my foot into the ground. Trying not to think about my presentation is making things worse. I hold my breath while my hands are on my malfunctioning knee trying to calm it down.

There's movement in the corner of my eye, and when I look, I spot Malika taking a seat next to me. "Morning," she says.

"Morning," I say.

"Hey," Bijal says at the same time, before adding a second later, "you're Malika, right?"

Malika nods, before turning toward me and giving me a frown, like, *Really?*

I shrug. *Clingy.* "We're still on, right?"

"Relax, we're still on. I just came over to say hey, and don't be late. I won't wait because I need just one night away from this picturesque cesspool."

"An oxymoron," Bijal says.

"A what?" Malika laughs. "You know what, doesn't matter. I'm going to take my breakfast to go. See you tonight, Ife."

I stare holes into her back trying to figure out how she does it. How she seems so poised when I've been off-balance from day one.

"Ife, hellooo," Bijal says, bringing me back to reality. "Hello? You alright?"

I turn to face Bijal, who's looking at me with the most earnest face. "Wonderful."

"You are the most sarcastic person I've ever met."

"And that is *truly* tragic."

"Yeah, yeah . . . Anyway, what's happening—"

Not doing this. I push out from the table. "Thirsty. You want one?" She nudges her cup toward me. Grabbing it, I drag myself over toward the drink dispensers.

"Ife, skirt!" Ms. Piddleton calls in a shrill voice from the teachers' table. If I were glass, I'd shatter into a mess of shards. "It's too short."

I nod. "I'll fix it when I get back to my table, Miss."

"Put the cups down, and sort it out. Now, please."

"Miss, when I'm at my table, I promise—"

"Uh-buh-buh. Now."

I look at the other teachers for some support. They keep their eyes on their food and my heart sinks. Mr. Ingham's already left. Clenching my jaw, I put the cups down. Soon as I do, eyes linger on me. I'm sure it's only one or two, but it may as well be the whole dining hall.

I don't want people watching me fix my secondhand skirt with its bleach mark and sewn-on patch. Imagining what

Zanna would do gives me the courage to plead one last time in my best diplomatic voice.

"Please, Miss. I appreciate that I've violated the uniform rules. But fixing my skirt makes me feel—"

Ms. Piddleton rises from her seat. She's tall and thin. Her skin is blotchy, her bark-colored hair tied in a bun. Looking at me through round-rimmed glasses, she frowns.

"Ife," she says. Two beats of my heart pass. I hear it in my ears. Feel it in my chest. "When I tell you to do something, I expect you to do it. Do you think it's smart to talk back?"

Silence.

She wants an answer. "N-n-no," I stammer feebly and far too quietly.

"Pardon?"

"No," I say, louder. Loud enough for those watching to snigger and giggle. I need to turn invisible. Right now.

"Well?"

I draw a breath and lift my shirt and leaf-green jumper up to get to the rolled-up waistband of my green plaid skirt. Adjust it so that the skirt is the perfect length. According to the Nithercott handbook they gave me, perfection is just below the knee. I go to rearrange my shirt and jumper, but Ms. Piddleton stops me with a glare that could freeze over hell.

"Until it's all unrolled, Ife."

"Miss, it's the perfect length. Why do I—"

"Uh-buh-buh. Skirts shouldn't be rolled up. It ruins them. Full stop."

I lean in close, so only she can hear. "Please," I beg. "This skirt was secondhand, so it's a bit big, and long. It'll go halfway down my shins and keep sliding down while I walk."

She looks at me without a single bit of sympathy. As if, somehow, I deserve this.

You don't belong here.

Ms. Piddleton sighs. "Any more back talk and you'll land yourself a week's house confinement." She titters. "You'll need to order clothes that fit. You're an ambassador for the school. In fact, make sure you get yourself to the school tailor before the first period. You still also need to be measured for a tailor-made skirt suit. For when the time comes. You'll have to wear one if we find you a sponsor and they ask to meet you. Now off you go."

"Yes, Miss," I mumble, blinking away the sting of oncoming tears.

Head down, I trudge back to the table. I slide Bijal's empty cup over to her and bury my head in my arms.

"Ife?" she whispers.

I don't answer.

After leaving the tailor's, I'm full of buyer's remorse because even though it's not my money, I know the meaning of overpriced. Dad's voice of shock when he sees the extra expense on my school fees is already ringing in my ears.

I take a deep breath, deciding those are Future-Ife problems.

Today, first period is chemistry with Dr. Butterworth, which I'm looking forward to. He somehow makes chemical reactions engaging. My guess is he sacrifices a good night's sleep to the "higher powers" of chemistry. He's always got bloodshot eyes, patchy stubble, and hair like a clump of cobwebs.

Next is maths. I manage to scrape a pass in my difficulty-adjusted oral test. One boy isn't so lucky and he goes red in the face begging the teacher to let him take it again.

By the time the bell rings, I'm ready to melt into a puddle.

My legs are noodles as I wobble to slay the dragon that waits for me in Mr. Morley's physics classroom. Ugh. I let the other kids rush up the outdoor stairs that lead to the door. When I'm sure I'm the last one, I climb and hold on to the banister for dear life. Most of the kids are already seated by the time I walk in.

"Christ, stop spacing out and take a seat," Mr. Morley says. I blink at him. "Sorry, is my tone out of order?"

"N-no, sir," I mumble. I want to say I didn't snitch, but I don't think he wants to hear it. Taking a seat, I end up wedged between a boy who picks his nose and eats it when he thinks no one is looking, and another boy who permanently has his hands down his trousers.

It really couldn't be worse.

"Stop leaning back on your chair, Chris. Right, today you'll be presenting your two-minute talks. First, we have Ife. Your presentation please. Quickly now."

Bijal gives me a thumbs-up and a smile from across the room. I look away. Everything feels stiff and tight. When I get to the front, I take a deep breath. It's taking everything in me to keep my legs from shaking. I pull out my notes from my blazer pocket, written on a few pieces of crumpled paper.

I scan my first page quickly, look out at the class, and

open my mouth. "When we think about atomic structure, we think about protons, neutrons, and electrons. Today I will . . ." Words on their way out sink into nothing. *Don't panic, you have your notes.* When I look down, my handwriting is suddenly jumbled nonsense.

Notgoodnotgoodnotgood.

"A-as I was saying," I say, attempting to improvise while I work out my next lines. "Protons and neutrons and electrons. I-I'll be comparing and contrasting the, umm . . ." My hands shake. "Th-th-the—"

The ground wobbles. I can't catch my breath. No matter how much air I suck in, it lasts a blink. *Not again.* Not here, not now.

"Is she okay?" a student asks.

"Reckon she's bottled it?" another whispers not so quietly.

Thoughts—twisted and cruel—flitter through my mind.

You're embarrassing yourself.

No one will ever understand you again.

You don't belong here.

You—

You—

You—

"Take a deep breath, Ife," Bijal bursts out.

CLANG.

She's standing up and her chair's toppled over. A finger and her signature bright smile are pointing in my direction. "You've got this!"

"Bijal!" Mr. Morley exclaims at the same time.

A few classmates giggle.

"We need stricter controls on our scholarship intake.

Hashtag *Make Cott Great Again*," Fran quips, before adding, "Jokes, jokes."

"You're one to talk," a boy retorts. Her face twists. "How much did your mother dearest donate to make you our year captain for the third straight year? But sure, stricter controls or whatever."

A few students fail to smother their laughs while Fran twirls her pink scrunchie around her finger. "Let's see," Fran starts with a smirk. "Take your dad's salary. Add it to your mother's. Double it. I'd say you're a tenth of the way there."

The students in the class let out a collective, "Oooooh."

She's obviously making it up, but her point is as clear as her white-pearl skin—she's obscenely rich and he isn't. Thing is, the boy isn't exactly poor. I've seen his dad pick him up in a different sports car each day. But here, there's always a bigger car.

Mr. Morley slams his hand against the desk and one of his rolled-up sleeves comes loose. His spiked hair bristles. "Enough. Can we get back to class, Bijal, or is there anything else?"

"Sorry, sir. Won't happen again."

While Bijal takes her seat, she gives me another thumbs-up. This time I smile back. My notes are readable again. My breaths, steadier.

"Sir, sorry, but can I start from the beginning please?" I ask.

"Fine. Off you go then."

"When we think about atomic structure, we think about protons, neutrons, and electrons. Today I will . . ."

Wednesday afternoons are for activities. I signed up for extra art. It's the only time I can work on stuff that isn't a pre-approved technique. I get to just be and create.

Predictably, Bijal signed up too. We're sitting next to each other in the sixth form's airy art block and she hasn't said a word to me. Her face is stuffed in a conspiracy theory maga-zine that's been ravaged by Nithercott collage-makers.

"Hey," she whispers, nudging me with her arm. My pencil tip strays off course and I acknowledge her with a grunt. "What did Malika mean when she said tonight was still on?" She lowers her magazine, looking me dead in the eyes.

"Uh . . ."

"It's okay, I promise I won't tell anybody. My lips are sealed."

I shrug and study the ugly pencil mark giving my work some surprising character. *Huh.* "We're planning to sneak out after lights out."

"Seriously?" Bijal closes the magazine. "To meet someone? Where are you going? If it's not too late, can I—"

"No," I snap. Bijal blinks at me in shock. "S-sorry. It's—you don't know them, so it would be awkward."

"Oh, okay. Yeah, you're probably right." She laughs weakly before brightening up with a fake pout. "So where are you and Malika going then? You have to at least tell me that."

I don't *have* to do anything. But if there's one thing Bijal is, it's that she's stubborn. So, I feed crumbs of the truth. Just enough for her to stop asking questions. "Just out into town with some friends. No biggie."

"Ife," Bijal sighs. "You're a terrible liar, you know that, right? Out into town?"

"Pardon?"

"When you lie, you blink a bit more and fidg—"

I stifle a laugh. "Fidget with my fingers." *Zanna said that to me a week after we met.* "Fine, you win. My best friend is meeting me halfway in Backemere."

"That's amazing!" Bijal bursts out. "I wish my friends back home would do that."

Suddenly I'm proud of me and Zanna, and our friendship. "Yeah."

I turn back to my sketch and let my imagination take the wheel.

An hour later and I'm biting on my bottom lip while looking down at what I've done. And frowning. Drawing is both solving and creating a puzzle at the same time. Until I put my pencil down, I don't know if I've cracked it. That's why art is such a rush.

There's a bang on the window in front of me, jolting me out of my reflections. Bijal gasps. Looking at us with the angriest face ever is Ben Small.

"Get the hell out here, Ife. Now. I swear."

"Wow," Bijal whispers to me. "What did you *do* to him?"

My mind jumps to the sheet of paper I stole, tucked away in a desk drawer in my room. "No idea," I answer, walking toward the front door.

The moment I step outside, Ben drags me from the front of the sixth-form art block to the side of Porthaven where the bins are.

"G-get off me!" I shout. The stale piss smell, mixed with rotting veg, wrinkles my nose, forcing me to hold my breath.

"Give it back." He doesn't even give me time to say anything before he says, "And why'd you do it anyway? He's a snake."

"I don't know what you're—"

"Don't lie. Someone from detention *saw* you take it and I *saw* you talking to Louis. Now there's a fresh post on Cotts-Lore about how Leon believed he was the Changing Man's follower and he ran after him?"

There's this tug of sympathy, but then it's gone because there's no excuse for him to straight up accuse me like that. I shrug. "Why the hell would I spread rumors about someone I don't even know?"

His face goes red as he kicks the big bin.

"You tell me. Are you really that desperate to fit in? It's like I'm the only one who sees the truth. He didn't run away. He was taken and I—I just want my brother back . . ." His voice is shaky and quiet. Like rustling leaves. "Whatever, just, give what you took back. Please."

I don't know what to say. The words won't come.

"Ife," he growls.

"Fine, I will. Sorry, it's in my room. But why are you getting so worked up anyway? Everyone knows CottsLore is just badly written, real-world fanfiction. I'm sure—"

"It's not *just* badly written." His face sours into a scowl. "It's playing with the truth and people don't really care. I can't believe you—Let me explain it for you, so you get it: This whole place is a massive bubble of privilege." He gestures with his hands. "And we're trapped inside it. Narrative matters way more than the truth. Even if it exposes warped perceptions and contradictions. God forbid someone would be taken in perfect ol' Nithercott."

It's the fact that he cuts me off to explain something to me like I'm a child that makes my blood boil and forces words to start tumbling out. Sharp and mean. I want them to hurt. "Well, I know that the police said your brother—" I stop myself, realizing I've said way too much already. "Ben, I . . ."

"Apologize," he snaps. The anger in his voice drills deep into my bones. "The cops don't know shit."

"I already did. I already said I was sorry. What more—"

"Properly," he says, cutting me off. "Like you actually mean it."

"Ohmyword, I'm sorry. I don't even know what else to say." He stares at me like he expects more. "I don't have anything to add."

Ben takes a deep breath and shakes his head. "That's not an apology and you know it, you pissant."

I pull back half a step and tilt my head. "What did you just call me?"

"What's going on here?" Dr. Butterworth asks, appearing from nowhere. He speaks slowly and deliberately. He turns to Ben. "Is she giving you a hard time about Leon?"

"It's nothing." Ben storms off.

Dr. Butterworth mutters to himself, scratching at his stubble, before looking me up and down. His watery, bloodshot eyes look weary and sleep-deprived. "B-be mindful. Please. He's hurting," he says before going after Ben.

I'm left standing there with my legs shaking and hands trembling. Being hurt isn't an excuse to be rude. Who even uses the word *pissant*?! This school wants to swallow me whole with its ridiculousness. I'm done.

I can't wait to see Zanna tonight.

CHAPTER 5

SNEAKY

'm lying in bed waiting for the lights-out check, tiredness sinking into my bones. My heart forces me to stay alert, pounding loud in my ears as I think about what I'm about to do.

"Alright, girls, lights out," Ms. Piddleton says, popping her head through the door. She taps Fran's shoulder, waiting for her to slip off her headphones. "Lights out. You're not exempt, Ms. Holding."

Fran nods and her phone goes dark.

"Wonderful. Good night, both of you."

Ms. Piddleton leaves, and seconds later Fran's face is illuminated by her phone. The sharp, blue light is just enough to help me climb down from my bed and get dressed for the breezy outdoors. *I can't miss my bus to Silkhead.* My index finger is a makeshift shoehorn as I slip on my Vans. After pulling on my warmest coat and placing a wig on a ball of clothes resembling a head, I turn to see Fran glancing my way with an unreadable face before going back to her phone. She couldn't be any more disinterested in me.

My plan is to go through the games room, which has a

door that is not alarmed. Malika said she's seen plenty of girls use it to sneak out to the hill for a drink on weekends.

On the balls of my feet, I creep down the dimmed hallway. Every single sound plays on booming speakers in my head. Ms. Piddleton's heels come clacking down the hallway and my nerves fray. She'll kill me if she sees me like this.

My heart clenches. To my right is the smaller kitchen that no one uses except when the large fridge is too full, and people use the squat, battered one in here. Everything in this smaller kitchen is out of time and shaded with rust and discoloration. I duck inside, swatting away the cobwebs so I can crouch under the counter and squeeze in behind the rusted pedal bin. I can just about see the open doorway if I close one eye and squint.

Creaking footsteps approach. I place both hands over my mouth, trying hard to control my breathing. Ms. Piddleton appears and looks into the kitchen. I wilt deeper into the shadow. She gazes right at me. I hold my breath. Her eyes are sharp needles pointed at my heart. I'm waiting for her to call me out, but she *just—keeps—staring.*

THUD!

She blinks. Her neck snaps toward the sound and then she is off, leaving me in total silence. I hear her telling off some other night owls. Crawling out, I dust myself off and get to the games room. Thankfully it's empty. Locking the door behind me, I pull and push the plush sofa and games cabinet out of the way, so I can get to the door. It really is unlocked. Just like Malika said.

Stepping out into drizzle, the wind whistles and loose leaves scuttle, scattering my drowsiness like cobwebs. A rash of goose bumps forms all over my skin, even though it's quite humid.

I wade through smokers' alley, which is full of weeds, strangled flowers, and dwarfed translucent mushrooms. My skin crawls. Damp mud squelches under my feet. The earthy smell invades my nostrils.

Several birds burst from the overhanging tree and I tense up for an instant, biting down the urge to turn back. Their flapping wings sound like rugs being violently beaten. A bird free-falls and lands in front of me, its wings broken. A messy chunk of its neck and chest are gone. I bite down a scream as I watch it twitch.

When I look up, two gleaming amber eyes gaze down at me. They belong to a cat perched on a tree trunk.

Gulping down my fear, I think about Zanna and press on along the grassy banks that slope down to the back fields. The wind blows through the trees that hem in the grounds from the A-road. They sway and fill the air with the sound of crashing waves.

Making my way onto the field, all that's left is to cut through the sea of trees in the far-right corner. A sudden thunderclap lodges my heart in my throat, and each step I take pushes it higher.

It settles back down when I emerge through the trees and walk down Old Glossop Road straight for the bus stop.

I'm really doing this.

A comforting gospel tune fills my head and a melodic hum escapes. It helps keep my fear of sandpapery darkness at bay. Until a shadow causes me to mentally press pause. An animal is perched on the upstairs windowsill of the massive house facing the bus stop. *An owl*, I think. It's hard to tell. The animal turns toward me and its eyes, large and bulging, glisten red like oily Nigerian tomato stew.

Suddenly the owl launches itself off the windowsill and glides silently into the night.

Majestic.

As cold and tiredness start to settle, the bus arrives. I hear it before I see the blaring lights. There's a drumming in my chest. I hop on, pay for my ticket, and breathe a sigh of relief as the bus pulls away lazily and bumbles down the sparse country roads.

As I gaze out the window, the open spaces combined with the still, featureless shadows creep me out. I miss Orlingdon, where there was just enough light to make you feel safe. Here, there's no telling what's hiding in the ocean of darkness. I look at the bus's digital clock and see it's 10:07. Plenty of time. Finally, finally, finally.

The stress of making it onto the bus without a phone pulls me in until I'm daydreaming and soon, I'm drift, drift, drifting . . .

When my eyes open, it's to the announcement that the next stop is Pickleham Lane. I blink. *Pickleham Lane?* The stop after the Silkhead one.

Panicked, I push the STOP button a few times, but the bus doesn't slow down. I squeeze my eyes shut. *No, no, no, this isn't happening.* As the bus pulls into Pickleham Lane, I check the time on the display. 10:15. I have five minutes. I creep up to the driver's seat.

"Ex-excuse me?" The driver grunts, not bothering to look my way. "If I wanted to walk back to the Silkhead stop, how do I get there?"

"Go back down the road."

"Oh . . . okay. D-do I need to cross or—"

"Back down the road."

"Th-thanks. Roughly how far is it?"

The driver shrugs. "Are you getting off?"

I curl my hands into fists, my nails biting into my palms. Slowly, I nod and step off. The door to the bus hisses me goodbye. Drawing a deep breath, I rush back down the road. The smell of wet earth gets stronger and stronger and I can't decide if it's pleasant or not. The one thing I know is that right now my tiredness has suddenly caught up with me.

When I arrive at the Silkhead stop, I have no idea if I'm late or early. But then I see a pair of fresh footprints on the mud leading to the back of the stop and I squeeze my eyes shut. I'm late.

I wade through the grass to the clearing behind the bus stop, expecting to see Malika waiting for me with a mischievous smile. Except there's no one there. Just green grass and . . .

Crouching down, I take a closer look at a bunch of small, translucent mushrooms that almost glow in the moonlight. Weird. They're clumped together and cut across the clearing toward the right. Wherever a mushroom exists, there's dark-speckled grass and blue flowers in bud.

My breath hitches as I remember what the lanky sixth former said to his girlfriend. *His steps come soundless* and *he leaves strange plants.* I jump to my feet, shaking my head when I see there's no footprint shape.

Get a grip, Ife. The Changing Man isn't real.

Looking around, I see nothing. No evidence that Malika was here. No evidence that someone else—supernatural or not—was here either. Only a hazy orange glow through the bushes. The air softly shimmers like looking at the space above a heater on a cold, cold day. When I blink, the shimmering settles. Clearly, tiredness is making me see things now.

BEEP-BEEP-BEEEP!

Tires squeal as I jump, biting down my scream. I turn back toward the road and hear the roaring of two cars going in opposite directions. After a moment, I remember to breathe again.

"Where is she?" I mutter. My jaw clenches. If I had a phone, it would be so easy to just check in with her. Then there's a sound to my left. The crunching of leaves. Through the tall bushes an animal skitters across my vision.

Nope. I don't want to think about whatever animals lurk beyond the trees and bushes. Instantly I head toward the bus stop bench and wait.

And wait and wait and wait.

Until I'm sure Malika isn't coming. Which means she left without me. I groan. I couldn't have been *that* late. She could have waited. My eyes sting and my vision blurs. Zanna's definitely going to be pissed. I was supposed to use Malika's phone to let her know when we were on our way. I kick out at a rock and head to the bus stop to wait for a bus back to Nithercott.

When I eventually sneak back into Beeton House, I am beyond drained and ready to collapse into bed. But first I need a phone to tell Zanna I'm sorry. I creep over to Bee's room, which, if my memory is correct, is the second room away from Ms. Piddleton's. I'm hoping she's awake.

When I knock, there's no answer so I try again and lightly push open her door. Her duvet rises and falls slowly. Snores are as gentle as her soul seems to be. Chewing on the inside of my cheek, I decide to let her sleep. Tomorrow is a new day.

In my room, meanwhile, Fran is still on her phone, probably video calling with a crush judging by the way she's giggling. Kicking off my shoes, I climb into bed and lie faceup, staring at the wood-panel ceiling.

I hope she's having fun. When I see Malika tomorrow, I swear she won't know what hit her. Then I think of Zanna and my stomach crumples. Rolling onto my side, I curl up and think about how I'm going to apologize to her.

CHAPTER 6

CONFUSION

"Malika?" Ms. Piddleton repeats. There's stone silence, which is strange. Whenever Malika goes back home for the night, her mum makes sure she's back in time for morning checks. Ms. Piddleton scans the room, titters, and then moves on.

After Ms. Piddleton is done, she moves on to morning announcements. The music studios are open again; the basement, where boarders keep our suitcases, is being fumigated, so off-limits; there will be a minute of silence at 10:00 A.M. for Alan Gopnik, a benefactor—presumably a dead one, though Ms. Piddleton doesn't say as much; and effective immediately anyone caught in possession of cigarettes will go on report.

When we are dismissed, the smell of coconut wafts under my nose and I already know who I'm going to see as I turn.

"Hiya," Bee says. Bringing her voice to a whisper, she asks, "How was last night?"

I sigh. "Uneventful. Only got as far as the Silkhead bus stop."

"Oh? How come?"

"Because Malika left me behind." I roll my eyes. "Hey, do you mind if I use your phone, please?"

"I—Well, I mean I guess but—"

"Please, please, please?" I push. "School sisters, right?" I argue, borrowing one of her lines.

Bijal frowns. "Yeah, but that's not—I—F-fine."

"Thanks! I owe you one," I chirp, navigating to QuickTalk. I search Malika's name and see she's green, which means online.

It's Ife, I'm on Bijal's phone

Where were you last night?

Malika Wardropper is typing . . .

After half a minute she's still typing and suddenly she's not. Probably thinking about how to come up with an excuse. I thumb the call symbol because I can't wait forever. It rings and rings and rings until I get her automated voice mail.

When I pull away from the phone, Malika's offline. She's definitely avoiding me, which is dumb because I'll be seeing her in fourth period for chemistry with Dr. Butterworth.

Sudden curiosity crawls through me and I open the web browser. Logging into Twitter, I see the preview of a DM from Zanna. By the nausea bubbling deep in my core, I know I'm not ready to face her just yet. Old me would reply—no hesitation. But now I'm overthinking things like . . . *What if she doesn't accept my apology?*

Taking a deep breath, I hand Bijal her phone. "Cheers. I think I'll need to use your phone later if that's okay?"

"Uh, I think I may—yeah, it should—but—yeah should be fine," Bijal stumbles.

"If it's not okay, you can just say it's—"

"No, no, it's fine. Sorry you didn't get to see your best friend by the way. Wanna do lunch?"

"Sure," I murmur, unable to stop my stomach tangling up like my thoughts.

I spend the first two lessons trying not to think about all the worst-case scenarios regarding Malika, giving up by the third. When the fourth period arrives, it's forgotten as I take my seat in chemistry. Anger bubbles through my veins as I keep my head on a swivel, waiting for Malika to walk through the door.

She doesn't.

After taking attendance, Dr. Butterworth asks, "Anyone seen Malika? She's not marked as absent in the . . . system."

"Nurse's, sir?" a classmate suggests.

"Definitely skiving, sir."

"Or maybe she's eloped to be with Leon?"

While my classmates descend into ridiculousness, my anger starts to drain and worry inks my thoughts. *What if she didn't . . .*

No. Malika was online this morning. She was typing to me.

But what if someone . . .

Fear and panic grip at my insides, overriding every instinct to breathe. My eyes lose focus and my mind is pulled all over the place. Tremors rattle every bone in my body.

Oh no, it's happening again.

And then the shattering of glass startles me out of my downward spiral.

"My bad, sir!" the culprit cries. "Beaker slipped out my hands."

By the end of the lesson, I've chewed my pen lid to bits. Mr. Morley appears just as the bell rings and we're packing up our stuff. There's a strange look of concern on his face.

I take my time leaving so I can listen, just in case it's to do with Malika.

". . . you sure?" Mr. Morley breathes.

Dr. Butterworth nods, positioning himself like he's trying to stop Mr. Morley looking at the folder on his desk. "I'm concerned."

"Then you need to—"

The words die in Mr. Morley's mouth. *Crap, crap, crap.* He looks me up and down, rubbing at his chin while staring at me. After a few quick blinks, he *tsks*. "It's rude to eavesdrop."

"Sorry, sir," I say quickly. Turning toward the door, I frown. The folder on Dr. Butterworth's desk was labeled NITHER- COTT STUDENT ACCOUNTS. It had a logo on it. Some sort of purple flower with a crown on top. I don't know what it means, but there's something off about Nithercott's name above a logo that isn't the same as the one stitched on my blazer pocket—a sparrow with its wings outstretched.

I step out into the midday heat and squint. Suddenly the optional summer uniform straw hats don't seem quite as silly.

The thought of adding the expense to my tab crosses my mind until a boy with a mop of curly hair lopes past my eye- line, texting away on his phone.

Louis.

I know I'm going to be late to my next lesson, but I'm worried about Malika. "Hey," I call as I half skip to Louis, who stops and turns.

A smirk builds slowly on his face and he runs a hand through his unruly hair. "State School. Whatever rumor you have to spread about Leon, I'm no longer interested. Old news."

I shake my head. "I'm not here about Leon."

"So, Franny then? I hear the two of you are roomies. Go on . . . Blanket immunity."

I ignore his provocations. "Have you seen or heard from Malika since yesterday after school? You're friends, right?"

"Malika? Have I heard from her since yesterday after school?" Louis pauses and then cracks a smile. "I think I have, and I'm sure I can help. But . . ."

"But?" I echo. When Louis's eyebrows jump up in expectation, I realize he wants a rumor. Something he can use for his hell site CottsLore. My jaw clenches. "Fine. Franny was video calling someone last night. Calling them 'Jelly Bean' and giggling a lot. I *think* it might be a . . . special friend."

"Now that is a surprise. The ice queen, who never dates, has a paramour. Did you happen to see—"

"Malika," I assert, surprising myself by how forcefully I say her name. I clear my throat. "You said you could help."

"Right, right. Let's see . . . so, she called me last night because she wanted company while she waited at the bus stop. But then she said she had to go." He shrugs. "If she's not in yet, she's definitely hungover."

"I see." The fizzing unease in my gut begins to settle. Louis is probably right. I take a deep breath. *Yeah, she probably went without me and had a big night.* "Thanks," I say to the space Louis was standing in.

He's already marched off.

Bijal and I take our seats and dig into our lunch—beef in a truffle cream sauce. A far cry from the humble soggy sandwiches and bruised fruit Dad used to pack for me.

"You're making a face. What are you thinking about?" Bijal asks after a comfortable food silence.

"Nothing." My face softens to sell the lie. But all I can think about is Zanna. I know I have to face her. I look off into space. "Just tired." Ben bulldozes into the dining hall, top button undone, hands in his pockets. "Leon really ran away?" I ask while my eyes track Ben across the hall.

"That's what they think . . ."

I turn to Bijal. One of her bushy eyebrows is arched. "But?"

"But I don't know. I mean, it doesn't make sense to me. I've examined all the angles. He was on track for head boy, his family is relatively well-off, and most people loved him. He literally had it all. Why run? I feel like there's a conspiracy here."

I remember the transcript. "Apparently people who knew him say he was acting strange. Maybe that was it. Something subtle."

"Maybe."

I'm not thinking of Leon anymore, but Malika. The worry returns. I know she and I aren't the closest, but the idea I missed some sort of cry for help makes me feel uneasy. What if she ran away?

"Are you okay?" Bijal asks. "Your breathing . . . it sounded like—"

"No, yeah, all good," I say, cutting in. "I just sometimes forget to breathe when I'm concentrating. Very inconvenient."

"How long?"

My head tilts. "How long what?"

"Since you've been feeling anxious. I noticed it during your physics presentation too."

Bijal's intense stare reminds me so much of Zanna's that I almost spill everything. How it started my first night sleeping at Beeton House and how out of sorts I feel.

Instead, I clam up. "I dunno," I breathe. "Anyway, I think I'm done. I'm going to get some fresh air." Pushing out from the table, I pick up the leather tray and head for the narrow exit. It's an alleyway to the left of these large windows that go from floor to ceiling and open up on the beautiful manicured back lawn, bursting with a multitude of flowers. A few students are gathered wearing "Find Leon" T-shirts. Judging by the time, they're about to head out and go look for clues. I wonder if they've had any luck in any of their searches.

My watching is interrupted by a Black girl with a fringe wig standing sideways. I stop mid-stride and my eyes go wide as I take in the girl's profile. *Malika?*

When she looks over her shoulder, I deflate. It's not her.

"Ife," a voice rumbles behind me.

Mr. Morley. Turning, I take in his scowl and his general couldn't-care-less attitude. I spy a tattoo peeking out from his collar. The jaws of a . . . dragon?

"Any reason you're just standing here, looking lost?" he snaps. I blink, frozen like a cat caught in the act of stalking. He sighs at my silence. "*Move*, you're in the way."

I don't meet his stare as I step aside. When I look back out the window, the girl I thought was Malika is gone.

The day wobbles by, slowly crumpling my chest like fabric after the thread is pulled too tight. I'm too distracted by the *what-ifs* to focus on anything. Before I know it, I am in detention, and Malika is still a ghost.

The idea she has a bad hangover has felt less and less true as the day has gone on.

What if she's missing?

I bring my pen to my mouth, flinching when I realize there's no lid to chew.

That's right, I chewed it to a pulp in my last lesson and threw it out. My eyes scan the room again, settling on Ben and the free space next to him. The teacher's still on his cigarette break, so I relocate next to Ben.

He peers up from his sheets of paper with those blue eyes of his and sighs. "Yes?" he asks, going back to whatever it is he was doing.

I swallow. "I, uh, wanted to ask about Leon."

"None of your business," he replies, not missing a beat.

Be brave. "I know that, but it's just what you said before about people not caring about the truth. I do. How did you know something was wrong?"

Ben sets his pen down and stares at the sheet of paper in front of him. "I just did."

"So, then you reported it straightaway?"

Slowly, he turns his head toward me and I know I've hammered a nerve. There's a pained expression on his face. "I didn't think . . ."

His voice loses all of its sharpness as it trails off. Without saying another word, he dips his head and starts writing. It's obvious I'm not going to get anything else out of him.

"S-sorry if I upset you," I mutter before heading back to my seat.

The rest of detention is a blur as I chew on my lip, worrying about Malika. Why isn't anyone else taking this seriously? A chilling thought crosses my mind. *Would anyone do this for me if I hadn't been seen for nearly half a day?* I push the morbid thought out of my head and clench my jaw. Malika has to be okay. I think about rushing out of the classroom and finding a teacher that might listen to me about my concerns.

And each time I'm frozen by an anxiousness that frosts my insides. My toes scrunch in my shoes. *What if I'm overthinking it?*

"But what if you aren't?" Bijal asks, pushing through the door to the dining hall. "Shouldn't you say some—"

"Bijal!" I exclaim after I slam into her back. "What are you—"

"Your two o'clock."

"My what now?"

She points and I follow her crooked finger over to a table near the floor-to-ceiling windows. Blinking slowly, I lower Bijal's arm because they're looking at us. *She's* looking at us.

Sound distorts as if I've suddenly been dunked underwater. Malika.

In the flesh.

Most of her piercings are out, except for simple studs in her earlobes.

Someone's rubbed out her *attitude*.

The Changing Man myth fills my head. It's not like I believe it. But a part of me won't let the possibility go. I remember when I didn't think demons were real, but Mum told me it would be a mistake to disbelieve in their existence.

All at once the noise of the dining hall rushes back.

"Is she really hanging with Fran? And is that a miniskirt and blazer?" Bijal scoffs. "You told me she thought their sense of fashion was giving basic-girl aesthetic?"

Stacey smirks in my direction, pulling Malika into a hug. Without thinking I stride over, a tangled ball of confusion and anger that wilts with each step. Fran and her girls all stare at me.

"Ife," Malika says, stepping toward me. A thoughtful look colors her face. "Everything okay?"

"Huh?"

She turns away and walks toward the floor-to-ceiling windows. "I sometimes forget how fortunate we are to be here. Porthaven House is lovely, isn't it, Ife?" she asks, her gaze fixed on the half of the orange-brick building visible. The blue flowers look velvety in the dusk light.

"I—I guess?" My eyes flick back to her. "Are *you* okay?" I bring my voice to a whisper. "Since when were you cool with Fran and them?"

"Yeah, funny, right? I never realized how cool they are. We just hit it off." She gives me a playful bump against my shoulder with hers. "Sorry about last night and the radio silence by the way. I'm feeling much more myself. I'll do better."

I blow out my cheeks, before releasing the air inside. "Are you, um, sure you're okay? I dunno, you're, uh, acting weird."

"Am I?" she asks with a grin.

I open my mouth to respond but close it without saying a word. My nails are digging into my palms. Suddenly my clothes feel way too small. *Am I overthinking this?* Heat flushes my face. "N-never mind."

Stacey loops her arm through Malika's and examines her face. "You look so much better without all those piercings." She turns to me. "Everything good?"

"Uh, yeah it is. I'm going to . . ." I let my words trail off as I walk away, utterly confused.

CHAPTER 7

ORIGINS

"Your food's getting cold," Bijal says at our table. "What happened with Malika?"

"I don't get it."

"Get what?"

"It's just so odd. Malika and Fran and her scrunchies. Suddenly friends. It's like she just flipped a switch." I scoop up a forkful of pigeon and lentils and bring it to my mouth. Grimace at how lukewarm it is. "Can you tell me more about the Changing Man myth?"

Bijal puts her fork down. "What do you wanna know?"

"I dunno." Malika's strangeness is fresh in my mind. "Do you think it could be real?" I bite the inside of my cheek. *Did I really just ask that?*

"Well, not in the way it exists now. But fundamentally, yes. It started, according to that article I found, back in one summer during the eighties, 1983."

"What happened in '83?"

"Come on, I told you this. Several students claimed someone was following them. All from different year groups.

They all said the same thing. No, they didn't see him, just his outline. Yes, they were sure they were being followed. The police never found anything though . . ."

"Yeah?"

"One by one the students withdrew their statements. Told the police to stop looking, so that's what happened. Then those students started—for lack of a better term—losing it. Some friends of those students began speaking out. Claiming that the person following them must have got to them somehow."

"Hence the Changing Man."

"Hence the Changing Man," Bijal repeats. A smile builds on her face. Braces showing. "So, from that point of view it feels very mundane. Very believable."

I lean forward in my seat. "But there's something else, isn't there?"

"You bet. I got talking to one of the officers who was working back then. All it took for him to help was a pledge to the charity of his choice. He's retired now and lives in the flats just behind the Butcher's Cleaver."

"The pub by the village shop?"

Bijal nods. "He said his memory was a bit hazy, but that he remembered something odd about their statements. Something that never got reported on. Each of the students said the same thing. It always smelled like wet pavement on a humid day when the man was near. Did you know there's a word for that—petrichor."

Wet pavement on a humid day. I recall how Malika stood me up last night and dread weaves a tight knot in my gut. It loosens when I remember the rain, how humid it was, and that I was walking down the pavement. Obviously, there would be a wet pavement smell. Still . . .

"He said he knew they were just messing about and trying to be part of the growing myth because in his words: 'smelling wet pavement on a *dry* hot day is impossible.'"

I *hmm.* "Would you really lie about being followed? Seems dismissive of him. I mean what if the man had really strong BO?" *Or what if everything they said was true?*

"Right?" Bijal shakes her head, stifling a laugh. "Honestly, he was nice enough, but not at all the sharpest. Anyway, what else, what else? Yes! Now, the Changing Man's name is used whenever someone is acting . . . off. Crops up a lot on CottsLore. Look, here's a recent entry."

Bijal hands me her phone and I take a look.

*Someone spread gossip about **Rupert** in **year 12***
WTF?

Hey, CottsLore. It's ya CottsBaddie and I'm back at it again. One of my frequent collabs—eaverSWay (catch her lurking in the comments)—shared this w/ me: "Lothario no more: Rupert turns over a new leaf." Recently caught dating multiple girls at once, he apparently now has a conscience. Sources say Rupert called a meeting to apologize to every girl he hurt at once. Seems like another victim of the Changing Man.

You think I'm all bark? A twister of the truth? A madman? Well then, take a look-see.

5 images

I open the images and recognize Rupert, who's addressing at least fifteen girls. He was the lanky sixth-form boy with the southern American girl. I go to hand the phone back to Bijal. Before she can take it, I snatch it back, squeezing my eyes shut briefly. *Zanna.* I really need to reach out to her. "Can I use your phone, please?"

"Well, uh, I—yeah go for it. Sure."

"Thanks!"

I open up the web browser and log in to Twitter. Go straight to my DMs.

> Ife ... I'm here
>
> Where are you?
>
> ???
>
> You better have portaled to a hidden world.
>
> That's the only pass I'm giving you for not replying ...
>
> Nvm.

My heart sinks like a stone. Zanna sounds so annoyed at me. I go full-on damage limitation.

> Hey ... finally got to a phone.
>
> Soz soz soz—my ride stood me up!

We need to catch up. So I can explain in full

You can call the phone I'm using.

Avolastic aeyastic asastic asastic asastic echmastic!

I look up from the phone. "Bijal?"

"Yeah?"

"Do you mind if my friend calls your phone? Can I give her your number?"

"Yeah, sure."

Bijal recites the number, and moments later her phone is buzzing. I take a deep, steadying breath and answer. "Hey."

"Explain. In full please," Zanna says. Curt. "What the hell happened?"

I walk her through exactly what happened last night and how Malika didn't show. When I'm done, there's a long stretch of silence. "I swear—"

"I believe you. Yeah. I knew in my bones you wouldn't have stood me up for any old reason. At all."

Her voice is flooded with warmth, but something's up. "What's wrong? What aren't you telling me?"

"Huh? I don't—"

I sigh. "You're doing that thing where you add extra words for no reason."

"Yeah." Zanna laughs. "I guess I am. Avoiding it. So, look

this isn't how I wanted to do this. I wanted to do this in person, when we met, but, well. My family are moving away from Orlingdon."

I feel a pressure in my chest. "What? As in—"

"Yeah, as in. Dad's brother isn't doing too well. So, we're moving there to be with him and offer support for as long as it takes."

"Where's *there*?"

"End of the rainbow . . . pot of gold."

There's a pinch in my chest. I swallow it down, my hands trembling. "Zee, don't play."

"Deadly serious. Dublin . . ."

She can't be moving away. We said we'd go to the same sixth form. My heart bangs against my chest. She can't be—

"Are you even listening to me? Ife?"

"S-sorry. I blanked. What did you say?"

Zanna *tsks* playfully. "Pay attention this time, yeah? I was saying that we're moving next month so we'll be having a going-away party. If you can—"

"I'll be there," I state. "I promise."

"Yeah?"

"Yeah."

"Awesomesauce! Also, you really need to get your phone back. I can't be waiting however long to get a reply on Twitter, 'kay?"

"It's confiscated." She's silent and I scoff. "What? You want me to take it back?"

"Duhhh. Remember when we snuck into Punter's office to change our grades? This is like that."

"Uh, not really?"

"Potato and carrots. The Ife *I* know wouldn't bat an eyelid."

Her words spark a fire deep in my belly. "I'm still me," I snap. Even if I don't feel like it.

"I know." I can hear the grin in Zanna's voice. "Oh, I need to go. Laters!"

The phone cuts and I instantly feel the void of Zanna's absence. I hand Bijal's phone back and she's smiling widely. My eyebrows bunch together. "Why are you giving me that look?"

"Becauuuse"—she slides her phone into her pocket—"I know how to get your phone back. Sorry, I wasn't deliberately listening to your conversation."

"So . . . how would you do it?" My heart thumps.

"It's easy. The confiscated stuff is in the back of the staff room and there's always a window open. You can get in that way. The door is to the left of the floral sofa."

"What about any locks?"

"Sure, there's a lock on there. But if you move the sofa, there's an air vent. This school has a lot of air vents."

"I-it's really that easy?" I answer. I pause to slurp down a spoonful of bloodred jelly. "H-how do you know all this?"

"You'd be surprised how much information they have in the library," Bijal says with a grin. "Just have to take the time to go through it. Anyway, here's how you'd get to the staff room without being seen . . ."

As part of my apology tour, I decide to face my parents after dinner, making a detour to the well-being booth inside

Porthaven House. I'm sitting inside and my stomach's all over the place. I wonder what I'm gonna tell my parents. Are they even going to let me defend myself? Or are they going to tell me I hate correction? *Ugh.* Doesn't matter. I'm going to tell them this place isn't for me and I want to leave ASAP.

I log in to my profile and tap Dad's number, pausing at the choice I have to make. Audio or video?

I choose video because it's the right thing to do. I guess I also miss their faces. It rings for a while and then connects. The first thing I see arc Dad's nostrils and I laugh.

"Hello? Hello?" he asks.

"Yeah, hi, Dad. I'm here."

"Okay good." He changes the angle of the phone so I can see his face better. "So how are you doing? Nice of you to call. Talk to me."

I hate when he does that. *Talk to me.* It instantly puts pressure on me to say something worthwhile. Not to mention . . . why? "I'm fine, thanks."

"Okay. So has anything happened to you recently?"

He always does this. "Like what?"

"Well, we got a call from the school the other day. They said you disrupted the class with your phone. Do you think it was smart to not own up that it was your phone?"

Obviously, it wasn't smart. I say nothing because it's one of those loaded questions. It's like if someone is pointing an empty gun at me and I hand them a bullet. Why would I do that?

Dad *hmms.* "Ife, I'm talking to you. Do you think it was smart?"

"No," I mumble, handing over the metaphorical bullet. I

want to roll my eyes, but if I do, I'm sure Dad would find a way to pull me through my screen.

"So why did you lie? Why wasn't it on silent? Ife, I told you when we got you that phone: Make sure it's off for lessons. Or, you should leave it in your room."

"I knowww, but it wasn't my fault." The words tumble out. "It *was* on silent. It must have somehow come off silent when it was in my bag. I don't know how but it's always doing that. I know it was wrong to lie, but the first time it went off I tried to put it back on silent. I just didn't get there in time and Mr. Morley was being unfair. I swear it was an accident."

"Swear ke? Ah, ah. There will be no swearing in this house," Mum says in the background.

I can't help but laugh. "Mummm! I was just trying to say that it wasn't on purpose."

"I know, dear. I've always said tell me the truth and I will believe you. What they're saying isn't like what you said just now. I will write them an email tomorrow."

"It's alright, Mum, you don't—"

She cuts me off and appears next to Dad. "Did you willingly disrupt the class?"

"No. I just—"

"Then I'm writing an email," she states before walking off.

"O-okay." My face gives nothing away, but inside I'm glowing like a Christmas tree. I don't say it enough, but I love her to bits. Even if she's always doing the most. I build up to say what I want to say, but Dad gets there first.

He's smiling in that way that makes me want to smile too. It's also the most cringe smile ever. "Ife. I didn't mean to sound upset. I'm not. I believe it wasn't your fault either, but when you give a teacher an inch, sometimes they can take a mile. Trust me, I've been there before. I just don't want you to make the same mistakes I've made. Your mum is writing the email but it will be from the both of us. We're proud of you and—Oh, there's no need to cry."

The tears drip off my chin. I wipe them away, and it hits me just how much I miss my family. So much has been going on I haven't had time to think about when I'll properly see them next in person.

I sniff. I'll tell them how I feel another time. I don't want to ruin the mood. My two-year-old brother's cheeky face appears in my mind.

"How's Ayo?" I ask.

"He's doing great. Not enjoying the cold of Stavanger. Neither is your mum, but they'll get used to it. How cold is it where you are?"

"Not too *too* cold. Summer's definitely gone. When am I seeing you guys again?"

"Well, we're going to be there for half term in like seven weeks. So, October twenty-first?"

My heart drops. Seven weeks is a lifetime away right now. "What about the exeat weekend?" The last few nights, Fran's been planning hers out. Her family can't decide between a shopping weekend in Paris or a spa weekend in Geneva. Which sounds great, but nothing beats *home*. "It's coming up. Can I come see you guys for the weekend?" I beg Dad.

"I wish you could, but it's expensive and we just paid for your school fees. Sorry o! Are you making friends?"

Malika flashes in my mind. So does Bijal. I hold back a laugh. "It's complicated."

I'm about to float the idea of going back to Orlingdon for Zanna's leaving, which is on a non-exeat weekend, but I hear Ayo crying.

Dad turns his head toward the crying. "Aahhh."

"Is Ayo alright?" I ask.

He grunts as he gets up. "Yes. Well no. He just bumped his head. I'm sorry, I have to go." He shuffles over to Ayo. "Oh dear," he adds, completely forgetting I'm still here.

I hang up.

Big silent tears run down my face. I feel so alone. Leaning against the side of the booth, I cradle my legs, close my eyes, and let the tears fall.

CHAPTER 8

IMPULSE

Dun-dun-dun-dun-dun!

My eyes burst open. I fell asleep. *Ugh*, I also drooled. Great. "Yeah, yeah, yeah. I'm done. Give me a second," I shout.

Wiping my mouth and doing my best to rub the sleep from my eyes, I get the door.

"This isn't a place to nap," the girl staring daggers at me says, rolling her eyes. Wait, I know her. She's one of the few Black people I've seen at the school—Rachel. She scowls at me like she's allergic to my existence before her face softens. "You're in Beeton House, aren't you?"

"Yeah."

"And you're new, right?"

"Yeah, why?"

"Because you don't look terrified and you're like half an hour late for checks."

Oh man, oh man, oh man. I rush past Rachel and head for Beeton House. I make it a few steps outside of Porthaven House before I trip, scraping my hands on the asphalt, my face over a murky puddle.

My wide-eyed reflection gazes back at me. Pain tingles in the palms of my hands. I pull myself up and inspect the damage. I'm bleeding. I make a quick detour for the nurse's office, thinking she'll be able to help with the pain and also give me an alibi for being late. But her lights are off.

Damn it.

Running back to Beeton, I prepare my body and soul, because I know I'm going to have to grovel until there are holes in the knees of my sweatpants.

I arrive out of breath just as the teacher on duty is leaving. I'm halfway through keying in the house PIN code when the door flies open. Ms. Piddleton strides out in a pink-sleeved windbreaker, bowling me out the way. She looks down on me and sighs.

"Ife."

"Miss." I give her my best sorry face and start groveling, ignoring the dull pain throbbing through my hands. "I'm *really* sorry."

Ms. Piddleton folds her arms. "You can't just turn up at whatever time suits you."

"No, it wasn't like that. I was—"

Her eyes narrow. "Don't argue with me, Ife."

"But, Miss, I promise it wasn't—"

"I'm warning you."

She raises an index finger and I know I shouldn't say another word, but I can't help it. This isn't fair.

"Miss, can I just explain—"

"Enough!" Ms. Piddleton snaps. "You'll be house confined for the next week."

House confined? As in all my free time—including break and lunch—belongs to the villain that is Ms. Piddleton?

My stomach hardens into stone. I'm now phone-less *and* freedom-less.

"Wipe that look off your face."

I had no idea I had a look *on* my face. "Sorry, Miss. I'm sorry, it won't—"

"Save it." She jabs a bony finger at me. "You've been here barely a month and yet this is the second time I find your name on my lips. And once again, not for the right reasons." A look of sympathy clouds her face and she lowers her finger. "I understand. When you come to a new school, you want to stand out, be noticed, be cool—"

I want none of those things. I just want to be where my friends are.

"—whatever. But let me tell you now. This is not a state school. Nithercott students are held to a higher standard. Don't ruin your potential. Do I make myself clear?"

Teachers like her like to be in control and make us feel tiny. She's doing a good job. I bite my lip. It's the only thing that'll stop the tears. "Yes, Miss," I manage to say.

"Good."

She doesn't wait for me to say anything, but spins and heads for her office. I glare hard at her back, wishing I could burn literal holes into her clothes. Nothing happens. Bijal comes up to me.

"Forget her. She's a bitch."

"Bijal!" I exclaim in a hushed whisper. But I don't disagree, and we burst into giggles.

Since Bijal doesn't have a roommate, we spend the night in her room applying a face mask and making dumb vids on her MacBook.

"I don't think I've ever been this relaxed at Nithercott." I lie back on her bed doodling flowers that morph into the one I saw on Dr. Butterworth's folder. I scribble it out, not wanting to think about anything strange right now.

Bijal takes a deep breath. "Me neither. As my parents like to tell me: 'We left Mumbai so that we could give you more.' That kind of pressure is heavy."

I get it.

We drown in silence. I want to ask her so many things, but I just can't bring myself to say the words.

"You know I joined in year eight," Bijal says. "My wannabe prep school back home only went up to the end of year seven. The secondary schools my 'friends' went to—the ones Mummy and Papa wanted me to go to—were way too expensive. When they found out *the* Nithercott was inviting any and all to take their exam to get into the Urban Achievers Program, they couldn't apply fast enough. Still those questions were . . ."

"Absurd," I finish, recalling my own exam. "How the hell were they able to choose when the questions were so out there? I mean I had no idea how to answer the question that literally said: 'A circle is over there and a square is over here. Where are you?' It made zero sense."

"Yeah, I didn't get a question like that. I got asked to articulate how unlucky I was and why."

"Ridiculous . . ."

"And yet, here we are."

"Here we are indeed . . ." She's teed it up perfectly for me to open up, but the pressure gets to me. "We should watch an episode of the *Social Media Experience*," I suggest instead.

I leave when it's nearly time for lights out. Rolling into bed, I think about home—Zanna, Orlingdon, and my family. I reach for my phone, sighing when my hand clutches at air.

Zanna's voice rings in my head and I remember how we snuck into Punter's office to change our grades in Archbishop's. It's then I decide.

I need to get my phone back.

After Ms. Piddleton comes to tell us it's lights out, I sneak to the games room and move the sofa and games cabinet out the way.

Stepping out into the crisp night, I shiver with excitement.

Following Bijal's instructions, I crawl through the bushes adjacent to smokers' alley. Feeble branches prod and poke at me, but I fight through. Arriving on the other side, I step to the wall dead ahead and keep tight to it so the cameras don't pick me up.

I shouldn't be doing this.

All that's left is to cut across the back lawn. Even in the dark of night I can tell how beautiful the layout is. The perfectly manicured grass is split into four quadrants, each one home to delicate ponds ringed by roses.

And looming tall is the moonlit back of Porthaven House.

Dim light from the upper windows makes it look like the building has eyes.

I step carefully across the carpet of grass, letting go of my breath when I reach the staff room windows at the back of Porthaven House. Like Bijal said, a window hangs open. Except it's one of those cat-flap windows and it's quite high up. Too high up.

I grumble under my breath. "Should I turn back?"

No, I need to do this. I look around and spot a bin. I drag it across, then awkwardly turn it upside down. Clambering on top of it, I reach upward. The windowsill is still out of reach. I'm going to have to jump.

"Am I alright?" I ask the wind. It whistles back as if it knows I am. I go for it and my fingers latch on, hold for half a second before slipping off straightaway. I try again and this time—

Got it.

Then the fun starts. I'll have to pull up my own body and squeeze through. ME. I've never done a pull-up in my life, but how hard can it be?

Answer: incredibly.

I grunt and wobble. God, I bet I sound embarrassing. After what feels like an age, I pull myself up until I'm half in, half out of the window. Frowning and nibbling on my bottom lip, I think of my next move.

Right below me are all the washed cups and mugs. Sending them toppling onto the wooden floor is not an option.

I take a few deep breaths and look around for a spark of inspiration. To the right something winks in the moonlight. It's the thing attached to the wall that's holding the curtain back.

Farther on is an armchair with a pile of A5 pieces of paper. An idea strikes me. If I can grab ahold of the winking thingy and hook my feet to the window, I might be able to somehow flip onto the armchair. Not the best idea, but the only one I can think of that doesn't end up with broken cups and mugs.

Okay.

Wriggling, I reach for the winking thingy and hold on tight. I shuffle so my feet are basically hooked on the edge of the window. This next bit of my plan needs my arms and upper body to be strong. But right now, from my core to my arms, I feel a bit jelly-ish.

Zanna always teased me over my lack of body strength, calling me her human version of Flubber from the movie. When I actually googled Flubber, I laughed and then pushed her over. Thinking about getting back to her gives me the strength I need.

Now!

My feet kick off the edge of the window. With all the grace of a bulldog on stilts, my back slams against the arm of the armchair and I fall onto the rug with a thud. In the process, pieces of paper go flying.

Rubbing my back, I fight the urge to swear and take the good with the bad. I'm inside and haven't broken anything.

The A5 pieces of paper are actually flyers for Nithercott Day. I arrange them into a neat pile back on the armchair.

Standing in the center of the staff room, I stifle a nervous giggle. I'm really doing this.

The floral sofa slides easily out the way and there it is—the air vent. With a satisfying click, it peels away and I climb into the vent. It's so narrow that as I crawl into the confiscation cupboard, my elbows rub against the metallic walls of the vent.

I cough. The cupboard's so musty and dark. Groping around, I find the light switch and flood the space with light.

A narrow walkway is sandwiched between towering shelves set above waist-tall cupboards. Lining the shelves are all sorts of stuff I'm not interested in. Walking down, I keep an eye out.

Until I find the label I need on one of the middle shelves— PHONES.

There's a huge pile of them in a clear plastic box and they all look like mine. How does everyone have the same clear case for wireless charging?

Set aside is a clipboard. Sliding it off the shelf, I can see it's a log of all phones with a number. Mine's the most recent entry—number 631—which means it should be one of the top ones. I get on my tippy-toes and ease the box onto the edge. *Easy does it*. It teeters and I bite my lip. *Easy does*—

It slides into my chest and sends me flying backward. I land on my back and the box spills its gut of phones. My eyes close as the rattling is barely dampened by the carpeted floor. I force myself to breathe and calm down. I'll find it. After I'm sure no one is on their way to check out the noise I made, I get on my hands and knees and trawl through phones trying to find mine with the number 631 sticker.

There it is at the end of the walkway. *At last*. It juts out from the gap underneath a wooden cabinet. Sliding onto my belly, I reach for it, my breath sending the dust bunnies scuttling away.

I pack away the spilled phones and put the phone box

back on the shelf. I crawl back into the staff room and make sure everything is exactly how I found it.

It's just a phone, but it's also everything. It's what keeps me connected to my friends and my old life.

I'm almost at the door when there's a rattle. My heart jumps up to my throat. Another rattle. Like an idiot, I stand there with my feet glued to the floor.

The door opens and someone emerges. "What the—"

"Fudge," I say.

CHAPTER 9

OUCH

The faint rustling of distant trees fills the silence between us as we stare at one another.

"Ben," I hiss, breaking the wordlessness. "What are you doing here?"

He keeps quiet. Frowning. Eventually he speaks. "None of your business. Question is, why are *you* breaking into the staff room?" I don't answer. "Whatever. What I really want to know is: What is your deal?"

"Huh?"

"I want you to explain yourself." Ben takes a few steps toward me with his hands in his pockets and looks intently at me. "By the by, you've got some pretty eyebrows."

"Whatever." My face is a radiator. *Pretty?* I shake away the words. "Why are you so annoying?" I shoot back.

Ben shrugs. "Just tell me why you did it. Then maybe—just maybe—I'll let you leave." He hovers a fist over the BREAK GLASS part of the alarm. "And you know I'll do it," he adds, smiling like the devil he knows he is.

I kiss my teeth and sigh. "Ben, look, I'm sorry I took your

piece of paper, but I swear, I didn't spread anything about your brother."

He laughs at me. "Seriously? You expect me to believe that? I saw you speaking with Louis."

"But I—Okayyy." My eyes close for a brief moment and I take a deep breath. "Yeah, I was talking to Louis, because he *bumped* into me. Then he was bigging himself up. He wanted me to know who he was. He asked me about you, and if you'd told me anything, but I just left because he's not worth it. I am sorry I lashed out though. I know I said some hurtful things."

Ben's face softens for a second and all the meanness is ironed out, until it crumples into an awkward smirk. "Well then, I seem to have . . . jumped to the wrong conclusion."

I bite down on all the names I want to call him and choose to raise an eyebrow instead.

"I . . . guess we're even." He shrugs. "No bad blood." He breezes past me and I turn my head to follow. He stops and walks backward. "Just one thing. You wanted to know about Leon. Why?"

"Malika. She was . . . acting different. *Is* acting different? Until I saw her at dinner, I thought maybe she'd run away. Like Leon."

Ben frowns and pulls at the peach fuzz under his chin. "Different how?"

"She's just not herself. Like suddenly she's friends with Fran and the scrunchies, except days ago we were in her room making fun of that whole lot. And then just her style and attitude are different. Maybe I got her wrong." I pull a face, not fully believing that. "The Malika I know would see herself now and think she's beyond boring. I just—"

"This is good," Ben murmurs.

"Good?"

"Yes . . . No. Look, here isn't the place to discuss this. There's something going on here, and I'm not talking about that Changing Man fairy tale. Leon was taken by someone, and maybe this person spooked Malika. I'll reach out, and we can talk then, okay?"

I nod, watching him move the floral sofa out the way. "Wait," I say. "When will you reach out?"

He pulls away the air vent. Pauses. Looks back at me with a crooked, moonlit smile and crawls in.

What the hell just happened and what does Ben know? And what is he looking for?

The questions bounce around in my skull as I leave Porthaven behind. As I step foot on the back lawn, I freeze and crouch down, running my hand across the grass. It's dry.

So why do I smell petrichor?

The smell is drifting this way from my left. *Smelling wet pavement when the ground is dry is impossible.* I should go. I know it in my bones.

So why am I just staring off to my left?

I get to my feet.

Turn around, now. The trees whisper as I step toward the smell that gets stronger and stronger. Until it's harder to breathe and my legs and arms are blocks of concrete. I round the corner and hold my breath. Goose bumps slide along the back of my neck.

The space in front of me is marbled with streaks of a thin orange mist. The air shimmers like a mirage. I shake my head.

I should go.

A giggle punctures the silence. Followed by, "Shhh, shhh, shhh."

"Stop . . . I said—" There's a smooching sound. "*Stop.* What if a teacher comes?"

I *definitely* should go. Whatever's about to happen here is none of my business.

A blur of movement stops me in my tracks. Someone else is here. They dip out of view suddenly. This school is not good for my heart.

I scan the area . . .

There.

Hiding behind the tree badly. There's a moment of still, and then the human shape I can see begins to shift and the streaks of orange mist get thicker. My mouth waters. I feel sick. Trembling invades my limbs.

I back away. Away. Away.

Crack. The snapping of a branch under my feet makes a thunderous sound.

"Someone's here," one of the voices says. The shape behind the tree moves ever so slightly and two eyes, glowing like magenta headlights, look my way.

The glare splinters every nerve in my body and a single thought digs deep into my mind: *the Changing Man.*

I sprint for Beeton with my heart beating in my throat and my stomach sinking all the way to my toes. I don't even care about avoiding the cameras. All the Bible verses to do with courage and comfort run through my mind like a bullet train.

ThenameoftheLordisastrongtower . . .

I just want to get back inside. A shrill scream fills the air, and I crane my head back.

Empty darkness. No magenta headlights.

As soon as I turn my head forward again, my foot clips a raised bit of the pathway and I'm stumbling forward. Heading straight for the concrete. I fling out my arms to break my fall and I clip the pathway again.

I'm sent flying headfirst toward a wooden bollard. There's no way I'll be able to avoid it so I squeeze my eyes shut and wait for—

I sit up in a dim room. I'm in a bed. Not mine. I wince at the throbbing pain in my head. Slowly, it all comes rushing back. I was running. I was falling—fell—into the bollard.

The walls are white and covered in posters. A colorful one catches my eye, and I squint to read what's on it. *Nithercott— where no door remains closed, no ceiling left unshattered.*

There's talking coming from behind the door of the room I'm in. I see a strip of light at the bottom that flickers. I tiptoe to the door and press my ear against it.

"It appears to be a slight concussion. I'd like to take one last look at her before I go. Don't worry, she's fine. Okay then. Bye-bye."

Steps clack toward me. I'm barely under the covers when the door opens. I see her afro first as the nurse looks at me through the doorway with a sweet smile. "Oh, you're up. Why didn't you say anything, love?"

"I just got up. How did I get here?"

"You don't remember? A student found you and got Ms. Piddleton to help bring you here after. You were in and out of it. How are you feeling now?"

"Yeah, okay. Alive." My head is pounding. This nurse gives me some weird vibes. There's something trapped behind her smile.

"Yes, you seem to be. Right, I've given Ms. Piddleton instructions. You'll need to take it easy. Avoid as many digital screens as you can. And make sure you stay hydrated."

The memory of the magenta eyes I saw emerges and fades just as quickly. I shake my head. "Can I stay here a little longer, please?"

"Sure you can, sweetie. Just pop out and see me when you're ready to leave." She closes the door behind her and I'm left alone. My stomach scrunches. Fear curls my hands into tight fists. I don't know what it is, but I can feel the wrongness in my gut. This whole place.

The kettle's haunting breaths, as it heats water, wakes me up. Yawning, I decide to head back to my room. I want to spend the time before breakfast in my own bed. On my way out, the nurse offers me tea and biccies. I shouldn't, but I do and it's instant regret. The tea is too sweet and the biscuits are stale digestives. Flip's sake.

"How are you finding it here? You're new, aren't you? One of our 'Urban Achievers'?" the nurse asks.

I swallow down a soggy bit of stale digestive (I'm a dipper). "It's okay. Yeah, I'm new. It's . . . different."

"Hmmm. Did you know I was once a student here? So, I get what it's like."

"Really?"

"Oh yes. I was just like you. Nearly thirty-five years ago now."

I burn my tongue when I over sip. *Ouch! But* . . . "Miss! Thirty-five years ago! You look so young though. Like what?"

"Black don't crack. At all," the nurse says with a wink.

Awkward silence. My hands drum against the mug while my eyes wander. They settle on a red puzzle book with worn edges and a mug stain on its cover. "You actually into puzzles, Miss? Or is it just an oversize coaster?"

She points a crooked finger at me. "Cheeky! I *love* puzzles. Crosswords, sudoku, anagrams. You name it."

Conversation blooms. We talk about our shared love of puzzles, her time at Nithercott, and how she ended up being the school nurse.

"Miss, so you and Dr. Butterworth were actually friends?"

"You can call me Elaine. And oh yes. He and I. We met in Learning Support actually. He told me his top-secret focusing trick—swearing quietly when his words or thoughts got stuck. I laughed and he smiled, and we were inseparable from that moment on. Not just us, but our families. Funny how we're both back where we started."

"Is it?"

"Strange though. He always used to say he couldn't wait to leave. And he did for a while. But someone, or maybe Nithercott duty, drew him back. I don't know, it's been a long while since we last spoke properly. He's a very busy man. Oh, and then there's Patrick."

"Patrick?"

"Sorry, Mr. Ingham. He always looked out for me like a sister. I think it's because he was an only child. Anyway, he wasn't always so popular. If I remember correctly, he was a couple of years above me and we were part of the skill 'n' tell club. Each week we'd challenge ourselves to learn something and then demonstrate to the members the week after. He was amazing the way he picked up things so easily." She mimics her mind being blown while getting to her feet.

"Really?"

"Hang on."

Elaine leans away from me and riffles through her middle desk drawer. When she turns to face me, I'm handed an old group photo taken by the steps leading up to the quad. Elaine's easy to spot, standing on the wall that guards the steps. I'm drawn to the smiling boy next to her with his arm slung over her shoulder. "Is that Mr. Ingham?"

"No." She stifles a laugh. "I do see the resemblance, but no, that's sweet ol' William Swan. We went out for like two terms, I think. The *longest* terms of my life. Mr. Ingham's this one over there."

She points to a glum-looking boy on the other side of the photo who looks a lot less like the Mr. Ingham I know. There's no warm smile or confident manner. Instead, he sits on the wall, glaring at the camera with a stony focus. Either side of him, two boys have the same stoic persona. "Oh. I never pictured Mr. Ingham as a student, but I didn't think he'd look so . . . cold."

"Well, it wasn't easy being the headmaster's son. It can go

one of two ways, where you're seen as royalty or as an alien of sorts. Tell you what though, he—"

Elaine stands up suddenly, looking past me. I turn around and see Mr. Ingham standing in the doorway with a soft smile. He's wearing a Barbour jacket over a set of striped pajamas. I glance back at that photo and wonder what changed.

"El," he says, stepping to her desk. "It wasn't easy at all. But enough about me. How is our Ife here doing? Evie called me."

"Oh, much better. She just bumped her head," Elaine replies, primping her afro.

"That so?" Mr. Ingham turns to me, his eyebrows drawing together. "Is everything okay now?"

I nod. "I think I'll be okay. Miss, can I go?"

Mr. Ingham raises an eyebrow. "Why were you out so late?"

I don't answer.

"Ife?" He frowns, then relaxes. "It'll be a lot easier for you if—"

"Homesick," I whisper. Which is a half-truth. Mr. Ingham nods and doesn't say a word. But I can tell he isn't impressed.

Elaine smiles. "Just make sure you remember what I told you. If you start to feel worse, come and see me straightaway. That reminds me, in your next free period, please come see me so we can undergo your mandatory new students' checkup."

Ah, yeah. I'd forgotten I still needed to schedule that.

I nod and squeeze past Mr. Ingham. I'm nearly at the door when his voice calls out to me.

"I—I don't suppose you can do me a favor?" he asks. A grimace on his face. "I was hoping you'd take a family on a tour of the school grounds tomorrow morning. They sort of arranged unconventionally, saying our school's warden told them it's okay. It's just that I'm busy with Leon's disappearance and there are other activities going on. Of course, if you're not feeling up to it, that's perfectly—"

"No, I'll do it," I answer.

Mr. Ingham breaks out into an approving smile. "Thank you so much. Ms. Piddleton will give you all the information you need. Speaking of, good luck."

I miss the warmth of Elaine and Mr. Ingham immediately. The clouds are gray and having a tantrum, spitting out uneven rain. As I'm walking toward Beeton, all I can think about is the orange mist, the shimmering air, the glowing eyes, and whether or not I imagined it all.

I don't think I did.

A flash of black appears by my feet and I jump. It's the hairless cat. It follows me all the way to Beeton, purring every now and then. I guess the cat wants to come and watch me get chewed out for the second time.

Sitting on the steps, and under Beeton's front door's cover, Ms. Piddleton is reading a book. When she spots me, she dog-ears her page, closes her book, and rises up. Not even her pursed lips and cold eyes bruise my composure. I'm too busy thinking about what I saw.

My head throbs as Ms. Piddleton turns away and heads

for the door. "I think you and I"—she keys in the code—"need to have a serious chat, don't you?"

I swallow, following her inside. But as I near her office, there's no space for remorse because a singular thought occupies my head right now.

I need to speak to Ben.

CHAPTER 10

INTO THE WILD

My phone buzzes by my ear, but I roll over in bed and ignore it. I've barely looked at my messages. I still don't know what really happened last night. What I saw. What I *think* I saw. I wriggle my legs against my bedsheets.

When I drop him a message on QuickTalk, he responds almost instantly.

Busy day—catch up in detention.

Zanna calls me after I message that the break-in was a success but ended with me in the nurse's office and in big trouble for being out late. After a few seconds I go to decline but accidentally pick it up. Slowly, I put the phone to my ear. "Hey, Zee," I say.

"Ife, there you are! Thought you weren't gonna answer," Zanna says in one breath. "Is everything okay? Tell me everything."

I frown up at the ceiling. The words are stuck in my throat. I'm not sure she'd get it if I walked her through last night.

Nothing about it makes sense.

"Ife," Zanna says thoughtfully, "when you're ready to talk, I'll be ready. Oh, before I forget, I'm craving tangies." Whenever one of us doesn't want to talk about something, the other person is owed a snack. It's such a silly rule, but it makes me smile. "Wait, no, I take it back, I want Twix."

"Zanna," I scoff. "Official rules state you can only switch within the same snack group. Twix and tangies are from different families."

"This is true. Are you alright though?"

Glowing eyes flash through my mind. I remember the shimmering air. *What* was *that?* "Yeah. It's just . . . complicated."

"Well, you can tell me anything, you know that, Ife. Right, I won't ask any more, at least until I get my tangies."

"Deal."

Zanna fills me in on the relocation—her dad's about to fly over to Dublin first—before hanging up, leaving me alone and scared. When I think about what I saw last night, my insides numb. None of this happened before I came to Nithercott.

It feels like I swallowed the red pill like that Neo guy from *The Matrix*.

Letting go of a deep breath, I roll out of bed and get ready for the day. I've got a tour to give before breakfast.

As soon as I step outside, everything comes rushing back. The smell of petrichor, the bursting pain of hitting my head. I flinch. The school feels like it's closing in on me one centimeter at a time. My uniform is suddenly way too tight.

I shudder, remembering the talk I had with Ms. Piddleton in her office. Before I sat down, she hugged me and asked if I was okay. It was both odd and nice. I also thought maybe, just maybe, I'd get off with a strong warning and no letter back home.

Nope. I got detention—indefinitely.

No leaving the school grounds—indefinitely. Even on the weekends.

Don't get me started on the lecture my parents gave me when she called them and put me on the phone. It's a literal miracle Mum didn't say they're moving back to the UK to keep an eye on me. At least my house confinement wasn't extended, and once I've served my time, I get to walk out and about on weekends within the school grounds with regular check-ins.

After a few minutes of waiting at the flagpole, an inter-racial couple emerge from Porthaven. The man is wearing large half-moon spectacles, while the woman—looking heavily pregnant—holds an umbrella up to repel the sun. I file away their looks for sketching inspiration.

"Hey there," the man says. His voice sounds like a hammer banging against a nail. It doesn't really fit anywhere. He holds out his hand. "Lovely to meet you . . ."

"Ife," I finish, taking his hand. He shakes it thoroughly. "Are you ready?"

"Indeed, we are. Lead the way."

I take them toward the quad and talk about how the days at Nithercott are structured.

The woman clears her throat suddenly. "Do you feel like a goose on a hot tin roof?"

"On a what?" I ask.

"Sorry," the man says with a chuckle. "I think what my life-helper means is that as an Urban Achiever, plucked from everything you know, how do you feel?"

I didn't even know they knew I was an Urban Achiever. Then I remember my green plaid skirt is the giveaway. "Uh, well, it's a great opportunity being here with my art scholarship." I pause, thinking seriously about their question. "I guess there's a lot to get used to. So it's strange. Yeah, I feel out of place." They stare at me with blank faces. "B-but that's just how it is. I know I'll get used to it. I've barely been here for a month."

"Splendid attitude," they say in unison. The woman smiles and inhales deeply, like she's smelling something pleasant.

"You *must* be talented. Utilizing the right side of your brain so . . . delightfully. Good for you."

"Thanks?" I say with a frown. We move on from the quad toward the art block, and they insist on seeing my art portfolio.

The woman looks overjoyed while the man stands in silence until he says: "Could you demonstrate?"

"Well, I'm not exactly prepared. I wouldn't know what—"

"Please," the man presses. "My wife and I would appreciate it awfully. A souvenir of sorts."

"O-okay." I grab a loose piece of paper and a pencil and get to work. I'll draw something quick and easy. A sketch of the two of them in a style the art teacher wouldn't like—a line drawing that I shade with scribbles. It's so much more interesting than the rigid, highly naturalistic work they want us to produce.

When I'm done, the couple shower me in praise. I can't lie, it feels good. And then, as we're due to move on, they excuse themselves.

"Thank you for your time, Ife. I think that'll be all from

us. We like you—a lot—but we ought to get going. Places to go. Others to see."

They thank me once again, walk off, and leave me alone in the art block where I sit for a moment before making my way over to breakfast.

An angry groan from behind me stops me in my tracks.

"B-b-blast it all to hell!" Dr. Butterworth exclaims, his voice carrying ahead of him, quick and frustrated. "Sensitive Alred. O-overreacting Alred. Blast it all to hell. They don't care. He'll . . . understand. Won't he? That we n-need to—"

As he emerges from around the corner, clutching a wad of files close to his chest, Dr. Butterworth jumps. The orange-rimmed glasses he's wearing jump with him. I spot a purple flower with a crown again, but I'm not close enough to read the words curling round it.

Either way, it looks official, and the cogs in my brain start working, spitting out a question: *What if the logo's bad news?*

Dr. Butterworth stands for a moment and takes a deep breath. "Yes?"

"Nothing, I was just—" One of the files slips free from his hands and I see an array of candid pictures spilling out. On the back of some, there's illegible handwriting. My body freezes, tingling with discomfort. I recognize some of the faces. I catch a glimpse of me and Malika smiling together.

"Sir, why do you . . ."

Exhaling, he calmly reaches down for the file. "They're for the new school prospectus. The school thought the more genuine the pictures, the better. House parents were supposed to give students a warning."

Before I can say anything, he walks off.

For a moment, I'm not sure what to think. Somehow what he's saying rings a bell. And yet, I don't believe him. There's something strange going on at Nithercott and he knows what it is. I'm sure of it. So I decide to follow him.

Following someone is a lot harder than the movies make it out to be. Dr. Butterworth keeps checking over his shoulder like someone is after him.

Guilty.

At times he disappears from view, but I find him again. And then I realize I was here last night. This is *couples' corner*.

Listen—the stories students tell make me shudder. If it's anything more than PG, I'm really running away.

I'm hiding behind a tree. Dr. Butterworth looks over his shoulder for the hundredth time before stepping into the bushes. For a second, I wonder if he's there to meet another teacher. But no one arrives. I give it a few more seconds before I creep closer.

Dr. Butterworth's crouching down, plucking the grass and looking at it in his palm. He jots down some notes. When he's satisfied, he stalks off. I count to ten and then I walk over to where he was and crouch down.

The grass is slick and dark-speckled. Baby, translucent mushrooms have sprouted. I recall the clearing behind the Silkhead bus stop. There's an expanding feeling in my chest. No way this is a coincidence. My eyes rove around the space, and an arm's stretch away, I spy small blue flowers halfway blooming.

Knew it. I pluck one from the ground and gaze at it.

His steps come soundless, and he leaves strange plants.

"Whatcha doing there, Ife?" Bijal asks, making me jump.

"I saw you come this way instead of brekky." I swivel and spot her walking toward me, her ponytail swaying with each step. "You're . . . you're not waiting for someone, are you?" she adds, coming to a stop in front of me.

I raise an eyebrow. "Waiting for—Oh! Hell no." I scrunch my face. My stomach turns itself inside out. Gross. "No, no, no. I was just looking at the grass and ground actually. Have you seen these before?" I show her the flower.

"Hang on. Lemme see that." Bijal takes the small flower and examines it. "No, I haven't. Why?"

"I see." My heartbeat pounds in my temples. I take a pic and make a note to tell Ben about the flower. Maybe he has an idea. "Uh, no real reason. Just seen them somewhere else before."

"Okey dokey. They're probably a product of the soil maybe." She points out how the soil here is a different shade and density to the rest of the school grounds. Except I'm sure the soil by the Silkhead bus stop wasn't like this. It was darker and more crumbly looking. "Now let's go brekky else Ms. Piddleton will go off!"

After breakfast we head back and chill in the common room before waiting for the morning attendance. Malika sits across the room all buddy-buddy with Fran and Stacey. She's got a pink scrunchie around her wrist. When Malika spots me staring, she smiles widely as if everything isn't completely different. Even though nothing's fine, I force a smile back.

I play with the pleats in my skirt, trying to loosen the tightness building in my chest. Malika was my one friend here. She had this whole place figured out.

What happened to her?

Ms. Piddleton rattles through the attendance, and when she gets to me, she looks up from her clipboard. "Don't forget, Ms. Adebola, you still have the remainder of your house confinement left. Not to mention detention and no leaving the school grounds for an indefinite amount of time. Understood?" I nod. "Good."

Nithercott School is now a fancy way of saying *prison*.

When the bell rings for the end of the day, I smile. I've been dying to talk to Ben all day, but today wasn't a physics day and that's the one class we have in common. I hang outside until Ben arrives.

"Alright?" He offers me his fist. I nod. When I reciprocate, he releases his clenched hand and smothers my fist. "Cabbage."

I burst into laughter. "Are *you* alright?"

"Let's grab our seats," he replies. "Much to discuss. Hit me. Figuratively please."

"Why would I think you'd want me to actually hit you?" I ask, taking my seat next to Ben.

"I've been told I'm quite . . . punchable. So, I didn't want to be misconstrued."

They're not wrong. "I wanted to tell you about what I saw. Last night, after we bumped into each other. I've been thinking about it *a lot*."

"What?" Ben asks.

I take a calming breath, fighting against the fluttering in my stomach. "He's real. Everything about the Changing Man's real."

I go into as much detail as I can remember from before I blacked out. Ben listens intently, asking questions every few moments, and I try my best to answer. Once I'm done, silence stretches between us like a never-ending yawn. Until he snaps his fingers.

"Interesting. Whoever's parading as the Changing Man thinks this is *Scooby-Doo*. Creating those weird special effects to make it look real." My heart deflates and I want to tell him the strange flowers and orange shimmer aren't special effects, but I can't find my voice. "You know, when you told me about Malika, it got me thinking: What if the two incidents are somehow connected? The way Malika is acting right now is similar to the way Leon was acting before he left—sorry, was *taken*. His texts started getting weird: no emojis, he stopped calling me Benny, and suddenly felt distant. Do you know who the couple were?" I shake my head. "No bother, it'll probably pop up on CottsLore. Plus, whoever is behind this is bound to slip up. In the meantime, we need to look back at the last time something like this happened."

"Summer of '83," I state.

Ben pulls his head back and nods slowly. "Exactly. How'd you know? They've tried to keep that kind of info buried. Reputation to uphold and what not."

"Bijal. She's a walking Nithercott encyclopedia."

"So look, I've been working through all of the info I can get my hands on." Ben hands me a list of names. Most have been struck out. Except the last two. One of which I recognize as Elaine's ex-boyfriend, William.

~~Sean Bolaji=no response~~
~~Lettie Wilson=stopped replying~~
~~Giveon Knight=dead~~
~~Preeti Edwin=stopped replying~~
~~Kevin Knapp=no response~~
William Swan—Sat 12:45
Amelia Haynes—Sat 1:30

"Stopped replying," I say aloud. Turning to Ben, I ask, "Why?"

Ben shrugs. "Hell if I know. Worst thing is, I didn't get anything from them I couldn't have found out online. But from what I've pieced together, I've got a theory about it all." My eyebrows rise, waiting for an explanation. He sighs. "The Changing Man story? A classic case of PTSD. Someone abducted and then released all those students. Like some sort of weird game. It's why they withdrew their statements. They were scared. And I think that same person has been doing it for years. Except now they've graduated to proper kidnapping."

I read between the lines. "And by kidnapping, you mean . . ."

"Bingo. I just need to find how it all fits." The hopeful urgency in his voice colors the space between us, and despite what's at stake, something tells me a deep-rooted part of Ben is relishing trying to solve this puzzle. "Why him?"

The question hangs in the air. *Why anybody?*

Ben claps his hands. "Anyhow, as you've seen, I've managed to find two alumni who are happy to talk to me in person. Want to tag team?"

"I . . . I'm not sure." My fingers fidget, thinking about how Ben is trouble. "Sorry."

Ben pushes the inside of his cheek with his tongue. "No, don't be. *But* it would be good to have you." He leans toward me. "Can you at least think about it?"

"Okay."

"Okay! I'm gonna stick around and make myself inconspicuous. Meet me at the log after dinner if you're in, and I'll go over the plan. I'm still figuring a few things out."

"Wait, I'm house confined for a week. Even if I were interested, I can't just come and go whenever. If I'm not back quickly, I'll get in trouble."

"Good thing I know just the word to get you off the hook. It's called diarrhea." *He cannot be serious.* "I guarantee Ms. Piddleton won't say a word. So you're in?"

The way he looks at me with sharp eyes and a crooked smile tell me he's deadly serious. "Ben," I breathe, doing my best to suppress my laugh. "I'll think about it."

"Fine, fine." He flashes a smile at me, his eyes ablaze with infectious determination.

I smile back and face my prep.

After I wolf down dinner, I head straight to the log with my mind made up, but full of guilt because I ended up lying to Ms. Piddleton. Turns out Ben was right about his excuse getting me off the hook.

Each step is a shot of adrenaline jolting through my body. I need to know what the hell is going on. Why Ben's brother?

Why Malika? Her transformation is too drastic for me not to take seriously.

Opposite the grass tennis courts, Ben sits waiting on the log that's ordinarily used as a balancing beam, chewing gum. He's got his arms crossed and is dappled by the shadows of leaves and the glinting of metal screws hammered into the lengthy trunk of the tree. Behind him is the back of the music building that also doubles as a climbing wall. I squint. In between the hand- and footholds are bricks that jut out with names printed on them in bold. Some I recognize as current students.

Sliding off the log, Ben stumbles but gathers his balance. "Hey."

"Bijal?" I say at the exact same time.

Ben scratches his cheek and squishes his eyebrows together. "Not quite. I know we both share a letter, but that's not my na—"

"No, not you. Behind you." He turns so he can see what I see: Bijal's head creeping out from a bush. She steps into view, looking sheepish. I hold back a laugh, smiling widely instead. "What are you doing here?"

"I—Uh, well you left dinner so quickly, and I thought maybe something was up, so I wanted to just make sure . . . just in case. S-sorry. I didn't mean to. I can go if—"

Ben claps his hands. "The more the merrier! A friend of Ife's is a friend of mine. She also says you're a walking Nithercott encyclopedia. I could use your knowledge. Only if you want to though. No pressure."

Bijal smiles and walks toward us. "Count me in. But, uh, into what exactly?"

"Why, solving the taking of Leon Small obviously. Right, so here it is." Ben hands me a couple sheets of paper stapled together. On the front it says *Operation Find Out More: Discussion Guide*. "It's basically a guide to use with William and Amelia. Have a look through, let me know if you have any questions. I'll wait."

I read through the discussion guide along with Bijal.

"Nothing from me," I say.

Bijal *hmms*. "I have one. Not a question, but a thought. Uh, more of a suggestion actually . . ." Ben puts his hands in his pockets and nods his head, indicating Bijal should continue. "What if we tweak the first question under the topic around the Changing Man—"

"Uh-huh," Ben says.

"And ask them what they believe."

"Right." He gets out some lip balm and applies it to his lips. Puckering them. *Rude.* "Uh-huh."

"Makes it a bit more . . . open. It means we don't come across like we're testing them or like there could be any wrong answers. What do you think?"

"I . . . I get what you're saying, but I've been looking into the most effective techniques for recalling past events and doing it your way might also give us more irrelevant answers than we want. So, I think if we keep it focused, that's best."

Bijal looks my way and I shrug, because I don't know what I'm supposed to do. My head shakes gently. *It's Ben's plan*, I try to say with my eyes. She presses her lips together in this determined look.

But when her mouth opens to speak, she hesitates. Finally, she says, "Yeah, that makes sense. Yeah."

I hold back a smile. Bee's nervousness reminds me of Zanna.

"Great. Let's meet back here tomorrow around three-ish." Ben turns to leave but stops. "Oh, and congratulations."

"On what?" I ask.

"Today, the Nithercott Three was born. Laters!"

I mock gag. "Do better."

"Whatever."

I would never have guessed he was *this* corny. The laughter trapped in my cheeks begins to fade. My feet scrunch in my Converses as I fix my eyes on Ben as he walks away.

Am I doing the right thing? Magenta eyes flash in my mind, and a shiver zags along my back. Could it really be someone with special effects? Bee loops her arm through mine and squeezes, catching me by surprise.

"You look so serious."

I relax my shoulders. "Just thinking."

"About?"

"Nothing important," I say, pasting a smile on my face.

CHAPTER 11

YOUR FRIENDLY NEIGHBORHOOD SHOPKEEPER

Bijal cracks her knuckles as she waits for me to climb out my bedroom window. "I'm excited," she says as we head toward the village shop. "To prep this morning, I—I tried to find out what I could about William Swan. Came across something he wrote in the local paper a few years after the summer of '83. It was about the weirdness of that year and the issues Nithercott had with kids getting in trouble, sneaking out, complaints and, oh man. I'm boring you, aren't I?"

A little. "Nah."

My head's constantly on a swivel just in case I need to dive into a bush to hide from Ms. Piddleton.

"Good. The 'secret' history of Nithercott is actually a big part of the reason why I've found this place bearable. Just knowing stuff, you know? People appreciate that. Also looking into stuff takes my mind off the stress of doing well. Not just for me but for my parents too."

"Yeah," I say, but my mind is drifting, which isn't fair. I try and focus. "I get it, my parents are similar. Now that I'm technically an inmate, I should find something like that."

"I mean you could always join me as my underling."

I wrinkle my nose and laugh. "No way in hell. What else do you like to do, besides read and talk about conspiracies?"

"Umm . . . Well, sometimes I like to tend to your every need? Jokes! I . . ."

Bijal's voice fades as my eyes scroll through the latest updates in the group chat. It feels so good to have my phone back.

> **+44700900824:** Hii gals! thx
> for the add! Ahooooo
>
> **Gina:** Ahoooo
>
> **Tola:** 🐺 🐺
>
> **Julie:** we love u Alice, we do!
>
> **Zan:** ✊🏽

Alice? They've replaced me already? I take a deep breath because I'm being way too dramatic. I'm about to send a message, but Bijal bumps my shoulder and I nearly drop my phone. When I look up to glare, she's staring at me with a pinched expression.

"What was that for?"

"Accident." She pauses. "So, I noticed you like art . . . well, I *know* you're good at it, otherwise you wouldn't be here on a scholarship. I've seen your drawings in the art room. They're amazing! You remind me of C. K. Henry."

I stifle a laugh. "Do you mean C. J. Hendry?" Bijal sticks her tongue out and nods. "How do you even know who that is?"

Bijal smiles. "I don't. Well, I didn't until a few days ago. But I got lost in an art rabbit hole. 'Cause you like art and I thought I'd try and make an effort and . . . and oh! Did you know that the *Mona Lisa* apparently is all about the number two?"

I switch to autopilot. *Cool. Oh really? Wild.* My eyes scan the group chat.

> **Gina:** @Ife—Alice could be ur twin! Except she's into graffiti! You guys together wuld be amazing.

> 👏 that's cool! welcome to the group :)

> **~Alice:** thx :D

> **Tola:** @Ife Gigi's right, I can't wait for you guys to meet! Alice is so cool. It's like we were separated at birth or something. Telepathy or something.

> **~Alice:** LOOOOOOL in sync 🕺

Rolling my eyes as far as they can go, I put my phone away and look up, expecting Bijal to be in the middle of some conspiracy theory. Instead, she glances from me to my phone and sighs.

"S-sorry," I stammer.

"For what?"

Damn. "For not . . . listening?" I shrug.

"Just say you don't want to talk next time." Bijal stares daggers at my phone.

"O . . . kay? What are you on about?" My heart thuds in my chest. Suddenly it's too warm and my scalp prickles. "I never said—"

"You didn't have to," she snaps. Her eyes squeeze shut for a moment before slowly opening. "Sorry, I—uh—I'm just hangry."

"I-it's okay," I mumble, knowing I'm the one who's not quite with it. The phone slips into my pocket as a peace offering. We're standing in front of the village shop. "I really am sorry. It's just—anyway, shall we get this over with?"

Bijal grins. "Let's."

I push through the village shop doors and the bell tinkles. The shopkeeper looks up from polishing the glass cabinet holding an array of wine bottles. The smile on his face is mostly hidden by a mustache thicker than a paintbrush. It doesn't reach his squinting eyes. He pulls out round-rimmed glasses from the pocket of the apron he wears. From Elaine's picture, I immediately know it's him. Except he's taller and more filled out now.

"Oh, students. Pizza slices have just gone in. If you're

after those, it'll be a—" He tilts his head when he looks at me. "Hey, weren't you here the other day?"

"No." I'm technically still house confined.

"Huh, maybe it was your sister, or cousin?" I shake my head. "You sure you don't have a relative or a friend that looks—not to say that all, uh—"

The way he struggles for words is painfully embarrassing. "I'm sure."

"Hi," Bee starts. "We were actually hoping to talk to William Swan?"

The shopkeeper frowns. "It's Morris now. I took my wife's name."

I step forward and smile. "Ben sent us." I glance down at the guide. "Thanks for taking the time to—"

"I agreed to speak to Ben," he states not unkindly. There's a pulse of silence. "Because he said it would be discreet."

"I—" I try and swallow the invisible lump clogging my throat. "Well—"

"It will be," Bee says, stepping in when my words fail me. She gives me an encouraging smile, and I remember the disclaimer in Ben's guide.

"Anything you tell us won't go beyond us. That is, Ben and the two of us," I add.

William continues buffing the cabinet, completely ignoring us. After a few seconds he tucks his cloth into his pocket and inspects the glass. "So, what is it you want to know?"

I clear my throat, take a deep breath, and read the words from Ben's guide. "So, we wanted to talk to you about the summer of '83 . . . mainly about what it was like to, uh . . . be there. Let's start with your school life."

"I'd prefer not to talk about any of that."

"O-okay. Is there anything else you'd prefer not to discuss?"

William looks at us and shrugs. "I guess when you ask the question we'll find out. Sound fair?"

I nod. My eyes scan the guide, trying to guess what kind of topic he won't mind us asking him about. "There was an article that said—"

"Lots of unqualified people had their say back then. I'm all too familiar with that. We should be careful about placing too much trust in such. When it comes down to it, what you think you know, you read in an article. What do you *truly* know?"

Again, my composure evaporates. I fidget and glance at Bee, who looks just as confused as I am. "Th-then let's look at what the social life was—"

"Let's *not*."

"Why not?" Bee asks.

"I'd prefer not to relive those years. They were hard for me. Look, I don't have much more time to give." He smiles politely at us and starts to buff the till's countertop, moving a few flyers out the way. I see one for the local grill, another for the taxi company, and a Nithercott Day one. I guess the school is sparing no advertising expense. "What else have you got?"

I flick through the guide and I'm not sure about any of these questions or topics. Before I know it, I'm sucked in by the mental quicksand of my mind. Then finally pulled free by Bee clearing her throat.

She gives me a grin before turning to William. "Can you give us just a moment?" He grunts *yes* and she leans in so only I can hear. "I think we should go open. It's clear he's got thoughts and opinions. Let's ask him what he believes."

"I dunno. Ben was pretty insistent we do it using his guide." I'm also not sure how William will react. He's been pretty temperamental.

Bee pinches her lips together before sighing. "What's the worst that'll happen? Come on . . ."

"But what if . . ." The words die in my mouth because she's right, worst he'll do is ignore us. Plus, Ben's guide isn't working. I nod. "Okay, let's try it out. Why don't you ask?"

"William," Bee says boldly. "Forget whatever we said just now. There's one question we want to ask you and that is— what is it you believe happened back then?"

Pausing, William lifts his head up and smiles. "Well, I thought you'd never ask. Where to start. I'd been in a few boarding schools. So Nithercott was just another beast to slay. But I think after maybe a couple of terms, I started to realize something about it was different."

"Different how?" Bijal asks as she moves toward the counter, and I follow.

The shopkeeper begins to answer, but like a moth to a flame, I'm drawn to movement in my periphery. I spy a vague reflection in the chrome fridge to my right. A Black girl, I think, behind the front windows of the shop. She's wearing the same thing as me—Nithercott trackies. I crane my head to get a clearer look, but whoever it was is gone.

I turn back too quickly, and all of a sudden, dull pain

builds where I hit my head, triggering the memory of the orange mist and magenta eyes. I flinch, returning to reality.

"And the police never asked to talk to you?" Bijal probes.

The shopkeeper pauses for a moment before nodding. "That's right. They said I wasn't needed. Even though I knew where the Changing Man lived."

"What?" I blurt. "Sorry, I just . . . you knew where he lived?"

"That's right," William repeats and chuckles. "I used to spend a lot of time in there—the library—and the moment I heard what students were saying about this urban myth, I knew it was real. There's a hidden room in the library. That's where he lived. I know because I smelled that wet-pavement smell too. It was faint, and I followed my nose to the wooden panel in the library. I'm sure that's where he was staying. Whoever it was behind everything."

"I've never heard of a hidden room before and I've read all the floor plans," Bee challenges.

William shakes his head. "I—"

From behind him, a stern-looking woman appears, paying no attention to me and Bijal. I'm guessing she's his wife. She has this royal air about her. As if we're beneath her.

"Willy Baby, are you telling your tall tales again? Here, take care of this order, please. It's for Mr. Green down in Little Forrest. Remember to use the gate down the little lane and ring the bell twice. Someone will meet you there." She places a slip of paper on the counter before turning to us. Her nose wrinkles. "And you are?"

"Students at Nithercott," Bijal answers.

The woman looks us up and down, and then breaks into a smile. "Wonderful. You must be on the financial aid scheme?"

"It's Urban Achiever, actually," I say. Even though I correct her, I don't feel any better for it.

"That's nice," the woman says, as if I haven't said anything different, before turning to the shopkeeper. "I need you to make this delivery now, please. Don't look at me like that." She turns to us. "He has his moments of . . . make believe. Don't you, Willy Baby?"

"Yes, that's . . ." William squeezes his eyes as if he's experiencing brain freeze. I scrunch my eyebrows together, but just as quickly, his face straightens and he smiles. "That's right. Oh my, was I doing it again?"

The woman is about to lead a muttering William away when the doorbell jangles and a tall, broad-chested man strides into the shop with tanned skin and cropped gray hair, dressed in a well-fitting suit. Age dances across his face like light. With each stride up to the counter I can't decide if he's nearer forty or seventy. I settle on somewhere in between. He spares a brief smile at us. "I came in to say that today's delivery isn't necessary."

"Understood, Mr. Green," the shopkeeper's wife says. Her voice is flat and monotone. "Anything else?"

Mr. Green knocks his fist on the counter. "Nothing else for today. Be seeing you." He spins and heads for the door, where he stops and looks over his shoulder. Right at us. "Nithercott students?"

"Yeah," Bijal says.

"On the Urban Achievers Program?" Bijal nods, and Mr.

Green smiles thoughtfully before departing without another word.

"Well. That was weird," I say, turning toward Bijal.

"Right? So odd. What now?"

I laugh, stepping outside. "Now we chill till Ben comes through. What do you think—"

Perched by the curb is a black car. Through the front window, I see a woman with red hair glancing at us. She's wearing a blazer, and on her lapel is a brooch: a purple flower with a crown on top.

The moment I step toward her, the car wheels away and U-turns, disappearing down Old Glossop Road.

"I've seen that before," I murmur.

"The car?"

"No, the symbol on her lapel. The flower. Dr. Butterworth has some files with the exact same thing. Something's happening here." I bite my bottom lip and do what I should have sooner. I google *purple flower with gold crown logo* and hit SEARCH.

I go to images and scroll for a few minutes but give up. There are a ridiculous number of results. None of which are useful. *Pointless.* I turn to Bee, struck by a sickening thought. But the words won't come out. *What if it's Dr. Butterworth who's responsible for everything?* The candid photos he had of students flashes in my mind. *What if we're already trapped?*

Bee and I sit in the art block, counting down the minutes until we need to go meet Ben. My pencil slides across paper like a scalpel. Bee scrolls through the rubbish that is Cotts-Lore. Still, her raw focus makes me pause in admiration. She is nothing less than earnest.

"Want me to draw you?" I ask, popping our comfy silence.

She nods slowly before her lips split into a smile. "Oooh, yes, please."

Hauling myself up from the stool, I walk a couple of steps to where the dip pens are. The best portraits are done with ink. My head turns. "So I'm—"

A strangled sound escapes from my lips. In full view outside the window are Stacey and Malika. Filming what I can only describe as a poorly choreographed dance routine. My first thought is, *Why?* And then, *Are they alright?*

Bee chuckles. "Hey, Ife, come look—"

"Looking." In seconds I'm alongside Bee, watching Malika and Stacey jerking in the most rhythmless way.

Stacey seems to sense us lurking, and stops mid-jerk to glare. Her eyebrows furrow and then relax before her gaze flicks between me and Bee. A curious smile blooms as she walks toward us, leaving Malika standing there.

"What now?" My nostrils flare. Bee shrugs.

Stacey strolls in and looks around the room. "We'd appreciate it if you didn't stare so much." Bee and I keep quiet. "Oookay then."

She sniggers and leaves.

"She's not okay," Bijal says, humming.

My eyes are on Malika, who stares into space with an unsure smile. Only looking half-alive when Stacey links arms with her. "Yeah." What happened? *They say he preys on the lonely in heart.* I turn over the words of the Changing Man myth, wondering if that's why Malika started acting differently. Because she was lonely.

A stab of fear shoots through my gut as I'm suddenly aware of how lonely I've felt here—even with Bee's best efforts. I don't want to end up like Malika—so far from who I know I am. My friends from home keep reminding me about how different Nithercott is. I know they're messing with me, but their words are paint knives mixing my anxiety and fears together to make something hideous and off-color.

I refuse to be someone I'm not.

"Whatever!" *Clear your mind, Ife.* "Bee, let me draw you real quick and then we'll head over to the log. It's almost time."

We're about to step onto the path that leads straight to the log, when pounding steps and heavy, whining breaths hiss through the air. I turn my head. A fox hurtles in our direction. It runs as if it's being chased, its legs pumping in powerful harmony. Blood drips from its face. I . . . I'm pretty sure its left eye's been gouged out of its socket. It whizzes by clumsily. Not even a glance in our direction.

I nudge Bee. "Its eye . . ."

"Yeah." She blinks at me. "Something must have . . ."

"But what? What would be so . . . so . . ."

Bee scrunches her face like she's eaten something sour. "Savage?" she whispers. "No idea," she adds. "Whatever animal it was, I don't want to meet it."

"Same," I say, not sure an animal was responsible.

We're still talking about what we saw all the way to the log, doing our best to keep the fear at bay. Ben's already there with his arms crossed, rubbing at his eyelids. He looks up at us, draws his breath, and releases it. "What you talking about?"

"Didn't you see the one-eyed fox sprinting past?"

"Uh-uh." Ben doesn't say any more than that. His lips are pinched tight as he waits for one of us to explain. He's defo not in a good mood.

"N-never mind," I say. "Don't worry about it. How did you get on?"

Ben rubs the back of his neck. "A dud. I—she just wasn't engaged. It is what is, I guess. On my way back, I saw someone posted about Leon on CottsLore again. Some bullshit about how he's an alien runaway who is—whatever. I digress. How was William?"

I can see why Ben's pissed. We run him through our encounter, and his eyes grow wide when we tell him William thought the Changing Man lived in a hidden room in the library. I don't get to the bit about William's partner because he's swearing.

"Shit! That's great." He whips out his phone and starts typing and scrolling frantically.

"What you looking for?" I ask.

"Anything to do with the school library. Anything that— hang on, this looks promising. 'Nithercott is extremely saddened to hear the news today regarding the passing of a beloved benefactor, Alan Gopnik. Widely known as a Christian philanthropist who supported a variety of causes, he is known for his commitment to ensuring schools could boast of impressive libraries, beginning in his beloved hometown of Cologne. In 2008 he set his sights on the UK and helped fund the renovations to our library and later, in 2011, we had the privilege of receiving a rare book to be stored there. Two years later he wrote a bestseller on the responsibility of the wealthy to view money as a good gift from God and therefore to use it wisely. To strive for a world where—' This isn't helpful."

We settle into silence while Ben goes back to scrolling and sighing.

"Holy smokes," Bee says, her fingers wiggling in the air. "Back it up. The article mentioned a rare book, right?"

Ben nods slowly. "Yeah, it—" He bursts into laughter. "Of course."

"Sorry for being slow, but why is that a big deal?" I don't like being left out.

"Becauuuse," Bee starts, "if there is a rare book, it would need to be preserved and definitely not on display. If it's stored in our library, then *maybe* there really is a hidden room no one knows about."

Which would mean William Swan wasn't telling tall tales. "Oh."

Ben snaps his fingers. "Exactly. Now then. I believe our next steps are finding out if the hidden room exists and how to get into it. There might be some more clues there about Leon." His blue eyes seem to glint like sunlight bouncing off the sea. "I'll think of a way in."

CHAPTER 12

HUNCHES ARE DANGEROUS

But only if you want to. I echo Bijal's words from just after Monday morning checks. They've been swimming in my head since she said she wanted me to ask if Ben had a theory about what we'd find. *Me.*

She thinks we have some sort of "rapport" and that if I asked him, he'd probably let me know. I don't know how she got that idea. My phone buzzes. It's her.

> **Bijal:** Did you have a think about what I asked? 🙏 p.s. No pressure :P x   *now*

This girl! I kiss my teeth, shake my head, and put my phone away for the start of detention. I press my lips together and get my prep out, thinking about how I'm going to ask Ben for his theory on the hidden library room. She wants to know if they're on the same wavelength. I'm curious too. Whatever we find, I just hope it isn't anything supernatural.

"What?" I ask, noticing Ben staring at me.

"Nothing," he sniggers. "Relax." There's a couple of seconds of silence before he leans toward me. He smells like vanilla and smoke. "I've been wondering. Why were you in the staff room that night?"

"My answer hasn't changed since the last time," I reply, shrugging and turning back to my prep. "Maybe if you tell me why you were there first, I'll suddenly have a change of heart."

"Such a perplexing Percy." He laughs and then sighs. "Fine. I was taking this back." He whips out an engraved brass lighter. The kind that can burn on its own once you spark it.

"You broke in for a fancy lighter?" I can't help the way my voice squeaks.

"It's not just a random fancy lighter, Ife. Leon gave it to me when I got onto the Urban Achievers Program, on the condition I kept out of trouble. That was before . . ." Ben stares at the lighter in his hands, pulling his lips into a half smile. "Never mind. All that matters is that it's important to me. Your turn."

"No, it's not."

"You said—"

"I said *maybe*." I'm about to get on with my prep, but I hesitate as Bijal's annoying face flashes in my mind. Wincing, I ask, "What sort of clue do you think we'll find in the library?"

"An excellent question. In any case, I'm hoping it brings me one step closer to Leon. If it truly was—or is—the Changing Man's lair, then I expect we'll find some stalking paraphernalia, a map or set of plans." I wonder if Bee will be disappointed that he doesn't think there'll be some sort of student shrine to the urban myth. I text her back. "Maybe some pictures of the victims and a reason why," Ben adds in a flat, monotone voice.

Anxiety blooms in the soles in my feet as I rock in place, remembering again the pictures Dr. Butterworth had of me and Malika.

Whatifwhatifwhatif—

I shake away the runaway thought. Because a new message from Bee has come through on my lock screen.

> **Bijal:** Awww, nvm! Ask him how he
> plans to get in pls pls pls x   *now*

"Any ideas about getting into the hidden room?" I ask.

Ben's eyebrow quirks. "Any ideas?"

"Yeah. As in how are we getting inside?"

"Getting inside?"

Is he being deliberately obtuse? I let out the breath I've been holding. "Are you messing with me?" I snap.

Ben looks up as if he's thinking hard and then smiles. "I don't know."

I frown. "You . . . don't know?"

"Yeah, that is what I said. Anyway, honest question: Why do you care about what it is we're doing?"

"Because I—I want to know what's going on," I answer.

He shakes his head. "I didn't ask what you *wanted*. I asked why you cared. If you can't tell me that, then . . ."

I frown, hard. "Then what? You can be so . . . Seriously, urgh."

Instantly I think of Dad, who's constantly trying to get me

to talk and share, even though he doesn't actually listen to what I say. Frustration washes over me and I kiss my teeth.

He holds up his hands in surrender. "Chill. If you're gonna get all defensive, then maybe us working together isn't wise."

My hands clench tight and I take a deep breath, holding it in. "I guess so."

Ben just shrugs. "Like duck backs in water."

That is not *how the saying goes.* I roll my eyes and get back to my prep.

Detention crawls by, and I soon give up on my physics prep. I'm about to DM Zanna a hilarious video of a boy brushing his teeth and blowing bubbles, when a preview of a new message from Bijal slips down from the top of my screen.

Bijal: Ife—do you copy? what's the
status? x *now*

I'm about to send a quick reply of *let's forget him and do it ourselves*, but I stop. Why does my chest feel so tight? *He's being unreasonable*, I tell myself. But then I think of Bee and how much she wanted me to do this one thing for her. She obviously believes in him. Maybe he isn't as useless as he looks.

Squeezing my eyes shut, I bite down on my bottom lip. "Why?" I ask in Ben's direction. "Why does my answer mean anything?"

He looks up from his desk. There's this fierce look in his eyes. "Trust. So, I need you to tell me. Right here, right now."

Why is he being so difficult right now, with a big fat stupid smirk on his face? "Okay fine!"

"Ife!" the teacher on detention answers.

I stop myself from rolling my eyes. "Sorry, Miss."

Ben stifles a snigger. He leans in toward me as soon as the teacher gets back to her romance book. "I take it you're ready to answer my question?"

"Yes," I force out. "I don't know what difference it makes, but if this is what'll float your boat, then whatever, I guess."

"Well?" Ben stares at me with his piercing blue eyes.

My feet fidget and I bite my lip. God, this is harder than I thought. I compose myself and go for it. "I care about finding out the truth. Something happened to Malika, and if it can happen to her, it can happen to me. I'm scared."

I wait for Ben to laugh or scoff or tell me I'm being childish. He does none of those things; instead he just gazes at me.

"Okay," he says softly. "I get it. But we do things my way. I have a way in. Keep an ear out."

"What do you mean 'keep an ear out'?"

"Trust me, you'll know."

The rest of detention goes by a lot faster, and when I hear the bell, it's like coming up for air. Being stuck in a classroom with the school's worst offenders is not my idea of fun.

As I trudge to prep, the smell of Zara fills my nostrils and a finger taps me on my shoulder. I know who it is and I'm not in the mood. "What do you want now?"

"Next time just ask," Ben says, thrusting a couple of pieces of folded paper toward me. I take it instinctively, and before I can even ask what it is, he's already walking off. "Look at it when you're alone," he says into the air.

He's a weird one. I want to open it up now, but I won't. I tuck the pieces of paper into my pocket and save it for later.

To be honest, I doubt he'd know if I took a quick look, but I can't help but want to feel honest. Silly, I know.

When I spot a waving Bee, I wave back and half skip to her.

"So, Ben," Bee asks once we find seats next to each other in the classroom for prep. She clacks away on her laptop. "What did he say *exactly*?"

I shrug. "That he found a way in."

"Did he say how?" she asks slowly. "Or when?"

"Only that we should keep an ear out."

"Well, that could mean a lot of things." She exhales, and a smile bunches up her cheeks. "Guess we'll just have to wait and find out."

"He's strange. What if his idea gets us in trouble?"

"I know, but I trust him the most out of anyone here. Once upon a time, we worked on the school mag together. The guy is legit. Plus, I checked my horoscope today and it was very profound. Talking about how there's irony in today's situation. I think going with it is how I'm supposed to bring myself into balance."

And yet somehow, she refuses to consider the Changing Man might be supernatural.

"I dunno, Bee, isn't that a bit risky? I can't get in more trouble."

"Don't worry about it." She puffs out her chest. "The remedy for such situations like this is to accept them and joke about it."

"That's not a remedy," I grimace.

"Anyway," Bijal sings. "Wanna watch a movie in my room after this? At least till we're summoned. I don't have any prep due tomorrow, and I feel so restless. For once I can't be bothered to read up in preparation for tomorrow's lessons. Can you imagine?"

I'm about to answer when there's a rhythmic tap on the door.

"Dun, dun," I sing dramatically after the knock.

"Come in," the teacher calls, sighing as she looks up from her book.

A small boy in a tartan scarf and camel coat steps into the classroom and just stands there for a moment. Probably soaking in all the attention from the girls of Beeton House who look up from their homework.

"Yes?" the teacher asks. "What is it?"

The boy blinks, and when he catches my eye, he smiles. Lifting his phone in the air, Ben's voice booms through the room.

"A tick or a tock for a minute. The place where pissants are born! Ticktock, ticktock, tick."

I turn over the words in my head and I decipher the beginning of the message. And how it links to the end of it. We've got five minutes.

"Right," the teacher mumbles. Before she can stand up, the boy has legged it and is long gone. "They don't nearly pay me enough for this rubbish." She tuts.

So, this is what keeping an ear out means. Only Ben would do this instead of messaging us on QuickTalk. Except five minutes doesn't give us a lot of time. There's still half an hour left of prep, and finding an excuse isn't the easiest—

Bee stands up suddenly.

"Miss! I know we should have let you know sooner—my fault, I said I'd take care of it, but I forgot—but Ife and I actually are late for our community service."

This is the third time the teacher's looked up from her book, and I can tell she's getting tired of it. "Community service?"

"For our Duke of Edinburgh, Miss." Bee smiles innocently. "We're already late as it is, but I'd understand if you said no. I'll just have to go and apologize to Ms. Haggerty later for not being able to help with her garden like we promised we—"

"Go, go, go. Just . . . no silly business. Okay?"

"Yes, Miss."

Gathering our things, we head out the door to where pissants are born apparently—the dumpsters round the side of Porthaven House.

CHAPTER 13

LIBRARY BREAK-IN

Our feet pound against concrete, and a stitch buds in my side, ready to blossom full of thorns.

How the hell can Bee run so fast?

We round the corner, and sure enough there's Ben. There's a wide smile on his face as his fist hovers over the BREAK GLASS part of the fire alarm on the wall. "Ladies. So nice of you to finally join me. Are you ready to rumble?"

"Bennnn," I warn.

"Yes!" Bee says at the exact same time.

My head turns in her direction and just as quickly back to Ben when I hear the crack of glass. There is absolute silence for half a second, and then the rude blaring of scattered sirens forces me to put my hands over my ears.

"Right then!" Ben shouts over the noise. "Let's get to work. We don't have long. By my calculations we'll have seven minutes."

"How the hell is all this necessary?" I shout after him as we follow his lead through the double steel fire doors. "Bee, please tell me you don't think this is a good idea. It—it's—"

"The only way we're getting into the hidden room," Ben

shouts back. "I cased the library. There's a PIN code panel. I followed the wiring and it's connected to the alarm system; therefore, the alarm . . . should override the locking mechanism."

Should?

I glance at Bee. Her eyes are wide and moony. "It's genius."

"Really?"

She nods as she rushes ahead.

The tight and winding hallways of Porthaven are lined with lockers and coat hangers and portraits of miserable-looking white men.

"Don't tell him I said this, but he's the one person I've thought was truly intellectually intimidating," Bee says as we follow Ben through another metal door.

"Oh wow, thanks."

"No—it's—I just meant that—like—"

"Bee, it's alright, I get it. I was joking. But seriously? Ben? Intellectually intimidating?"

She opens her mouth but walks straight into Ben's front, bouncing off him and against a wobbly table that's home to a potted plant. It slides toward the edge and Bee stops it from falling off just in time.

He puts a finger to his lips. "Mr. Morley and Dr. B." Ben swears and mutters under his breath. We peer round the corner to get a closer look.

"You know what, John," Dr. Butterworth says, striding up to Mr. Morley. "You think you know best because what? Because you're more . . . senior?"

"Jesus Christ, I think I know best because I follow the rules. They're called rules for a reason, Alred. If we have any concerns, we're supposed to escalate it to safeguarding. You *know* this."

"You . . . you sanctimonious prick. How dare you—" Dr. Butterworth turns away.

"No, say it," Mr. Morley spits. "Since you came here on a mission. How dare I, what? You think I don't want what's best for my students?"

Dr. Butterworth spins around and walks up to Mr. Morley. Silence hovers between them. And then, "How *dare* you pretend like you care about your students. You're failing them and that's what really eats away at you, isn't it? The fact you can't stomach being here." Dr. Butterworth jabs a finger at Mr. Morley. "I—I can't ignore it. Patrick won't either. Louis *needs* us."

"Alred, drop it. There are policies in place for a reason." Mr. Morley shakes his head. "I know you went to school with him, but Ingham's just going to tell you to do the same thing. Besides, what can he actually do? You're wasting your time."

With those parting words Dr. Butterworth storms off, leaving an angry Mr. Morley swearing colorfully. He goes and sits on the guest sofa, ignoring the blaring alarms.

"I take it this wasn't part of the plan?" I ask, unable to resist.

"Ha-ha. No, it wasn't." Ben bites his lip, deep in thought.

I wonder what Louis has got to do with them being so annoyed at each other. Maybe someone's finally coming after him for all the crap he allows to be posted on his little hell site.

Bee and Ben seem to be thinking about how we can make it past Mr. Morley. But the longer we wait, the more likely we'll run out of time, and I can't get in trouble again. Ms. Piddleton already made it clear I'd face an external suspension.

Taking a breath, I step in so they can make space for me. "Maybe we should do this another time," I announce.

"Why?" Ben asks.

"I just . . . don't think this is the right time. He's obviously waiting for something, and if we stay any longer, then—"

Ben sighs and looks at me pointedly. "I thought you wanted to find out the truth."

"I do, but—"

"Doesn't sound like you do." He turns away from me. "Well, you know where the door is."

I'm getting really tired of Ben cutting me off like he knows me. My jaw clenches. I think about what I can say to make him understand why, but all I feel is frustration and annoyance. "Bee?" I ask, stepping backward. She sighs heavily. Opens her mouth to speak, but no words come out. "Alright. Well, let me know what happens." I pivot to turn around and a sharp pain blooms in my side as I bang into the wobbly table.

The potted plant teeters on the edge before hurtling to the floor. I draw in a deep breath as the tinkle of exploding ceramic fills the air.

Mr. Morley exclaims and swears so loudly for a moment he drowns the alarms.

"Okay, so here's what I'm thinking," Ben says hurriedly. "We trap him in the closet." He opens the cloakroom door and fishes out an umbrella. "You two get ready to slam the door shut, okay?"

The hallway creaks as steps move toward us.

Me and Bee are out of sight around the corner, waiting for Ben's signal. My chest tightens while my heart kicks against it. Taking a deep breath, I glance at Bee, whose smile never shifts, and her eyes stay alight. She's headfirst down the rabbit hole.

"*NOW!*"

Bee and I emerge from our spot and push hard against the cloakroom door. Keeping it shut. Mr. Morley swears at the top of his lungs and bangs against the door. Mumbling and moaning.

It takes all our strength to make sure the door stays shut while Ben wedges the umbrella under the door handle.

"I swear, if I find out who you are!"

We leave Mr. Morley's voice behind, letting it get drowned in the sound of alarms, and stalk across the Porthaven foyer. Down the hallway to the library. A door on our right opens, and our heads swivel.

A small year-seven girl appears with her black hair in pigtails, which pop against her fair skin. Ben steps forward. "You didn't see us, okay?"

When he winks, her face flushes, and I contain the urge to gag. She nods and walks past us. This boy can wrap anyone around his finger.

Ben nudges Bee. "Don't get jealous," he says. This time I *do* gag.

"D-d-don't make me sick," Bee splutters.

Down the hallway we go, and within seconds we reach the library. The door is open and the librarian's voice blurs into the droning alarm bells.

Why is she still here?

Ben reaches into his blazer pocket and pulls out a paint-brush.

"A paintbrush?" I hiss. "Seriously?"

"Don't question my methods, Ife. Simply observe them."

"Put it away. I have an easy solution to our librarian prob-lem," I say confidently. "Bee, I think you should draw her out. Tell her there's a teacher trapped in the closet."

"Why me?"

"Because if anyone knows how to schmooze and people-please, it's you." Like a bolt of lightning, a flash of hurt colors her face and I instantly backtrack. "Bee, I didn't mean—"

"No, no it's fine. Don't worry about it. You two just bet-ter be quick, okay?" Sucking in a breath, she steps into the hallway and says, "Miss! Miss! I—I—think there's a teacher stuck in the cloakroom and . . . and I don't know what to do and . . . and—"

"Okay, *calm down*, child. Show me where this teacher is."

After Bee leads the librarian away to an angry Mr. Morley, Ben and I slip inside. I follow him to a dark brown door that's a few shades darker than me and slightly ajar.

My heart thumps. Ben was right. Triggering the alarm has automatically unlocked it. But as he pulls on the handle, it won't budge.

He hisses out several swear words before looking around for something. A word flashes into my mind—*leverage*. I start looking too, and quickly my eyes settle on a cobwebbed broomstick behind the librarian's desk.

Ben's one step ahead of me. Vaulting the desk, he grabs it, thrusts it into the narrow opening of the doorway, and pushes. The door inches open. He grunts until the gap is wide enough to slip through.

I hesitate. The first thing I see is a faded orange haze and I take a step back. It's gone when I blink.

"Come on, princess, we don't have all day. You coming or not?"

I step inside, and the coolness of the room hits first. There's a stale, earthy smell in the air. Goose bumps pimple my skin. My eyes dart about. The whole room is lined with books. Dust hangs in the air, but every now and then, an iridescent glint slashes through the dust, making the room come alive.

"How long left?" I ask.

"Four minutes. Let's split up."

I wander around, not finding anything. Until I come across dry, speckled grass sprouting through a crack in the wooden floor surrounding a lone, wilting mushroom. There's a disconnected trail that leads around the corner. My heart clenches. He's been here. Every few steps I spot crinkled blue petals and dying mushrooms. I crouch down and find a relatively fresh petal, its edges brown. When I take a closer look, I can see it has this dimpled texture like a golf ball and an iridescent powder on it. Just like the dust settled on the dying mushrooms. I think it's some sort of pollen. I slip the petal into my pocket.

As I follow the trail, a blur of movement catches my attention. In the frosted window up ahead, there's a figure. From the shape I can tell it's someone in a pleated skirt. They don't move, and a twisting panic takes over my entire body.

Can they see me?

Sound falls away as I move toward the window. The figure moves too, mirroring me. Getting closer. My heart's pounding so hard my rib cage vibrates. I try to take deep breaths, but it's like I'm swallowing tiny pins.

I lift my arm and the figure doesn't move.

Instead they step right up to the glass, placing their hand against it. Their hands are small. As small as mine. I step forward, pressing my hand against the glass.

"Can you hear me? Do I know you?"

A craggy, birdlike sound escapes, warbling into a word I can't make out. My skin crawls.

"Ife!" I pull my hand back sharply and turn around. Ben's grinning at me. It morphs into a frown. "Are you alright?"

"Huh? Oh, yeah, I—I think so."

"Over here, I've found something."

He leads me to a carving in the wall. When I glance back, the figure is still standing there.

Ben clears his throat. "Check it out."

"What is it?"

Ben is beaming. "Took me longer than I'm willing to admit, but *E* for east." There's a slender book in his hand, which he uses to point toward a cabinet that's obviously been moved. "It was tucked away behind that."

I'm starting to see how Bee finds him intellectually intimidating. Just then his phone alarm goes off and he swears. "Time's up." He holds the book out to me and I take it.

"Okay."

"Look alive, Ife. Tuck it into your waistband or something and let's get going."

Ben pushes the cabinet back into position and we make our way through the library. Out the open door. Right in front of the librarian.

"What on earth are you two doing?" she demands, adjusting her round-frame glasses with her index finger. Even behind glasses, her eyes are strikingly sharp and gray. "Well?"

I panic. "I—we—it's not—"

Ben steps in to stop me sounding like even more of a joke. He gives me a gentle smile and reaches into his blazer. He pulls out a carrot. Even he looks puzzled by it, but he quickly fixes his face.

"Have you seen Nibbler? White bunny, floppy ears, got a bit of an overbite like Mr. Morley?"

I bite down on my laugh while the librarian draws in a sharp gasp. "No, I have not, Mr. Small. And don't you think it's quite irresponsible to have a—"

Ben points past her. "Oh, there she goes, Miss! Never mind." Grabbing my wrist, he drags me along with him in a mad dash. We burst out the front of Porthaven in a fit of giggles. My heart is racing.

"Meet me at the log after the fire alarm checks. Bring the book. Ciao!"

Before I can protest, he runs off.

Thankfully, I'm not the only one to arrive late to the fire alarm meeting point. Ms. Piddleton just tuts in my direction and moves on with her checks. Snaking through the crowd of bodies, I get to Bee and hook my arm through hers.

"Hey," I say.

"Hey. What did you guys get?"

I give Bee a peek under my school shirt, flashing the slender book. "Ben wants to meet at the log as soon as we're done here." I pull out the petal. "Also took this. I think it's to do with the Changing Man. Remember that flower I showed you at couples' corner?" Bee doesn't look excited like I'd expect her to be. "What's wrong?"

"I guess you overestimated my schmoozing. Librarian and Mr. Morley didn't buy it and gave me detention. See you in detention tomorrow." She shrugs and leaves it at that, allowing worms of guilt to wriggle in my stomach.

"Elaine . . . Carter?" Bee sounds out as Ben reveals who the book was last checked out by. "As in the nurse?"

Ben flips the book around and shows us the checkout card glued to the inside cover. "The one and only. That's her name in her ghastly handwriting."

On the opposite page, the title of the book is printed on thick, premium paper. Similar to the kind you'd use for watercolor painting.

The Hidden World: A History of Ciphers

I'm so focused on the beautiful font that it takes me a moment to realize the paper has been altered below the writing. I run my finger along it to make sure I'm not imagining what I'm seeing. "Can I borrow your lighter?" I ask Ben.

He whips it out and holds it up to me along with a cigarette. I take the lighter and ignore the cigarette.

With all the concentration in the world, I wave the flame of Ben's brass lighter underneath, warming it up, while making sure I don't set the page alight. Scribbly handwriting that looks like it was written in a hurry appears.

fc ky ooxo skf dgfvo mweo
[A pony, A Sonnet, Sudoku, Neon]

It matches Elaine's handwriting on the checkout card.

Bee squeals. "She left a ciphered message."

"Well, would you look at that," Ben muses. "The bit in brackets must be the key. How'd you know to do that, Ife?"

I shrug. "My bestie and I used to do the same thing back in the day. We came up with our own secret ways of communicating."

"Amazing," Bee marvels.

"Yeah. Thinking about it now actually, it was Zanna's idea. I've always been a bit . . . nervous about things. I was freaking out about joining the art classes of the years above. When she found that she'd be having art class in the same room before me, she started leaving me these encouraging notes and Bible verses and jokes. All in code. Man, some of them were terrible. But she helped me feel less powerless and disconnected."

Ben *hmms* deeply, and when I look his way, he's staring into space. "I like that. Leon was the same. He . . . I . . .

uh . . ." Ben sniffs, and when I see how close his straight face is to cracking into pain, I look away and think of how I can change the subject.

Before I know it, I'm telling Ben and Bee about Zanna and all the little things that are unique to just us. I even tell them about our snack-for-feelings thing. When I'm done, I know I've been waffling. "Sorry, got carried away there."

"She sounds so amazing," Bee says, her eyes bright. "I wanna meet her."

Ben shrugs and clears his throat. "Cool. Now then, shall we get back to the shift cipher at hand?"

Shift cipher?

"Neon's easy," Bee replies. "That's ten." *Ten what?* "And a sonnet is fourteen, but it—"

"Could also be three," Ben finishes. "Since it has three quatrains."

Quatrains?

"Exactly."

They go on for a few minutes, just going back and forth, finishing one another's thoughts. A slither of jealousy wiggles in my stomach. The way their minds work is so far removed from mine. All logic and reason.

My ears perk up when they get stuck on the sudoku clue.

"Ninety? Number of squares?" Ben suggests.

"For a shift cipher, that seems too high and"—Bee taps something into her phone—"yup, doesn't fit. I was thinking nine, for the number of regions or three, for the number of larger boxes that make up one side of the perimeter?" *Tap, tap, tap* on her phone's screen. "But no dice."

I have a think too, trying to find an angle they haven't

thought of. But no ideas come to me. My uselessness swells up like a soaked kitchen sponge.

A sudden detail from the conversation I had with Elaine punches through my inner negativity, and I force my way into their conversation.

"I think I know what the last number is."

Ben smirks. "Oh yeah?"

I nod. "Pretty sure the number you're after is seventeen."

"Seventeen?" Ben raises an eyebrow and tilts his head. "You can't just say a random number and act smug. Why is it seventeen?"

"It's seventeen. I *know* this because when I spoke to Elaine the other day, she mentioned sudoku being her favorite puzzle. When I asked why, she said there was no real reason. Only that she was born on the seventeenth and that seventeen is the minimum number of hints for a sudoku to have a single solution. She thought it was poetic or something. Any other questions? Or can I return to being smug?"

"Touché." Ben half smiles. "I—I think he would like you." Ben clears his throat again and turns to Bee. "Well then, we've got twenty-five, fourteen, seventeen, and ten. Bijal, if you please?"

"Already on it," she answers, frantically typing away on her phone. "According to this decoder, her message says: Go to page two three nine."

Ben's already flipping through the pages. He goes still as a statue.

My stomach twists. "What does it say?"

"It's a message. Words are underlined—sloppily. She did this in a rush. Trapped, magenta, eyes, watching." I take a deep breath, recalling the night I hit my head. My throat clamps shut, and there's a lightness in my head. *Keep it together. Breathe.* "Seventeen. One." He flips to page 171. "Orange, strong, smell, arriving. Ac. Knowledge. Ment. S . . . Acknowledgments!" Another flip of the pages. He takes his time piecing the underlined words and letters together. "Running, out, of, time. Changing, man, coming. Follow. The. Flower. Person."

Ben clamps the book shut, draws a deep breath, and exhales. "I need a smoke."

CHAPTER 14

INTO THE DARK

We thought that something was up. This is good. Right?

It's the question I ask myself. It must be like 3:00 A.M. and I haven't even changed. As I lie on top of my duvet overheating in my blazer, I think about *everything*. The figure behind the frosted glass. Elaine's message. Dr. Butterworth's strangeness and whatever it is he's hiding.

Something's going on, but I'm not sure how anything fits together. My mouth waters at my nausea. I suddenly feel light-headed.

Bursting to the front of my mind is the myth of the Changing Man. He fills up the space in my head and scrapes at the edges. I see his glowing magenta eyes. My breaths are rapid and my head hurts. Why Elaine? Why Malika? Why Leon?

I google and a few things pop up—fae folklore, doppelgängers, and multiverse theory. None of them quite fit, but none are easy to shake as impossible.

They say he preys on the lonely in heart.

Maybe they were all lonely and it attracted his attention.

Maybe Dr. Butterworth's helping him. I wring my hands. *Maybemaybemaybe.*

Something cracks inside me and the nausea erupts. My hands clamp over my mouth and puke blows up my cheeks like a balloon.

Hopping out of bed, I sprint to the toilets and let it all out. I gargle out my lunch and drop to my knees. Energy fizzes out of me and I feel like a flat Coke. "Urgh."

Prayer comes easy, and even though my hope and trust is real, it doesn't stop my heart being pummeled by an imaginary hammer. I focus on my breathing and place my hands over my heart. Something crumples inside my blazer pocket. I fish out the folded pieces of paper. The ones I got from Ben.

It looks like the other pages of the transcript:

This is why the truth matters to me ;)
—Enjoy, pissant

TRANSCRIPT-PAGE 1

Key:

```
A = Angela Anne Small
B = Ben Small
DW = Detective Wilson William
```

DW: This interview is being recorded. I am Detective Wilson William and I'm based at ▇▇▇▇▇▇ which is with the Surrey Police. What's your full name?

A: Angela Anne Small

DW: Okay, you said earlier I can call you "Angie." That's correct, right?

A: Yes.

DW: Okay, thank you, Angie. And present is Ben Small. The date is Wednesday 10th September 20XX and according to my watch it's 14:27.

A: Why are we here . . . again.

DW: Well, we thought it best to speak to you again. Covering all bases, as it were. As you know, we don't have any leads at the moment.

B: An understatement. You're not doing your jobs.

DW: You heard from him that night, didn't you Ben? Can you please respond verbally?

B: Yeah, I did.

DW: Did he seem strange to you?

B: Yeah, but I thought he was high or drunk. Or both.

TRANSCRIPT-PAGE 2

Key:

A = Angela Anne Small

B = Ben Small

DW = Detective Wilson William

DW: I see. And why do you now think otherwise?

B: I know my brother and hindsight is a bastard. I should of seen it. I . . . don't think it was him texting.

A: Language.

B: Sorry, should have seen it.

DW: Angie, do you share Ben's perception?

A: I–I'm sorry, but none of this matters. I don't care about what happened before. My boy is missing–taken by someone.

DW: Yes, some have mentioned the name . . . Changing Man? Can you talk me through that?

B: This is bullshit.

DW: Pardon?

B: We've already told you what she thinks. Mum, this is a waste of time.

DW: For the record, Ben Small has now left the room. Apologies if you find the questions cumbersome, Angie, but I assure you we are doing everything we can. If Leon were here, what do you think he'd say right now?

A: I don't understand the question.

DW: Did you consider yourself and Leon close?

Key:

A = Angela Anne Small
DW = Detective Wilson William

A: You already asked me that. Why am I
still here? You should be finding out
who took my son.

DW: We're doing our best, Ms. Small. I
hope you can appreciate that. Are you
sure he wasn't displaying any signs of
unhappiness?

A: Are you saying I didn't know my own
son?

DW: His friend, Henry, reported that before
Leon ran off, he was acting odd. That
he was easily startled whenever someone
mentioned the Changing Man. He even
accused Henry of following him as a way
to mess with him. People were starting
to tease Leon. Is it possible the
teasing got too—

A: I told you already. He didn't run.
We're done here.

That's it. The whole transcript. Understanding bleeds
into me about why Ben is so driven to find his brother. He
feels guilty. That if he'd just said or done something the

last time he heard from his brother, Leon would still be around.

I'm reminded of the last time I felt guilt. Nowhere near as deep, but a few years ago I got caught aiding and abetting some ex-friends who shoplifted. My mum cried, and the guilt was a lump clogging my chest. To this day I'm still ashamed.

There aren't any words I can say to Ben, but I'm glad he shared this.

I just want to find him and tell him he's not alone. I can't imagine what it must be like to deal with the regret, the fact the police were so unhelpful, and a brother who's still missing.

Slowly I get to my feet to make my way back to my room. The glint of the moon on the mirror stops me. My mind goes back to the village shop, the school's rare book collection room, and curiosity fills my thoughts like billowing smoke.

What if?

I take a tentative step toward the mirror. My heartbeat rattles every bone in my body. I close my eyes and take another step. An invisible force tugging at me.

Until I'm in front of the mirror, looking down into the sink. My teeth pull away the dead skin on my lip. The moment I look up and gaze at my reflection . . .

Relief gushes through me. There's no eerie figure lurking behind. Just me in the mirror.

The taste of metal fills my mouth. I take several deep breaths and splash water over my face.

Be brave.

CHAPTER 15

ELAINE

have never been so nervous to knock on a door before in my life.

Ben, Bee, and I make our way over to the nurse's during the first break, having agreed we'd try and find out what Elaine knows. We think she was a prisoner and, in desperation, thought of writing out the code. But we have no idea what she means by *follow the flower person*.

"Just a thought, but we should be gentle with her," Bee says before my knuckles hit the wooden door. "There's no telling what's what in this situation. We need to be careful."

Ben yawns, wiping the tired from his eyes. I nod. There's a tightness in my chest that's been there since last night. I should tell them about this feeling of being followed. Observed. But now is not the time. After.

The door rattles, and soon after, it opens wide to a smiling Elaine.

"Ife! It's you. Nice to see you again. And so soon after your checkup. Oh, you've brought friends. Wait, I know who you both are. You're Bijal and you're Ben, yes. What can I do for you? Is it your head again?"

"Uh, no. It's . . . I—we wanted to ask you a few questions," I say. "If that's okay?"

Elaine smiles and says, "Five minutes, but then I'll have to get back to work. Tea? Biscuits?"

"Yes, please," Ben and Bee reply.

The kettle bubbles on the table by Elaine's desk while she sits in her chair chomping on a digestive biscuit. "You said you wanted to ask me a few questions?" Crumbs fall out her mouth as she speaks.

"Yes, we did. We wanted to ask you about your time at Nithercott," Ben answers.

Elaine looks at the three of us and the silence is long. It's broken with a sigh. "It was so long ago, but I will try my best. Would you like to know about what the teachers were like? Or maybe—"

"Sorry, Miss, but could you tell us about the message you left behind?" Ben asks. Bee gives him the coldest be-careful stare ever. He brushes it off and goes on. "I know you know something. What did you mean by 'follow the flower person'?"

The smile is wiped from Elaine's face and it's replaced with a blank stare and rapid blinking.

What the hell is he doing? This wasn't the plan.

"Ignore him," Bee says quickly to Elaine. "If you could tell us about what the teachers were like, that's fine. I-it's for a school project."

Elaine's smile returns. "Why certainly. Now, there was this teacher, Mr. Spinfoot. He used to wear the most extravagant blazers and they were all picked according to his mood that morning. Yellow meant—"

"Do you remember writing this?" Ben holds out his

phone. "I need to know if you met him. Or—or if you know anything. Please. Who is the Changing Man?"

"Ch-Changing Man?" Elaine asks. Her face is scrunched in confusion. "I—"

Ben nods. "Yes, yes. That's right. You left this message. Is the hidden room in the library where he kept you?"

"I—What?" Elaine looks around as if somehow we can help her out. "Who kept me?"

"The Changing Man," Ben snaps.

Elaine blinks at us and . . . this is getting us nowhere. Maybe she didn't write the code. Maybe she doesn't want to tell us anything. Or maybe . . . maybe she just doesn't remember. An idea forms. I remember the petal I slipped into my blazer pocket and pull it out slowly. Maybe seeing it might spark her memory.

"Ife, don't," Bee warns.

When she tries to stop me, I brush her off. Her narrowed eyes and pinched expression are enough for me to instantly regret it. I open my mouth to defend myself, but there's a raking pain in the back of my throat. I take a deep breath and try again.

"If this means we find something out, then what's the problem?" I whisper.

"What's the problem?" Bee whispers harshly. "Oh, no problem, just that she's clearly confused. We need to get back on track. Let's not—"

"Oh, what's that?" Elaine asks. She takes the petal from my hand. Rising from her seat, she examines it. Utterly entranced. The pollen clings to her fingers and she rubs her thumb and index finger together. After a moment she sneezes, and then she looks at us oddly. Sniffing, she tilts her head a little while her left eye twitches and her smile fades into emptiness.

"I *told you*," Bee hisses first at me, then at Ben. "I told you both."

"Miss?" I ask.

Elaine's breaths are shallow. "*Let me out*," she erupts suddenly, banging her fists against her temple. "*Let me out!*"

Her voice is hysterical and scratchy.

"We're sorry. Miss, we didn't mean to—"

Elaine grabs me by the shoulders and grips me hard. My blood chills as I look into her eyes. There's something not right with them. They're halfway between empty and petrified, alive with feral urgency. She huffs and puffs as if fighting some invisible beast in her mind. "Vol ow . . . sor . . . P-p-paper trail."

What the hell is happening?

Bee—or Ben, I don't know which—pulls me from her grasp. I come to my senses, running out of the nurse's office and into the fresh air.

"What was that?" Ben gasps, right behind me. "Why did she suddenly switch like that?"

"This is why I said be careful," Bee says. "That was probably some form of PTSD. Whatever happened to her as a student was probably locked away deep down. We shouldn't have pushed her."

They go back and forth, but I'm not paying attention. My fear's caught up to me, turning my legs and knees into mash, and I'm using all my strength to stay standing. To not plunge into an ice-cold panic. Would the same thing happen if I showed Malika a petal?

A thought spears through everything.

"She was trying to tell me something," I blurt. Both of them look at me. I take a deep breath. "I—I think the old her was trapped inside. I don't know."

"What do you mean 'the old her was trapped inside'?" Bee asks.

"Her eyes. They were so . . . so, I can't explain. Intense. Trapped. Sh-sh-she said something about a paper trail?"

Ben laughs. He's soon gritting his teeth because Bee's kicked him in the shin.

"So-sorry," he says, scowling at Bee.

Bee is deep in thought. "Paper trail?" She turns to me and I nod. My mouth is so dry. "I think we should go to the ancient data stores next. It's the first thing that comes to mind when I think about a paper trail. I think it's as good a place as any."

"I'm not sure that's the right call," Ben asserts.

"Why?" Bee challenges.

"It's . . . I have a hunch." He paces. "Besides, she could have meant anything when she said the words 'paper trail.' *Anything.*"

Bee presses her lips together. For a moment I think she's going to back down. Instead, she steps toward Ben. "Hunches aren't true or false. They just are. The *only* reason we knew about the hidden room was because *I* was right. And *I* was right about being more careful with Elaine. I deserve to be taken seriously."

Sucking in his cheeks, Ben folds and unfolds his arms. He shakes his head before looking my way.

I shrug. "I think we should follow her gut on this one."

A smirk builds on Ben's face. "Fine."

"Fine," Bee parrots.

"What do you think we'll find in the data store anyway?" Ben asks. "Apart from inches of dust and mildew?"

Bee fixes him with a hard glare. "You're silly and being narrow-minded. The data store is an *archive*. That means it has original docs from over the school's history. I'm hoping we can find out what she meant by *flower person*. There must be something. Tell you what, if you have a better idea, I'd like to hear it."

"I . . . am outnumbered it seems. In that case, I know the way in."

"Do tell," Bee answers, taking his olive branch.

Ben nods. "I'm a well-connected fellow and I make it a point to befriend the staff here. Chefs, groundskeepers, receptionists—they are figurative flies on the walls. Did you know a lot of them post on CottsLore?"

"Huh," Bee acknowledges.

Conversation soon turns to their shared interest in Nithercott trivia, broken when the bell rings for the end of break and we go our separate ways.

On my way to PE, I look through the group chat with my friends.

~**Alice:** Ahooooo!

Julie: Ahoooo

Zan: 🐺 🐺

I roll my eyes at this new wolf-howl greeting thing everyone is now doing. Even Zee. I obviously don't get it.

> **~Alice:** @Gina I'm still
> crying @ the way Ms. Bryton
> went red when her phone
> went off!

> **Gina:** 🤣 I mean I don't
> blame her! I'd go red too if
> my ringtone was im a savage
> at 50 plus

> **Zan:** No wayyyy!

> **Tola:** I'm a savage yeah…classy,
> bougie, ratchet!

> **Julie:** Sassy, moody, nasty!

Shaking my head, I close the chat and take a deep breath, letting my shoulders relax. *I'm just irritable because they don't know what I'm going through,* I tell myself. *It's not their fault.* I drop Zee a message.

> Video call tonight? Rewatch
> Lord of the Rings? Been ages
> since we've done that! Avolastic
> aeyastic <3

Zan is typing . . .
Zan is typing . . .
Zan is typing . . .

Sorryy! I would but me and Lisa
are checking out this new film
by Tosin. Children of the light.
We can do another night. I'll let
you know! Xoxoxo

Of course she's already found someone new. She didn't
even respond to my use of our secret language. My stomach
sinks like a stone. Whatever. I put my phone away.

On my way to the pavilion, I spot Mr. Ingham standing in
front of Porthaven House, watching over his school in one of
his elegant three-piece suits.

When he catches me staring, he gives me a slow wave and
a big smile.

His mouth opens, but nothing comes out. Something
catches his attention—an approaching police officer. He
steps out to meet him.

Dr. Butterworth rushes by me at a brisk walk. I do my best
to keep up with him as I follow. This time I don't care about
hiding because he's going in the direction I need to be going.
He goes left, toward the Butcher's Cleaver and Pickleham Village, which is in the opposite direction of my next lesson.

Who needs to learn how to hold a hockey stick properly
anyway?

I'm about to follow him when my phone buzzes.

Bijal created group "Nithercott 3"

Bijal has added +447700900149 to the chat

Bijal: Old data store tonight?

~Benny: 👀 Is water wet?

Bijal: Well ... water isn't wet by
itself, so are you in or out?

~Benny: Touché. I'm
obviously in.

Bijal: Yesss! Ife?

Lol, do I even have a choice?

Bijal: Nope.

~Benny: It's a rhetorical type
of day so my answer is ... can
pigs fly?

😆 Weirdos. Let's do it.

When I look up from my phone, Dr. Butterworth is
gone. I sigh at the missed opportunity. Hopefully, whatever we find in the old data store gives us a clue about

why Elaine lost it. Then a thought crosses my mind and the uncertainty becomes a great big weight pushing down on me.

If we work out the truth, what happens next?

CHAPTER 16

THE OLD DATA STORE

"Night, you two," Ms. Piddleton whispers.

"Night," I reply, fully clothed under my duvet.

After I've been in darkness for what feels like forever, I'm ready to hop out of bed, but Fran whispers into the dark.

"Hang on."

I listen. Sure enough, our door creeps open. I close my eyes until they're nearly shut. I can just about see Ms. Piddleton looking back into the room. Finally she leaves, happy we're not up to no good.

"How'd you know?" I ask, finally getting out of bed.

"Call it a feeling. I didn't like her look." She unlocks her phone, the light illuminating her face. "Enjoy your night out. My lips are sealed."

"I see . . ." I pull on my puffy black parka coat and slip on my Doc Martens. The sturdiest shoes I own, because who knows what state the data store is in? The door edges open again, and I freeze. My heart pinballs all the way to the back of my throat.

A shadow stretches into my room.

"Pssst. It's me," Bee says, slipping inside.

I exhale. "You scared me. I thought you were Ms. Piddleton."

"Nope. She's in her flat already. Heard her lock her door. You ready?" she asks.

I nod. Let's get this over with.

"Something you said has been stuck in my head," Bee huffs as we move the sofa. "You used the word *trapped*. When you showed her the petal, do you think you caused her old self to reappear?"

"I'm not sure. It was weird. I think so." I chew on my lip. "Do . . . do you think something like that's possible?"

"Yeah, without a doubt. I mean, suppressed memories *are* a real thing." She glances at me. "Ife, what aren't you telling me?"

I take a deep breath. "I think I'm being watched. Followed."

"By?"

My teeth pull at the dry skin on my lips. "The Changing Man."

"I don't even know what to think anymore, but I guess we can be extra careful and keep a lookout." Bee frowns. "Why do you think the Changing Man would be after you?"

"I've been thinking about the myth . . . where it talks about how he preys on the lonely in heart." I pull and twist on my hair. "I think my homesickness attracted him."

"Like a shark to blood?"

"Yeah, exactly. Maybe that's how the Changing Man picks." I start sliding the cabinet aside to reveal the exit.

Bee tilts her head in thought. "Well, my horoscope said to stay optimistic . . ." She launches into how this is down to the moons and planets and . . .

I zone out, focusing on getting the cabinet out the way. I step toward the door. "Oh no."

"What?"

There's a new, shiny lock hanging from the door bolt. No doubt this was Ms. Piddleton's doing. Bee pulls up next to me and I demonstrate the locked door. "Window?"

"Window?"

"Yes." I'm sure now. "Window. The kitchen windows are massive, and unlike the front door, they aren't alarmed. Right? You told me that."

We put the games room back the way we found it and sneak into the moonlit kitchen. My heart swells and pushes against my chest when a shadow appears from nowhere.

Bee puts a hand on my shoulder and points. "Just the lamppost."

I see it flicker, watching a shadow grow from one of the chairs. I sigh.

"Right, let's break out of here," Bee says.

Hands in the pocket of my coat, I nod. *Let's get this over with.* I'm already thinking of everything that can go wrong—what we might find in the data store. I follow Bee's lead past the front of Porthaven House, where dim light bursts through the ground-floor windows. There's a faint squeaking sound that fills the air, and I stop.

Movement strobes the light coming from under the front doors. Someone was standing there.

Bee tugs on my arm. "It's just the doors, come on," she says. A rush of wind rattles the doors, and the squeaking noise sounds again. "See? Now come on."

My heart races. I know what I saw. A shock of static zags down my back and I shiver. Bee's by my side, pulling at my arm again.

"Scared? It's okay, we won't get caught. Trust me."

"Y-yeah." My fear hardens. "I guess I just freaked out a little."

"You're late," I say to Ben.

He's pulling up to the log with his hands in the air and yawning widely. "I needed to piss. I am allowed to piss, right?"

I roll my eyes hard.

"Did you bring it?" Bee asks.

Ben reaches into his blazer pocket and pulls out a flashlight. "Of course. Shall we?"

"Let's," Bee sings.

We walk along the perimeter of the back fields closest to the school, round the back of Mr. Ingham's house, and into the adjacent woodlands. The flashlight flickers on and Ben leads the way, Bee and I on either side of him.

We make a left down a worn path, and in two steps, Ben stops suddenly and colors the night with multiple swear words. Bee gasps. I go still as a tree trunk. Off the path to the left lies a boar on its back, its stomach split open.

"Jesus," Ben says. "I wouldn't want to meet whatever attacked that."

"*Attack* is an understatement, don't you think?" Bee breathes. She steps toward the boar. "This is . . . Wait. It doesn't have a *heart*. Like it's been taken."

"Taken?" I think of the fox who had a missing eye. If so, the real question is, "For what?"

Bee shrugs. "Nutrition. Maybe this wasn't an attack. I bet this boar died of natural causes. Bloating caused it to split open and some animal scavenged it, and the heart was the easiest, most accessible organ."

Ben's flashlight roves around the boar's corpse and settles briefly on a path of moonlit mushrooms and barely blooming blue flowers an arm's length away.

It leads into the engulfing darkness of the woodland. I swallow. "It's the Changing Man's work. I've seen those flower and mushroom combos before. In couples' corner where I saw—I don't know what I saw—and that night Malika stood me up and reappeared different. I think the urban myth is right. That the Changing Man can grow strange plants."

"Coincidental," Bee says quickly, with a slight shake of her head. "Look, there are scuff marks and paw prints. See, something probably brought it here or scavenged here. Yeah, it's probably not *that*. There's nothing supernatural about this."

Ben *hmms*, but doesn't say anything. I know he doesn't believe me either.

Whatever happened to the pig was deliberate and way too precise to reduce it to a series of coincidental events. Since when do scavengers act in moderation? I want to believe her words, but the signs of the Changing Man are too fresh to be dismissed. I don't care if they refuse to believe he's got strange abilities; he was here. And judging by the wetness of pooling blood, it wasn't that long ago. Still, I keep the thought to myself and nod. I don't want to ruin anything. They probably think I'm already doing the most by believing in this stuff.

Gathering my courage, I follow Bee and Ben as we continue down the path. In moments we're in front of the old data store.

It's a box of a building, overgrown with leafless vines and fenced by tall grass. There are twin outdoor lights on either side of the door. They look almost identical. Except the glass on one of them is fractured.

"It wouldn't be an overstatement to say this building may or may not collapse on us," Ben says, striding up to the front door. He lifts up the ancient plant pot and produces a key. "Bingo. Just like the groundskeeper let slip once."

"What do you mean it may or may not collapse?" I ask. "Are you sure it's safe?"

"Exactly that. And no. But when are we ever sure about anything? Now, if you're quite done pussyfooting"—Ben unlocks the door—"let's get what we need and get out of here before we're riddled with asbestos in our lungs."

"Asbestos?" I ask Ben's back as he slips inside. Bee sighs deeply as we follow. It's too dark to see.

I go to flick on the lights, but Bee says, "No."

"No?"

"We don't want to draw attention to ourselves."

The rotted walls of the old data store imprison rows and

rows of filing cabinets. The stench of mold has me holding my breath for as long as I possibly can before I exhale. I can't think of many other places that would be worse than this space.

"Exactly what do they keep in here?" I ask as we walk down the aisle that splits the room in two.

Bee turns. "Student records going back before the nineties, old reports, old schedules, old everything. Elaine's file should be in here. Let's start there. See if there are any flower links." She sighs, having a quick look around. "Doesn't look like it's organized in any sort of way. We're going to have to split up. Ife, you go take the back three rows, all across, Ben the next three, and I'll do the next. We'll go from there."

We head to our designated rows and begin the painful work of going through the cabinets. It's slow work because Ben's the one with the flashlight. Which means I have to use my phone light and it can only illuminate so much. After a short while, Ben saunters over.

"Shouldn't you be going through your designated rows?"

He pries open a stiff cabinet drawer. "I wanted to . . . apologize to you. Properly."

I don't say a word.

"I know, I know, I've been rude at times. Erratic." Ben swallows and pulls out his brass lighter. "Leon. You would have loved him. He understood who he was. Always . . . had an answer for everything. That was the most annoying thing about him, you know? You could tell him *anything* and somehow he'd turn it back on you. No wonder the teachers found him 'bright but difficult.'"

I look up from my filing cabinet. *Why is he telling me this?*

"The night he started acting off . . . I should have said something. It was so obvious. The way he'd stopped calling me Benny, and all the little things . . . and I just—it doesn't even matter." Ben sighs heavily. "If only I'd told someone when he started acting strange. If I had then—I mean, I never got to . . . I just want him back."

He slams the cabinet drawer shut suddenly and a thunderclap of noise bellows.

"Ben . . . ," I whisper. I watch the tears fall. He sniffles and wipes them away.

"You're *everything* he wanted me to be. You're determined and brave, and I guess you remind me of every way I messed up before he was taken. But that's not your fault, so I'm sorry."

The words of the transcript flash in my mind, and my eyes sting. "Th-that's not true." I haven't felt like me the whole time I've been here. "I feel like I'm suffocating," I admit. "Nithercott is really a lot."

"Yeah. I get you. I used to be a weekly boarder, and I remember running after Mum's car when she dropped me off on Sundays."

"Seriously?" I laugh while picturing the image.

He nods. "Not my finest moment, but all of this is a lot. Especially when you're not really born into it or used to it. They expect you to act a certain way. So I feel you."

Bee appears round the corner with a wide grin. Her face shifts. "Am I interrupting?"

"I'm just unloading emotionally while apologizing," Ben says with a laugh. "No biggie."

"Right. Odd beans. Anyway, I found something big. Follow me."

She leads us to her row where multiple sheets of paper lay strewn on the floor. "I found something in Elaine's file."

Bending down, she picks one up and reads aloud:

June 30, 19XX
CONFIDENTIAL AND CLASSIFIED

Dear Mr. & Mrs. Ayodele,

After Elaine's recent disciplinary record, Nithercott is so pleased you have accepted our invitation to partake in our King's Mentor Scheme, and I am writing to confirm arrangements.

During her time here, she will be under the stewardship of one of our patrons (see below) who will act as her exclusive mentor throughout the rest of her duration at Nithercott School as well as any higher education she pursues post leaving.

Commitments made by mentors may only be terminated with thirty days' notice in writing. This notice period enables us to pair the student with another mentor within the allocated window.

Whilst we take all reasonable care to ensure students are fit for mentorship, we are not liable in respect of expectations not being met.

This agreement cannot be altered or amended except in writing and signed by both parties.

Signed and agreed on behalf of
Nithercott School . . . J. Ingham. . . . . .
Date: 30/06/19XX

Jonathon Ingham
HEADMASTER

Witnessed by: Mr. Russell Walton
WARDEN

Witnessed by: Mr. Orchid Green
PATRON

Witnessed by: Mrs. Annabel Johnson
TREASURER

Bee and I share a look. I bet we're both thinking about the name *Orchid*. It can't be a coincidence, surely. He must be the flower person Elaine said to follow in the code she left. But . . . "Why didn't she just say 'Follow Orchid'?"

"Judging by how badly the words were underlined," Bee starts, "she probably didn't have time."

Ben swears under his breath.

"What is it, Ben?" I ask.

His head shakes slowly and he pulls out his phone. "I know that name. Orchid Green." Silence reigns until Ben looks up from his phone. The color drains from his face. "He held a meeting with Leon about being his sponsor. It was around the time he started acting off . . . But—I—How is he—ugh! I'm so confused."

190

"Deep breath, Ben. You're spiraling, and that doesn't help us, or Leon," Bee interjects. Ben nods and Bee continues. "Let's see if we can find any records related to Orchid Green."

Back to the cabinets we go, poring through the absurd amount of paperwork. My eyelids are heavy as stone and I'm struggling to keep them open. I've reread this sentence like five times. When the words sink in on the sixth time, I sit up straight. "Holy—guys! Guys!" Bee scuttles over. "I found something to do with Orchid Green. A memorandum."

MEMORANDUM

NITHERCOTT SCHOOL

DATE: 24 September 2000

TO: HERCULES GRET
FROM: RUSSELL WALTON
CC: ORCHID GREEN
SUBJECT: Dissolution of King's Mentor Scheme (24/9/00)

I, along with the board of governors, have carefully considered the position in which Nithercott School finds itself, having just obtained emergency funding. Simply put, we are burdened financially. Our donors are giving less collectively—they've developed a bystander culture. Meanwhile our boarding school houses are half empty and somehow are running at a deficit. We need more students. Therefore, the board, for whom I speak, are of the opinion that we should pursue the dissolution of the King's Mentor Scheme.

No doubt this would cause a large vacuum in the very essence of what makes Nithercott great—its ability to reduce errancy and reform minds. But fear not, for we have carefully considered the consequences of such a step. We think it right to repurpose the scheme in favor of a more wide-reaching program that will promote our good works as an institution and fill our boarding houses. Orchid Green has generously agreed to fund and spearhead this new initiative—the Urban Achievers Program.

Hercules, as headmaster, if you accept this dissolution, please make sure that proper credit goes to those who helped develop this concept.

Bee scans over the piece of paper again as if there's some clue hidden between the lines. "There's something we're missing," Bee mutters. "I don't get this—"

"Orchid Green is the Changing Man," Ben states. "He's the one who took Leon," he adds, out of breath, waving a wad of papers about. "Every single one of the students who complained in the summer of '83, *and* who was a King's Mentor at the time, had Orchid Green as their patron." Ben picks up another sheet of paper. "Records state they all had one-to-ones with Orchid Green days before they all retracted their statements. There's nothing linking the students who weren't King's Mentors to Orchid, but I'm sure they're tied to him somehow. Think about it. Leon—and Lord knows who else—had Orchid as their sponsors under the Urban

Achievers Program. I think he created the program to get away with everything more easily."

"But why those particular students?" Bee says quietly. "Because it's not everyone in the program."

The silence bloats as we think about her question. And then an answer comes to me. I connect my thoughts in a flurry. "They didn't quite fit in maybe. It made them lonely too. So the Changing Man went after them. It would explain why the school didn't notice if at the end of the day, they were changed for the 'better.' Made more Nithercott."

I take a breath. Ben and Bee look at me, probably sharing the same focused thought: This is real.

"I think we've found our smoking gun," Bee whispers. "So what now?"

"Find more proof," Ben states, raking his hands through his hair multiple times, focused on steadying his breathing. "It's getting late, and I need space to think. Let's think of a plan tomorrow."

We take the key letters and records with us and leave the data store in the same state it greeted us in. As we head back toward the main part of the school, a voice calls out.

"Who's there?"

It's Mr. Ingham. We rush for the thick woodland. Blinding light bears down on us, scanning the area. We burrow into a bush and hide.

"The longer you hide from me, the worse it's going to be," Mr. Ingham states. "I know you're there and I will wait."

Ben swears under his breath. "If he sees me, it's over. I'll be expelled."

"Mummy and Papa are going to kill me," Bee breathes.

I curl my hands into tight fists. There's a lightness in my chest. "I'll deal with this. He doesn't seem to know how many of us there are. No reason for all of us to get caught."

"But why? You could get in serious trouble," Bee whispers. "You're still supposed to be house confined."

Why? Because I want to be the old me again, and I can't do that if I'm always afraid or hiding. A smile blooms on my face. "When it comes to schmoozing Mr. Ingham, I might be the best. Plus, I have an idea. I think he's one of the few adults who would *actually* care about what we found."

I pick up the wad of records and letters we took and head out from the bushes. I step into the light, shielding my eyes with a hand.

"What the devils are you doing here?" Mr. Ingham's wearing a purple bathrobe and tartan slippers. His eyes are bloodshot, his hair all over the place. "You know better, Ife. You're already on thin ice."

Right. My punishments.

"I—" Disappointment is carved deep into his frown. It swallows my words and floods my thoughts. Suddenly, talking my way out of this situation sounds like a bad idea.

"Well? Out with it," Mr. Ingham says with a frustrated shake of his head.

Deep breaths. I channel the confidence of my old self. "I was in the old data store, sir."

He bunches his eyebrows tight together. "How did you—" Curiosity creeps into his expression. "What on earth for?"

"Sir, how much do you know about Orchid Green?" I ask. "Truly?"

Hairless meows, slinking out from the shadows to scratch at Mr. Ingham's robe. He attempts to shoo the cat away. "Well, his funding is one of our main means of making our education affordable. *He's* the reason you're here on our Urban . . ." His words trail off as he runs a hand through his hair and frowns. "What exactly are you asking?"

I thrust everything we found at him, and Mr. Ingham takes it. "He's been involved with Nithercott since 1972. He was the assigned patron of every King's Mentor student that filed a complaint in 1983. He created the Urban Achievers Program. He was Leon's assigned sponsor. Before Leon went missing, they had a meeting. I'm sure if you look at all the incidents involving students from Nithercott, he must be tied in some way to every single one of them. He's bad news, sir."

I leave out the fact he's literally the Changing Man.

"I see." Mr. Ingham flips through the sheets of paper until he pauses. Muttering under his breath, his lips pinch together as he looks me up and down. He smiles, but it's dim and fragile. And just like Ben, there's a tightness in his eyes. Mr. Ingham's been through some stuff.

"Are you okay, sir?" I ask.

"Y-yes. It's just . . . someone here is very familiar to me." He shows me the record he was looking at. There's a picture of a frowning boy with brown skin and short, dark hair swept to the right. I recognize the face from the picture Elaine showed me.

"Skill 'n' tell club," I say.

Mr. Ingham tips his head to the side. "How did you know that?"

"School nurse, sir. She showed me a picture and I just remembered his face."

"I see. His name's Ramesh, and we used to be really close. My best friend, I suppose. But we suddenly drifted apart. It was like overnight he changed, and I felt so powerless back then. Like maybe I'd done something wrong. But if you're saying what I think you're saying . . . maybe it wasn't me. Who knew . . . This might be the lead we need to kick Detective William into gear with regards to Leon. While it's not too late." Mr. Ingham pulls out his phone and after a moment places it to his ear. "Ah, good evening, Detective William. Yes, I am aware of the time. However, a student of mine has come across something that may be of interest in the investigation concerning Leon. I suggest you pay us a visit tomorrow morning. Yes, that's all. Good night."

Mr. Ingham puts his phone away and takes a deep breath.

"Ife, go back to Beeton. I really shouldn't, but I will overlook this offense, just this once. But I do not want to catch you, or your friends, whoever they might be, outside your house again after lights out, otherwise I will not be so lenient." Hairless hisses and Mr. Ingham laughs. "Enough of that. Next time, if you"—he glances toward where Ben and Bee are hidden—"have suspicions, please inform senior leadership or contact the police."

"Y-yes, sir."

"Good." Mr. Ingham turns to walk away. He pauses, his back half to me. "Still, nice work. I'll be reviewing everything on my end too."

When I can't see him anymore, I let out a breath, placing my hands on my chest. My heart is punching against my rib cage. A rustle catches my attention. Emerging from the darkness are Bee and Ben.

"Nice one," Ben says. He squeezes my shoulder, and warm pride pulses from my chest. "He let you off? Just like that?"

"I told you, schmoozing Mr. Ingham is my thing. I showed him what we found."

"What'd he say?" Bee asks.

"Speechless. Called Detective William. They're going to be looking into it."

"Least it's something." Ben flashes an empty smile. "Look, we can't leave it for them to cock up like they always do. It'll lead nowhere with Leon still out there." He sighs and opens his mouth. But nothing more comes out.

Right then Ben is the most readable person in the world. Tangled emotions dance across his face—anger, pain, loneliness—in the form of wide eyes and frowning eyebrows.

"Ben," Bee and I say together. I take a step toward him, and he takes a step back.

"I—okay—I'm sorry. I . . ."

I frown. "Are you—"

"I'm fine," he snaps, his eyes wet and breaths heavy. "Can you just—I need some—We'll sort stuff out tomorrow—today. Right now, I just need sleep."

CHAPTER 17

NITHERCOTT 3 PLOT

slide into my bed, ready to drift into a deep and undisturbed sleep when my phone buzzes:

Nithercott 3
attachment: 1 image

The image loads. It's a luxury house that is all concrete and glass and polished wood paneling. Thorny bushes and small trees tightly packed together ring the house, held at bay by a lush carpet of grass.

Nice house, but . . . ??

Bijal: It's where the Urban
Achievers offices are and it's
only down the road.

I look at the image again and zoom in on the words embossed on the gate—*Little Forrest*. I sit up straight in bed. The name rings a bell.

But from where?

> **Ben:** jinx. I was looking at the
> same thing. Couldn't sleep. It's
> built like a fort though ...

> **Bijal:** No way in except through
> the front gates. So they can't be
> caught lacking.

> **Ben:** To find a way in and get
> proof Orchid is the Changing
> Man, and clues on Leon's
> location, we need to be
> meticulous in our planning

> **Bijal:** Exactly

That's right. When we were in the village shop. The woman.
She said: "Remember to use the gate down the little lane and
ring the bell twice. Someone will meet you there."

> I think I know a way in

> **Ben:** Go on ...

> **Bijal:** 😈

CHAPTER 18

UNINVITED GUESTS

Instead of attending our Wednesday activities, Ben and I are tucked in some unruly bushes across from the gate into Little Forrest.

Bee's keeping watch from the village shop. The bag of sweet and salt popcorn between us rustles as Ben grabs a handful and shoves it into his mouth.

"You alright?" I ask.

He reaches into the bag again. "Never better."

I nod, checking my phone. Waiting for Bee's message. A few hand grabs of popcorn later, it comes.

All clear

"All clear," I parrot.

Ben takes another handful of popcorn. "Here. We. Go."

"You know it's a share bag, right?" I sigh as Ben gets to his feet. "Key word *share*."

"Just get ready to play your part." Ben pulls on an all-white mask he stole from the drama department. Then he flicks a piece of popcorn at me before leaving.

"Very mature," I murmur, and start counting to ten in my head.

. . . *Seven Mississippi, eight Mississippi, nine Mississippi* . . .

Fractured pieces of stone crunch under my feet as I walk down the little lane carrying a crate of random fridge and cupboard items we took from various boarding houses. The side gate into Little Forrest is matte black, smudged with rust at the edges. Smoothing out my clothes, I take a deep breath to calm the way my heart thunders at the bottom of my feet.

I press the bell twice. After a while, the clack of heels rings through the air. There's a mechanical buzz, and a lady with a mound of gray hair, tied into a bun, steps out to meet me.

She's in a violet dress, and her ears and neck shimmer with diamonds.

"Yes?" She glances down at the crate of snacks and recoils, drawing back. "Are you lost?"

"Not at all. This crate is courtesy of the village shop. For your continued support."

Violet Dress titters. "They should know we don't eat . . . those."

"Those?" I ask. She points at a jar of gherkins. "Ah, I see. Our mistake. I'll remove them. Oh, you might want to check on your front gates. I saw a student looking suspicious. I think she was planning on vandalizing them."

"What?"

"Where shall I put the crate?"

"Just drop them inside the door." Violet Dress isn't really paying attention to me. "You said something about vandalism?"

I nod. "Yep, at your front—"

Violet Dress power walks down the little lane muttering

under her breath, and a smile creeps onto my face. I ping a message to the group chat.

Me: Incoming

Moments later two figures run up the little lane. Ben and Bee. Energy crackles all the way through to the tips of my fingers and toes. Together we step through the side gate onto Little Forrest's lawn. With hoodies up, we creep across toward the door that's been left ajar.

When I step inside the building, I'm taken aback by the interior floral design. Vines with blooming orange flowers crawl along the walls and up the ceiling. Different kinds of potted plants are on nearly every raised, level surface.

One pot catches my attention. The turquoise flowers have an uncanny resemblance to a scorpion tail. It's beautiful, and in my mind, I'm already mixing the watercolors needed to paint them.

"They sure love their flowers." Ben half laughs.

Bee and I don't laugh. There's a lingering, earthy smell. I inhale deeply. *Petrichor.* And as we round the corner of the hallway, a thin, orange mist carpets the floor. So thin it seems to flicker in and out of existence. But it's there.

In the air, iridescent pollen hangs. With each step, color shifts.

None of us say anything. Even though we have different thoughts on who or what the Changing Man is, I know we're thinking the same thing—*this building has to be connected to everything.*

We're forced to hide behind large potted plants of

speckled grass when the sound of heels slapping wood heads toward us. The lady I distracted earlier walks swiftly by and heads into a door on the left. She reappears seconds later with a wad of files.

"We need to get into that room," Ben whispers. "It's got to be where all the files are. And files mean clues. And clues mean Leon."

Bee nods. Soon as we're sure the lady won't be returning, we edge toward the door.

"Let's convene in the sorting room," a voice booms nearby. It's both sharp and soft, and scrapes at my insides.

We all share a glance and rush into the room on the right instead. A conservatory.

"Let's—"

The words die in Ben's mouth when the handle of the door we just closed behind us rattles. I dive for the space behind a tall cabinet. Bijal hides in the space underneath the canvas sofa. I don't see where Ben goes, but I think that's a good sign.

"How are you feeling?" the sharp and soft voice says. It's disquietly familiar, and when the man we met in the village shop—Mr. Green—strides into the room, my pulse quickens. *Of course. Mr. Green is Orchid Green.* He takes a seat out of view.

"Good, thanks, sir. Excited to hear who my sponsor is." I recognize the voice and I swallow as the man is followed inside by a smiling Louis and his curly mop. "I hope it's you. Usually when people get you, they go on to do great things."

I press record on my phone.

"Please, call me Orchid. And you flatter me, boy. It's your

hard work that's gotten you here, and while unfortunately I am not your sponsor, I am truly interested to see just how you'll flourish. Would you like to know something else interesting, Mr. Kimble?"

Louis nods. "S-sure."

Without warning the air is thick with the stench of petrichor. And a curling orange mist seeps toward Louis. He looks at the tendrils of mist with an open mouth.

"There is no sponsor." I hear the smile in Orchid's whisper. Louis touches the back of his neck and his frown is fractured by a sudden yawn. "There are simply"—Louis slumps in his seat, looking fast asleep—"buyers."

Orchid comes into view and towers over Louis's body. He reaches his hand out, freezing when thundering bangs and high-pitched screams can be heard from behind the door. Orchid's hand curls into a fist and he leaves. The moment he does, the three of us burst out of our hiding spots.

Every swear word under the sun escapes from Ben's lips. Bee inhales sharply and scrambles for her phone. She puts it to her ear.

After a few moments, she takes a deep breath. "Hello. I'd like to report a . . . an, uh, attempted abduction . . . Little Forrest, Old Glossop Road . . . No, I don't . . . It's a student . . . fifteen minutes? That's too slow. You need to get here *now*!" She hangs up and turns to us. "We need to get him out of here."

"Do what now?" I shake my head. "Did you not just see the same thing I saw? He created the mist from nothing. Orchid could come back at any minute."

"You're always making excuses."

"What?" A booming bang makes me clap my hands over my ears. "Look, the best thing we can do is leave whatever madness that's happening and show my recording to the police when they arrive. That way we—"

"Girls!" Ben shouts. He's dragged Louis's body halfway out the conservatory onto the grass garden. "I have no idea what's going on in there, and I hate to break up your little moment but . . . can I get some help?"

Bee rushes to his side to help out. But I don't. *I'm not always making excuses.* Her words are fresh in my mind and I hesitate. Then I see movement in the bushes. Someone's moving round the perimeter. They stop and look around.

Louis?

It's hard to tell from here, but it looks exactly like him. When they see me staring, they step back into the thick of the bushes and disappear. *Why is there someone who looks like Louis?*

The sudden smell of fire catches my attention.

"Ife!" Ben demands.

I shake away the moment and rush over to help. Sharing the load between the three of us, we head toward the side entrance, heading round the back of the building to the other side.

"Not everything is about you," Bee breathes.

My eyebrows bunch together. "Huh?"

"You don't see it, do you?" Her voice rises.

"See what? What are you talking about?"

"You say *we*, but really everything is always about you. It's always been about you." Her bottom lip wobbles like a guitar string and her eyes water. I have no idea where this is coming from all of a sudden. "This is so much bigger than you getting what you want. People's lives are at stake."

"That's not—I'm not—" The excuse is ready to fly from my lips, but I stop myself. It'll make things worse. Gaining my composure, I realize she isn't angry. She's disappointed. *Because I think it's better to get to safety first?* I adjust my grip on one of Louis's feet. But . . . "You're not being fair."

"Ladies, can we not do this now? Maybe *after* we get Louis to safety," Ben says with a sigh.

Bee laughs, brushing him off. "Of course I'm the one not being fair. Why is it so hard for you to admit you don't care about anybody but you?"

"That's not true."

"Just admit it! You only came to me when you *needed* something. And whenever I tried to say no, you'd push and push and push." Silence. "Oh, *now* you don't have anything to say."

Another beat of silence.

"You could have said no." I swallow. "You're the one who chose to try and make me your friend any way possible. That's not how friendships happen, Bee. You can't *make* people like you. It's suffocating!" I squeeze my eyes shut. "I'm sorry . . . I'm sorry, I shouldn't have—I didn't mean—"

A high-pitched squeal splinters the air and stabs at my eardrums.

Another loud burst of sound is accompanied by another squeal. All of us bring our hands to our ears and drop to our knees.

Louis's limp body thuds to the ground, and I silently apologize for the bruises he's going to wake up to.

The ringing in my ears has barely died down before Ben's helping me to my feet. "Get up," he orders. "We need to get out of here."

We pick Louis back up but don't make it much farther before the smell of petrichor wafts our way. Heavy and suffocating.

CHAPTER 19

SNAPPING AND CRUNCHING OF BONE

"fe . . . Bijal . . . Ben," calls a rumbling voice through the air. Thick as smoke, jagged as rock. We look back toward the house where Orchid stands. Except he's different. Even though the glare on the windows makes him hard to see, it's not enough to hide the way his eyes glow in our direction. There are no whites to them as they blaze fierce magenta. Every nerve in my body frays like an old shoelace.

Even though the glare on the windows makes him hard to see, it's not enough to hide how wrong his silhouette is.

"Please do not take what is not yours," Orchid grumbles.

Suddenly Louis gets heavier. No, Ben's let go. He reaches into his inside blazer pocket and pulls out a fountain pen. His hands tremble. "I'll hold him—it—off; you girls take Louis away."

"Don't be an idiot," I hiss. "The hell are you going to do with a fountain pen? You'll get yourself killed."

"To be blunt, if he wanted us dead, then we'd be dead. Orchid wants Louis."

There's a squeal as a man with clumped hair and uneven

stubble comes crashing out of the window to our left, showering the grass with glass shards.

"Why are you three here?" Dr. Butterworth asks, getting to his feet and breathing heavily. His Nithercott tracksuit and sports jumper are matted with his blood. In his hand he wields a weapon that looks a lot like a chrome Super Soaker. Attached to the top of it is a gold canister. A purple flower is etched into its side, a crown stenciled above it.

He aims his weapon toward the window he crashed through and pulls the trigger. A burst of flame roars toward Orchid, who cowers and hisses. Dr. Butterworth takes in our faces, eyebrows bunching when he catches sight of Louis. "You sh-shouldn't be . . . here."

Ben steps forward, his hands constantly smoothing and resmoothing his blazer. "What the fuck. Sir, what the—"

"Language!"

"Who gives a shit about language! He—it—tried to take Louis. It took Leon, didn't he? I . . . Sir?" Ben pleads.

Dr. Butterworth looks Ben up and down before glancing toward the building. Orchid no longer stands by the window. "We don't have much time." Dr. Butterworth pulls a key from his pocket and hands it to me. "Here, t-t-take this. The hill where the cherub points. Now go, get Louis somewhere safe." Dr. Butterworth swallows hard and takes a deep breath. "Rose, twelve. Very . . . important. Repeat."

The key is cold in my palm. "What?"

"Repeat to me. It's . . . up to you now."

"I—" Dr. Butterworth's stare is so intense. "Rose, twelve. Very important."

"Good. Now all of you quickly, go. Quickly. He can help you."

"Who can—"

"*Go!*"

Ben, Bee, and I carry Louis as fast as we can. A crow flies free from the bushes. I glance over at Ben, who's taking deep breaths. His eyes are wide and his head is shaking. "What the hell is happening?"

We stop as we see Dr. Butterworth rush into Little Forrest.

"I thought we had an understanding?" Orchid's voice echoes, sounding like there are many of him. "You will regret this, you insignificant human. You should have let things be."

Ben won't stop swearing. Bee lets out a sob before quickly covering her mouth with her hand.

I pinch Bee and Ben hard. "We need to go, now," I say in response to their glares. Moments later, Dr. Butterworth's scream bursts through the calm of Pickleham Village. Sounds of snapping and crunching soon follow. "Now!"

I swallow down my fear, unable to get rid of the sound of broken bones ringing in my ears every step of the way back to the grounds of Nithercott.

The key is heavy in my trembling hands. A chill snakes through me as we camp in what Ben calls his secret spot. An open space of grass, ringed by bushes, with a tree stump in the middle, which Louis is now resting against.

"Ife." Bee's quivering voice shakes me out of my spiraling

thoughts. "Ife, you need to breathe. We need to go and tell the police exactly what happened, we need to—"

"No." I squeeze my eyes shut, trying to catch my breath. I gasp. "He . . . he gave me this key. Someone can help us."

"Key? Ife? You know what, it doesn't matter. We need to be there to give our statement."

I sink to my knees, until I'm sitting, and exhale. "He knew our names. He killed Dr. Butterworth."

"I know." Ben sighs. He won't stop running his hand through his hair and sighing.

"He knew our names," I repeat. "You saw his eyes, didn't you? I *told* you the Changing Man was real." I can't keep a hold on my breaths. Every breath I take escapes straightaway. I draw my legs up to my chest and half sniff, half laugh. "I told you! We need to go where the cherub points. Dr. Butterworth gave us a key. It's important."

Ben mutters under his breath, pacing around while Bee sits cross-legged. She's stone-still, except for the gentle rising and falling of her shoulders. Thinking.

Something sparks and she tenses, looking me dead in the eyes. "Ife. You recorded what happened in the conservatory, didn't you?"

I nod.

"Good. Then we *have* to go back. We'll show them the recording. They can't just dismiss it. Let's go now."

I shake my head as a wave of chilling heat flushes through me, knotting my stomach. My toes curl in my shoes. I can still hear Dr. Butterworth's screams. The splintering of bones. I don't want to go anywhere near that place.

"Ife?"

"No. We're not going back there," I manage to say. "We should get Louis somewhere safe first."

The sound of distant sirens rings.

Bee reaches out to take ahold of my hands, and I don't let her. "We have a chance to blow this whole thing out of the water if we can just get them to believe us."

"Don't push her," Ben says, lighting a cigarette. "She doesn't want to go, and I kind of agree with her. They can't help us. Not with this. They'd probably laugh us away. We should go find where the key Dr. Butterworth gave her leads. I don't think it's smart to go back toward the lion's den."

Bee looks at the two of us. Her eyes are wet with the promise of tears. Her eyes settle on me. "This isn't about getting Louis somewhere safe, is it? Why can't you just be honest for once and say you're scared. We're not monsters. We're not going to disown you because of that."

"Because what? You're such a shining example of honesty?" I snap. "You let everyone trample over you, and you ignore it, calling it 'banter.' Are you really that desperate?"

She opens her mouth to say something. Instead she purses her lips and leaves.

"Bee," Ben calls. "Hey, Bee, wait. You can't just—"

Anger simmers and my nostrils flare. "Let her go. If she wants to die like Dr. Butterworth, then that's on her."

"You don't mean that." He's right, I don't. Regret is bitter in my mouth. "Also, I hate to be that guy, but she's right."

"What?"

"You know exactly what. Go, I'll make sure Louis is taken somewhere safe."

Ben can be serious when he wants to be, I think while

walking toward Little Forrest. Kicking a pine cone, I practice what I'm going to say. But nothing feels right. It feels too forced, too fake.

A sudden squeal sends birds flying, and I burst into a run. *Bee.*

"Bee," I call out. Her shoulders swallow her neck while she stands rooted to the spot. She swivels and glares at me. "A-are you okay?"

"No." She sighs. "I stepped in some dog poop." Relief washes over me and I stifle back a laugh. She's trying not to laugh too. "It's not funny. It's gross. Anyway, why are you here?"

I smile at her, the way she's smiled at me before. Bright and wide and honest. I take another breath and open my mouth. "I'm . . . uh."

Her eyebrows jump up and she tilts her head before bubbling into laughter. "You're so bad at apologizing. Like what?"

I rub my hand all over my face, absolutely mortified. "I—what I *wanted* to say was that"—I walk toward her and take her hands—"I am sorry."

"Yeah?" she asks with a frown. But she doesn't pull away.

"I'm sorry. About everything. You're right. I've been self-ish and it's not an excuse, but honestly, I've been so scared about getting swallowed up by this place . . . and turning into someone I'm not. I'm . . . I'm sorry for the mean things I said"—tears well up in my eyes and I wipe them away—"that I didn't mean. I didn't see it then, but I see it now. I was too stubborn to realize, but you and Ben are my friends, and I hope I haven't messed things up and—"

"Don't be silly. You haven't messed anything up." Bee

sighs heavily, her face wet with tears. "I'm sorry too. I wasn't being entirely fair. Plus, you were right. I wanted you to like me so much." A pause. "Even though you were ice cold."

I fake gasp. "Ice cold?"

"The coldest. But, I could tell you were real. Even though you were going through it."

I hold out my arms and I pull her into a hug. For a few moments we just squeeze and squeeze and squeeze. "Did you speak to the police?" I ask, nuzzled into her shoulder.

Before she can answer, the sound of sirens heads toward us.

A bald police officer steps out of the car with his partner. He strides in our direction. "I'm Detective William. Did you call in the abduction?"

"Yes, we did." Bee steps forward. "We have proof. Show them."

I whip out my phone and hand it over to Detective William, who lets his partner watch too. A few agonizing moments drift by.

Detective William scratches at his scalp. "You do know wasting police time is an offense, girls? Punishable by law."

"What?" I blurt. "Did you not see the video?"

"I did. And all I see is a boy falling asleep and some special effects. You called about an abduction. There's nothing to investigate here." He turns to his partner and smirks. "Unless hypnosis is a crime?"

"B-b-but the words of the man. He—said something about buyers."

Detective William sighs. "What words?" He hands me my phone back and I rewatch the video. I put the volume to max and swallow hard. There's no audio.

Detective William's partner steps forward. Her snarl really brings out her badly drawn eyebrows. "I know you Nithercott kids feel entitled to everyone's time," Bad Eyebrows huffs. "But we don't stand for that, okay? So the next time you want to call the police about nothing, think long and hard because we won't forget this. Do you understand?" Bad Eyebrows speaks slowly as if we're dumb, so I refuse to answer.

"We understand," Bee says, answering for us. The officers glare at us all the way to their car and drive off. "What are we going—"

The buzz of both our phones cuts her off.

Nithercott 3

Ben: Louis safe and sound . . . for now.
Also I'm 99.9% sure I know where the
cherub is. I'll meet you both outside
Beeton tonight at 1 am.

CHAPTER 20

THE HIDEOUT

My hands tremble as I fumble with my coat zip. Every fiber of my being ripples with anxious energy. A nervous laugh escapes that I quickly stifle, flashing a look toward Fran, who looks up from her phone with a smile.

On the fourth try, I manage to zip up my coat. I step out of the room, and Bee's waiting for me with a dim, just-for-show smile.

"Ready?" she asks.

"As I'll ever be," I say, pressing my nails into the palms of my hands. Keeping my trembling in check. We climb through the kitchen window, dropping into the bracing cold.

For once Ben is on time. He nods our way. An owl, perched on an overhanging tree, hoots, and we all flinch. *Don't do this*, my inner voice screams. I ignore it because if we don't do this, no one else will.

Ben leads us across the front lawn into the copse of trees that sandwich the school entrance. Behind them is a brick wall and, some way along it, a hole. After squeezing through the gap, we end up in a large, perfectly mown garden. On the other side of that is another gap in the wall, which leads to a sloping open field. At the other end, there are swaying trees that are so thick with leaves, they swallow the night. But every now and then, I see specks of light escaping.

"That's the hill, where we'll find the cherub," Ben announces.

"Waheyyy," a boy slurs, smashing a bottle of beer against a tree trunk. People cheer.

"Don't mind them, bunch of idiots," Ben whispers, stepping us through "the regulars." They seem so comfortable out here in the dark. So unbothered by what could be lurking on the hill. They wave at him, calling him all sorts of names, and he waves back. *El Capitan, Big Ben,* and . . .

"Songbird?"

Ben shrugs. "Yeah, I write poetry. This way."

The regulars don't flinch like we do when a bottle smashes, when someone shouts into the silence, or when someone vomits.

"Bennyyyy," Stacey calls. I hear her but don't see her.

From nowhere arms wrap around him. "You're here," she breathes. My nose wrinkles at the strong smell of alcohol. "Come, come, we're just vibing and drinking for Leon. God bless his soul." She pulls him. Stopping when she notices me and Bee. She glares at us both before rearranging her face into a frown. Pointing at me. "You were . . . you were—I swear I just saw you . . . Whatever." Shaking her head, she turns to Ben. "Drink? For Leon."

"Actually, we're just on our way elsewhere, thanks though. Be seeing you," Ben answers for us. His fists are clenched tight.

Stacey shoves a canned cocktail at him. "You can't just not drink. How would Leon feel?" Her words are slurred and all over the place.

Ben sighs and takes the can. She watches him pop it open, down it, and smile. She smiles back and gives me a shallow nod, turning around and dancing her way offbeat back to the crowd.

"She is something else," Bee says.

"Agreed," I say.

Ben laughs dryly. "Sometimes, I truly think I hate this place. None of them care about Leon. Not really." I nod in agreement. "This way."

We follow Ben deeper and deeper into the dark until we're in front of a massive tree. The kind that looks like it's been around forever. Its roots stretch far beyond its broad trunk. Ben shines his phone light at the bottom of the tree, revealing a moss-stained cherub that's pointing eastward. Its face has been worn down by time. What was probably a pleasant smile is now something twisted.

"The pointing cherub," I mumble. "How did you know where to find it?"

"Uh, Leon used to mention he and his friends would follow this path of ferns to find their way back down the hill. Said they would see the strangest things: a tree wrapped in several school ties, standing stairs that used to be part of a home, a strange statue."

"Uh-huh. Well, whatever Dr. Butterworth wants us to see is around here somewhere."

All three of us have our phones' lights on. We start kicking away leaves and twigs and a vodka bottle that was obviously left here months ago. Other than that, there's nothing else.

"Maybe we should come back during the day when it's brighter out," Ben suggests.

Bee gasps. Starts tapping my shoulder. "What was it Dr. Butterworth told you, Ife?"

"Where the cherub points."

"Right, right, so what if it's not where the cherub points but *where* the cherub points?"

I squish my eyebrows together. "I don't . . . get it?"

Crouching by the cherub, Bee points in the same direction it aims. "*Where* the cherub points. We should be looking over there."

I follow her finger and see through low swinging branches the outline of something large and solid. Ben's already walking in that direction.

"Guess we better do as the cherub commands," he says.

The large and solid shape turns out to be an abandoned cottage. Crooked like the branches in Susanna's Yard, its roof is half gone and vines cover most of the front. We wade through tall grass to get to the doorway without a door and step inside.

There are no words for the way I cringe at the rotting, peeling walls. The furniture—a couple of chairs and a table—is as crooked as the cottage itself.

After nosing around there doesn't seem to be anything in here to be unlocked by the key I was given. The cottage is abandoned for a reason.

Ben sighs. "Let's come back and look around properly when it's light out."

"Yeah," Bee says.

"Wait," I say as we file out through the front. I see a distortion in the tall grass where it's been trampled. I walk toward it and hear something that sends a jolt through my spine—the sound of something tinny under my feet. "Both of you . . ."

They turn around at the same time and say, "Yeah?"

"I think I found what we're looking for." I stomp a few times so the tin-like sound rings out. Dropping to my knees, I brush away the clump of leaves, trample the sprouting grass, and point my phone light downward.

My breath hitches in my throat. There's a keyhole. With trembling hands, I lower the key Dr. Butterworth gave me into the keyhole. It fits. I go to twist, but the lock is stiff and it won't turn. "I'm trying but it won't—"

"Let me do it," Ben says, taking over from me. He manages to turn the key a bit. "Just needs a bit of force."

"Not too hard," Bee warns.

"Almost got it, just a little . . ." He grunts as he puts all his weight into it and the key snaps. "Balls."

A small part of the snapped key juts out but it's way too small for us to use our hands. I sigh in frustration.

Locksmiths cost a fortune. Why pay, when I can do it myself? Dad had said when he'd snapped the key in our home door lock. Even though Mum begged him to just call. Eventually he unlocked the door and got the snapped key out with a pair of knives he borrowed from a neighbor.

"We need knives or something sharp," I say. "Ben, you

happen to have a pair of knives in those endless pockets of yours?"

He shakes his head. "Didn't pack them today, sadly."

The sound of shenanigans nearby sparks an idea, and I turn to Bee because she'll definitely know the answer to my question. "Glass is sharper than a blade, right?"

She takes a moment. "That's right. It can have a cutting edge up to five hundred times sharper than a very sharp scalpel, and—"

"We'll use glass," I say, cutting Bee off. The adrenaline surges through me. The vodka bottle. I run back to the cherub and bring it back, handing it over to Ben, who nods.

"Stand back."' He smashes the bottle against a nearby tree and shards of glass go flying. I find two shards on the ground and use the sleeve of my hoodie to pick them up. One of them snaps when I try to turn the key with them, and I'm forced to look for a thicker piece of glass.

Delicately this time, I use the glass to turn the key the rest of the way. It clicks. The hatch pops open.

"Bingo," I mouth, using the glass to pull out what's left of Dr. Butterworth's key.

Ben swears while Bee makes a squealing sound. There's a metal ladder that leads down into pitch black. Drawing a deep breath, I start the climb down. Slow and steady. The smell of metal is strong. Automatic light flickers on.

At the bottom, the tunnel opens up into a big enough space for us to stand side by side. Up ahead is a green door and it has a purple flower with a gold crown on top. *That symbol.*

I reach out and twist the golden doorknob. My heart sinks. It's locked. And the keyhole isn't made for the key we were given, even if it hadn't broken.

That's when Ben, with his criminal ability to pick locks, gets to work with a couple of bobby pins. There's a click and the door swings open.

"Ben. I hope you know that it's never anyone who's good that knows how to pick locks," Bee says.

"I beg to differ," he replies smugly. "What does that make you two then?"

I close my eyes and take another deep breath. He's an idiot. I focus on the room behind the green door and step inside. Light flickers on and the room is . . . not as high tech as I thought it would be. In fact it looks old and antique. There are messy desks at both ends of the room, bookshelves, another desk with an old-looking computer, and adjacent to both, a cozy sofa with a throw.

Rose, twelve.

We each go for one desk. As I'm riffling through sheets of equations and scientific jargon, shuffled with takeaway menus and a Nithercott Day flyer, looking for anything that has the words *rose* and *twelve*, a sadness washes over me. Zanna would be interested in those scientific pieces of paper on the desk. She wants to be like Maggie Aderin-Pocock and take on her dream of making it into space. *I miss her.* She's probably starting to pack up her stuff for her move. The urge to text her right now is huge, but then Bee comes up beside me.

A loud but brief tune makes us both jump. It's just Ben booting up the computer. I get back to the papers on the desk and nothing seems to be useful. A lot of technical stuff that makes zero sense.

Ben groans. "Ugh, it's locked."

My eyes go wide. *Rose, twelve.* It's a password.

I stride over and type in *rose12*.

Invalid password. Attempts
remaining: 4

Warning: After **5** consecutive
unsuccessful login attempts,
your account will be locked

After a couple of variations, I'm down to two attempts. *Think, think, think.* My eyes scan the room for anything that'll help. On the desk is a rose bookmark with a quote. I pick the twelfth word and type it in.

Invalid password.

Down to one attempt. My heart races.

I look around again and one of the books on the shelf catches my eye. Broad and blue, an intricate pattern of red roses covers the length of its spine. Striding over, I yank it free and flip to page twelve. Stuck to the page is a Post-it with a series of letters and numbers.

E99sh3lls!

When I enter them into the password field and press enter, the screen flickers and the last thing Dr. Butterworth was looking at appears:

Ministry of Interdimensional Defense 13th Ward

*CHIEF OF INVESTIGATIONS
JOHN D. MORLEY

CASE TITLE: LAB REPORT

REF	DATE	TIME	DAY	LOCATION
0307	3/9/XX	2130	TUE	N/A

SUBJECT(S): MORITZ BECKER; MALIKA WARDROPPER; EMILE ELBURN; PHOEBE ODDFELLOW; SHINJI IGARASHI; JUSTYNA RICA; NIKOLA LILOU; OPHELIA MALDEN; RINAT YASHIN; REBECCA IRIS; ARNOLD NOAD

PATHOLOGIST: ALRED R. BUTTERWORTH

FINAL CONCLUSION
MOST RECENT STUDENTS (LAST 3 MONTHS) LOST TO THE ENTITY KNOWN AS A THERIMORPH (what is colloquially called the Changing Man)

1. THE ABOVE-MENTIONED STUDENTS ARE CONFIRMED REPLICAS
   A. SAMPLE INDICATES A PROBABILITY OF 23.0248%, WHICH CONFIRMS THE ABOVE STUDENTS AS BEING MINIMAL BIOLOGICAL REPLICAS.
   B. THIS MARKS AN INCREASE OF 12.748% IN A BIOLOGICAL MATCH, COMPARED TO THE LAST SET OF TAKEN STUDENTS.
   C. ORIGINAL STUDENTS ARE CONSIDERED MISSING.

"Holy smokes." Bee grabs my upper arm and squeezes. "No way. No, no, no. There's an interdimensional threat *and* the government are aware of it, *and* Morley's in on it with Butterworth? Also a *therimorph?*"

I narrow in on the word *missing.* My head shakes, unable to process what I'm reading. The Malika I saw in the dining hall with Fran—dancing with Stacey—wasn't real then. The words on the screen are a thunderbolt through my chest.

I take a breath at the words, reading them again, remembering Dr. Butterworth's words. *He can help you.* "We need to—" Ben's muttering to himself.

"Ben?" I ask.

"He's not there," Ben whispers. He swivels so he's facing us. "He's not on this list. Leon's alive." His eyes grow wide and glisten under the dull light. "He must have known. That's why he was odd. Different. Because he knew he was next and . . . and . . ." Ben slaps his palm against his forehead. "He really did run. *Shit.*"

"Then why hasn't he gotten in touch?" I blurt. The moment I do, I wish I hadn't because the hope on Ben's face wrinkles with doubt. He doesn't answer. "S-sorry, I—"

"Because it wasn't safe." He stares right at me. "He can't come back until he's safe."

"Y-yeah," I say. "That's probably it."

Regret mingles with a flash of anger when I think back to the candid pictures Dr. Butterworth had and the way Mr. Morley treated us.

They *knew* what was happening.

Ben runs his hands through his hair and draws a deep, deep breath. "But biological replicas? Like . . . clones?"

I clear my throat. "It's got to be." The pieces come together. The Changing Man—Therimorph—Orchid—whatever he's called—is taking people and putting replicas in their place. I remember the emptiness in Elaine's eyes. The sudden strangeness in Malika. How he tried to take Louis. How he mentioned buyers.

I shudder at that word—*buyers*. What do they do once they "buy" the student? Suddenly it's hard to breathe when I think of all the possibilities.

Ben looks in my direction. "Ife?"

My eyes close and everything comes spilling out like water. The feeling of being followed. The ominous reflections. The boy I now know as Louis's replica.

"I have one." My breath trembles.

"Why didn't you say something?" Ben asks, traces of an accusation in his voice.

"Because I wasn't sure. I thought I was imagining it at first and . . . and I was scared." My hands curl into tight fists. My blood is boiling. "But I'm not anymore. We need to talk to Mr. Morley. He'd know what to do."

Bee whips out her phone and sighs. "I'm looking at his calendar on QuickTalk, and he's got a meeting early tomorrow so he'll probably be at breakfast. We'll have to catch him then?" Bee suggests.

In agreement we make our way back down the hill in silence.

I stumble over my thoughts.

Orchid. The Changing Man. Therimorph. He's the reason for everything messed up at this school. For Malika's disappearance. Ben's brother. For all of it.

I have a replica. My mind becomes a stuffy room full of anxious thoughts. Because if I have a replica, it means I'm on borrowed time. *How long before they come for me?* As the students who are out and about drink, and smoke, and chill without a care, I wonder how many of them have been replaced already. How many more of us at Nithercott are in the Changing Man's sights? Waiting to be taken.

I'm unable to keep my legs steady against the tides of fear crashing into me. *Why did I have to get wrapped up in this?* A sick, twisted feeling wriggles in my stomach at the thought of being surrounded by forgeries—replicas.

I glance across at Bee and Ben, and my heart aches.

What if we can't stop him?

It's nearly 3:00 A.M. and I'm still not asleep. I'm in Bee's room; she didn't want to sleep alone. I couldn't say no to her. Not after the day—night—we'd had. It just means I need to be up in a few hours so I don't get caught. As Bee's room is only a couple of rooms away from Ms. Piddleton's flat, it's one of the first rooms she checks in the morning.

"You asleep?" I whisper loudly.

Bee snores in response. I sigh and sit up. Check my phone. Zanna's left me a few messages—GIFs. One of Mary Poppins sailing on a kite and another of a wiggling cat. Except there's no context.

What the hell am I looking at, Zee? P.S. all packed? evulastic eiyastic xo, I text before putting my phone to one side.

Tiredness is making everything feel heavy.

I just want all this to go away. To fall asleep and wake up and realize I was dreaming this whole time. But I know I'm not. This is real. Deep in my stomach, anger I never knew I had sparks. I don't want to think about all the students taken without anyone knowing to mourn them. My blood curdles at the thought of Ayo cuddling with my replica while I'm gone forever. *Would he notice?*

"We need to stop him." The words feel strange coming out of my mouth. I don't know if they're brave or reckless, but it doesn't matter. Here they are.

But what if you can't?

I push away the thought and collapse back onto the bed.

CHAPTER 21

SUMMONS

My phone's buzzing by my ear. I yawn and turn off my alarm. I need to get back. I leave Bee's room and head to mine. My fingertips slide against the walls while I walk, thinking about the mess of thoughts in my head. Always coming back to: *What are we going to do?*

As I search for the answer, I jerk my fingers back from the walls. "Splinter." I seethe.

I'm in the middle of biting it out when, up ahead, I see Malika's forgery. She doesn't have the baby hairs the Malika I know cherished. My heartbeat pounds throughout my body, flaring my nostrils. I take a deep breath and I stride up to her.

"Where's Malika? The real one," I demand.

Fake Malika searches my face, ignoring my question. My boiling anger reduces to a simmer.

"Wh-what is it?"

Her hand reaches for my shoulder and I'm too scared to stop her. When I glance, I see there's some iridescent pollen on it. It must be from when we snuck into Little Forrest. When she touches it, something shifts in her eyes. Her hand grips my shoulder tight. A chill ripples through me. In a gentle voice, she speaks.

"I . . . Ife?"

My breath catches. *It's her.* "Ma-lika?" Even though I'm looking at a forgery, a part of her is still there. Scared. How is that even possible? For two people to be inside one body?

That moment with Elaine flares in my mind and I get an idea. A way to bring the original all the way back. "Wait here." Rushing into my room, I open my desk drawer. The blue petal sits on my pile of pens and paper. "Malika, here you—"

I burst into the hallway. She's gone. After I sulk back to my room and take a seat in my chair, there's nothing to do except exist before it's time to head to breakfast. Voices mutter outside my room. Stacey and Fran.

"You really think I should give him a chance?" Stacey asks.

Fran *hmm*s. "Why not? I mean if you like him, then go for it."

"He's in sixth form though. Isn't he a bit too old?"

"Old? Who's old?" a voice squeaks. One of Fran's minions, I guess.

"None of your business," Fran answers. "We'll see you at brekky. Stacey, look, okay. Life's too short, do what you wanna do. The both of you would be a power couple though."

The door pushes open and Fran steps inside.

"Ife."

"Fran, you—"

My words are swallowed by Fran's big smile. "Wild night last night on the hill. I saw you showed face. No hangover, I hope?" She smells like a fragrant garden.

"N-no?"

"No worries, darl." I didn't thank her for anything? "Now then, brekky? I could eat a moderately sized pony," Franny declares with a wide smile.

I'm not sure if she's joking or not, but I laugh anyway. So does Stacey, who's just there. Lingering. That's how Bee and I end up going to the hall with Franny and the gang and even sitting with them.

The conversation soon slips into gossip and stuff drier than yam. Mainly what's up with CottsLore and how there haven't been any new posts for a while now—*Louis*.

Bee catches my eye and the same concern is etched on her face. I shoot a quick text to our group chat.

> **Me:** Ben, you able to check on Louis?
> Got a bad feeling. Apparently CottsLore
> is down . . .

Ben responds almost immediately.

> **Ben:** Yeah, heard. See him now
> actually. He's just standing on
> the lawn in the sun like he's
> photosynthesizing.

> **Ben:** Someone asked him why
> posts weren't appearing on
> CottsLore anymore.

> **Ben:** He's crying

Ben: Apologizing for the hurt
it's caused.

Ben: Says CottsLore is dead. No
more posts. Crap, I think they
got to him anyway.

A shudder rakes me out from the inside. Fighting to take
deep, controlled breaths, I stifle my body's instinct to break
into trembles at the dining hall table.

Staring at the back of Mr. Morley's head is a good distrac-
tion from my guilt. Until I think about Malika, who isn't at
breakfast.

If I'd made it to the bus stop earlier, then maybe . . .

My appetite slips away and my crunchy cereal is now a
bowl of lukewarm mush.

Fran gets up to go and pour herself a drink.

"Being Franny's roomie doesn't make you anything," Stacey says. "You're still just an Urban Achiever."

I frown right back at her. It's too early for this. "What?"

Stacey's lips curl into a smirk as she ignores me and turns
to Bee. "Was bribery part of the online friendship course?
How much did you pay her to act nice, Bijal?"

"It was actually the same amount you paid Fran," I snap,
rolling my eyes. Stacey looks at me with her mouth open
like she didn't just walk into that. "You trying to catch flies
with your mouth open like that?" I add, surprising myself. If
Zanna were here, we'd knock shoes under the table twice. A
footshake to celebrate shutting Stacey up.

My gaze rolls back toward the back of Mr. Morley's head

that's now rising. *He's leaving.* I go to make eye contact with Bee, who's already giving me a look. She's seen him too. As I get ready to get up, a shadow looms over me.

"Ife. Bijal." A stony voice crackles through the air—Ms. Piddleton. I look up, expecting her to tell me off. About what? I have no idea, but instantly I'm thinking of every little thing I've done. She stares at me, as if considering my sentence.

Is this because I'm wearing Tesco socks that don't have the Nithercott emblem on it?

After an eternity she says, "Mr. Ingham spoke to me this morning. He'd like to see you now, please. He called it a pastoral meeting."

"Oh, okay, thanks," I murmur, pinching my lips together. Bee catches my eyes, knowing we're going to miss our chance to speak to Mr. Morley this morning. We'll have to catch him in physics.

Before leaving, Ms. Piddleton tells off Franny and her scrunchies for their nonregulation use of makeup. Her lips curl up into the faintest of smiles, I'm sure of it. But I quickly forget Darth Piddleton because the headmaster wants to see *us*.

What for?

I close my eyes and take a calming breath before entering Porthaven House. "Hey, Miss," I say to the receptionist, who's typing away on her phone.

She glances up and quickly sets her phone down. Giving me a great big grin, she replies, "Hey, Ife. Bijal. How goes it?"

"Alright thanks, you?" I reply, wondering how she knows our names.

"Yeah, not too bad, thanks. Bit of a slow day today. What can I do you for? Oh wait, you're here for Mr. Ingham, aren't you? His eight fifteen?" I nod. "Right, you both can head up. There should be some seats just outside his office. He'll call you in when he's ready for you."

"Thanks." I step past her desk and climb the fancy wooden stairs. I slow down as I near the top section, taking in the big board that's on the wall displaying past head boys and girls. The amount of head boys and head girls who were Butterworths is wild. I had no idea. Since the earliest year (1970), I count something like ten boys and fourteen girls. Except for one year—1980—where I see Mr. Ingham's name.

We get to Mr. Ingham's office and spot Ben already seated there.

"You too?" Bee asks.

He nods as we take seats.

A soft purr catches my attention. Hairless is on the seat next to me. I go to give the cat a stroke, and it flinches away from my touch. "Not a fan of me, are you?" I ask.

The hairless cat licks its paw before slinking off.

Several minutes go by. Whoever is in there with Mr. Ingham is taking their time. Laughing and joking. I can see two shadowy figures through the frosted glass.

Twiddling my thumbs, I get up and stretch my legs. There's an article pinned on the notice board across the hallway titled *Headmaster's Note*. There's a square picture of Mr. Ingham looking glum, just like the photo Elaine showed me. I start reading:

> *It hardly seems possible that Leon has been missing
> for nearly a quarter of a term. The day we learned of
> his disappearance still feels so fresh. But since then,*

our pupils have shown tremendous resilience and I am so proud of them.

The local papers have since stated Leon is unlikely to be found, given how long he has been missing. Simply put, they have given up. But Nithercott never has. Volunteers spend their weekends supporting the efforts of the Missing Persons Bureau. That includes myself, some of our own staff, several students, and many in the local community.

As we press on, I know that anxiousness is at an all-time high, making the days, the weeks, and the term feel so much longer. However, we have reason to keep going, like Jacksage and Zipley in The Curious End, *collectively we can get the Guffin down into the valley. It is not a task we wanted, but it has fallen upon us, and I am hugely proud of the way everyone in my orbit—students, parents, members of staff, and governors—are rising to the challenge.*

Yours ever,

P. Ingham

Heaviness threads itself through my bones. No wonder Mr. Ingham looks so glum in the picture. I can't imagine what it must be like for him. Having to both look after the school and at the same time handle not giving up on Leon.

There's movement just behind Mr. Ingham's door.

"Thanks for your time, and thank *you* to you and your staff for the wonderful job you're doing instilling the Nithercott way into these kids. Honestly. I mean that. I want you to know I was not one of the ones who ever doubted you. Your response has been stupendous," says a bald-headed man with a bottle of water in his hand as he emerges from the room. The warden. He reminds me of that really old prime minister. Winston Churchill. There's something off about him.

It's in the way that he moves. Like he's one misstep from unraveling.

Mr. Ingham appears soon afterward wearing a tight grin, his teeth white like pearls. "Always a pleasure to have you, Warden. What's happening around getting extra funds to subsidize the search?"

"Yes, yes," the warden says, gesturing with his cane. "Soon."

"But you said that last time, and at this rate—" He stops talking when he sees us. Gives us a hollow smile and finger. *One minute.* Leaning in, he whispers something to the warden, whose wrinkled, bulldog face sinks into a deep, rippling frown.

Mr. Ingham grimaces and quickly says something else. An apology, I guess. The warden's face rearranges itself into a big, slobbery smile. It's the ugliest I've ever seen.

The warden sizes the three of us up. "You students sure are lucky to have a head like Mr. Ingham. An astute man." He waves his cane with a flourish and totters away.

Mr. Ingham mutters the word *prick* under his breath while he stands by his open door. "Right. Ready when you are, you three." He gestures for us to step inside.

The inside is fancy with loads of gold-framed paintings on

the avocado-green walls. Big floral-print plant pots sit in each corner. No idea what the flowers are, but they're the prettiest yellows and reds I've ever seen. Behind Mr. Ingham's desk is a marble fireplace that he partially eclipses as he sits down in his seat. Adjacent are shelves bursting with plaques and medals and pictures with important-looking people. A shrine.

"Oh, that was my assistant's idea," Mr. Ingham says, latching on to my gaze. "It started off with just one picture. That one there"—he points to a picture with himself and the warden—"which was taken on my first day as headmaster. A way for me to celebrate the small wins and, well, it's taken on a will of its own." He stares at a medal with a satisfied smile before reaching out to adjust its position slightly. "I'm sure you're wondering why I've asked you all here today," he adds, sinking into his chair with a sigh.

I nod. *Yes, I am.*

"Don't worry, you aren't in trouble. I just wanted to give you three an update in terms of your findings after your escapade the other night. Oh, don't look at me like that. Contrary to CottsLore, we do actually review security footage every once in a while."

"Update, sir?" Bee asks sheepishly.

"Yes, I said I would ensure we looked into our sponsorship system. And it turns out you were right. There were irregularities in the way the Urban Achievers system and Orchid, especially, operated. He engaged in lying about the extent of the sponsorship, unprofessional behavior in mentoring assigned students, as well as unethical practices. We'll be launching a formal investigation and informing all the parents of Urban Achiever students."

He then goes on about how he will be checking in with all students who had gained sponsors through the program and ensuring they will now be sponsored by the school itself.

I know Mr. Ingham is well intentioned, but it's taking everything in me not to flare my nostrils or flatten my expression into a scowl. He has no idea how serious everything really is, and I know he wouldn't believe us if we told him.

"You three have been selected to help me pilot a new initiative. I'm eager to get your input. I'd quite like to avoid another instance of . . . well, Nithercott wants to do things right this time. With transparency and robust safeguarding in mind. I'm thinking of providing internships driven by the nature of one's scholarship or one's interest. What do you think?"

"That sounds like a good idea, sir," Bee states.

Mr. Ingham's face lights up. "Yeah? You think?"

"Absolutely."

"Great. It's been quite hard recently, but I have a good feeling about this." Mr. Ingham relaxes into his leather chair, and in the brief moment of still, he looks aged and weary. "This might be the light at the end of the tunnel Nithercott needs." He chuckles, explaining his plans and ideas further. "Well. I'm sure I've talked your ear off. You don't have to return to your first period. If you need anything—*anything*—do not hesitate to come up to my office. And if I am not in, just leave a message with Janice downstairs."

On our way out, I lock eyes with Ben for a split second. His eyes are all puffy, and it looks like he's about to say something, but he just looks away with a weak smile.

"You okay?" I ask.

He nods at me, his eyes hollow. He's anything but okay, and I hate that he's pretending.

I stride up to him and get on my tiptoes so I'm at his eye level. "We'll find Leon," I declare. "Whatever it takes."

His pinched eyebrows don't relax as he lets out a hard sigh. Then a shallow nod as he heads off. Predictably, Bee takes Mr. Ingham up on his offer of skipping the first period so she can spend time in the library. She wants to see if she can find out anything useful. She thinks maybe there are patterns we're not seeing. Before she rushes off, I ask her how she's feeling.

"On top of the world," she replies dryly.

"Brilliant," I say, beaming. "Good to see you're finally getting the hang of sarcasm."

Bee sticks out her tongue and heads off.

All the way back to my room the only thing I can think about is what I can do.

We know the *who*: The Changing Man. Orchid Green. A therimorph.

We know the *what*: real students being replaced with biological replicas—clones.

We think we know the *why*: to give students to buyers who find their loneliness appealing.

What's missing are the practicalities. The *how*.

I need to clear my mind.

Grabbing a scrap piece of paper, I fix my eyes on my lamp and, without lifting my pencil or glancing down, begin to draw.

A sudden yawn overtakes me. First, a power nap.

When I collapse onto my bed, I let out a great big sigh. I nestle my head into my pillow, roll over, and fall asleep.

My eyes fly open. A fit of coughs erupts from the window. I sit up and crane my neck and see someone in a Nithercott uniform dashing out of view. The sudden urge to climb out the window and follow overwhelms me, but it settles quickly when the smell of cigarette smoke wafts in and I hear a teacher telling off a student.

Slowly, slowly my eyelids close and I drift.

My phone buzzes, and with tired eyes I look at my screen before sitting up quickly. It's a message from Bee.

> **Bijal:** Where are you? Ur late to
> history? I told the teacher you had a
> meeting with the headmaster x   *now*

"Ah, fudge, fudge, fudge." Scrambling out of bed, I grab my blazer from the back of my seat and rush out the door. There's a tug and the tearing of fabric. My blazer pocket snagged on my door handle.

I'm going to have to take it to the uniform shop to get it sewn back up. Knowing Dad, he'll dock it from my pocket money. *Sigh*. At least the walk to the tailor's means time to scroll socials. A post from Louis denouncing his past actions stirs my curiosity.

I land on the now dormant CottsLore page and the way . . . I can't. Stop. Reading . . . fills me with slight shame while I wince, grimace, and shake my head at other people's shamelessness.

One of the posts catches my eye.

> *Someone spread gossip about **Zola** in **year 8***
> *listen yeah, i swear Z is a villain—all tht nice stuff he has is DEFO stolen. & I know where-ish he keeps his stash. his lair is sumwhere behind the pavilion. Do ur part and get hunting!*

My eyes grow wide. *I need to do my part.* And I know just the place to start.

I fire back a quick reply to Bee, making an impulsive decision.

> Overslept 😃 Going back to Butterworth's hideout. Be back for physics & Mr. M 🤜 🤛

I head out of Beeton and veer off course. Phone buzzes.

> Why???

> Hunch. I reckon Butterworth knows all about CM's hotspots

> Oooh, good idea! Stay safe!

> Thx! Will try x

CHAPTER 22

BEYOND THE BOUNDARY

'm really doing this. I half run, half skip, putting a timer on my phone. I need to be back before my next lesson.

My thoughts are disrupted by the tangy smell of weed. There's someone in the bushes to my left, smoking. On school grounds? They have no fear. I don't look because it's not my business, and I walk quicker.

"Hey! Hey, wait up!"

Ben. I turn to see him running after me. "Shouldn't you be in class?"

He takes a long drag. "Right back at you. Wait. Your blazer. You're going to the uniform shop?"

"No," I say. "Back to Butterworth's hideout." I continue walking, but he grabs me by my wrist. I snatch it away and snap at him. "Don't you ever do that again. What the hell is your problem?"

"Jeez, relax. I'm sorry—sorry. You're right, I shouldn't have done that. I just—but why?"

"Why what?"

"Why are you going back there?" Ben folds his arms against

his chest. "We found what he wanted us to find. There's no need to go back."

"There's something I want to know," I admit. "I once saw Butterworth examining couples' corner, which was where I saw . . . what I saw. He must know where the Changing Man likes to strike."

Ben coughs. "Right."

"Ben, what's going on with you? You're not you."

"Ife . . . I just—What the hell is going on? Nothing makes scnse and . . . and I still can't. Leon. He's still out there. Alone."

I take a quick look at my timer. I don't have a lot of time. I grab his hand and squeeze it as hard as I can. Whenever I felt overwhelmed, Zanna would squeeze my hand. I don't have the words yet, but I hope it helps Ben. "Come with me."

"What?"

"Back to the hideout. Let's see if we can find out—"

I spot Ms. Piddleton and pull Ben into the nearest bushes.

Ben gasps. "What the—"

I clamp my hand over his mouth and whisper, "If she catches me, I'm screwed. I'm supposed to be in class right now." Slowly, I remove my hand. We wait for Ms. Piddleton to move on. But she's just standing there. Waiting.

And then an impossible voice rings through the air. Everything in me curdles like gone-off milk. *He should be dead.*

In the flesh, and looking very much alive and healthy, is Dr. Butterworth. Great big smile on his face.

". . . Ms. Piddleton. A pleasure to see you."

"Why did you call me out of my lesson, Alred?"

"I—" Dr. Butterworth freezes the same way Elaine did

back then. Frowns and then smiles. "I owe you an apology. I seem to have forgotten."

My heart sinks. *He's a replica*. The Dr. Butterworth I knew spoke slowly and measured and with a quiet confidence. This impostor sounds forced. Not quite sure how slow or measured to be.

Ms. Piddleton sighs heavily. "Did something happen?"

"I can a . . . ssure you. I am fine." Dr. Butterworth walks by her, leaving her alone.

Ms. Piddleton shakes her head before going in the opposite direction.

When she's gone, I turn to Ben. "Coming?"

"Nah." He snaps a twig beneath his feet. Determination swims in his eyes. *Good*. "I think I'm going to try and see if I can put together where Leon might be hiding out."

Saying our goodbyes, I make my way to the cherub. Halfway there, I stop suddenly and quickly look behind me. Nothing but yawning greenery. I look ahead and almost jump out of my skin. Hairless stares me down, its orange-ish eyes eerie as hell.

"You're far from home, aren't you?" I chuckle. It blinks at me, bored-like, and slinks off.

Get a grip, I snap at myself, even as anxiety billows like wolf-gray smoke through me, clogging my mind, throat, and nose.

I continue walking and my breath hitches. Slightly out of sync, I hear faint footsteps. When I stop and turn, the sound stops and there's no one there. When I start moving again, it takes a while for the offbeat footsteps to return.

I'm being followed.

"Not today," I say under my breath. I recite all the Bible verses I know about protection. I reach into my pockets, but I don't have anything that'll help me out. Taking a deep breath, I look around. Various scenarios play out in my head. *Orchid?*

My head shakes. There's no petrichor smell. I think about the coughing I heard earlier. What if it wasn't a smoker?

I don't think, I run. Faint footsteps build into loud, careless ones that hammer into the crinkled leaves. I don't bother looking back.

Moments later I realize looking back would have been pointless. Standing in front of me is . . . me.

My replica.

A childlike smile blossoms on her face as she tilts her head. She steps toward me. I step back sharply and her expression changes to one of hurt. Her fingers fidget just like mine, but the way she stands, and how she's drawn her hair into puffs are completely different. A chill zags down my spine. I'm looking at something that isn't *quite* me.

"You," I breathe. "Why are you here?" Louis's replica appeared when he was the one about to be taken. *Is it my time?*

Her smile makes my skin crawl. *Skin!* This isn't a dream . . . The detail is too real for this to be some sort of dream, and yet, it doesn't feel real. I don't think there's a word for the way my mind feels like a big bubble of gum. It pops when my replica speaks in my voice.

"I have waited a long time for this." My hands curl into fists and my replica laughs. *Is that what I sound like when I laugh?* "Don't worry, I am not here to take you."

I cock my head and frown. "You're not?"

"No." She wrings her hands. Her smile sets itself into a serious stare. "I came to warn you. Before it's too late."

"When is it too late?" I take a step toward her. This time it's her turn to take a step back. "Please," I rasp. My mouth is as dry as Domino's Pizza crust. "How long do I have left? And . . . and why are you telling me this? Wait, no, how are you here and what does he want?"

"He—"

A rustle from the bushes bunches my replica's shoulders by her ears. Her eyes dart around before settling on me. When we lock eyes, she fidgets and my stomach scrunches up. "Don't."

My replica doesn't listen. In the time it takes me to blink, she's already sprinting into the heart of the trees and bushes.

How long do I have left?

The question sticks with me like a piece of popcorn shell between two teeth, all the way to the cherub, where I follow its pointing finger to the hatch. Lifting it open, I clamber down the ladder and step into the unlocked hideout.

Shaking off the strangeness, I riffle through the piles of papers, looking for a shred of information about where the Changing Man operates. "There's nothing here," I grumble. I fling a wad of files onto the desk and accidentally send a teetering pile of stuff onto the floor.

A small but thick-looking raven-blue book catches my attention. I crouch down and pick it up. The title is in wonderful gold lettering—*A. B. VOL. 1*. It must have belonged to Butterworth.

I open it and read:

*This is a story without a satisfactory beginning.
In fact, there is no enjoyable middle either. There
is only the present.*

*Those are my thoughts when I consider the
entity that haunts Nithercott. I often look up at
the stars and wonder about fate. That I would
find my way back home. But not to any home I
knew. Not anymore. It's changed.*

*Strangeness is nothing new to me, of course.
The ministry has taken care of that. But creatures
that can alter their atomic form at a whim is not
"nothing new."*

*And that is what I crave. The things that
are beyond the boundary of understanding.
So here I am. Back home, in a sense. Some
might call it a coincidence I am back at the
very school that made me who I am. After all,
before I took this assignment, I had no idea it
was here. But when I chose, there was burning
conviction. I am sure now that in my choice,
there was providence.*

*This is our protagonist: a journeyman.
Nothing inherently special about him. That was
the unsatisfactory beginning, and unenjoyable
middle. Now, the present begins . . .*

What have I just read? My heart won't stop banging in
my ears. I flip through the pages and find illustrations and
notes and fact files. It's a treasure trove of information that

reads like a story. When I read that the replicas are made from animal parts, saliva builds in my mouth. The bird without a throat, the one-eyed fox, and boar without a heart flash in my mind. I feel sick.

"Volume one of how many?"

I check my timer. Barely have any time left. Pillaging the room, I find two more volumes and a business card. I hold my breath at the symbol that is striking against the white. A purple flower with a gold crown.

I turn it over.

MINISTRY OF INTERDIMENSIONAL DEFENSE
AREPO BRANCH
Command
+447700900698

Without hesitation I call. They pick up on the second ring but don't say a word. Just steady breathing.

"Hello?" I ask.

"Who is this?" The voice is all hushed tones and secrecy.

"I'm a student at Nithercott and—"

"Unfortunately, you've dialed a—"

"Don't you dare hang up. I know who you people are. You need to bring every person you can spare down here and end the Changing Man."

"I don't . . . follow? Is this a prank? You must have the wrong—"

My alarm goes off, but I ignore it. "You don't get to patronize me, like I have no idea what's really happening at my school. I don't care if you're not even in control of anything, but trust me when I say you *need* to listen to me. Dr. Butterworth is *dead*. There's no excuse to do nothing. So, get off your backsides and be useful." My breaths are ragged. My hands tremble. "Please," I add, breathing down the phone. "I-I'm next. I'm scared."

After a few moments the voice on the other end of the line sighs. "I'm sorry, I can't help you."

The line disconnects.

My eyes squeeze shut and I suppress the swear words that try to force their way out.

CHAPTER 23

THE GAME IS AFOOT

"What did you find in Butterworth's hideout?" Bee asks with big eyes as we take our seats for physics. She sniffs. "Wait, were you *smoking*?"

"Listen, I found something amazing." I show her Dr. Butterworth's journals. "And no, that's because of Ben."

Bee tilts her head at me. "Ben? Why were you with Ben?"

"He happened to be around."

"Cool," she says, pretending not to care, completely unaware of the way her face flushes. "Anyway. What's in them?"

"I'll tell you in a min, but . . . I saw my replica."

"You mean . . ."

I nod. "Yep. No word of a lie, she said, 'I came to warn you.'"

"Damn."

Mr. Morley slams his hand down on the table. The one with his ring finger. His signature move. "Christ, this isn't a social club, girls." In the same breath, he glares across the room. "Sort your top button out, Edwards," he barks at one of our classmates, making me jump. It's mad he's supposed to be the one person we can talk to about this.

I bring my voice down to a whisper. "It's just lots of facts and illustrations about the Changing Man. Like how the replicas are made up of animal parts—eyes, vocals, heart, etcetera. It's mad, but I think we can use them to come up with a plan."

There's silence as my eyes lock with hers. Then her lips curl into a smile. "Brilliant."

"Right?"

"We need to speak to Mr. Morley straight after this lesson." Bee scrunches up her face. "*You* should speak to him."

She's not making sense. "Why should I be the one to talk to him?"

Bee puts her hand up and answers a question before turning to me. "Honest answer? He terrifies me, and besides, don't you want to be the one to see the look on his face when he finds out you know his secret?"

"Fiiine," I huff, glaring at Mr. Morley. I notice for the first time his face looks like he's always on the verge of swearing at something or someone. Bee is right. I do want to be the one to tell him I know he's involved with the Ministry of Interdimensional Defense. I want him to feel small the way he made me feel small.

Just before the bell goes, Mr. Morley clears his throat and stands before the class. "Right, a brief note from me before I dismiss you to carry on with your mundane lives. Jesus, Perrie, will you shut up for one moment, please, thank you. As I was saying, a brief note from me. I shall not be present for the remainder of the term." For a moment, there's a flicker of sadness in his eyes. "I will be going on sabbatical, effective tomorrow."

I sit up straight in my chair. "What does that mean, sir?"

"It *means* I won't be your physics teacher for a while. Can't say I'll miss you all, because I won't. So, see you—maybe—next term. I'll enjoy the peace and quiet of my four walls."

He can't just leave. He's the only adult left who can help us. Dr. Butterworth *said* he would.

Mr. Morley doesn't dismiss the class. He just walks swiftly out the door without a word. By the time Bee and I realize we need to go after him, we're a step behind, fighting our way through the bodies in front of us spilling out of the classroom. Mr. Morley is long gone.

Bee whips out her phone and after a few taps says, "He'll be on prep duty, which means he'll have to stay for dinner." I am both impressed and weirded out at how she can find out pretty much anything.

"Catching him at dinner it is," I breathe.

The day goes quickly, and all I think about is my replica and the need to speak to Mr. Morley. Detention and prep fly by and soon it's time for dinner. The smell of schnitzel hooks me from a distance and reels me in until I hit a wall of boarders talking in their own groups. They haven't opened the doors yet, and if I'm this far back there's no guarantee there'll be any schnitzel left. Or that I'll be able to catch Mr. Morley. I *have* to speak to him. Even though it's schnitzel for dinner and I am *starving*, I know he comes first.

Time to get moving.

Convos start and stop and start up again. People gossip. Completely ignore my existence as I dip and weave through, jumping the line. It's kinda amusing. That's my superpower: seeing things clearly because *I* am not seen.

I'm almost at the pearly gates when my power fails. I don't know how, but it does, and an arm locks with mine.

"Roomie!"

All my energy is sapped away like I've just found out halfway through a drawing that the shading is all wrong. I stop myself sighing and perk up. "Hey, Fran."

"Heya," the pink scrunchies all sing back before their lead vocalist, Fran, steps close to me. "Where you going, love? Not cutting, are you?"

"Just—no, well yes. I was looking for you of course," I lie. "Hoping you'd do me a favor. It's schnitzel day and I don't want to miss out."

"Oh . . . yeah?" Fran's eyebrows jump up to the top of her head. "I guess you can jump in with us, then. If it means that much to you. Sit with us?"

"But I—sure," I answer, smirking at Stacey, who's glaring at me. The smirk's wiped from my face when I spot Malika gazing at her reflection.

With perfect timing, the jangle of keys has everyone looking up like meerkats. I'm not as near to the front as I would like, but I'm close enough that I'm confident I'll get a schnitzel before they run out.

"What's it gonna be?" Al asks, once I'm at the front of the line. Always the same question.

"I'll have the . . . schnitzel."

"Bold. True to form as always, Ife."

"Not having schnitzel on schnitzel day? What kind of degenerate do you think I am?"

"Yeah, yeah," he says, dishing my schnitzel, roast potatoes, and drizzling it in a creamy sauce. "And if hunger beckons—"

"There's always seconds!" I finish. A few of the kids look at me like the weirdo I am, but I don't care because Al is great. He's one of the few people in this place I wouldn't rub out if I could redraw everything in my image.

I take my tray over to Fran and her girls and sink into a world of mind-numbing gossip. My ears twitch when I hear Ben's name and I bulldoze my way into the conversation. "What was that about Ben?"

"Ooooh," they sing. Then Stacey pipes up saying, "Someone's keen."

Blood rushes to my face and heats up my ears.

"You and Ben up to no good, yeah?" Fran adds, smirking.

Clearing her throat, Stacey says, "We were just saying that he wasn't in today and it was so much more peaceful. You know? That boy can disturb the peace like nobody's business. I'm just curious, but would you say you're used to it?"

"Excuse me?"

Stacey plunges her fork into a stem of asparagus. "Oh, you know. Aren't state schools notoriously feisty?"

Feisty? "Not in my experience. I don't know if you've noticed, Stacey, but Nithercott isn't exactly rainbows and sunshine."

"Huh," she says with a tight smile. "I guess *some* people would disagree with that statement."

"Guess I'm not some people," I snap. A pause. "And while I'm—Hold that thought."

I'm forced to stuff the words down my throat because Mr. Morley is halfway out the dining hall already and I can't miss him. I don't even bother looking back at Franny and her scrunchies.

I practically throw my tray into an empty slot in the

trolley and break into a run. "Sir!" My hands thrust at the closing door as I chase. "Sir!"

He turns and it's subtle, but I see his face rearrange itself into his trademark scowl. Now that I know who Mr. Morley is, I can see it all now. He's playing a role. Just like almost everyone else at this school.

"What? Christ, speak up, girl. What is it?"

"I know who you are," I start.

"What the hell are you on about?" he blusters. "Ife. Look. I don't know what you're playing at, or who put you up to this, but my patience is running thin. So if you don't have anything to say, then—"

"I know you and Dr. Butterworth were working together," I say in one breath. I show him the business card I swiped from Dr. Butterworth's hideout. The angriness on Mr. Morley's face slips off and is replaced with a look of worry. But he doesn't say anything so I keep talking. "I need your help. Please. He killed Dr. Butterworth, I'm one of the next, but you probably know that. We need your help." I take a deep inhale of air. "If we can—"

"Come with me."

That's all he says. Seriousness invades his voice and his lazy posture straightens.

He turns away from me and I skip after him. "Where are we—"

"Not another word." His voice is a stencil knife, etching fear into my skin. I follow him in silence until we're in front of his car. He opens the door to the front passenger's seat and says, "Get in."

For a second, I think of refusing. But something in his face makes me trust him. I get in, even though I really don't want to. I watch him walk round and get in on the driver's side.

"Who else knows?" he asks.

"Only me, Bee, and Ben. No one else. I promise."

"Bee? Oh, Bijal, the know-it-all?" I nod. "Well, okay. This is less than ideal. I'm sorry, there isn't much I can do for you. If they've decided you're next, then you're next."

His bluntness sucks, and if my mum was here, she'd say he has a rotten attitude. "Are you serious? Dr. Butterworth was right. You really don't care about us."

His face is a watercolor of shock and interest, and I can't stop a smirk appearing on my face. "I—I do—but it's not— It's complicated."

"No it's not. I'm telling you now that we need your help. We need to do something. *You* and the people you work for need to do something. We need to stop the Changing Man. How is that complicated?"

"Christ. Okay, look. Dr. Butterworth was a stubborn man who wouldn't listen. And he is now *dead* because he bit off more than he could chew. Look, what's happening here isn't anything we can just stop." His words don't match the way his face grimaces. He doesn't even believe what he's saying. "Not right now at least. I know it's not what you want to hear, but that's what it is. We monitor and make sure the Changing Man doesn't overstep. We make calculated decisions based on risk."

My phone *dings!* I ignore it. "You *do* know what he's doing, right? Students are taken and replaced with replicas that have boar hearts and fox eyes. How is that not overstepping?"

"Yes, I'm well aware of Alred's conclusions, thank you.

But these matters require a bit of finesse, a bit of delicacy. We just can't go charging in all gung-ho. We have to consider the wider population's safety. The last thing we need is our foe instructing his replicas to go on a killing spree, which we are very much ill-equipped for. He—and the worst part is we don't know his face—is a bomb we have no control over."

I don't believe it. "We need your help—*I* need your help. We need to defuse the 'bomb' now." The silence is chalk scraping against a blackboard, until Mr. Morley decides it's enough. His nostril's flare as he starts the engine and backs out of his parking space. "Where are you taking me? What's your part in all of this?" Silence as he turns out of the school entrance and heads down Old Glossop Road. I don't say a word until he pulls into a secluded lane and the car rolls to a stop. "Are you finally going to tell me what's—"

"This is your stop," he states.

"Wh-what?" Words fail me as I process what he's just said.

Mr. Morley sighs. "I said this is your stop. Walk it off. Run it off, hell, skip it off, I don't care. Whatever you need to clear your head and drop this. I can't help you."

I glance at him. He's staring straight ahead and nibbling at his nails. Then I put it together. Dr. Butterworth's death. The sabbatical. *Coward.* "You're running away."

"Don't you dare tell anyone else about me, or this. Just leave it alone," he adds as I'm halfway out the car.

"Yeah, yeah." I slam the door on him and his uselessness. The moment I do, his tires squeal and he speeds down the lane. Shaking my head, I take a moment to check my phone. It's a message from Dad.

Good afternoon, daughter, and trust you
had a productive day. Next weekend I
have a surprise. We will be taking you
out for exeat weekend. We will stay at
the local Travelodge.

My heart levitates. I've missed them so much. But then
my joy plummets, realizing how useless Mr. Morley is. I glare
back at where his car just was. There's no way I'm leaving
this alone. If anything, it's only just beginning. Looking at my
phone again, I send a text to the group chat.

Me: Morley was useless. We need to
meet at the log

As I'm walking through school to the log, my phone
buzzes. And buzzes. And buzzes. I pick up.

"Hey, Zee, kinda in the middle of something right now,
what's up?"

"Nothing, stranger, just checking in. We've missed each
other the last few days. You been busy?"

"Yeah, you could say that."

"Good, and also I'm glad you're doing better."

"Better?"

"Yeah, I dunno you just sounded down last time we spoke,
and I'm getting some tangies out of it, but you're my bestie
and I always feel sad when you feel sad. I get it, moving
school's been tough. I understand. Also I'm only gonna say
this once, but not having you here has been tough for me too.

Especially as my whole life is now more or less in cardboard boxes."

Wow. "I had no idea, Zee, I thought . . . I thought maybe you were fine. Maybe you'd moved on from me or something. I—"

"Nah, don't be silly. You're my bestie. Anyone that's fine not seeing their bestie as much as possible is not normal. Plus, why should I have told you if you didn't tell me." She laughs. "Anyway, I was calling just to call so I'll leave you to it."

"Okayyyy and Jaffa Cakes."

"What?"

"I want Jaffa Cakes. I'm invoking our snack-for-feelings rule. When we catch up, we'll have a feast!"

Zanna snort-laughs down the phone. "You're so silly, but fine. See ya soon."

She hangs up. I close my eyes, my limbs suddenly heavier. "Miss you, Zee," I whisper.

When I finally get to the log, Bee and Ben are waiting for me and they're having a debate of some sort. Ben's playing with his lighter, flicking it on and off. When he spots me, he smiles.

"Hey, you look . . . healthy."

"Thanks?" I pull out Dr. Butterworth's journals. "It's up to us now. The ministry is useless and Morley's a coward. We need to come up with a plan to stop him taking me. To stop him taking anyone else." I turn to Ben. "To find out where Leon is." He nods. I hand a journal to each of them. "We're looking for anything that can help. Let's get cracking."

After a while of book-absorbed silence, we begin flinging

out useful tidbits at one another about the Changing Man that snowballs into a plan.

Ben: "Says here therimorphs have a visceral fear of fire. It appears to be an instinctive reaction that cannot be easily suppressed."

Me: "Explains why Dr. B had a flamethrower at Little Forrest then."

Bee: "True, true. Well, I know how to make a homemade flamethrower."

Ben: "Oooh, Dr. Butterworth did some tests on some therimorph matter. Sustained burning can cause irreparable damage to their cells."

Me: "What does that mean?"

Bee: "It means death by fire."

Bee: "Therimorphs don't like loud noises. Which makes sense. Remember those noises we heard at Little Forrest?"

Ben: "Oh yeah. Loud bangs always followed by squeals. I have a stash of fireworks that pack a wallop. Soon as we get a clear line of sight, we launch them."

Me: "Glorious."

Me: "Butterworth writes that the petrichor smell is actually part of the orange mist. It's what induces tiredness."

Ben: "Nose plugs!"

Bee: "Nose plugs!"

Ben: "He's getting hungrier according to this. It says that his attacks are now more frequent, distributed across Little Forrest and a patch of greenery known as couples' corner. Occasionally he will operate outside of school grounds, but these are few and far between."

Me: "We already know that Little Forrest is out of the question. So we need to stake out couples' corner."

Ben: "Sounds like a plan. Does it say anything about the conditions he prefers to make his move?"

Bee: "Uh, very good question. I actually know the answer to this. He acts on Thursdays."

Ben: "You sure?"

Bee: "Obviously there are a few anomalies, but nearly all incidents and reports and the dates in the journal are on Thursdays. It fits. He acts with clockwork precision according to Butterworth's notes. Verified by spikes in CottsLore activity over the next couple of days. He says as well that his theory is that Thursday is a special day to them somehow."

Ben: "Maybe it's their version of Throwback Thursdays, but like Thieving Thursdays?"

Me: "Ha! It's a bit more than thieving though, isn't it?"

Ben: "Abduction-and-then-murder-and-replacement Thursdays isn't alliterative."

Me: "I can't. We need to find a stake-out spot around couples' corner."

Bee: "Let's scope it out tomorrow, so we can be ready for next week."

Ben: "Till then, let's stay alert over this next week. Any signs of trouble SOS the group chat."

When we're done with the finishing touches to our plan, there's a fluttering in my stomach that builds into a jolt of excited energy. I say a silent prayer of thanks to God. For the first time since I've been here it feels like I'm standing on solid ground.

CHAPTER 24

FLAMES AND FIREWORKS

Next Thursday evening comes, and I can't believe nothing happened. The first couple of days after we sculpted our plan, we were on a knife's edge. *What if we got it wrong? What if we were waiting too long?* But thankfully we're still here, it doesn't seem like anybody's been changed (we've been on the lookout), and we could not be more ready.

We found the perfect vantage spot relative to the growth of speckled grass, blue flowers, and translucent mushrooms. From here we should see the Changing Man coming. Bee's made some makeshift flamethrowers from spray cans and lighters and other bits and bobs. When she gave a demonstration, it was *wow*.

All that's left to do is wait.

The moment Bee goes to take a leak, her bag of sweets rustles as Ben grabs a couple of tangies and throws them into his mouth.

"She's going to know you took some." His fingers tap against his thigh. "You alright?"

He reaches for the bag again but pauses. "Nervous."

"Ben Small being serious for once?" I suddenly look up at the sky and gasp.

"What?"

"Pigs. Flying."

Ben laughs. His mouth opens to clap back, but no sound sprouts because he's smiling widely. "Leon said to me once, 'Benny, when you shut yourself off like that, it's like you're going through life wearing damp socks and turning down everyone who offers to give you a fresh pair.' I didn't really listen at the time. Thought he was just being weird. But I should have. One scholarship review, a few suspensions, and two mad girls later, I'm thinking he was onto something."

"He definitely wasn't onto anything by calling you Benny though. Or using a sock analogy. I don't get it."

"Well," Ben starts with a smirk. "Creativity wasn't his strong suit. Logic was. Anyway, *you've* been going through Nithercott in damp socks and it's time to be honest with yourself. Take our offer at a fresh pair of socks, Ife. I know you want to."

For a second, I don't say anything because it feels weird for Ben to say my name, let alone say it in that way. Like he cares.

"I—I dunno what you mean. But"—I bite my lip, knowing how silly I'm about to sound—"what if they don't fit, or I'm allergic, or they feel funny, or—"

"You're over-metaphoring. Bottom line is, Bee and I don't bite."

"Oh."

"Get it now?"

"So how do I . . . I have a stupid question. How do I take them? The socks, I mean."

Ben lets out a chuckle. "Honestly, the best answer, which

is also the most unhelpful answer, is it depends on the person. How you go about taking the socks is up to you."

"You're right." I nod.

"See?"

"What's he right about?" Bee asks while walking back to us, dousing her hands in hand sanitizer.

"He's right about being unhelpful." I ignore Ben's eye roll and think about the socks metaphor. *Ben can be wise when he wants to be.* "Bee," I say confidently. "I'm . . . socks."

Her eyebrows jump up and she tilts her head before bubbling into laughter. "What?"

"Wait, no. I—What I *meant* to say was that I accept your socks."

"You're not making sense," she says with a frown.

"And that's okay," I answer, turning to Ben. "It's metaphorical."

He shakes his head. "I don't think that's entirely what—"

Whatever point he's about to make dies in his mouth and for good reason. *Someone's here.* Sure enough, a girl leads a lanky boy, holding his hand. When she gets closer, I realize it's Stacey. She leans against a tree and pulls him in for a kiss, but he steps back.

"Troy?" Stacey says. The lanky boy stands still, looking over his shoulder. "What? You're suddenly scared now? You're the one who suggested we come here."

"No," the lanky boy answers.

"No, what?"

I sit up straight and glance at Ben and Bee. Surely, they can smell the subtle, wet-pavement smell too. That's Ben's cue to get the fireworks ready.

"This was a mistake." Stacey sniffs, finally noticing the smell thick in the air. "What's that smell? And why is . . ."

The air begins to shimmer, marbling with swirling orange mist. But where is he? I don't see him behind any trees or anything.

"It's okay. You're okay." The lanky boy smiles as Stacey yawns. Everything slows and sensations fade. I blink. Behind his eyes there's a faint, growing glow. *It's him.*

I text Ben.

NOW!

Are you sure? I don't see him and we need to be sure. If we're wrong, we're finished.

Because it's the boy! I'm sure. Do it. Trust me.

The moment I hit send, Stacey crumples to the ground like a bag of yams. The soft *thud* is followed by the fizz of fireworks screaming high above. Seconds later there's a barrage of explosions as the raven-blue sky is splashed with brilliant flashes of light.

The Changing Man claps his hands to his ears and staggers around like my uncle Olu after he's had too much to drink. I squeeze Bee's hand and plug my nostrils. She does the same.

"Here we go," I murmur.

We spring from the bushes and charge at the Changing Man, who glares in our direction with large eyes that glow faintly through the orange mist. The air around him shimmers and thickens. I wrinkle my nose when I smell petrichor seep steadily through my nose plugs.

Another round of fireworks color the night with pulsing light and a thundering *BOOM*. The Changing Man lets out a strangled gasp, dropping to his hands and knees. The edges of his form seem to flicker.

I shake the spray can and press my index finger down on the trigger. A burst of flames roar toward the Changing Man like a baby dragon breathing fire. Bee roars fire at him too. It's not nearly as impressive as Dr. Butterworth's flamethrower, but the Changing Man cowers all the same, his hand raised to defend himself, illuminated by the glow of his eyes.

Ben joins us, and the three of us force him scampering back, back, back.

Until he's pressed against the trunk of a tree. Right where we want him. All that's left is for Ben to tie him up so we can find out what he knows about Leon.

As Ben approaches with the rope, a high-pitched squeal from the therimorph sends the three of us reeling backward. My flamethrower drops to the ground as my hands instinctively fly to my ears.

When I look to the Changing Man, I'm crushed with a fear that squeezes my heart like it's a stress ball.

The Changing Man flickers into a deformed version of Orchid before shuddering into the shape of a young boy. Except he's unfinished. Half of his face is honeycombed like a natural sponge and one of his eyes is large and bug-like. There are no whites to it as it glows. My skin prickles all over and my breath quickens.

I blink, not sure what I'm looking at. Maybe the fire affected Orchid's ability to change into his commanding self?

Suddenly it dawns on me that I'm wrong.

The way the boy stands. Scared almost. It's as if it's a different person entirely and not Orchid in a different form. The unfinished boy doesn't move. Keeping his glowing amber eyes trained on us.

Amber? I frown and then I understand. It doesn't feel like Orchid because it *isn't* him. *There's more than one*, my inner voice screams.

I glance at Ben and Bee, who are rooted to the spot like me. None of us dare reach for our makeshift flamethrowers. Then the unfinished boy talks. Cold and breathy.

"All that we do has never been personal. But when your times come, I am going to enjoy watching you suffer. Very, very much."

"What the fuck are you?" Ben calls out.

My insides squeeze. My clothes and shoes are way too small. *Ben!*

There's no answer. Instead, the unfinished boy runs awkwardly away into the dark of night. I let out a breath and grip Bee's arm.

"That wasn't Orchid," I rasp.

"But—"

I shake my head. "Soft orange. Orchid has magenta eyes when he's in his therimorph form. Whoever it was we saw just now, when they shifted within their therimorph form, the eye color didn't change. They stayed amber. And they said *we*." I draw a deep breath. "There's more than one of them."

"Orchid isn't operating on his own," Ben says blankly. He spins his lighter in his hand without glancing down.

Bee sucks on a tangie, shaking her head in disbelief. "Holy—"

"Smokes," I finish. An idea strikes. "How do you two feel about spending exeat with my family?"

"I'm in," Bee answers.

"Why?" Ben retorts at the same time.

"Because we need a new plan and we need to be able to plan in relative safety. We really pissed them off tonight. But we didn't get what we wanted. We didn't *kill* them."

"K-k-kill?" Stacey asks from the ground, propped up on her elbows.

"You passed out and we happened to be around." Ben holds out his hand.

Her gaze flicks between the three of us, clearly lost. She doesn't take Ben's hand. "Where's Troy?"

"Not here," I answer dryly.

"Oh." Stacey gets to her feet. Dusts herself. "Well then, thanks I guess. For sticking around. Uh." She scurries off and it's just the three of us.

I clear my throat. "We're safer together."

"Fine," Ben grumbles.

With a great big yawn, I step into the video call booth early Friday morning and call home. I'd rather do this from bed, but the Wi-Fi in Beeton has been acting up and my data's running low. It takes a few seconds before I'm staring up

Dad's bottomless nostrils. It's like they've been shaded in with charcoal. Finally he adjusts the screen and it's him and Mum sitting together on the sofa in front of the TV. They're doing their best *Gogglebox* impression. Mum's not even paying attention to the call. Her eyes are glued to the TV screen.

"Hey, daughter," Dad says with a wide grin. "Talk to me."

"How are you, Ife?" Mum chimes in, finally noticing I'm here.

"I'm alright, thanks," I reply. "How are you both doing?"

"We're well, we thank God." Mum loves answering for both of them. "Excited to see us this weekend?"

"Of course," I say with a smile. "About that, I . . . Well . . . I was hoping that—"

"Speak up, Ife, we can't hear you," Dad says.

"I was just saying that . . . th-that could Ben and Bee come stay with us for the exeat weekend . . . Pleeease?"

"Who is Ben?" Dad asks, ignoring Bee. "Is he your boyfriend?"

I see Mum's back straighten as her focus is ripped away from what I know is CNN. "Eh? Boyfriend? What do you mean boyfriend?" She's staring so seriously at the screen I'm expecting her to reach out through it and flick my ear.

"No! He's just a friend. Bee too. She's a girl in my class who's helped me a lot. But they need somewhere to stay this weekend. Please. It's important."

Dad *hmm*s deeply. "Okay . . ." That's his way of saying *I'm not buying it.*

"Please, Dad. Pleeease."

"But why? Why is this important to you?"

"Because I'm trying hard to make friends, and you always

complain that my friends don't come to our house. And you never meet them." I sigh and go for my secret weapon. "Please, Dad. They're really nice and won't be any trouble. Ben's an entrepreneur." All I can hear in my head is: lies, lies, and more lies! But if there's one thing about my dad, it's that he loves anything business and I can see it in his face. He's interested. "Bee is so sweet too. You'll love her."

Mum scrunches up her face. "Ife, that's not nice. We're coming today to take you out. So we can spend time with *you*. This is not nice at all. Be honest: Is something going on with you and Ben?"

"No, Mum," I drawl, struggling not to roll my eyes. "He's just a friend."

All of a sudden Mum and Dad switch to Yoruba.

"Ṣé ọ̀rẹ́ Ìfẹ́ lè dé sí ọ̀dọ̀ wa tí ó bá wá kí Ìfẹ́?" Dad turns his head to face Mum.

She shakes her head with her eyes closed. "Mi ò gbà."

"Kí ló dé?"

"Mi ò kàn fẹ́ ni," she replies, shaking her head even harder.

Dad grimaces and squeaks like a mouse. "Àh, f'ara bale, mo ti san owó yàrá fun."

"Nígbà wo?!"

"Má bínú aya mi, ọjọ́ mìíi, màá bá ẹ sọ́ kí n tó ṣe é." Dad wraps his arms around Mum and puckers his lips while she squirms in his grip.

"Stop it. Ah, ah, Dotun, *stop*!"

I pick up fragments of meanings, but when Dad says "aya mi," *my wife*, in his sweetest voice, I know I've won. Dad looks at me as if he's suddenly aware I'm here.

"H-hello? Ife."

"Yeah, Dad?"

"They can stay with us for the weekend. But we need to talk to their parents about it, okay? Can you give us their details? Thanks."

"Yeah, I will." My face is super calm, but I'm holding my breath and tensing my stomach. I can't break into a smile, in case they snatch away the good news. "Alright, well I'm going to go now and send you their parents' details. Have a blessed day. Bye!"

I hang up, let myself do a little jig, and immediately text Ben and Bee, before putting my room as the next destination in my internal sat nav.

I shove open the door to leave and thud into a body that cries out in a squeal. It's Franny. And I've knocked her over. Off to her left her handbag's the wrong way up, spilling its textbook guts.

"OhmyGod. I'm so sorry. Are you okay?"

"Splendid," she groans. Her words are coated in sweet frosting, and her smile is all sunshine. "I need to text and walk less. Help me up, will you."

"Of course." I scramble to help her to her feet. When she reaches out her hand, I take it and flinch. A visceral feeling of being watched overwhelms me. An instinct. I look around, trying to see if I can spot where my replica is hiding, if she's here.

"Everything okay, babe?"

"Um, yeah. Sorry, sometimes I get this weird feeling." I help her up before I drop down to shove her textbooks back into the Hermès stomach. My hands tremble as I pick up her handbag and hand it to her. "Sorry again."

I don't wait for an answer as I'm on the move again. I just want to get away from there. The hope and excitement I had has been rubbed out. Replaced with panic as I find it difficult to breathe. This is way too much! I pump my arms faster, trying to outrun this blanket of fear.

By the time I reach my room, I'm huffing and puffing. Lord, I'm really out of shape. I hope my lungs know how pathetic they are. An image comes to my head, and I imagine myself sketching angry lungs, complaining about me making them work so hard.

I step inside and start packing for exeat. My phone buzzes. It's from Dad.

> ... looking forward to seeing you later
> today 🏃

CHAPTER 25

IMPOSTOR

The end of the day comes at a crawl. But I'm glad it's finally here. We all are.

Ben, Bee, and I are perched on the low wall that curves around the front of the school flagpole. Waiting in silence for my dad. He shouldn't be much longer. Any. Minute. Now.

I'm still thinking about last night.

"Thanks," Ben says, crumpling the awkward silence. "I know I wasn't initially keen on it, but you didn't have to. Mum passes on her regards. Says she's glad she can finally have a weekend all to herself. Free from my supposed 'moping.' So . . . thanks."

I let myself smile. The boy actually has some form of manners. "You're welcome. As I said before, safer together. Even if you are the most annoying person ever." I look between Ben and Bee. "Plus, this will be a great opportunity for us to plan something spectacular. We've got to find a way to finish this."

Bee grins. "Defo going to have to leave out stuff when my parents ask for a full debrief after this weekend."

Getting Bee's parents to agree was touch and go. They wanted a whole itinerary—times, locations, links, foods expected to be eaten, etc. Things my parents definitely didn't have. Thankfully we share dads who love dead jokes, and mums who know the struggle. Mutual respect was quickly established. Terms were agreed and negotiated. And here we are.

We settle into silence for a few more minutes before the car Dad's driving chokes its way onto the school grounds, stopping with a squeak. I do not trust this car one bit. It's a death trap. He rolls down the window and he's wearing the biggest grin. "Hey, guys, hop in." The boot pops open.

We put our stuff in and get in the back. Just as I'm about to strap in, Dad chuckles.

"So. Am I your driver now?"

I've heard that chuckle too many times to know it's a varnish covering the coldest of threats. I smile at my friends and say I'm going to keep Dad company at the front.

"Cool," he says, all smiles again.

The conversation during the ride is completely one-sided. Dad keeps telling all these jokes and stories that are so unfunny and boring I feel bad for Ben and Bee. They aren't used to such an onslaught.

"Here we are," Dad finally announces as he turns into the parking lot for a Travelodge.

"And this is your room, Ben." Dad clears his throat. "It's adjoined to ours. Just knock if you need anything. Here's your room key. Don't lose it, otherwise they'll charge me and then I will have to find you and make you pay me . . . with

275

interest." Dad's laugh makes me cringe as I watch him hand it to Ben. "We'll come get you for dinner, okay?"

"Sounds good."

Ben disappears into his room and it's just me and Dad and Bee. He's grinning at me.

"So—"

I cut him off before he can launch into cringe territory. "Don't. You always do this."

"Do what? What do I always do?"

"I'm not doing this," I mutter, knocking on the door.

"Who is it?" Mum sings from behind it.

"It's me," I reply. The door opens, and Mum is looking up at me with a smile that reaches her eyes. My heart does cartwheels of joy. I've missed her so much. I have the urge to sketch her, but the thought is squashed by her big hug.

"Praise God for your safe arrival! We've missed you. Come in, come in. Go say hey to Ayo, he's just getting ready for bed. Nice to meet you, Bijal."

Behind Mum, Ayo pokes his head from behind the corner of the wall. He's got a cheeky smile on his face. "Ife," he giggles, saying it like *If-ayyy*.

"How's it going, bumblebee?" I reply with a grin. When I take a step toward him, his smile gets wider. "You're getting more teeth!"

He notices Bee for the first time and waves at her before pointing to his crowning tooth. "Ook! Toof!"

I stretch my mouth with my index fingers and bare all my teeth. "More teeth," I counter, and Ayo giggles so hard he falls over. It's nice to be appreciated for the funny person that I am. Scooping him up in my arms, I let our noses kiss. "I've missed you, bumblebee," I whisper. He burps in response.

Wonderful.

"Right, let's sort your hair out," Mum says to Ayo, taking him from me. He wiggles about before snatching Mum's wig off her head and throwing it to the floor. It takes everything not to laugh at his unprovoked violence on her Brazilian-haired bob.

I bend down to pick it up and rise to Ayo's tears. I bet all Mum did was look at him crossly. That usually sets him off.

The moment becomes a still-life portrait, and I take in all the small details. Ayo's squished face, Mum's *don't test me* face. A bag of peanuts propped up by a bottle of Schweppes Tonic Water. No doubt Dad's.

A big palm on my shoulder shakes the stillness to life. "You good?" Dad asks.

I'm on the verge of tears and I can feel one stinging my left eye. But I hold it in. "Yeah, all good, thanks."

"Good, good. There's a Nando's round the corner. Up for that?"

"Always."

We catch up a bit (Bee gets grilled of course), and make fun of the faces Mum's pulling as she does a wall squat. She says it's to help her as she nears midlife. I have no idea why she'd willingly subject herself to torture for the sake of something she doesn't have to think about yet.

Once Dad and I bond over Mum's pain, he goes on about the politics in America like he's USA born and bred. He literally has no connection to the place. He's never been and doesn't have any family out there. I think he secretly hopes for a USA acceptance letter or something.

"You know, I think they need a better foreign policy, because if you think about it—"

"Dad, we're gonna go hang with Ben." Before he can protest, Bee and I are already moving toward the adjoining door. "Let us know when it's time for dinner," I say as we step into Ben's room.

"Ben?"

"By all means, don't knock on my account," he responds. He's doing his hair in the mirror. Who knew making your hair look a ruffled mess required actual effort. When I don't say anything, he looks our way. "Yeah?"

"We should brainstorm," I say. "I wasn't joking. If we're going to put a stop to this, we can't go one at a time. We need to nip this in the bud. We need to think *big*."

"Big?" Ben asks with a smirk. "How big are we talking?"

"I'm talking about driving out the Changing Man, and whoever else with him, for good." My fists clench as I think about putting a stop to everything. "So, any ideas? I'm thinking we could find a way to expose them. I don't know how, but that'll force the ministry to act. They won't have a choice."

Ben runs a hand through his hair. "No, that'll just make things messy. I think we need to get rid of them ourselves. I don't trust the ministry. We should just set them all on fire. A good place to start would be—"

The door opens and Dad steps in. He looks at us, his frown lines out in full force. They soften and he bursts into a gap-toothed smile. "Let's go."

As he opens up the doorway farther, my attention is caught by what's behind him. I see the impossible. My legs are deboned and I nearly tip over and stumble into Ben's chest. Tears well in my eyes.

"Easy," he responds, steadying me.

"Ifeee!"

Zanna rushes toward me. The first thing I think is that she's changed. She's so much more put together. I clench my teeth, willing the burning feeling in my chest to fade. The Zanna I left always had something out of place. A hair bow that was frayed, mismatched earrings, that sort of thing. I push away the dumb thoughts because when we do our footshake, I know it's still her.

"Surprise!" Zanna exclaims, wrapping her arms around me.

CHAPTER 26

CONFRONTATION

t's so confusing. We're sitting in Nando's close to the windows at Dad's request. He wants to catch as much natural vitamin D as possible. Mum's at the hotel watching Ayo.

And Zanna's really here.

"So," she starts, "how have you been? What's the goss? Is he your . . ."

"No, he isn't. Just a friend."

"What's up, Fae? Why are you staring at me like that? You seem . . . off?"

Fae is her nickname for me. I love how it means fairy, even if it is also the second syllable of my name when said incorrectly. An inside joke that makes my insides lift. I exhale. I've missed her so, so much. "I—but—"

Zanna spears a piece of broccoli from my plate and brings it to her mouth. My stomach churns and alarm bells ring. The Zanna I know hates broccoli with a passion.

"Got you," Zanna says, stopping short of putting the piece in her mouth. My heart deflates all at once. *Not funny.* "Is everything alright?" I nod, forcing a smile. "Well, before you glitched, I think you wanted to ask about why I'm here? It's called a surprise. I'm surprised you didn't catch on."

"Huh?"

"I gave you *hints*."

"When?"

She whips out her phone and shows me several messages—namely the GIFs with no context—that are about as close to being classed as actual hints as Jaffa Cakes are as close to being classed as actual cakes.

I'm about to tell her what I think when I have the urge to pee. "S-sorry. I—I need the toilet."

On my way back, I see movement in the front windows, and out the corner of my eye, I think I see my replica. *Why would she follow me this far?* When I take a step toward the entrance, I thud into the path of a Nando's waiter on a mission.

"Are you okay?" the waiter asks.

"Y-yeah." I nod and look past him at the window. But there's no sign of my replica, only a young Black girl on the phone. I shake my head and walk back to my seat.

"Zanna was just telling us about how before art you thought about dance," Ben says the moment I slip into my seat. "Can you confirm these allegations?"

My face becomes a radiator. "Seriously, Zee?"

She shrugs, totally unapologetic. "What? We *bonded*. These guys are great."

"Ditto," Bee singsongs.

Well, it's good to see everyone getting on so well. I clear my throat. "Yeah, I, uh, can confirm. B-but I don't dance anymore."

"So," Ben starts, "if I play some fire tunes, could you still tear it up?"

"First, never say 'fire tunes' or 'tear it up' again. Embarrassing. Second, I don't dance on demand. Third, I'm shutting this whole topic down."

Zanna lets out a tuneful hum. "So, anyone wanna see a video?"

"Show that video and I will go nuclear," I snap, before Ben or Bee can answer. "Don't think I haven't got any ammo."

Zee and I stare at one another like that Diddy GIF until the moment is snapped by our laughter. *I've missed her too much.* Conversation between the four of us flows easy like the brushstroke of a broken-in paintbrush.

Soon it's time for dessert. I order a Naughty Nata. The rest of the table goes to get some frozen yogurt from the machine. While I wait, I scroll through my socials but quickly get bored. Looking around the restaurant, my heart clenches when my gaze settles on the front window.

Curiosity wriggles in my stomach. It drags me to my feet and through the entrance into the crisp air. The breeze permeates my bones and helps calm me down. *In. Out. In. Out.* There's no petrichor smell. No distortion in the air. I think I'm safe. But there's also no replica. I look up and down the street.

Did I imagine it?

"Ife, what's wrong?" Zanna asks. She's followed me outside. "You've been odd the whole time. Did I do something? I was saving this for my big finale but"—she digs into her coat pocket and pulls out a mini packet of Jaffa Cakes—"maybe you're hangry? But for something not on the Nando's menu?"

"It's hard to explain."

"Ife, I'm not even really sure how to say this, but you don't need to act weird because you've made two amazing friends. Or that you're thriving. It makes me happy to see things are going well for you at Nithercott." The memory of magenta and amber eyes curls my hands into fists. "I know it's silly, but I was worried that you might . . . like, leave me behind or something. If that makes any sense? But you're the same Ife I said bye to!"

Despite how hard I try, I can't stop my cheeks bunching like puff puff and smiling as wide as I can. Zanna's wrong though. I'm not quite the same. Not after everything that's happened here, and that's okay. Because it's through the strangeness—being tried and tested in a lot of ways—that I've changed, and not because I let the school swallow me whole with its self-serving appetite.

"But there's something I want to know. So"—Zanna takes a deep breath—"I'm invoking triple truth. You remember what that is, right?"

The truth, the whole truth, and nothing but the truth. "Are you sure? Once you use it, that's it for the next decade. Zee, you sure?" I want her to question herself, but there's not a single bit of hesitation in her stare.

"I'm sure. Now tell me, what's got you so worked up?"

"I . . . I . . ." My words are gulped back down when I spot her. My replica peering out from around the corner. Her eyes suddenly go wide and she hides. *I need to speak to her.*

"Ife," Zanna says, snapping her fingers in front of my eyes. "I invoked triple truth; you can't hold out on me."

"S-s-sorry," I say, rushing off. "I promise you, I will explain everything. I just—I—"

Nothing I say will be good enough, so I give her a quick hug and rush off after my replica. I round the corner. At the end of the lane, she stands, as if waiting. She moves out of view and I chase after her.

"Wait!"

I follow her through narrow alleyways to a secluded bit of greenery until she stops with her back to me. "I thought you weren't going to follow." I can hear worry in her voice. The voice that is exactly like mine. Slowly, slowly, she turns.

"L-last time." I step toward my replica. "You . . . warned me. Why?"

"Because, I . . ." Her eyes grow wide before softening. "I wanted to. I . . . wanted to keep on learning from you. There was something about how you acted. I . . . I wanted to be around you. I didn't want to *be* you. Even though I knew it would make him upset. There are rules."

"Who would be upset? What rules?"

"Silly." My replica sighs. "I can't tell you. He'd find out and he'd get rid of me."

I step toward her. "Who?"

"Orchid." She says his name in a whisper, as if saying it too loud might summon him.

"Wh-what if I promise to protect you from him? Will you tell me more?"

"You"—she turns around with an innocent pout—"promise?"

"I promise."

She bounds toward me with a big smile on her face. She takes ahold of my hands. "Okay then. If you absolutely promise. He sets the rules. If we disobey, he says he will cut our strings. He says only he has the power to do that. He says we need to observe and learn, but we aren't allowed to be seen. Not until the *very* end."

"What happens in the end?"

"He—I . . . I replace you. That means there is someone in his world who wants you. I don't want to talk about it. The other rule: We must not go near certain flowers. These blue ones. They are dangerous."

"Because the original person comes back." She nods. "How does he do that? Make it so there's so much of the original person in the replica's body?"

My replica opens her mouth and nothing comes out. At least for a few seconds. "I . . . am not entirely sure. I've never seen it. But I do know that it requires both the original and the replica. And he added a new rule, well, an order actually. On the upcoming day of celebration, we mustn't cross over. Because that's when everyone leaves the heart."

"What day of celebration?"

"I don't know."

My head tilts. "How are you doing that? Acting so much like me?"

"Through watching. *But*, I've always felt like"—she gestures up and down with her hands—"this. Like this is who I am." She shrugs. "Oh, you're my first friend." She frowns. "What do friends do? I don't know."

I can't help but laugh. "Friends?" I shake my hands and snatch them away. "We're not friends."

"Ife—"

"Don't!" My anger bubbles like a fresh pepper blend over searing-hot oil. It's misplaced, I know, but I don't hold back.

"You're a fake. A puppet. There's no way I could be friends with someone like you."

My replica goes still. Rapid deep breaths escape from her mouth. Suddenly her knees buckle and her eyes are wide. She's trembling all over, tears spilling. She has no idea what's happening to her.

But I do.

She's having a panic attack, and the memory of the few I had in the days leading up to arriving at Nithercott is like a shard of glass to my gut. A million paper cuts. Thousands of splinters. I remember it clearly. How alone I was as I lay curled up on my bedroom floor. How my anger boiled over. How I lashed out. How I—

Guilt tightens my chest.

Without thinking, I go over to my replica's side and put an arm around her shoulders. "It's okay. We're going to do this. Take my hand." She does. "Breathe."

I stay with her like this until her breathing evens out and she wobbles back onto her feet. "Thanks," she says, smiling at me. I smile back.

"You're welcome."

Suddenly, her face gets serious. "Listen, you need to run away."

"What do you mean run away?"

"You can't stop him. They're a lot more—"

She doesn't finish as Ben barrels around the corner. "Piss off!" he shouts.

My replica scowls, then runs, faster than I can keep up.

"Ben," I gasp.

"Hey," he replies. Bee is by his side. "Your friend Zanna

told us you just ran away. She thought something was off and, well, seems like she was right. Thought I'd give a helping hand. You okay?"

"You dumbass!"

Bee flinches while Ben looks at me dumbstruck with his eyebrows lifted. "I—I thought—"

"She was about to tell me something important, and you went and scared her off. I was *calming* her down. Whatever." Taking a deep breath, I let go of my annoyance and look around. "Where's Zanna?"

"Enjoying the dessert I should be enjoying right now," Ben says.

We head back inside and finish the meal. Behind every forced smile, and fake laugh at Dad's jokes, all I can think about is how we're going to stop the multiple Changing Men and my replica's warning. I shake my head. Running away isn't an option.

Right?

❀

After dinner, I say my goodbyes to Zanna, who hugs me a little less tight and smiles a little less wide. All of me wants to explain everything to her, but the words don't come. I watch her leave with a sinking feeling in my stomach.

For the rest of the evening, Bee and I chill in Ben's room. We watch mind-numbing TV and avoid the elephant in the room. Choosing instead to debate if a fish is wet in water (it isn't, I don't care) and recasting our favorite movies.

"We need a plan," I say finally. "You were going to say something, Ben, just before my dad interrupted for us to head to Nando's."

"I was going to say we should set the whole place on fire," he says. "Little Forrest *and* Nithercott. Molotov cocktail it. That'll close the school down for good probably."

"It'll also have us staring at, like, at least three years in prison," Bee counters.

"Only if we get caught."

"*Ben*," I laugh. "We are not burning down the school. We aren't arsonists. What we need is to force the ministry to get involved."

"How would we do that?" Bee says. "And why haven't they acted before? Even Mr. Morley's run away. But I'm wondering what about if we *don't* burn anything but we expose the school and its celebrated Urban Achievers Program? Bring a massive media storm on their head."

"I think we have the same issues as involving the ministry," Ben says. "It wouldn't be Nithercott's first incident and they've weathered all previous storms. Which brings us full circle. Burn everything. That solves the fundamental problem."

This boy. "Ben, I—"

"Hear me out. We burn the school, lessons can't take place. They'll have no choice but to send us all home. We burn Little Forrest, and we burn their way in and out. I've been rereading the journals. Butterworth thought that's where their portal was and I think so too." Ben mimics dropping a mic.

He's right, but still . . . "What if we don't burn the school, but we only burn Little Forrest. The school isn't *really* part of the issue."

Ben sighs. "I guess that makes sense."

"Don't sound too enthused," I say to Ben. "Bee?" I ask. She nods. "Good."

"When?" Ben asks.

I remember what my replica said to me. "That's what we need to figure out. My replica said something about the *day of celebration*. That's when everyone leaves the 'heart.' I think by 'heart' she means Little Forrest. That's when we need to carry out our plan."

CHAPTER 27

DISASTER AND SWITCH

I spend the drive back to Nithercott on Sunday afternoon nibbling at the dry skin of my lips—thinking. Guilt somersaults in my stomach when I remember how I left things with Zanna. I make a mental note to drop her a message.

Be brave, I whisper to my soul. It's not by chance I'm here. Still, anxiety plunges into my gut when I think about if I'm actually ready for this. Squeezing my eyes shut, I try to grab at all the hope I can muster. Mum's favorite saying finds me: *There is nothing you can't handle in Christ.*

My toes curl in my shoes with renewed determination.

We know the *who* and the *what*.

We just need to work out the *when*. My eyes open and I take a deep breath.

"Tonight, at your secret spot," I tell Ben just before we drop him off on his road. He nods in agreement before saying bye to my parents and briskly walking down the street in the opposite direction to the car.

"You enjoy yourselves?" Dad asks me and Bee as he drives away from the curb.

"Yeah. I had fun," Bee says. I nod.

"Tired?" Mum follows up.

I *hmm*, because I'm too drained and angry to answer with words. But when Bee answers, it earns me a stern look of disapproval so I drag the words out of my mouth. "Yes."

The car pulls into school and it's so bittersweet. Like putting beetroot purple next to an earthy green. When I see my family next, everything will be over. One way or another. The invisible chill of fear sneaks into the gaps in my clothing when I step on the land mine thought that is: *What if I never see them again?*

". . . and don't forget, remember the child of whom you are," Mum says as we arrive at Beeton House. She hands me my weekend bag. "Because God never forgets those that are His."

"Thanks. And always." We hug. I could just crumble in her arms. I can feel the bones in my legs crack like dry paint. But they hold.

It's Dad's turn next. Pulling me into a big hug, he asks, "Are you okay? Your mum and I have been worried about you lately. How you're not replying to our texts and even how distracted you've been this weekend."

"I'm fine," I say, burrowing deeper into his arms. My eyes squeeze shut briefly to make sure tears don't escape, before opening again. "Honestly, I'm fine."

This can't be the last time.

He steps away and, after studying my gaze, nods. "Be good. We're going to miss you, but half term will be here before you know it! Keep up the hard work. I know it's not easy being away from home. I had to do the same when I was around your age."

"Really?" I reply in shock.

"Ah-*ah*!" Mum interjects. She kisses her teeth. "Ife, don't mind him. He thinks being sent to live with his uncle in another state because he was a troublesome boy counts as 'doing the same.'"

Dad just sticks out his tongue and Mum laughs. "Right," he huffs. "Let's get you checked in."

"Welcome back, Ife and Bijal. I hope you both had a good time away," Ms. Piddleton says from behind her desk. I do my best not to roll my eyes as I stare at her, adjusting my weekend bag that swings off of one shoulder. There's a hint of a smile, and I don't know why but it irritates me.

"Yes, I did, thanks." Bee's already zoomed off, and I'm halfway out the door when Ms. Piddleton clears her throat loudly.

"I . . . uh, hope you can see that I meant what I said. I hope you had a good time." A few seconds of awkward silence. "I know things haven't been easy between us."

My fists clench and I spin around, ready to speak up. Ms. Piddleton is leaning back now, a fully bloomed look of remorse on her face. The harshness of the words dies in my mouth. "Why do you pick on me?"

"Pardon?" Her eyebrows shoot up in surprise.

"Is it because I came from a state school?"

"I don't feel like that is a fair question, Ms. Adebola." There's a flicker of something unreadable. "Nor do I like what you are insinuating."

"What does that even *mean*? How is it not a fair question?"

She sighs. "Believe it or not, I know what it's like to not quite . . . fit in. It's never easy. I don't apologize for being hard on you. Because it's only ever been for you to fulfill your potential. I . . . don't want you to leave here feeling anything but ready."

"Miss, I—what are you on about?"

"Doesn't matter. Anyhow, I almost forgot I have some news. Nithercott Day is right around the corner. You've been given the honor of chaperoning on that day. Here's the brief." She hands me a single sheet of paper.

I read while I head back to my room.

Overview:

This coming Wednesday is our annual Nithercott Day, one of the most important dates in the school calendar. All pupils are expected to attend this special event, and parents, patrons, and local residents are also warmly invited to attend.

We request guests arrive by 10:20 A.M. ready for a 10:30 A.M. start. Refreshments will be served throughout this special event, as will lunch—on the back lawn (weather permitting) at approximately 1:30 P.M.

As a Chaperone:

You have been given the honor of accompanying patrons and local residents. As part of this responsibility, you are encouraged to engage with them as often as you can, and answer the many questions I'm sure they have. Please remember that in all you do, you are representing Nithercott.

CHAPERONE NAME: . . . . IFE ADEBOLA
DESIGNATED GUEST(S):. . . . . . MR. & MRS. WHITE

My designated guests have a color for a surname. It *could* be nothing, but one thing I've learned in my time at Nithercott is that there aren't any coincidences. The dots connect.

Nithercott Day must be the *day of celebration*.

It *has* to be. What's Bee like to say? When you get rid of all the possibilities, then whatever is left, however improbable, must be the answer. Or something like that.

My insides tremble as fear quakes through me. This coming Wednesday is days away. A part of me screams *get out!* But I take deep, deep breaths and recite a Bible verse about courage, trying to feel the power in every word, before I place the sheet of paper on my desk.

After unpacking my stuff, I hop into bed, where my fear returns and simmers. The moment when we saved Stacey and poked the bear in the process flashes in my mind. After a moment, I text Zanna.

Hey

She starts typing and then stops, leaving me on read. I wait a few minutes before sending through another message.

Sorry about running off like
that

Again she leaves me on read.

Maybe she's busy. *Or maybe she doesn't want to speak to*

me. The thought scares me more than being taken by the Changing Man ever could. I remember her invoking triple truth, and send her a five-minute voice note explaining *everything*. A couple of minutes later my phone is buzzing. Trust Zee to not listen to the whole thing.

"Hi." My mouth is dry all of a sudden.

"Are you serious, Ife? Don't play with me."

"I'm serious."

"You need to get the hell out of there. All of you do. Like right now."

I reach for a Jaffa Cake and stuff the whole thing in my mouth. I chew quickly and swallow. "I can't just leave," I say. "Besides, we have a plan."

"We? *We* better mean you and a whole damn army."

"Ben and Bee. Chill, we've got this. Trust me."

Zanna sighs. "Well . . . what are you going to do?" I walk her through our plan and how it's perfect. Loud silence buzzes in my ears. "You need more than that."

Not the reply I was expecting. "More? We're burning down their way in and out. What *more* is there?"

"It's all well and good burning their gateway, *but* if they're not there to burn with it, what's to say they don't say 'screw it, let's return the favor'?" I nearly choke on a Jaffa Cake because she's completely right. We didn't think about that. "So . . . I propose a disaster and switch."

"Disaster and switch?"

"It's like a bait and switch, except switch out the bait with disaster. You need to draw them in with a disaster—so set off their alarms. Make them think *what the hell is happening?*"

"Right, right. We could douse the whole place in, like, oil so when they arrive we light the match and then—flames . . ."

Sustained burning means death.

"Flames," Zanna repeats, then makes a raspberry sound. "It's going to be okay. Look, you know I love you and I miss you loads. So, I'm going to need you to be careful, okay? If it looks mad, then you need to just run, I don't care. You, Bee, and Ben."

"Love you too, and we will."

"And try not finish my Jaffa Cakes all in one go."

"How did you—"

"You're not subtle, I hear you munching." Zanna laughs. "Anyway, I gotta go. Mum's figuring out stuff for my going-away party. Be. Careful."

After she hangs up, I lie in my bed for a moment, thinking about everything she said. I don't hear it, but I feel it. The ticking of time. The jaws of menace closing in. I pop another Jaffa Cake in my mouth. Our plan has to work.

It has to.

The night is fresh as I walk through the school and make my way over to Ben's secret spot.

"You're late," Ben says. Then he shines the light of his phone at my eyes and laughs. "Not good enough."

"Sometimes I wonder about you," Bee says.

Ben shines the light upward across his face. The shadows are all wrong, settling in a way that pinches my chest. "Me too," Ben says. "Me too."

"I'm *late* because I had a bit of indigestion. But let's get down to it. I've got some updates." I explain how I'm now a chaperone, why I think Nithercott Day is when we need to act, plus Zanna's disaster-and-switch plan. "Well?"

"I, too, had a chaperone letter waiting for me at home," Ben says simply. "I guess Nithercott Day really is the day. Also, I endorse Zanna's amendment."

Bee holds up her hand. "Same and seconded! Gutted I'll be missing out on all the student stalls. I had my eye on the tarot one."

"A small price to pay for survival," I say. "So. When's the best time to carry out our plan on that day?"

"Probably shortly after Nithercott Day starts," Ben answers. The sparking of Ben's lighter pierces the brief silence. He takes a long look at the flame before extinguishing it. "We're going to be like lambs to the slaughter. We're up against something organized. At least now we know how to spot the enemy. We'll have to be ready, maggots. Nose plugs."

"Nose plugs," I affirm. "But, Ben, maggots? This isn't a wartime movie."

He shrugs. "I've also got some of those bangers you throw to the ground. Small enough to fit in your pocket. Doesn't make that loud of a noise, but might give us an extra second if needs be." Ben scrunches up his face and puckers his lips. "See you hellcats later."

CHAPTER 28

NITHERCOTT DAY

report to the front of Porthaven at 10:10, where the receptionist gives me a name tag to clip on to my uniform. She looks me up and down, lingering on my blazer's partially detached pocket.

It is what it is, my stare back says.

Once she's done judging me, she tells me my number. I make my way to stand with the others when she clears her throat suddenly. I turn.

"I've been told there's been a change of plan. When your number is called, please take your designated persons to"—she refers to a piece of paper—"the purple marquee. It's past the oak tree."

Standing with Bee and Ben, I watch as a procession of black cars drop off our designated person or persons. Numbers soon start getting called.

"So it begins," Bee says ominously.

Ben sighs. "Yeah."

"You've got—" Bee's number is called. "That's me." She's chaperoning the warden, who has a big, greedy smile on his face. She gives my hand a quick squeeze. "You've got this."

Ben's called, and his designated person is an elderly woman who trembles with every step. But the way she smiles with the hungriest of eyes cements her as suspect. He shoots me a smirk. "Godspeed."

"Number five!" The receptionist announces.

That's me.

Just like we planned, I set my phone timer for ten minutes, flipping the switch to silent before slipping it back into my blazer pocket. I step forward as another car trundles to a stop. The interracial couple I showed around a while back gets out. They smile and wave at me.

"Ife! It's good to see you again," the man says.

I plaster on the fakest smile I can, knowing the two in front of me could be therimorphs like Orchid Green. From here on out, I need to get away. "Thanks. You too."

"Have you been keeping up with your art?" the woman asks. She stands next to me—too close—and pulls out the sketch I drew of them the last time they were here. "Your talent is just so delectable."

Delectable? "Yeah, I have. And, uh, thanks. Shall we make our way to the back fields?"

I'm not ready for what's in store when we make it to the edge of the fields. The smell of cotton candy sweetens the air as students, staff, parents, patrons, and local residents flow in all directions. They stream in and out of gazebo tents that come in a multitude of colors.

This whole thing is an *event*. I pull out my phone to take

a picture to send to Zanna. My attention is captured by the stage that's being filled by an orchestra. There's a moment of still, and then they burst into the most soulful instrumental of . . . "'Redbone'?"

"Huh?" Mrs. White asks.

"N-nothing. I just recognized the song they're playing, that's all. I've been told to take you to the purple marquee"—I look in and around the large oak tree and point—"over there."

As we make our way against the grain, my stomach grumbles at least three times before we reach the marquee. Every time I think there's an opening for me to disappear, Mr. or Mrs. White are right by my side. A knowing smile on their faces.

The orchestra finishes "Redbone" just as we step inside to the empty space. No, that's not quite right. It's just that sound is swallowed in here.

I need to leave.

"Apologies, but I—"

"Why don't you have a seat," Mr. White says, cutting me off and gesturing to one of the comfy-looking chairs. "We have so much to ask you. Feel free to take off your blazer. It's quite stuffy here."

"No, that's okay. I really—"

My hand is taken by Mrs. White. "Such delicate, inviting hands. How often do you draw?"

"As much as I can. Look I—"

"I'll cut to the chase," Mr. White says with a warm smile. "We are enamored with you, quite frankly."

I frown as my heart stalls in my chest. "Enamored?"

"You are so . . . well put together," Mrs. White gushes,

moving toward me. "I mean, I can tell. I've had so many like you before, but none quite as remarkable. As defiant. He has outdone himself yet again. So much so, I just *couldn't* wait for you to be delivered."

I take a step back and stumble into a seat that wasn't there before. Perfectly placed by Mr. White. He holds me in place. Pressing down on my shoulders. There's no way I can reach for my nose plugs or the bangers.

"Don't fret. It'll be painless." An earthy smell fills the shimmering marquee. It's not as strong as the Changing Man, but I know it'll be enough. Thin streaks of orange swirl. "Like going into a deep sleep."

My heart sinks to the soles of my feet. Every fiber in my body trembles. I gnaw at my bottom lip, trying to keep the tiredness at bay. I cry for help in desperation more than hope.

"Soundproof." Mrs. White strokes my cheek. Her fingers are cold. "I know this is a shock."

"Please," I whimper.

"Like my partner said, pain—"

My phone alarm goes off. Rip-roaringly loud. They squeal and flinch. Enough for the pressure on my shoulders to loosen. Enough for me to shrug his hands off me. Just as quickly they reach for me, but I duck and roll out the way. Springing to my feet, I sprint for the marquee's exit.

I slip through the entrance flap and slam into tides of people, pinballing off a middle-aged man, a young girl, and the edge of a kiosk, before I gather my bearings. Glancing back toward the marquee, I see the man emerge, his head on a swivel. He spots me, and my breath hitches. With a gentle tilt of his head, he smiles wide and strides toward me.

Pins of fear prick me all over, causing my arms and legs to shake and shudder.

Movemovemove, I scream at myself.

The standing crowd up ahead erupts into thunderous applause, simmering into silence when Mr. Ingham, who ascends to the stage, raises his hand. "Thank you, and welcome to Nithercott Day. It truly is a great honor to stand here before you all: students, parents, esteemed guests."

"Sorry—excuse me—oops," I say, weaving in and out. I place my phone in my skirt pocket and slide off my blazer, dropping it to the ground.

"I have a simple question for you all: Why are we here? Perhaps if I phrase it differently: What *is* purpose?" Mr. Ingham continues.

Next to come off is my jumper. I tie it around my shoulders.

"I'll tell you. Purpose is what *we* receive. And while we often see it as some far-off thing, it isn't. In fact it's—"

"What the hell!" squeals a voice.

All heads turn in the direction of the noise. It's Malika. The man's got his hand round her wrist. Realizing he's got the wrong girl, he lets go and laughs awkwardly, holding his hands up, as though he's made a harmless mistake.

As gossipy murmurs fill the air, that's my cue.

Pushing my way through the squeezing crowd, I head for the front of the school, making sure to stay out of the view of the few functioning cameras on the school grounds. Ben and Bee are waiting for me. He's carrying all our equipment in his rucksack.

"Why are you down a blazer? And why's your jumper tied around your shoulders like that?" Bee asks.

"Circumstances," I answer.

She doesn't push me, only nods.

The walk to Little Forrest is somber, the air filled with the pitter-patter of our feet against the pavement. We've rehearsed this plan so many times I could say it with my eyes closed.

Still, my heart beats like a hummingbird at the back of my tongue. I recite the plan in my head over and over.

Bee and I to the side gate. Ben to the main gate. Cut the wires so the electronic lock fails. Enter. Douse the grounds with oil. Throw rocks at the building to trigger the alarms. Wait for the Changing Man and his minions to come. And then—

I stop dead in my tracks. The unmistakable smell of wet pavement clings to the air. Emerging from the left, Franny bursts into view. Her face is bright coral and tears stream down her face, making her mascara run. "St-St-Stacey."

"What about Stacey?" Ben asks. She doesn't answer. "Fran, *what* about Stacey?"

"We were hanging out, and . . . and she just collapsed. I saw orange and—and there was this smell and—"

Ben nods. "Fran, listen, it's important that you tell us right now where she is. Which way?"

Fran is losing it now. She moves her hands around as if they're on fire and she's trying to put them out. "Th-th-that way." She points. "OhGodohGodohGod."

We follow her lead into the thicket of trees and all I can think is *why now?* I push the fear away. I'll have plenty of time for that later. Right now, we need to save Stacey.

"Which way?" Ben demands. "Left or right?"

"R-right."

Ben sprints a couple of steps to the right.

"Nobody move." Ms. Piddleton appears. "That's enough," she snaps. I swallow.

We are royally screwed now.

All at once, Franny stops sobbing and the coral in her face fades.

Bee takes a step forward. "But, Miss, you don't understand. There's—"

"Really?" Franny says, cutting me off. Her voice is odd. Mangled. "I can *finally* stop pretending? Thank the moons! I'm sick of this form."

"Franny?" I ask, even though I already suspect the truth.

She turns to me with a big fat grin. "My name is Carnation Sapphire and you'll address me as such. Or don't address me at all, you inferior being. You've really gone and done it now. I chose mercy when you came for me with the fireworks. But upsetting our buyers for no good reason crosses a line."

I gasp as Franny's clothes and skin bubble as one. She melts into a puddle of gunk and in a blink morphs into the shape of a hairless cat, jumping onto Ms. Piddleton's shoulder.

We were lured here.

Bee falls back and presses into my side. Ben's breaths are ragged.

Stacey was never in danger.

My stomach drops. There's so many of them working for the Changing Man. Did they know we had something planned?

How?

"Now, now," Ms. Piddleton says. "Don't speak to her like

that. It'll stimulate the toxins that'll worsen her texture. There's still time to appease your buyers. I think she gets it. How hopeless her situation is."

"No, I don't think she does," Carnation taunts. "Do you honestly think I haven't been aware of your movements from day one?" Carnation slides off Ms. Piddleton and then takes on various forms. First turning into an owl, then wobbling into the receptionist, before twisting into the lanky boy Stacey was with, and then the warden.

Each transformation weakens my knees as numbness spreads from my stomach. All that time we spent piecing it all together and looking outward at the sponsors, and the monsters have been right there among us all along. Solid bitterness burns the back of my throat.

Finally, Carnation transforms into Fran. "Get it now? You could never win." They swiftly return to being a hairless cat.

"B-but—no—it can't—" I trip over my words.

"Don't you see?" Carnation says, stalking toward me. "All this time I've been watching."

Taking a step back, I struggle to control my breathing as the bass of my heart rattles through me. We can't win. Tears sting my eyes. Bee squeezes my hand.

"Carnation," Ms. Piddleton says.

"What?" Carnation hisses. "Well?"

"The—uh—well. We owe him a favor." Ms. Piddleton picks Carnation up and whispers something.

Carnation, now sitting on her shoulder, hisses. "Orchid's not going to like this, but fine. Go ahead."

Orchid. I swallow. That must be the one who stands at the top of the pyramid. That's the one we have to stop.

"Silence. We have a proposal." Ms. Piddleton clears her throat. "No need to look so glum," she adds with a smile. Carnation sits by her feet.

Time stops and my mouth hangs open. This is how it ends.

"What proposal?" Ben spits out, breaking his silence.

"Turn yourselves in." Ms. Piddleton points at us. "If you come with us, in return we will ensure your consciousness will remain intact. You will still be you in a true sense. You'll think the same. Act the same. All in a new body. The best of both. You have our solemn word. This is the best we can offer you. You have won yourselves a free future."

I look at the smirking faces in front of me. Barbed wire in my gut. Their confidence infuriates me. Because they think they're offering us some kind of sweet deal. I already know if we accept, they won't hesitate to break the agreement. I *hate* them.

"Screw that," Ben says, stepping in front of me. "You couldn't get Leon and you won't get any of us."

Carnation flowers into bloodcurdling laughter. "Couldn't get Leon? My boy, we devoured him. The transfer of his partial consciousness, however, was defective. His replacement had too much of a conscience and ran off before it could take Leon's place. By the time we found it though, this whole narrative around Leon had been created. It gave us no choice but to put it down. Truly inconvenient. It has made things harder for all parties involved."

"Devoured him?" Ben repeats, and his hands rub against his chest as though it burns. "What are you talking about? He got away! And you . . . and you—"

Ms. Piddleton doesn't even look in Ben's direction when

she answers. "He's gone, Ben. The Leon who texted you that night was the replacement."

"B-b-but he worked out what was happening. He's different," Ben argues. "You're lying!"

Carnation sniggers. "The *only* thing he worked out before he went into a deep, deep sleep was that it was over."

Nononono.

The revelation is a knee to the thigh that leaves Ben speechless. The despair on his face twists my stomach out like a soggy cloth. My breath hitches. "B-Ben—"

"Dead," he mumbles, his breath shaking while tears streak down his face. Bee goes to rest a reassuring hand on his arm, but he leans away from her. "If I . . . If I . . . If I'd paid more attention, then Leon wouldn't have died."

Bee clears her throat. "That's not true. You—"

"It was my fault." Ben rubs his face with his hands. "He was always watching out for me. If I wasn't so needy."

Damn it. He's spiraling. "Listen, Ben, it's not your fault," I state.

"I killed Leon."

"*Ben.* No, you didn't. *They* killed Leon. *They* took him."

"But . . . But . . ."

There's a loud bang that makes me and Ben jump. Bee's thrown one of the bangers Ben gave us onto the ground. That wakes him up. With a vicious snarl, Ben whips out his flashlight and shines it in Ms. Piddleton's face. She shields her eyes as he strides up to her and sprays perfume at her point-blank.

I've never been more thankful for Ben's bottomless pockets of stuff.

"What in the—Argh!" Ms. Piddleton coughs and sputters.

"Ife, my bag. Front panel pocket," Ben orders, his face reddening. "Now, now, now."

I do as he says and feel at the makeshift flamethrowers. I pull one out but instantly drop it when Carnation scratches at my hand. Flickering into Franny, Carnation wraps two hands around my throat and squeezes. Fearful panic overwhelms me as I struggle to breathe, watching anger and joy shimmer in Carnation's eyes.

When I try to breathe, the pressure increases and my eyes sting. My hands claw in desperation.

"You truly are insufferable," Carnation spits. "Why must you—"

Bee sprays fire at Carnation, who cowers. Bee's mid-spray when the flamethrower falls apart and Carnation swats her away. Another flicker, this time into the lanky sixth-form boy. Only now the fingers in his left hand stretch and twist into something slithery-sharp. The lanky sixth-form boy lumbers toward Bee, nothing but menace in each step.

Bee scrambles away from him, kicking out when he grabs her by the ankle. He doesn't let go. I swallow. The urge to run pulses through me. My body is full of tremors, my heartbeat thrashing in my ears. I squeeze my eyes tight and take three deep, deep breaths before I rush at him. He lashes out and I'm sent backward. Landing flat on my back.

There's a loud boom. One of Ben's bangers.

Crawling over to Ben's rucksack, I rifle through it, looking for something to use, and pull out a jar of pickles. They're the same jar from when we snuck into Little Forrest. I remember the woman at Little Forrest recoiling when she saw it, and an idea hits.

I wind up my arm and launch the jar at the lanky sixth-form boy's head. The jar smashes against his back instead, soaking him in pickle juice. He turns, flashing bug-like eyes that glow amber.

For an endless instant there is unbearable nothingness.

Then the lanky sixth-form boy . . . melts. Hisses. Steams. His shape jittering as he drops to his knees. Holes dimple flesh and eyes sprout into glowing amber moons too big for a human face. When Carnation reaches for me, Bee lands a kick in the chest of Carnation's horrific form. Tentacles sprout from the neck. Carnation flickers into a hairless cat. Meows and groans and shudders all at once. A mouth becomes visible on the rib cage. The cat form limps a few steps, slowly dissolving into a pulpy mess. Finally, it goes still.

Meanwhile, Ms. Piddleton is on her hands and knees writhing around like a bug. She flickers. Ben makes this weird gesture. Like he's doing the *A* from that old, old, old "Y.M.C.A." dance. Then he points into the distance. I get it.

The hill!

I take one last look back, and every bone in my body shivers. Holes of different shapes and sizes cover Ms. Piddleton's flesh. Her eyes bulge. Glowing bloodred. Slowly, slowly, her face twists into a deep and wide smile.

I drop my head and sprint away.

CHAPTER 29

TAILSPIN

My lungs are on fire.

Ben, Bee, and I have been running nonstop. Well, *moving* nonstop. I'm barely fast walking. My arms and legs are heavy as stone. We're halfway up the hill, and thankfully we haven't bumped into Ms. Piddleton or anyone like her.

Even though I'm not moving fast, the thoughts in my mind are. Everything is such a mess! They were supposed to be caught completely off guard. *How didn't I see it?* Stupid question. I know how it happened. They were always watching us.

And now we have no answers and no plan. The temptation to swear out loud is huge.

But—*but*—we are okay. We're still alive and kicking.

The relief I have swirls with annoyance and frustration. My mind right now is a Georgia O'Keeffe canvas—a spiraling, abstract masterpiece of every thought.

I drag myself the rest of the way. When I look up, using all the muscles in my neck, Ben and Bee have pulled farther away and I'm forced to speed up.

They've stopped for breath.

"H-how?" I splutter. Oh man, I need to exercise more. "How are you guys this fit?"

Ben has a big, hysterical smile on his face. "A smoke a day makes everything okay."

My face wrinkles. "I beg to differ. There's nothing 'okay' about it. I doubt a scan of your lungs would back that up." Ben says nothing. I think deep down he knows I'm right. "Anyway, did you see what your pickles did? Who knew it could kill them? I thought at best it would buy us a bit of time."

"I was saving those for later. Victory pickles."

Course he was. I burst into laughter and pull him into a hug. "Idiot."

Ben doesn't resist. But he doesn't hug me back either. "But who knew indeed," he starts. "It was like a slug in salt."

"I think that's it. The high salt content must do something destructive to them. Did you notice how sluglike they looked while changing shape?" Bee chimes in.

I nod. Before I can say anything, there's a rustle in the bushes to our right, and I grab my breath. An oldish woman in green hunters, gilet, and bucket hat appears. There's a dead, lumbering look in her eyes.

Oh no.

From the left, Elaine emerges. Her wide smile is laced with wickedness.

Oh no.

The librarian is next to arrive. Tilted head. Empty smile.

Oh no no no.

Instinctively, I put myself in front of Bee and Ben.

"Ife?" Bee whispers.

I swallow.

The replicas walk toward us so calmly, each step they take is an ice cube down my back. Suddenly they all stop. Except for my replica who arrives. Clearly different. Clearly the messenger. She whistles and more shapes appear. When they come into focus, I gulp down as much air as possible, unsure about what's happening. I thought my replica wanted to *help* me. My heart sinks.

Ben laughs out loud. "What the hell?"

"It's us," Bee breathes, and I can't tell if it's fear or fascination in her voice. Which is insane. If it's fascination, she is not alright.

Bee's replica is the spitting image of her, except there's no signature smile.

"This can't be my replacement," Ben says, sizing his replica up. He scoffs. "I'm definitely taller than that. Not to mention better looking."

"Not the time," Bee utters.

"Or the place," I add.

My replica clears her throat and begins to speak. Her voice scrapes against my skin.

"Please stop this futility and come with us. We have been directed to use force. Do not make this any harder than it needs to be."

They take a menacing step toward us. My replica looks around quickly and pushes her eyebrows toward her hairline. She mouths a word to me. *Up*.

She's right. The way out of this situation is to climb higher. "Up," I gasp.

All three of us make a break for it. Ben leads the way. We

end up at the viewpoint with hands on our knees, gasping for breath. The view is amazing. From afar, our replacements, and the puppets, slink toward us. That's when Ben stands up straight. "I have an idea. It's not great, and you're probably not going to like it."

He's not inspiring confidence. "What's the idea?"

"I can draw them away. Then I'll lose them. I know this place like the back of my hand. I'll circle back and we'll finish off what we started. We need to destroy Orchid and their way into this world."

"Ms. Piddleton is still out there. She's different. She's not a replica who's blindly following orders. What if she realizes you're alone?"

"Then we outmaneuver her. There's a route you can take that I'm sure you'll be able to lose her on. I'll deal with the rest."

My heartbeat increases in an instant. "What?"

"Don't worry about it. As I said, there's a route you can take her on. I'll—"

He's smiling at me like this is a good idea. "It's a bad idea," I say out loud. "What if she goes after you instead?"

"I know this place like the back of my hand," he reiterates. "There are two routes we can take. We'll be fine."

"We should be sticking together, not splitting up. Have you never seen a horror movie? Ever?"

"I know what I'm doing. I know this place like—"

"The back of your hand, we know. Just . . ." I shake my head and sigh. He really is an annoying somebody. "Just stay safe."

"But of course." Ben smirks at me before giving Bee a

wink. He points to a faint path. "Head that way, you'll come across a signpost. Take a left, and when you see the tree with a red paint stroke, there's a hiding spot opposite it."

"Little girls. Little boys," Ben's replica sings as he emerges. "Seriously, making me run like this? It's a bit rude."

Ben nods at us. "Now!"

Bee and I sprint away, and I notice how her head cranes back even after we're out of sight. "Seriously?" I ask her.

"What?"

"Ben?"

Bee scoffs unconvincingly. "It-it-it's not like that. I'm just worried. That's all."

"Hey, no judgment here. Just surprised, that's all. But it makes sense. He is Mr. Intellectually Intimidating, after all."

Bee sucks in her lips like she's applying lip gloss, completely ignoring the way I'm looking at her. When she finally makes eye contact with me, we burst into a fit of giggles. We turn left at the signpost.

"What are we going to do?" I exhale.

"I know. This is so messed up."

It's more than messed up. The Changing Man and his minions are way too powerful. There's a sinking feeling in my gut. "I don't think we have a choice, Bee. We need to finish it. Today." Zanna's promise rings in my ears. *If it looks mad, then you need to just run, I don't care.* But I can't. I can't. I—

There's a bloodcurdling scream. It's Ben's voice. No doubt about it. I look at Bee and she's already turning back. I grab her arm.

"What if it's a trap?" It's a valid concern, but the words

taste of guilt in my mouth. I know I say them because I'm scared. I don't want to find out.

Bee's eyes are fierce. Blazing. She pulls away from me. "What if it isn't?"

"B-but if it *is* and we get caught—everything is for nothing." I need her to understand. To see I'm right. That I want us all to make it home. That I need to see my friends and family again. That this is the best thing for us. "Two of us surviving is better than none of us." The words slip out before I can sense-check them. "I—What I meant was—"

"He's our friend, Ife." She frowns, defiant. "I know it's a risk, and crap, we might not make it, but I wouldn't leave you behind and I know you wouldn't leave me behind either. Right?" I freeze. Bee searches my eyes and I look away, because right now I don't know what I'm doing or what I'm thinking. I'm scared.

Use your words, I scream at myself.

"Ife?"

My throat clenches. *Speak!* But the words won't come out.

"Seriously? I thought—" Bee shakes her head. Takes one last look at me and breaks into a run.

"W-wait," I shout after her. She stops and turns. Once again, I can't say anything. My throat is clogged. I move toward her, pushing through the fear. Even though every nerve is screaming at me to run. There's no way I can let her go alone. She and Ben are the jewel in the crown of everything good about Nithercott. "You're right."

We run back the way we came and down the path Ben took.

It's there we see Ben standing in our way. Smiling. No, it's his replica. The way the replica smiles is too straight and perfect. I smirk. Ben was right, he's better looking.

It releases another bloodcurdling scream while stepping toward us. "How nice of you to come to me."

"Ife," Bee whispers. "You go and I'll—"

I shake my head. "I'm not leaving you alone."

"Go. One of us needs to finish off the job and that's you."

"But—"

She gives me a firm shove. "*Go.*"

I'm already on my way, fear slamming into me like waves. I barely make it a few trembling steps before I stop. My eyes close. *I can't.* I turn, and that's when I hear the snapping of bone. Like the crunch when you bite deep into a firm apple.

Sound blurs. My eyes snap open.

A scream.

Bee's.

Ben's replica crouches over her. "Give up resisting. I was told not to make you suffer any more than necessary." The smell of petrichor swarms the area and the space behind Ben's replica begins to shimmer. He rises. "Give up." Orange mist marbles the air.

"G-go!" Bee croaks.

Fear overtakes me and my legs move without thinking. I run as fast as I can back down the hill. But instead of running toward Little Forrest, I find myself running straight for Beeton House.

CHAPTER 30

ESCAPE

After stuffing as much as I can—as quickly as possible—into my weekend bag, I sprint to catch the bus. It doesn't take long before I see its blaring lights. Swallowing back the panic, I take deep, short breaths. At the same time, some of the people drinking and chattering away outside the pub opposite me stop what they're doing and look toward me. My insides squirm and I look away. I hop on and pay for my ticket.

A few onlookers rush toward the bus but they don't reach it in time, and I breathe a sigh of relief as the bus pulls away and bumbles down the country roads. Finally, finally, finally. I close my eyes and wait. When they open again, rain thunders down like metal screws being poured onto the bus's roof. The window rattles as heavy winds thrash against it. I shiver as my toes curl. My vague reflection sulks at me. I close my eyes and concentrate on the sound of the rumbling engine. Propelling the bus toward Nithercott Station.

I should probably tell my parents to be at Orlingdon Station to pick me up. I can't wait for the fun conversation that'll be. I fish out my phone with trembling hands, only to fumble it and watch it plop into my open weekend bag. Blindly I reach in to pick it out: Instead, my hands find the cold glass of the snow globe Zanna got me before I came to Nithercott. I pull it out. Look at her handwriting on the bottom.

If Nithercrap gets mega hard,
think about all the good reasons
that make it worth it
EvUL / 4vuru Fae xx

My eyes shut and I let the gravity of her words pour down on me. Heavy like the winds outside. A shallow smile lifts my lips. Ben's smirk and Bee's smile flash in my mind.

What am I doing?

Mr. Morley comes to mind and how I called him a coward. I squeeze my eyes tight. He was never a coward.

Only scared.

I stare out of the window at the blurring landscape passing by. My mind's elsewhere. Full of worry for Ben and Bee. The pattering of rain stops. There's a choir of voices in my head.

Bee first. *That's what friends are for.*

Take our offer at a fresh pair of socks, Ife. I know you want to. Ben's advice.

I turn to my phone and scroll through my gallery until I find the picture I took of the bottom of the snow globe I gave Zanna. *True friends are never apart. Maybe in distance, but never in heart.* The words I wrote.

The bus slows to a stop and an announcement fills the stuffy space.

"The driver has been instructed to wait at this stop for a short time to help even out the service."

The doors hiss open and a gust of air slithers up my sleeves and down my neck. The wet pavement glistens. All I'd have to do is get off.

Damn it.

I probably haven't wasted too much time. Ben and Bee could still make it out alive.

Damn it.

Energy flows through me.

Damn it.

Reaches my toe tips.

I stand up, grab my bag, and make my way to the doors. The blustering wind slaps me in the face. I jump off and splash onto the pavement. The bus back toward Nithercott is approaching on the other side. If I run, I should be able to make it. I have never felt so fit, or full of purpose as my legs get me down the stairs, along the tunnel, and onto the other side.

Right as the bus pulls away from the stop.

I check the bus times. There isn't another bus for thirty minutes. So I start jogging. Everything in me is telling me this is stupid and dumb. To run for the hills.

So why won't my feet stop moving? Why am I heading back? Why do any of this at all?

Because this is what friends do.

My friends back home haven't forgotten me. But the fact

is, I'm not there anymore. They're getting on with their lives. I need to do the same. No more running away.

I think about a plan as my legs work.

What do I know? Well, I know that they have my friends. I know that every second I'm not there, they're one step closer to being gone forever. If I'm going to end this, I need to destroy the heart, and that's at Little Forrest.

A thorny stitch sprouts in my side, but I swallow the pain and tell myself to keep going.

I get to Little Forrest and then what? Maybe there's another way inside I haven't thought of. But then what? Always *and then what?*

Deep breaths, Ife.

When I hear the rumble of a car fast approaching, I crane my neck. The car squeals to a stop in front of me and my head jerks back as I gasp, nearly choking on my disbelief. The disheveled man looking at me from the driver's seat?

None other than Mr. Morley.

The car's not the one I've seen him drive as a teacher, but it's just as bad. It makes Dad's car look pristine. Even though the door lifts upward like wings.

"I call him Knight Rider," he says, sounding like a proud father.

"They don't pay you much at the ministry, do they, sir?"

I can tell my reaction isn't the one he wanted. "Get in."

CHAPTER 31

HOMECOMING

The inside of his Knight Rider is just as disappointing and bland as its exterior, with broken buttons, wrinkled leather seats, and scratched metal details. I shudder, even though the vents are blowing hot air. The inside only *feels* as inhospitable as the Antarctic.

"You should be on your sabbatical," I blurt, my voice way higher than it usually is.

It looks like he hasn't shaved or showered in days. In fact, he smells like it too. My nose wrinkles. Mr. Morley sighs. His grubby hands grip the steering wheel tightly. Does he not know his fingernails are caked in dirt? I crack open the window.

"Hey, Ife. You okay?"

I don't want to breathe in the stale air just yet so I half nod, half shake, because honestly, I'm not sure if I am okay.

"I get it. Running away is hard." Mr. Morley takes a deep breath. "I miss him, you know."

"Wh-what?"

"Alred—Dr. Butterworth. He was the most infuriatingly brilliant person ever. He was also my best friend. The hardest thing about this whole situation is I never got to say goodbye. Never got to apologize."

"B-but this was my fault. I *left* them. *I* left. You don't get it. I had a choice and I did the wrong thing. I got scared and I—Why are you here?" My eyes narrow at Mr. Morley when he doesn't answer. I reach for the snow globe in my bag. "Sir, how did you know I would be here? Where are you taking me?"

Mr. Morley chuckles. "Relax. I'm not a mindless drone."

"Could have fooled me," I bite back.

"Ha. I found you because as you know, I'm not *just* a teacher. But you're just a regular girl." Mr. Morley's suddenly serious. He glances toward me. "I'm taking you to Nithercott Station. I know it's hard to swallow, but don't go back. Go home. You can't save them."

"They're my friends."

"You are not listening to me. You can't save them."

I shake my head. My nostrils flare. "Yes, I am, and I'm saying I made a mistake. I have to."

"Look. I know how much you want to do this, but they *will* do much worse than kill you. All of you."

"I know," I breathe. "You're right. Alone it feels pretty hopeless, but I know you can help us. You guys have the tools. Please. I need your help, sir. If you could—"

"I get it. I know how much you want to make them pay. To hurt them. I can see it in your eyes." I think he's lying. I think these words are more for himself. "But they are untouchable. You can spray fire at them and they'll hurt, but it's not enough. It's never enough to kill."

My fists are clenched so tight, they're shaking. I relax them. "But they aren't untouchable. Trust me. I killed one."

I lock eyes with Mr. Morley. His frown unravels like badly tied shoelaces when he realizes I'm for real.

"Seriously?" he asks, his eyebrows pushing up toward his receding hairline.

I nod. "Pickle juice got over one of them and they died."

Determination sparks as he swears under his breath. "And you're sure that's what killed it. Pickle juice?"

There's a long stretch of silence. "It did. We think their natural form is sluglike. It's the high salt content that kills them."

"Even if I go with you, it won't be enough. I'm not Superman."

"You mean you're not from the planet Krypton?" I can't help the smirk that forms on my face. "But whatever, that's not why I'm asking you. I'm asking you because when I asked for help the first time around, I thought you were just a useless coward."

Mr. Morley swallows. "Okay."

"But that day, you found out what had happened to Dr. Butterworth, didn't you? That must have been really hard."

"It—Yes." Mr. Morley is looking at me like no one's ever empathized with him before. But I'm only just seeing it now how he and I, we're two peas in a pod. Both haunted by the decisions we've made.

"You regret not helping him."

"Yes," Mr. Morley forces out.

"That's why I'm asking you, sir. Because I know what that feels like too. And I know I would do anything to make it right. That's why I'm going back. I made a mistake. Please. You have to help me. We can end this once and for all."

Mr. Morley turns to me. "Hold on to something."

I do as he says. "Why?"

The engine revs and roars and tires squeal as Mr. Morley drives away at a speed that is definitely not safe. He shrugs. Like not even he's sure. His eyebrows push up. "We're headed to Tesco and then to Butterworth Manor."

"I see."

Mr. Morley grunts and does a reckless U-turn that re-arranges my insides.

After buying balloons, salt, and enough jars of pickles to fill the boot, we zoom to Butterworth Manor. It's everything I could imagine and more.

Gray and stony with endless windows, it clutches at the sky with multiple spires that can't decide on whether they are elegant or scruffy, sharp or dull. It's so large and unwelcoming I can't imagine anyone having fond memories here.

"Is this where Dr. Butterworth grew up?" I ask.

Mr. Morley nods, popping open the boot. "It's our local HQ now. But it's also where he lived. Something of a privileged upbringing, you could say. Still, it's pretty hard to enjoy it when you're watching your friends change. You know about Elaine, right?" I nod and he grunts. He pulls out bolt cutters. "This way." Mr. Morley leads us away from the house and to a large padlocked shed. In one squeeze of the bolt cutters, the padlock slips off. When he flips on the lights, they illuminate a vault of some of the strangest weapons I've seen.

There's one that looks like an iron attached to a silver canister. Another weapon looks like a cross between a light-saber and a chainsaw. There are so many others, but Mr. Morley boringly grabs a flamethrower off the wall and hands it to me. He runs through how to use it. We then spend what feels like hours filling up all the balloons with pickle juice reinforced with extra salt.

He laughs once we're done. "Pickle juice and salt? Christ, it can't be that easy."

Mr. Morley swerves in and out of traffic as we hurtle toward Little Forrest. I text Zanna.

> eanggastic nteuastic hutastic
> ullybastic feastic uostbastic.
> Love you the most x

I turn my phone on silent straightaway, knowing as soon as she deciphers it, she'll want to call. I tell myself, *I'll call her once this is all over.* I chew on the inside of my cheek, trying to believe my thoughts. Once we get closer, Mr. Morley finally slows down and my stomach settles. He parks in the stony turnout of an overgrown country road that looks like it hasn't been driven on in ages. The doors open and my feet squelch onto the muddy grass.

From the parked Knight Rider, it takes about four minutes to reach Little Forrest from the back. I feel like such a badass as I carry a flamethrower with one hand. I also have a belt of pickle juice bombs around my waist. Plus more in a rucksack. We're ready. I'm ready.

We go over the plan one more time: get in, find Bee and Ben, destroy everything we can along the way. I take a deep breath and follow Mr. Morley as we move in. Out of sight and out of mind, creeping carefully toward the fortress-like building. Movement rustles the greenery ahead of us. My gut twists while Mr. Morley tenses. Ready and willing.

Emerging from the thicket is my replica. She's got her hands raised. "I'm here to help."

Mr. Morley glances at me, and I nod. *She's good.* "Why?"

"Th-th-they thought you might come back. So people are on the lookout. I don't know how, but I just had this feeling—a sense—that you were near and, well. I think that's how they made us. We can sense the original. I can get you in." I raise an eyebrow. "If I pretend like I've caught you, then we can catch them by surprise. There's two of us inside at the moment. Everyone's on the other side or on the lookout for you in and around the nearby area."

"That could work," Mr. Morley huffs. "Ife, gimme your gear. Other Ife, lead the way."

"L-Layo," my replica says softly. We look at her with blank faces. "I want to be called Layo."

"Layo then." I smile. Ifelayo is my full name. I guess she liked Layo more than Ife. "Lead the way."

"Ouch." I grimace as Layo leads me forward with my arm behind my back. "Can't you be gentler?"

"It needs to be believable," she whispers back, before ringing the side gate twice.

The lady with the mound of gray hair who answered the side gate last time appears. She's in a burgundy dress today, a wide smile plastered on her face. "Wonderful," she says. She shows us in, spinning on her heels, walking back toward the main building. "You've caused quite the stir. Well, it doesn't matter. You're here now. He'll be so—"

Mr. Morley sprays her with fire. Ablaze, she spasms and writhes and staggers toward the building as though in a shower that's gone from hot to ice cold. Layo releases me, races ahead, and drop-kicks her to the floor.

The lady squirms and gasps. Clawing for the steps up to the door. Gagging for breath. Mr. Morley towers over her and douses her in pickle juice. At first there's a low hissing sound like opening a can of Supermalt. And then there's a gurgling sound. Her expression says it all as the pain etched on her face slashes through the air. Wobbles my eardrums. Makes me shiver.

Tentacles sprout but quickly wilt. Bits of her pulpy flesh fall away like over-chewed gum. Whatever's happening is breaking her apart. Soon she's a gooey mess of sludge at my feet. It reminds me of okra soup. Except it doesn't make my mouth water when I look at it.

Mr. Morley puts an arm on my shoulder and swears. He hands me my flamethrower and brine. "Now then, shall we?"

My heart is nothing but slush in my chest. "Let's."

CHAPTER 32

INTO THE BELLY OF THE BEAST

As Layo leads us boldly into Little Forrest, the receptionist walks toward us with files in her hands. She freezes and looks past us. I turn, and from here you can see what's left of the lady, dead on the steps.

When I turn back, Mr. Morley's already lifting his flamethrower.

"Don't bother, she's a creation," Layo says, deadpan, before addressing the receptionist. "If you don't want to end up the same way, I suggest you don't interfere."

In the same breath we edge around her desk to get to the stairs.

"A creation?" I whisper to Layo.

She nods. "Basically, fake humans that aren't replicas of anyone. Puppets with an artificial consciousness. Flesh robots . . . ish."

"Oh."

"I can't let you go upstairs." The receptionist blocks our way up.

"Really?" Mr. Morley flashes a smile that is two thirds cringe, one third haunting. "Not even for me?" he coaxes.

She shakes her head. "I can't. Please lea—"

All of a sudden, Mr. Morley steps to the receptionist and wraps his arms around her neck. Just like that. No warning. Just *boop*. My mouth drops open as her face goes bright red.

Her eyes water and her limbs are splayed everywhere. "I can't," she splutters.

Mr. Morley doesn't let up and catches her rigid body in his arms. He lays her on the ground.

"It's only going to get worse from here on out," he says, while we climb the stairs. "You ready?"

"Nope. You?"

Mr. Morley shrugs. "Not in the slightest."

We enter a room that's completely empty, barring a single bookcase. Layo strides up to it and grabs ahold of the edge. She pushes, and it budges the tiniest bit. A few books slip off their shelves. "Help. It's behind here. The door."

Mr. Morley helps her out, and there's a small squeak as the bookcase moves. I join in and as we push, a door is slowly being revealed. One without a lock.

I twist the doorknob and pull it open. The stale smell of petrichor washes over me, and for a moment my legs wobble. I take a deep breath and step through the doorway. It takes everything for my mouth not to drop open.

A pebbled beach stretches out in front of me. There are stone steps leading down to it. On it is the beginning of a bridge. The rest of it is swallowed by a thick orange mist. A whole world hidden behind a door. No word of a lie.

How is this even possible?

Mr. Morley does this weird huff, blowing air out of his nostrils. "Seven years."

"What?"

"We have been looking for the entrance for seven years. We suspected, but to see it . . . to get this far. You're really something."

I smile at him. Thinking about all the atrocities the Changing Man has gotten away with. "I'm their worst nightmare."

As we take the steps down, tall silhouettes emerge from behind the mist. Mr. Morley crouches and Layo and I do the same.

A figure pockmarked with bottomless holes steps out from the bridge onto the pebbled shore. The therimorph's skin is bleach white, and octopus-like tentacles burst from its neck. Two eyes glow forest green. It gasps and shifts its shape into a slender man in a Barbour jacket and green wellies.

Another therimorph appears, shuddering into the shape of a woman with impressive bangs.

"Where in the moons is he? We're due to confirm and undergo the transfers. How can we do that when he isn't here?" Green Wellies asks.

Impressive Bangs frowns. "I—I—"

"Go. And. Get. Him."

"B-b-but Anemone, she said no one should—"

"I don't care *what* she said. *I* said go and get him. She's not the one whose neck is on the line here. I've been doing this a long time. Not once has there been a delay to the program, or any issues. Now *go*."

"But she expressly forbid—"

"This is more important! This—"

I adjust my position as a cramp seeps into my thighs.

My phone in my hoodie's front pocket slips out and dances down the stone steps, *thunking* loudly along the way. My heart expands inside my chest. I swear my ribs are about to splinter.

The therimorphs look up at us. Grow and shift in shape. They shudder into large, four-legged beasts, an assortment of teeth bared. Drool drips from their mouths. I blink, not sure what I'm looking at.

I—I think it's what they think a wolf looks like. Maybe. The almost-wolves are all wrong, with snouts that look more like beaks, extremely hunched backs, and corkscrew tails.

A moment of stillness lasts for a single, never-ending instant. Then everything is all action. They gurgle howls.

"*Go, go, go!*" Mr. Morley shouts. "I'll cover."

I turn my head around. "Go where?!"

"The bridge!" Layo replies.

I do as I'm told. Skipping down the steps, I grab my phone and run toward the bridge. Even though the two snarling therimorphs block our path.

But I don't hesitate. I can't. Not now. Only thing I can do is trust Mr. Morley isn't sending me out there to die. The hiss of the flamethrower fills the air as heat warms my skin. I let out a howl that smothers my fear. The sound comes deep from my gut. Wild and free. And then I feel two hands on my back and I'm sent flying down on the ground. Pushed.

I crane my head, ready to scream at Layo, but my mouth drops open. She's being squeezed by their tentacles. A blur of green and red and blue and purple flash in my periphery, whizzing by.

Balloons filled with pickle juice slam into the almost-wolves. They steam and stagger toward me, looking drunk as they crumble.

Two more balloons fly by, and that's more than enough to stop them dead in their tracks. They collapse into a pulpy mess, releasing Layo, who doesn't move. I rush over to her side.

"You saved me," I breathe.

She nods and smiles weakly and sits up. "I did." Her eyes are wide and wet. I don't think she understands what pain is. Her breath is slow, and as she takes a few more deep breaths, she giggles. "I . . . am." She swallows. "I am your friend after all. We need to go over the bridge."

I laugh and help her to her feet.

"This is only the start," Mr. Morley says. "Let's go."

We make our way into the mist. The air changes instantly. It's thinner. Harder to breathe. Drowsiness starts pulling me down, pushing me back, but I use every fiber of my being to stay in the moment. To keep putting one foot in front of the other.

Until we come out on the other side, gasping and breathing heavily. We're in some sort of crypt. The light here is bright and the air is fresh. Looking up, I notice the ceiling is full of dancing patterns of interconnecting golden vines painted on an obsidian background. Numerous pillars support the multiple sections of arched ceiling. It's beautiful.

"So many layers," Mr. Morley says.

To my left there are stairs. We climb them and reach a shallow tunnel opening. Walking through, we come out into a forest of shrubbery dappled with color. Out ahead is a black door with golden details. It stands freely with seemingly nothing around it. There's a rustle to my left.

A great big therimorph emerges from nowhere. *Layo didn't mention a monster.* It has too many legs to count sprouting out of a sluglike body that has an iridescent purple shine. Apricot-orange bristles and maroon eyes cover it all over. Black pincers flare as it hisses.

"Yoouuuuu shouldn't be hereeee."

"Gorlab," Layo says grimly. "An experiment."

The color combos are sublime. Would definitely appreciate it more if a prickly leg wasn't stabbing at us.

I jump out the way and run to hide behind a squat tree. I look across, and Mr. Morley, joined by Layo, is doing the same. We make eye contact.

What now? I ask him with my face. I gesture with my flamethrower. *Do you think we can shoot it down?*

He shakes his head.

Well, this is great.

Hiss! Bark splinters by my face. Some of it cuts me. I close my eyes and sink to my knees. Guess this is it.

"Ife! Move. What are you doing?"

I tried.

"IFEEEE."

You should have walked away, a voice whispers. Funnily enough, it snaps me out of my daze of self-pity.

NO!

No to the stupid little voice, and no to giving up. My eyes flash open and . . . FUUUDGE. I'm staring at two mean-looking pincers. I dodge at the last minute. Where my head was, the pincer is buried in the tree's trunk.

God, please, I plead as I reach for my flamethrower. Silent prayers flow through my veins. I aim. It's knocked out of my hands.

Whatever, I just have to keep it moving. I run through the shrubbery forest not knowing where I'm going. But something feels off. I can't place it. Until I stop for a breather and gulp in the air. It's only now that I realize I can't see Mr. Morley anywhere. I can't hear the slug-spider either.

A sick feeling in the pit of my stomach bubbles. I turn around and run back. We're both getting out of this place. By force and by fire. No idea how, but we'll figure it out.

We have to.

After I've run for a while, noise trickles into my ears. Hissing and groaning and the breaking of things.

The sounds are getting louder and louder and—

Something yanks me from nowhere and immediately I lash out. My arms and legs fly all over the place. *You. Will. Not. Kill. Me.*

"Ife it's me—ow!—stop."

Layo's voice gets through to me. It just takes my body half a second longer to process it. She's joined by Mr. Morley.

"Y-you're okay?"

"Yeah. Course we are," he says. "Not an easy one to get rid of."

There's loud hissing. Louder than anything we've heard. But it sounds different. Strangled in some way. It's hurting. There's another hiss and then silence.

"Are you alright?" he asks, checking me over.

"Yes," I answer.

"Good. Christ, this place is horrible. Let's get a move on."

All the adrenaline is punched out of me as I'm winded by my own anxiety.

"You're shaking. What happened?"

"Pa-pa-panic—"

"Hey, take it easy." Mr. Morley steadies me.

In. Out. In. Out.

I wipe away my streaking tears. Deep breath. "What if I can't save them? What if this is the end? What if I never go home?"

Mr. Morley scratches at his stubble. "That's a lot of *what-ifs* that may never happen. Look, the hardest thing to accept in life is that you can't save everybody." My shoulders slump. "But you can try. You can *always* try. Now then, Ife. Tell me, what are we going to do next?"

My lips quirk into the smallest of smiles and I sniffle. "We're going to try bloody hard to save my friends."

"Bingo. Now where are we going, Layo?"

"Beeton House."

CHAPTER 33

SO IT BEGINS

We step through the black-and-gold door, and on the other side is a world of orange mist that hangs over a vast bit of marshland that's full of translucent mushrooms and speckled grass and budding blue flowers. Goose bumps slither along the back of my arms. The marks of the therimorphs are everywhere.

I have no words. Neither does Mr. Morley.

It's Porthaven House. Beeton House. Otto House. I blink a couple of times, and then the weird pieces all fit together. It's the whole school. No, it's all of Pickleham Village sitting on a marsh. Only the buildings though. There are none of the roads or trees.

Did the therimorphs create it intentionally? Or was it something else, and their presence turned it this way?

Mr. Morley swears so colorfully I forget for a moment we're in a blanket of orange. "It's only a matter of time before they come for us."

A sudden coldness shudders through my body. Is this what they want? They want our world? But . . . I puff out my chest. "We came here for a reason, and excuse me if this sounds petty—I don't care by the way—but we're going to bring their world crumbling down."

Mr. Morley laughs out loud. "Would you consider interning with the ministry?" When I frown, he huffs. "No need to give me an answer now. Think about it. Right, ready for absolute mayhem?"

Nope. But it's a bit too late for that. We step onto the marsh. The grass sludge under our feet squelches and rearranges at will. I take a step and half my leg drops into the marsh. Layo stops me from falling headfirst.

"Careful."

"Thanks." We're almost at the school grounds. It sounds like the start of a really bad joke. A fake teacher, a replica, and a student walk into a school. As we get nearer, we see therimorphs galore. Too many to take on at once.

Layo takes the lead as we dip and shuffle and edge around the therimorphs on the premises. Just when I think we'll need to use our flamethrowers and go all action-hero, luck goes our way. Except I know it's not "luck." Not really. I can't explain it, but this is how it's supposed to go. Hiding in the bushes by a fake replica of the King of Beelsalam Garden, we look out toward Beeton House.

There are two therimorphs standing there in front of a van. They both have glowing eyes, bleach-white flesh riddled with bottomless holes, and tentacles bursting from their neck. This must be the therimorphs' natural form. Not as sluglike as I thought.

I lead us through alleys that exist between bushes and buildings. I wouldn't have known about them if it wasn't for Bee.

"That woman, she scares me," the one with the larger head says.

His colleague with squat legs frowns. He's looking down at a clipboard in his hands and shaking his head. "Yup. Scarier than Orchid, maybe."

"No one is scarier than Orchid. But she's insane. Unhinged."

"Well then, do you want to go in and ask what the ETA is till we need to head to the processing plant?"

"Me? Why me? I had to deal with her last time."

"Smorg, bander, voral?"

Big Head nods. "Smorg, bander, voral."

"Smorg, bander, voral," they sing in unison. And when they say the last word, they both shift into two different things. Squatty shudders and flares into this shape that looks like a cabbage plant. While Big Head sharpens into a tree with a lot of branches. If those branches were thorns.

"Bander trumps smorg," Big Head sings. "You're up. I'm going to get a bite. Have glorious fun."

"Go dissolve yourself."

Big Head walks off while Squatty psyches himself up outside the replica of Beeton. Mr. Morley rises slowly. Signals for me to wait as he creeps up on the lone therimorph. His hands are lightning fast, there's a flash of blue, and before I know it, Squatty clutches at his throat unable to make a sound as he's doused in salt-enhanced brine. Soon after, he's collapsed in a gooey mess. Mr. Morley waves me over.

"Like spreading butter over toast," he says, examining his handiwork.

I roll my eyes and smirk. Mr. Morley is a badass therimorph

killer and I am here for it. Who would have thought I'd be admiring him?

There's a keypad on the door. I key in the combo I know and twist. It works, and the door creaks open. We step inside. It's still Becton House, but everything is wrong. Grayscale roots grow over everything. The lights flicker and there are strange flowers and mushrooms growing out of unusual places.

"Bloody hell, this place needs a makeover. Right, I think from here on out, keep behind me. Who knows how many—Oh, a rabbit." Mr. Morley reaches out toward it. But I don't hesitate. I belt it with a brine bomb. It starts to steam and hiss and scream before collapsing into a mushy heap.

"Instinct. Can't be taught," I say, breaking the silence.

Mr. Morley looks at me, then chuckles. "The internship's yours if you want it. The ministry needs more people like you."

Again with the ministry internship. "Let's survive this first."

We step around the body and turn the corner. At the end of the hall is the office. Someone's in it, speaking. We approach the door slowly. Before we have a chance to decide how to play this out, the door opens. Ms. Piddleton is smiling at us. "Ife. John and . . . you." Her voice sounds like dry hands in winter. She laughs softly when we aim our flamethrowers at her. "How can I help you both?"

"How many therimorphs are there in the house?" Mr. Morley asks.

"So that's what you call us." Ms. Piddleton smiles. "It was just me and Petunia. Now it's just me, seeing as you killed her." She turns to me, a wicked smile on her face. "She was

Carnation's sweet, and one of Orchid's favorites, you know. He won't like that."

Mr. Morley chuckles. "I don't give a rat's arse what Orchid does or doesn't like."

Ms. Piddleton smirks. "You really should."

"The kids you've taken. Are they here?" Mr. Morley asks.

"Yes."

"Release them."

"I can't do that. They're to be prepared soon." She glares at Layo with a smile. "You've done a treacherous thing."

"I don't think you're in a position to say no." Mr. Morley steadies his flamethrower. "We know all about your weakness."

Ms. Piddleton bubbles into laughter before stopping suddenly. Abruptly.

"Sir," I say. A terrible feeling invades my joints. "We need to—"

Too late. She's already rippling. Stretching. Smiling so widely I will not sleep for days after seeing it. "Come then, swine. It's been a while since I showed my form. Let me show you that your time is up. Let me show you true fear. True terror. Anemone Vermilion is here." Ms. Piddleton changes before us. She's wearing Bee's skin. Wearing her voice. "You. Do. Not. *Learn.* You humans never do. What must I *burn?* Who must I *woo?*" She cracks and twists into a beautiful, plump woman.

"Jane," Mr. Morley gasps.

All at once Jane is gone. She is shapeless and inhuman. Skin punctured by irregular-shaped holes and oozing tentacles sprouting all over like a forgotten potato. One tentacle

340

wraps around and smothers Layo. Ms. Piddleton's eyes glow bloodred. Before a word can come out of my mouth, she rips Layo apart. Her body splatters everywhere. Chunks hit my face. Get caught in my hair. Her right hand lands at my foot, flinching as if it's still connected to a functioning body. It has the same faded scar I have on the skin between my thumb and index finger.

Burning bile claws its way up the back of my throat as my mind stretches. I can't escape the image of seeing my body being torn apart.

Thehellthehellthe—

My breaths are deep. I squeeze my eyes shut, knowing I don't have the luxury to grieve. Anger and fear intertwine. She just wanted to be her own person. My hands curl into fists. Nails digging into my palms.

"Come. Let me crush you. Once and for all. Bugs beneath Orchid's being."

We spray fire and miss the target. Ms. Piddleton is insanely shifty as she changes shapes like *that*. Slithering and squirming. Getting closer and closer. Mr. Morley lobs a few balloons in her direction.

"Run!" he booms.

I do as he says and sprint back down the hallway. Mr. Morley is behind me shouting curses. The smell of brine mingled with wet pavement stuffs its way up my nose. I take deep breaths to keep the dizziness away. All the while Ms. Piddleton giggles to herself. She's enjoying this.

Then Mr. Morley shouts at me. "Go find the kids. I'll hold her back."

"But—"

"Damn it, I'm not asking you." He dodges a claw. "GO!"

I know better than to argue with him. While he holds off Ms. Piddleton, I rack my brains. *Think*. Where would she keep abducted children? The answer comes to me. "Basement! Where all the boarders keep their suitcases and stuff. It's . . . it's back this way."

This has to be it. Otherwise there's no other place for them to be. Unless Ms. Piddleton was lying and they're not here? No. This is it. Sprinting back down the hallway and turning toward the shorter hallway leading to Ms. Piddleton's flat, I spot the hatch in the ground with its gold handle that looks like the tab of a tin can.

I pull the hatch open, revealing stairs. Time slows. I take a deep breath and head down. When I reach the bottom, lights flicker on and I look around. Scared faces turn in my direction to stare. Each student looks like they're in their own isolated classroom, surrounded by bars. There's a desk and chair with its own small bookshelf. Some of them have certain add-ons like painting easels or sports items.

I spot Ben in the far corner, lying on his back and looking up at the ceiling of his cage. "Ben!" I shout. "Ben!"

He rushes to the front of his cage.

"Ife? Is that really you?" Ben asks.

"The one and only," I say. I've got a great big grin on my face. "Thank God you're okay."

When he is close enough, I know something's wrong. His eyes are puffy. There's a slight tremble in his lips. "They took her with half of the others."

He doesn't need to say a name for me to know who he's talking about. Bee. "Where?"

"I—I don't know. I—They mentioned the processing plant—"

There's a big thud and rip-roaring squeal from above that makes everyone gasp or scream. The dim lights above our head flicker and one of the bulbs shatters.

"First things first, let's get you out of there. Keys?"

Ben points over at the wall. As I go over to unhook them, a loud "Oi!" stops me in my tracks.

I turn. It's one of the few Black girls at the school—Rachel.

"Yes, *you*. Is there anyone else worth shouting at? Anyway, I saw how you rushed to his cage. You better be letting us out too. Your name's Ife, yeah?"

"Yeah."

"Right. I remember you. You're the girl who fell asleep in the well-being booth." She looks me up and down. "I'll overlook your lack of impressiveness. Hurry up and open the cages."

I fumble at the keys and unlock the cages one by one until everyone's free. There's five of them in total. A young boy comes up and hugs me, treating me like some sort of hero. I'm not though. I'm just as scared as he is.

"What's going on?" he asks, looking at me like I have all the answers. "Why did they bring us here?"

"All I know is—"

There's another big thud. Another high-pitched squeal.

This time it's followed by the slamming shut of the hatch. Slow footsteps. A strange shadow stretches into view.

"Everyone, get behind me." As ridiculous as I feel, I point the flamethrower at the staircase. I take deep breaths, but it doesn't stop my hand from shaking.

Mr. Morley appears. His clothes are torn and bloody. Half his face looks burned as he wheezes like Muttley from *Wacky Races*, barely holding on to the flamethrower in his right hand. What I'd do to just be watching cartoons in my pj's right now. I lower my weapon.

But relief tangles with confusion because something isn't right. I lift the flamethrower again and aim it at Mr. Morley. "Prove it."

He tilts his head. "We don't have time for this."

"Prove that it's you," I demand.

"H-how?" He sounds exasperated. "What can I do to prove to you that it's me?"

"You can die!" I shout, throwing a brine bomb. Proud of myself. Mr. Morley's definitely left-handed and this fake is holding the flamethrower in his right hand. For a second there's nothing, and I fear I've embarrassed myself. "Sir, I—"

But then it begins. The unraveling of everything that keeps a therimorph together. An earsplitting screech echoes through the room. Tentacles burst from nowhere like popcorn. Mr. Morley becomes Ms. Piddleton plus a mess of tentacles.

"You-ou-ou-ou unspeaaaaakable cretinsss!"

I reach for my brine bomb belt. But I'm out. I whip off my rucksack to grab more, but a tentacle flashes from nowhere and knocks the bag out of my hands. I fall onto my backside and scramble backward. A tentacle wraps around my ankle and lifts me up until I'm hanging upside down.

"I care not that I am supposed to spare you. I so, so, so very much will enjoy your taste. Oh, how I grin. Now then, no time to waste."

Craning my neck, I am staring down at her great big mouth full of lots of different teeth that rearrange themselves. Wriggling bits, that I guess are strange taste buds, swell. I squeeze my eyes shut.

There's a huge roar and then I go flying across the room, slamming against the cages. All the breath is knocked out of my body. I sit up sharply and gulp as much air as possible.

Ms. Piddleton is writhing in the middle of the room, frothing and foaming. Ben's by my side.

"Are you okay?" he asks.

I nod. "Wh-what's happening?"

"I threw your rucksack into her mouth and she swallowed it whole. I think the bitch is dying."

"You're alright, you know."

Ben laughs. "You really know how to make a guy feel special. Cheers."

"Ding-dong, the witch is dead," I whisper.

Orchid's next.

CHAPTER 34

AND THIS IS HOW IT ENDS

We emerge from the basement and creep down the hallway where the real Mr. Morley is lying on his back with his eyes closed. His chest rises and falls. When he opens his eyes, they are wet.

"Sir," I say softly. That's all I can say. I can't really wrap my head around what I'm looking at—the huge hole in his lower abdomen. The nausea surges and I slap a hand over my mouth.

His eyes lock with mine and a slow smile builds. "I knew you'd finish her off." The words are slow and heavy. "Get them out of here. Don't even—" Mr. Morley erupts into a coughing fit.

I crouch down by his side and shake my head. "He has Bee. I need to stop Orchid."

"Run. It's only going to get harder. Listen, you can't save everybody. Go."

Tears well in my eyes as I shake my head. "But you can try. You can *always* try."

Mr. Morley smiles, this time showing his teeth. They're stained with blood. "Which senile bastard said that?" I purse my lips as he takes my hand. "You're so stubborn. You would have got on well with Alred. Ife . . . Ife . . . bring his world crumbling down. Left pocket."

He's looking past me now and that's how I know it's ending. His chest is barely rising. Barely falling. I reach into his left pocket and pull out a small canister that fits snug in my hand. Its head reminds me of the metal bit that goes into a car's petrol hole. There's a smooth button near the top.

". . . It's yours . . . ," he mumbles. "P-push to start."

I push the button and a jet of blue flame lances forward like a blade.

"Sir. I'm so—" The look he gives me stuffs the words I want to say back down my throat. Then his hand goes limp. He takes another short breath. I stiffen.

"Ife . . ." There's a flicker of wonder in his eyes as he says my name. Like he's seeing me. I have goose bumps all over. And then he exhales—lets go—before going still.

He's . . . gone. Just like that. My head shakes. *No.* I can't stop blinking. *Why is it so blurry?* I look up and around at all the kids looking at me. Looking *to* me. I let go of Mr. Morley's hand and wipe away my tears with my forearm.

"Pen and paper. I need a pen and paper." I mutter to myself and run back down to the basement cage with the painting easel. When I find everything I need, I draw. The paths, the routes. Everything. It comes flooding out. Each pencil stroke is a mathematical equation considering angles and distances. I even account for the marshiness of this place.

I can picture everything unfolding in my mind. The path they'd take. The scenery they'd see when they arrive and . . . "Done!"

I head up from the basement toward the entrance, where I tell everyone to hang back. I creep up to the door and look through the eyehole. Big Head stands outside. My heart thunders in my chest. An idea strikes. I rush back to the basement and grab what's left of Ms. Piddleton's head.

"What are you doing?" Ben demands. "And why do you have Ms.—"

"Just trust me. Don't come out till I say so." I step out the front door toward Big Head, who looks up.

"I—I don't know you?"

"Your friend's dead," I say, deadpan. Just like Mr. Morley would. Big Head stands up straight, looks around. He's about to call for help, but I get there first. I show him what's left of Ms. Piddleton's head. "I wouldn't do that if I were you."

"Wh-wh-what do you want?"

"I want you to find me a way to sneak into the processing plant."

"I . . . I can't do that. Orchid would kill me."

I shake my head. "Not if I kill him first. Find me a way in. That is all I'm asking you to do. Can you do that for me?" There's no response so I make of show of displaying the capabilities of the weapon Mr. Morley gave me by burning out Ms. Piddleton's eye. "Can you do that for me?"

Big Head draws a deep breath and nods. "Y-yes."

I hand the map over to Ben. "Use this to get them out of here and back to school."

"I'm not leaving you or Bee," Ben states. "Wherever you go, I go."

"Not today, you don't. They need someone to get them back safely. And that's you."

"But—"

"No buts."

Ben sighs. "Then allow me to say something to you that's unrelated."

"Make it quick. We need to keep it moving." There's awkward silence. "So . . . is this where you tell me you're madly in love with me?" I joke.

He laughs. "Be serious."

"That's rich, but alright, alright. What do you want to tell me?"

"So . . . I—Well I was—I—Thank you."

Thank you? For what? "But I haven't done anything," I reply.

Ben laughs in a really annoying way. It's as if he knows something I don't. "Don't worry about it," he says.

Before we separate, Ben gives me a look. I nod. I need to do this. It feels right this way. "I'm sure." My words come out all jittery. My throat's all dry. "Don't worry about me. I'll be fine."

"Well. Alright then." He pulls out his brother's engraved brass lighter and hands it to me. "For luck. When you're safe and sound I'll be expecting it back. So, look after it."

"But it's important to you. You can't just give me—"

"Yes, I can. And I just did. Look, my brother . . ." He clears his throat. "Sorry, it's still . . . Christ. Just bring it back," he sniffs.

I push the lighter back into his hands. "I don't need it. But I promise you, I'll come back in one piece."

He nods. "Fine then. Oh, and this. It belongs to you." He brings out my phone. "Fell out when Ms. Piddleton threw you like a rag doll."

"Thanks."

"Well, um, make sure you—"

"Stay safe. Yeah, I know. You too."

Ben smirks. "No, I was going to say keep an ear out. But stay safe works too."

Then there is just me. That's when the nervousness pulses through me from my stomach. Everything is real now. Not that it wasn't before. I'm seriously getting the shakes. Is it too hot in here? Why do my clothes feel way too tight?

I recite Philippians chapter four from the last bit of verse five all the way to the end of verse seven.

Do not be anxious about anything . . .

Yeah, sure. It says don't be anxious like it's the easiest thing in the world. As if I haven't tried that before. But this verse and its truth has gotten me through some of my hardest moments. So I give it a go. "God, please. Don't let me be anxious. I just want this to be done and over."

I sigh. All the signs of my anxiety are still there. I still feel like the world is closing in on me like four walls. But there's this weird peace. It tells me I'm getting through this. These feelings are real and scary and I hate them, but I won't let them define me. Not when I have hope.

It's time to go save Bee.

The walk to the processing plant is uneventful. It feels weird to walk next to a therimorph who's scared of me.

"Why us?" I ask as Big Head keeps us out of sight.

Big Head keeps his eyes glued ahead. "What?"

"Why do you take humans? Why not animals? What did we do to you?"

"You taste better."

I sigh. "I see."

Big Head points up ahead at a replica of the old data stores, except it has an extra floor and a large chimney. Plumes of billowing smoke climb high into the sky. There's a faint smell of petrol. "That's it."

As we approach, Big Head says there's a way in around the back. It's where they dump the human waste. The parts that the buyers indicate they don't want when they select their "cuts." I'm reminded of Mr. and Mrs. White, shivering at the thought they'd already chosen what parts of me they wanted, and what parts of me they didn't.

"Just go ahead. You'll see a tree with blue flowers. Opposite it, there's a bush of purple berries. Crawl through that and you'll be in the waste area. The door is unlocked." Big Head sizes me up. "You're really going to try and kill Orchid?"

I nod. "Don't have a choice. It's the only way."

Big Head gazes at me with his luminous eyes. "You won't do it." He shudders into a lopsided rabbit and bounds off. I compose myself and take a deep breath. This is it. This is how it ends.

I follow Big Head's instructions. When I'm done crawling through the purple berry bush, there's this rotten meat and petrol smell in the air. I blink. Look around. The space is cluttered with barrels of various sizes and black bags. I see a fox's head bursting out of one of the bags and a glimpse of a Nithercott blazer.

But up ahead there's a door. Just like Big Head said. Faded silver letters are printed over it.

ORCHID & CO.

I gulp and take a step toward the door.

It bursts open and a woman comes walking through. She slings a bag onto the large pile to my left. The bag splits. Innards spill out, blood drips. I gag. And when her head swivels to face me, she blinks with a vacant stare.

"Hey," I say.

"You are?"

The lie comes quick. "It's me, Anemone Vermilion."

The woman, whose blank look makes me think she's a replica, cocks her head. "A-Anemone? Why do you . . . look like that? And what is that thing in your arms?" She's talking about the flamethrower I'm carrying.

"I was attacked and I, uh, needed to remain nimble. This is one of their weapons. You need to take me to Orchid, at once. It's important. Intruders."

"Intruders?"

"Petunia's dead." I channel my inner Ms. Piddleton. "We don't have the time. Quickly now, take me to him."

"Oh my, oh my. Y-yes. At once. This way."

The inside of the processing plant is stifling. The farther she takes me, the heavier I feel. The harder it is to breathe. But other than the discomfort I feel, that's where the similarities end. There are corridors and stairs where they don't exist in my world. After we go through the second door, we end up in a large, decadent space. It's so floral and immersive, full of carefully placed mirrors. I'm transported into a unique vision of endless reflections. Up above there's a massive wooden chandelier, held up by the thinnest of threads and hemmed in by several balconies that protrude quite far inward. To one side of the room a group of Nithercott students are huddled together, and on the other, their replicas stand in single file.

In the middle of the room, I see two identical girls trapped in glass cylinders, connected by a tube. One slams her hands against the glass, tears streaming. While the other stands passively.

My stomach somersaults. *It's Bee.*

"We will wait until the transfer is complete," my guide says. A therimorph with larger holes covering its white flesh pours some liquid into a hole. The smell of petrol fills the air. After the cover is screwed back on, the therimorph pushes a button.

There's a low hiss and a purple mist seeps into the cylinder with the Bee I know. She starts to scream and gasp, and when she does, the mist changes into a murky green and swirls toward the replica.

I don't think. All I know is whatever's about to happen isn't good. I break from the edge of the room and spray fire at the therimorph by the controls. When they squeal and cower, I ignore the fact my eardrums are close to bursting and push the button they just hit to start the process. The mist stops rising. I bang the flamethrower against the glass cylinder, trying to smash it.

"P-purple lever," Bee rasps.

I spray fire to keep another therimorph away while I pull down the purple lever. The glass cylinders begin to rise. *Too, too slowly.* Two therimorphs face me down. Using fire, I move them out the way so I'm between them and the students they've taken.

"Enough!" thunders a voice, hoovering up all the noise. "This is . . . unexpected." I look up. The voice is distorted. But the glowing magenta eyes that emerge from shadow are bone-chillingly familiar.

Orchid.

His bleach-white flesh is full of bottomless holes. Except for the left side. It's like he's been cut up and stitched back together badly. Dr. Butterworth must have really done a number on him. He peers over on one of the balconies.

"I presume you do not come before me to offer your life?" Orchid asks.

"I'm here to stop you. I know how you prey on the Urban Achievers. How you set up this whole thing."

"Prey?" Orchid tilts his head. "I have no need to *prey*. Watch how you speak to me, human." Menace *bleeds* into his voice and I flinch. "If I wanted, I could devour whomever I please."

I don't doubt it.

"If anything, this is mercy."

What? "That is absurd. What makes you think—"

"Shut up. I do not owe you pathetic humans an explanation. You live for our consumption."

My mouth hangs open for a moment. "Someone once told me no one gets to tell you who you are," I say, regurgitating Mr. Ingham's words. "What you're doing isn't merciful."

That's when Orchid bubbles into raucous laughter. It makes my ears tremble and goose bumps break out all over my skin. For a moment I think he's going to drop down, and I hold my breath.

Instead Mr. Ingham steps out from the shadows by his side.

My thoughts fracture like glass, and my throat crumples.

"That's enough, Orchid. We have an agreement, do we not? Let's not sully those terms here today," Mr. Ingham says, before looking down at me. "You're a sweet girl, Ife. We have similar outlooks on life. We're both willing to fight for the things we hold dear. I think that's why, deep down, against my better judgment, I let you be for so long."

"Huh?" I don't get it. My focus switches between Orchid and Mr. Ingham because there's just *no way*. "What is this?"

Nothing makes sense. He *cares* about us. If this was the real Mr. Ingham, he wouldn't say any of this stuff. He wouldn't be hand in hand with literal monsters. He wouldn't just reveal himself.

Mr. Ingham must see the look on my face and guess what I'm thinking, because he shakes his head. "I'm not a replica. I am as much me as you are you."

I frown and swallow. "Then . . . why?"

"Why indeed?" Mr. Ingham says with a watery smile. "Imagine you're watching a runaway train. It thunders down the tracks. Straight toward a horde of people who can't escape. People you care for. And you see this happening. By your side is a switch that'll divert the train onto another set of tracks. Except that track also has people on it too. Also those you care for. Just far, far fewer. What would you do?"

The question hangs in the air unanswered because truthfully, I don't know. None of those choices are good. "I—I don't want anyone I care about to die."

"That is not the way the world works, Ife," Mr. Ingham says not unkindly. He sighs. "The monsters hungered. The way into our world is here. And I made the best possible decision I could when *they* stood by idly." Anger stains his every word and I understand he's talking about the ministry. How long was he waiting for Morley and Butterworth to take this choice out of his hands?

But . . . "Letting them target lonely students *you* bring in on the Urban Achievers Program so others live isn't the best possible decision, and it's definitely not fair."

"Lonely? They don't care about who's lonely or not. *Listen* to me. I pulled the switch because this is about making the right choice. Grow up. You can't save everyone." He smooths down his blazer. "Neither could I."

"Could?" I frown. "Are you talking about people like Ramesh? Your friends from back then?"

Mr. Ingham's stare hardens for a flicker before he smiles. "I can't believe someone could see me so clearly, they were able to push me so far."

"Th-then why the Urban Achiever students?"

"It was the right play." There is no guilt in his voice. Only cold frankness. "Nithercott was failing and before long would have fallen into financial ruin. I couldn't let that happen. Nithercott is not a place that fails. *I* don't fail. I needed a way to bring in more students, more income, and ensure Orchid and his people would not overrun us. I gave him assurances he could take his pick. You are right, it isn't fair. But this way,

I can save a great deal more people. This way Nithercott, and all it stands for, endures."

My blood boils, heating me all over and tying my tongue. How can he not see how dumb he sounds? How his perspective is so warped and untrue? Ben was right. The narrative means more than truth.

"I had no idea of your remarkableness until the day I heard you temporarily stopped Louis from being taken. Honestly, I was surprised. The fact you forced my hand. I thought by dissolving the sponsor system, it would be enough to get you off the scent. But then there was the debacle that night at couples' corner with Stacey, and I knew you were determined to see this through.

"Orchid said you would be trouble. That I should do what needed to be done. But I didn't listen. And oh, what havoc you have caused. Orchid was quite annoyed at me for not keeping you in check. I still don't know whether I should be annoyed at you or impressed."

I'm an idiot. The words drill into my mind. How didn't I see it? Maybe I did, and I didn't want to accept that the one person other than Bee and Ben who looked out for me was a monster. My eyes water.

"Now, now, don't cry. I don't want to end on a note of bitterness, so allow me to say this: You interfered with my plans, true, but you are truly a marvel. You have my word, I'll ensure it's quick." Mr. Ingham runs a hand through his hair. "Now then," he starts with his arms outstretched. "Are you going to cooperate? Or will you continue to defy the inevitable to the bitter end?"

CHAPTER 35

YOUNG KIDS RUMBLE

can't breathe.

Someone squeezes my arm. It's Bee.

Her eyebrow lifts. *You do* not *look good.*

My lips curl into a narrow smile. *I know.*

"Ife . . . what now?" Bee asks. She's not looking at me but at the students still in the corner. I keep a steady stream of fire from the flamethrower in front of us. She waves them over behind our defensive line, and they oblige. "We need to find a way out of here. We can't"—I let the fire roar harder when Orchid's minions attempt to get closer—"stop him."

"I need to get up there and burn Orchid to a crisp. I have no idea what to do about Ingham though."

"Except we've got more pressing issues right now. Look."

More therimorphs have appeared, and they step toward us in their natural form, free from their humanlike shell. They have us cornered, but they can only get so close. The fire's too fierce for them to overcome. When one therimorph tries to push through, it ends up on the floor squealing in agony.

Another stretches out a few tentacles that slip past, but the heat makes them wilt and recoil. That gives them all ideas. The tips of their tentacles shift into sharp instruments and spear at us.

"Alive!" Orchid booms. "I need them alive!"

The tentacles miss, except for one that nicks Bee's arm.

She cries out in pain and I glare at the therimorph responsible. But Orchid's instruction gives us time. All around us, the therimorphs attempt to ripple into shapes and things that may help them get to us. It's no use though, because it doesn't matter *what* they turn into, it's still their body. When they see and feel the heat, they have no choice but to back down.

Still, I know soon my flamethrower will run out. An idea sparks from nowhere. Well then. Here goes nothing. I lower my weapon and look up at Orchid and Mr. Ingham. "Tell them to stop," I shout. "I surrender. I'll give myself to you. But I need you to do two things for me."

"I don't *need* to do anything," Orchid hisses.

Mr. Ingham says something to Orchid, who grunts. A moment later, Mr. Ingham is leaning over the balcony. "What are these two things?"

"First, I need you to promise you'll only take me and no one else."

Mr. Ingham gives nothing away. "And the second thing?"

"I want Orchid to tell me something. Face-to-face. None of this across-the-room stuff."

Before Mr. Ingham can answer, anger invades Orchid's face as he roars. Claws and talons and tentacles burst from his flesh as he jumps down from the balcony. "Enough of this charade, you insolent human. You think you can summon me?" His voice sings. Echoes. Scrapes. It is fear itself.

"While I can preserve you, allow you to live through one of my creations, I will not. I refuse. You have upset me in a way unforgivable. You have killed too many."

My legs wobble as he approaches. *This is how it ends.*

The therimorphs make way for him. Each step he takes plunges a shard of fear into my gut. My hand tightens around the last thing Mr. Morley gave me. I hide it in the front pocket of my hoodie.

"Now you are not so brave. Not in the face of one such as I." I can see the trace of a smile smothered by tentacles on Orchid's face. "Now then, prepare to—"

When he's close enough, I thrust at his heart with Mr. Morley's canister.

But before I can press the button, Orchid knocks me over easily. Lowering himself onto four thick tentacles, he crawls over to tower above me, eclipsing the light of the chandelier. His face snarls. "You infuriate me. You have shed innocent blood. You have killed my sweets. And for what? All your struggling and all your defiance—all of it—ends now. And when I am done with you . . . when you are nothing but crushed bone and marrow . . . I will *end* your friends and your family."

He lifts a sharpened tentacle high above his head. In the metallic reflection of the tentacle blade, I see movement and the flicker of a flame. Bright and brilliant, I see the wooden chandelier burning.

This is how it ends.

I smile at Orchid and his face twists in confusion.

"Look up," I say.

He turns to see Ben leaning over the edge of the balcony,

sawing away at the threads holding the chandelier up. I reach for the canister and plunge it into his heart, just as the chandelier comes crashing down on top of Orchid, splintering into a thousand pieces of burning wood and melting glass.

This is how it ends.

The whole room lights up in a blaze of flame that spreads like wildfire. Orchid screeches, but he can't escape the inferno. I struggle onto my feet and look up to the balcony. Mr. Ingham is no longer there. I get to Bee's side. "I know a way out. Everyone, follow me." I lead the way through roaring flames, heading back the way I came. The heat chokes my breaths and warms my skin.

On the way, we come face-to-face with Ben, who grins ear to ear.

"It actually worked!" he exclaims for the hundredth time as we find our way out into the waste area.

I shake my head and shout over the flames. "Ben, you might *actually* be a genius!"

"I made Rachel lead the others to safety and I followed you instead. You see? You'd have been therimorph meat if I hadn't completely ignored every word you said! Anyways, never mind that. We need to get home."

I tell the students with us to crawl through the purple berry bush quickly. That this place is a mirror world. I explain the way back and make one of them repeat the route until they've nailed it. I tell them not to trust Mr. Ingham if they see him. "Now go!" I order.

Suddenly Orchid explodes through the burgundy door. "I have worked and toiled. You will not take this away from *me*! It is my right!"

"It's over," I say. "Leave us alone."

Orchid shakes his head. Wrenches out pieces of glass from his chest with his tentacles. "No. It's not. It's never over. I will not lose. I cannot lose. Now give yourself to me. Give. Yourself. To. Me."

I shake my head. I have no idea what he's on about, but I'm done running. I'm done giving up. I'm done making the wrong decision. "No."

"Very well. Then you leave me no choice." Orchid grows and stretches until he resembles a monstrous spider with so many tiny tentacles, it looks like fur. He knocks over barrels and metal drums. Crushes wooden crates under his size. Splits open black bags.

Tentacles surge at me suddenly, and Bee shoves me aside.

"Smell that?" Ben asks as we dip, dodge, and dive Orchid's lumbering attacks.

Bee sniffs. "Is that . . ."

"Petrol," I state. "Yes." The fuel for their mad machine. I spot the leaking barrels below and around Orchid. I remember Ben's fun fact. *Sustained burning can cause irreparable damage to their cells.* I guess the chandelier wasn't enough. One of the barrels is small enough to pick up, and an idea forms. I hurriedly explain my plan to Ben and Bee. We share one deep breath. I give my friends a devilish smile. "Buy me ten seconds, and then you throw the lighter on my signal. Just make sure the flame is burning, okay?"

I don't wait for their answer. I run past Orchid's hulking mass while Ben and Bee take all of his attention. But the tentacles seem to have a mind of their own. One catches me in the side. Another grazes my arm. But I keep running. I just need to get to the barrel. I grab hold and—

From nowhere, a tentacle claws into my thigh and wraps itself around my waist, lifting me off the ground, the barrel in my hands.

I hover above Orchid's gaping mouth. This was not the plan, but beggars can't be choosers. "*NOW!*" I shout while throwing the barrel into the deep darkness.

In the same breath there's a sudden blaze of heat that engulfs everything. Orchid screams and wails. He lets go of me, tossing me aside. This is the second time I've been sent flying by a tentacle, but I don't feel any pain because there is nothing but relief in every fiber of my being.

At last. *This* is how it ends.

With us.

Ben, Bee, and I are the chaos, the wreckage, and the judgment.

We look at one another and smile. Three friends who beat a whole other world. Well, it feels like it. And as Orchid burns, I can hear the beat of my heart in my ears. It says, *Rumble, young kids, rumble!*

Then there is silence.

No more screeching.

Only the massive burnt corpse of Orchid. I swallow. Stagger backward. Take in the mess and then empty my stomach. I look at Ben and Bee with tears in my eyes. "It's really over."

"We've got to go." Bee takes my hand, but I don't budge, still looking down at what's left of Orchid. "Ife."

"Hang on." I climb into the mouth of Orchid and rummage

around until I find what I'm looking for. Ben's lighter. "I believe this is yours?"

"I believe it is."

"Oh, one more thing." I find another small barrel of petrol and carry it with me. "We're going to need this."

After we're done dousing the whole of Little Forrest in petrol, we pour a trail all the way to the side gate. Once we step outside, Ben produces his lighter.

"Who wants to do the honors?"

Bee raises her arm, and I'm not about to deny her. Ben hands over his lighter and she lights it. "Before we get this over with, I wanted to say a few words."

"This isn't a memorial." I sigh. "But why not."

"I—I just wanted to say that we did it. We *actually* made a difference. And I never thought I'd be an arsonist, but well, before you came, Ife, I never thought about a lot of things. And, Ben?"

"Yeah?"

Bee doesn't say a word, she throws his lighter at him and as soon as he catches it, she rushes him with a tight hug. "Set the whole thing ablaze."

For a moment Ben's speechless. His mouth opens to say something, but the words don't come. Instead he smiles, crouches down, and says something under his breath. Words just for him.

And then the petrol ignites.

CODA

SHOCK AS POLICE LAUNCH INVESTIGATION INTO 'UNEXPLAINED' COMAS IN PICKLEHAM VILLAGE AT THE SAME TIME LITTLE FORREST GOES UP IN FLAMES

by Filmore Oduwole

Police have launched an investigation into the unexplained comas of residents, school staff, and students, whose bodies were found littered all over Nithercott School on Wednesday evening.

Dozens of bodies were discovered on the premises of the prestigious independent school after officers responded to reports of sudden collapses.

Emergency services rushed to the scene at around 7:40 P.M. as witnesses described a large police and ambulance presence around the vicinity of Nithercott School.

One student, who we cannot name, said: "One moment I was hanging with a group of friends, the next there was loads of screaming and shouting. Even one of my friends just fell to the floor and wasn't moving. It was so scary. It was like she was a puppet and someone cut her strings. My parents are coming to pick me up soon."

A local homeowner told *The Observer* that all-black vehicles had been stationed outside Nithercott School throughout the night. "Routinely people would emerge and knock on doors," they said.

The homeowner, who did not wish to be named, divulged that they were suspicious and had never seen the symbol stitched on the lapels of the people who came from the mysterious vehicles—a purple flower with a gold crown on top. My money is on a secret branch of government.

Lettie Fraser, who runs the local bakery, said: "It's quite alarming. The poor souls. I was talking to my neighbor about it, we're not sure what's happened. I left my shop around 8:15 P.M. and there was a police car and a black van across the road. The car and the van were still there the following morning. It's such a shame. Everyone that fell into a coma—they were pillars of our community."

The Observer understands that of those who collapsed, none have woken up.

Two Months Later

Droplets of water condense on the window of the coffee shop as the cold of outside battles the warmth of indoors. Nervousness and excitement intertwine in me. We've been texting nonstop, but it's been a long while since the three of us have been together.

Nithercott doesn't exist anymore. A warrant was issued for Mr. Ingham's arrest. But he's nowhere to be found. Go figure. A police search is currently underway and the media are calling it the biggest boarding school scandal in history. Loads of students and teachers left. Or are in comas that they still haven't woken up from.

All the boarders were allocated to new schools in the area temporarily. For the past couple of months, I've been boarding at Bonneville. Somehow, it's even posher than Nithercott. Mum and Dad insisted I come home, but to their surprise, and mine, I respectfully said no. Convincing them I'd be fine was tricky, and while I had to give them certain assurances—two phone calls a week, and a longer, monthly video call—it was worth it. Because even though Ben and Bee are at different schools, they're no more than five bus stops away each.

My phone vibrates in my hands. I look down and stifle a laugh. It's a quirky GIF of a dancing hot dog captioned: Good evening.

Alice is so random, I love her! I search for a GIF, something just as random as her. I grin when I find it. Per-fect. It's a girl jumping over stuff like she's a horse. I press send and take the time to reply to Zanna. I've got a video call with her later. Can't wait to go see her in Dublin next half term. I was so relieved when I saw flights are really cheap.

Everyone else in my messages wants to know about all the absurdity to do with Nithercott and how I'm coping with the fact that a lot of people have suddenly become Sleeping Beauties. Once I'm all caught up, I tuck my phone away and go back to staring out the window.

My mind presses play, and the events of the past few months run like a movie. A surreal movie. Orchid defeated. Mr. Ingham in hiding. Mr. Morley lost. No, not lost, dead. I still think about Layo too. All she wanted to be was her own person. Like I said, it's been a long few days. Months even. My sense of time is all over the place.

I rub my eyelids and sigh, before sprawling myself over the table. I think I'm going to rest my eyes. Just for a bit. I'm way too early, after all. I'll count to thirty and then . . . and then . . . and then . . .

I'm woken up by a bang on the table. My eyes creep open and I'm staring at a steaming to-go cup. I look up into the bluest eyes I've ever seen. They belong to a man with pale skin, yellowed teeth, and messy purple curls that brush his shoulder. He leans on a cane in his right hand and is wearing the most extravagant-looking coat. It's red on red velvet with gold buttons and black-fur lapels.

"Hot chocolate," he says with a smile. "For you."

"Who are you?" I don't like being approached by strangers.

"Who I am doesn't matter."

I shake my head. "I think that's up to me to decide. You're the one giving me hot chocolate, and I don't even know you. So, who are you?"

The man doesn't answer. Instead he reaches into his coat and produces a card, places it carefully on the table, and then slides it across to me. I hold my breath at the symbol that bursts from the white. A purple flower with a gold crown.

I turn it over.

MINISTRY OF INTERDIMENSIONAL DEFENSE
Lelouch Pope
Commander in Chief
+447700900327

I look at the man named Lelouch. "I called your ministry. Did they tell you I called?"

"They did indeed." Lelouch runs a hand through his hair. "But it seems you did not need us, after all, to destroy one of their nests." There's a great big yawning silence before he continues. "Mr. Ingham is in our custody. Rest assured he cannot come back from this. The therimorphs on our side of the breach are also being hunted. They probably won't act, but still, be careful."

"Oh."

Lelouch smiles. "Mr. Morley told us about you."

"Did he?"

"A rose. That's what he called you. Said all you needed was some watering. I'm here to offer you an internship. With us."

"An . . . internship?"

"Correct. There is so much of this world that is unknown. So much to see. What do you say?" He holds out a hand. A warm smile on his face. "It would be my pleasure to welcome you to wonderland."

Yeah, no. I've had enough shenanigans for a lifetime. I check my phone. Five minutes until we're supposed to be at the cinema. "I think . . . that my friends are waiting for me." I sling my bag over my shoulder and hesitantly take a sip of the hot chocolate, bringing it with me as I head for the door. Leaving the card behind. "Thanks for the hot chocolate though."

"Think about it, Ms. Adebola."

I have to say, I'm impressed by how well he pronounces my name, but it changes nothing. "I won't. Oh, that reminds me." Malika's been on my mind a lot lately too. "Will they wake up? Can you make them more themselves again?" Even though they're replicas, there's still a part of their original selves in there. If there's even a chance they can wake up and have normal lives . . .

"We . . . don't know." Lelouch sighs. "We are working on understanding exactly what's happened and exploring all avenues. We're thinking exposing them to the pollen of those blue flowers may help."

"I see. Well. Thanks."

Dusk is getting a grip over the sky in the form of colliding orange and purplish-blue colors as I walk briskly toward the cinema. God this hot chocolate is good.

I spot Ben across the road as he spots me. He's in a puffy orange jacket, his hair cropped short as can be. In one hand he's got a chocolate bar, in another, a stapler. I really don't understand this boy.

A huge grin plasters his face as he makes his way toward me in this loping walk. At that moment I think only he can make walking look effortless. He offers me a bit of his chocolate and pockets the stapler.

We walk to the cinema in silence until he finally says, "Well."

I take another sip of my hot chocolate. It's so addictive.

"You think it's over?" Ben asks. "I mean, there's no reason for them to come back, right? They wouldn't dare now that their weakness is known. Not to mention I'm pretty sure the Ministry of Interdimensional Defense will finally be pulling their fingers out."

"Yep," I say, taking another sip.

"A woman of many words, I see."

I finish off the hot chocolate. "Can I ask you a question?"

"Shoot."

"Am I the only one who's not okay?" I throw the to-go cup into a bin we pass by. "I haven't slept properly since I came back. Whenever I close my eyes, I see him."

"Mr. Ingham?"

I shake my head. "Mr. Morley."

Ben stops suddenly and draws me into a big hug that startles me, before he awkwardly pulls away. "It's okay to not be okay, and it's going to take some time, but trust me when I say one day it'll be a bit easier."

"What if I'm not strong enough?" Panic begins to bloom from deep down inside.

"We never are, Ife." He puts a hand on my shoulder. "I'd be a liar if I said the whole Leon thing hasn't messed me up still, but you and Bee are . . . everything. You see me and you understand me. Because of you both, I'm understanding that what I feel isn't supposed to shrink. Instead, I'm supposed to outgrow it, weird as that sounds. Thanks for being a great friend."

Right. Friend.

"Now then, I think we've dallied enough. We're here. Knowing Bee, she's probably waiting for us already. Shall we?"

He offers his arm. I laugh and slide my arm into his as we step through the doors of the cinema.

Bee's the first face we see when we step inside, her signature smile as warm as one of Dad's hugs. "About time! I took the liberty of buying us tickets already. Both of you can pay me back within the week, please. I'm not very liquid right now."

I laugh and take my ticket. "Yeah, yeah. But I swear, if this film is dead, you're not getting a single penny from me."

"Never! *Ferris Bueller's Day Off* is a classic. If you don't like it, then I don't know what to tell you. Did you know it took the director six days to finish the script?"

Ben yawns. "Bee, I beg you, promise me you won't spout trivia while the film's playing. Alright?"

She sticks out her tongue at him and then asks why he has a stapler sticking out of his coat pocket. They go back and forth, and I burst into laughter.

"What?" they both say to me.

I shake my head and wipe away the wetness filling my eyes. "Nothing, it's just . . ."

"Go on," Bee says.

Ben smirks. "Use your words."

"Ha. It's just, I was thinking about it on the way here. You know you guys are my home, right? No matter where you are."

THE END

ACKNOWLEDGMENTS

And exhale!

There are so many people I need to thank, so I'm going to get right to it.

First and foremost, thank you, God! Everything happened too perfectly and pleasingly. All glory goes to You.

Mum, Dad, and Temi. You three are my heart and my *home*. No matter where we are in the world.

My deepest appreciation to my literary agents, Claire Wilson and Pete Knapp. I am ever grateful for your support and wisdom. Thank you both for believing in the story of my heart. Thank you for your consistency and integrity. I could not ask for better for what is now, what is next, and what is beyond. Thanks must go to Safae El-Ouahabi and Stuti Telidevara for the work they do seen, and often unseen; and to the teams at Park & Fine, and RCW for their professionalism, care, and know-how.

Words cannot express my gratitude to my editors, Foyinsi Adegbonmire and Emma Jones. You pushed me to make *The Changing Man* the very best it could be. In your care, my words and ideas were sharpened. Most of all, they found a safe haven.

A heartfelt thanks to the teams at Feiwel and Friends and

Macmillan UK who have shown me nothing but enthusiasm and love.

To Rach, a million thank-yous. Simply put, *The Changing Man* does not exist without you. Finding you on Twitter all those years ago is what I call my "second beginning" on this whole writing journey. Look at us, eh. Who would have thought?

A tremendous thank-you goes to Tols who cheered for *The Changing Man* long before I did. Your encouragement got me through that first rewrite. I'm so blessed to know you. Keep on killing it!

Special thanks go to the writers who provided their input along the way. Ruona, huge thanks for your excitement and sincerity. It is infectious! I see you, I believe in you, and I can't wait for your stories to be out in the wild. Many thanks go to Tyler: elite CP and high-concept queen. Keep on writing— we're ready for your stories. Maria-chan, you are my anime twin. You just get it, and I am glad for all that you are. I appreciate you immensely. I may not have known you at the very start, but you were there at the end. To Samara, thank you for your kindness and energy. Your joy is everything and has lifted my spirits more than you know. To Bella, thank you for casting your eyes over *The Changing Man* when I needed fresh eyes.

Thank you to my writing community, who in a multitude of ways have encouraged and inspired me: Ayana Gray, Hannah Gold, Louisa Onomé, Aisha Bushby, Lucia Nobi, Ben O'Hara, Laura Martens, Mary Ojino, J.A. Moy, Isi Hendrix, Kereen Getten, Katherine Webber, Rimma Onoseta, Saara El-Arifi, Shani Akilah, and J.P. Rose.

To my day-ones who never stopped asking me how my writing was going—Henry, Quashie, Ope, Safian, Rachel, Persis—I love you all.

My church family—thank you for your prayers and your love. What a blessing it is. Thanks especially to Simon and Ashley, Dave, Patrick and Beth, Mark, Alex and Naomi, Reuben and Ruth, and Alastair and Eleanor.

To Krishna, Nadia, Becca, and Reanna—thanks for your kindness. Your next McDonald's breakfast is on me.

Last, but not least, to everyone who's supported me, but I have forgotten to name, thank you, thank you, thank you.

Thank you for reading this Feiwel & Friends book.
The friends who made *The Changing Man* possible are:

Jean Feiwel, Publisher
Liz Szabla, VP, Associate Publisher
Rich Deas, Senior Creative Director
Holly West, Senior Editor
Anna Roberto, Senior Editor
Kat Brzozowski, Senior Editor
Dawn Ryan, Executive Managing Editor
Kim Waymer, Senior Production Manager
Emily Settle, Editor
Rachel Diebel, Editor
Foyinsi Adegbonmire, Associate Editor
Brittany Groves, Assistant Editor
Helen Seachrist, Senior Production Editor

Follow us on Facebook or visit us online at mackids.com.
Our books are friends for life.

If you made it this far, then you're a real one. Which is why I want to do something different. A post-credits scene, so to speak:

Bee was right—*Ferris Bueller's Day Off* is an absolute classic. As we make our way out into the cinema's foyer, I bump into a fast-walking man. My half-finished popcorn flies into the air and comes showering down. Ben swears at him for me, but I tell him it's not that deep. Somehow there's at least a few handfuls of my popcorn left. And beside the tub is a card. The image of the purple flower with a gold crown sends a zag of energy down my spine.

A smile builds on my face. No doubt Lelouch planned this.

I glance at the card for a moment before picking it up and slipping it into my jeans pocket.